STORM FORGE

STORM FORGE

PAIGE L. CHRISTIE

To Neville —
Words & Magic
forever

PROSPECTIVE PRESS
Winston-Salem

P ROSPECTIVE P RESS LLC

1959 Peace Haven Rd, #246, Winston-Salem, NC 27106 U.S.A.
www.prospectivepress.com

Published in the United States of America by PROSPECTIVE PRESS LLC

ʎ TRADEMARK

STORM FORGE

ISBN 978-1-63516-014-7

First PROSPECTIVE PRESS trade paperback edition

Printed in the United States of America
First printing, September, 2022

The text of this book is typeset in Athelas
Accent text is typeset in Scurlock

PUBLISHER'S NOTE

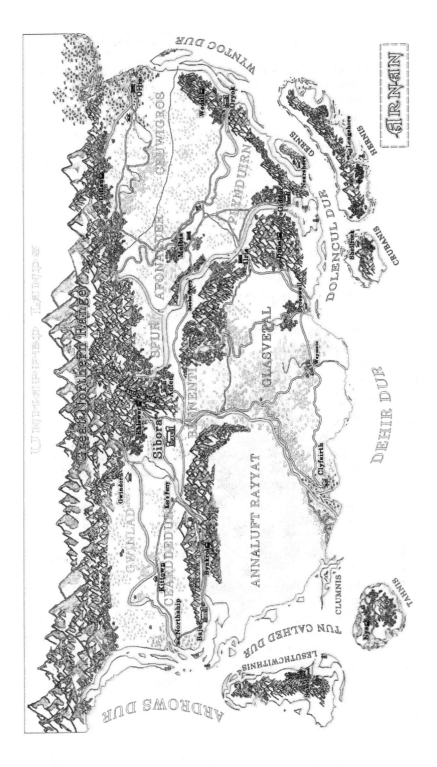

Thanks is Given to The Following Amazing People

Rebecca Sanchez Hefner & Ellen Morrissey, my fellow Blazing Lionesses who've been with me on this grand adventure through all the ups and downs, and who are always right when they say, "Woman, you don't need that chapter."

Patti K. Christie, who remains 100% the best Mama in the universe. Thanks for love, support, humor, history, laughter, good eatin', and always being AMAZING!

MultiverseCon Tater Squad without whose love, support, strength, friendship, (and terrible jokes), the last three years would have been unbearable. You are a blessing.

> **Jesse Adams & Allison Charlesworth,** for all the love, and for starting this wild ride
>
> **Holly Hogan,** for being a rock, always
>
> **Mason Adams,** for creative energy, and bright and endless inspiration
>
> **Liam Fisher,** for honesty and humor in all things
>
> **Ris Harp,** for showing the world what fortitude looks like
>
> **Besse Rawitcsh,** for quiet lessons in big strength
>
> **Leigh Boros,** for always seeing the bright side
>
> **Robby Hilliard,** for continuous insight
>
> **Rob Gilmore,** for stunning grace in the toughest of times
>
> **Richard Fife,** for inviting me to MultiverseCon in the first place (So much woot!)
>
> **Darin Kennedy,** for ALL the puns
>
> **Dee Norman,** for standing up and stepping forward
>
> **Brent Peters,** for believing and sharing
>
> **Alex, Chelsea, Venessa, Angelina, Ross, Ariel, Cooper, Henry, Kerney, Gerald, Nicole, Marcus,** *and everyone else along the way, and yet to join.* Thanks for being part of this relentlessly kind community!

The Community Table Team: Gary Wood, Ski Brominski, Renada Davis, and Jon Davis, for all your stunning hard work and dedication through the toughest of times.

Jerry Hefner and **Joe Barrett,** for your support of the Lionesses, and being awesome humans.

TWT – The Writing Tribe group, especially Vennesa Guinta, Sean Hillman, Rachel Brune, Joe Compton, and Joelle Reizes, for smart discussions, lots of wordy time, and upbeat support no matter how tough things get.

Janny Wurts, Steven Poore, and **Lucy Holland,** for being early supporters of this series and always believing that I could do it.

And most of all **YOU,** the readers who have believed in this series and stuck with it to the very end. I wouldn't be here without you. Enjoy!

For

Ellen Morrissey

and

Rebecca Sanchez Hefner

Perhaps all the dragons
of our lives are princesses
who are only waiting
to see us once
beautiful and brave.

Perhaps everything terrible is
in its deepest being
something helpless
that wants help
from us.

~ Rainer Maria Rilke

1

Leiel – 39 Years

AN OLD THING, TO WAKE FILLED WITH FEAR. SO OLD THAT MEMORY cut twice as sharp—of a moment-to-moment churning of gut and tightness of chest, of pain and anxiety so much a part of morning as to have been reborn with each waking, usual as breath, sad and tiring as passing time. Leiel lay motionless, staring into the still-dark sky, wide and bare overhead, sparked with the flung dust of stars. Only a faint paleness edging the east hinted that dawn poised to break over the horizon. Nothing stirred in the stark heat, not bird, not bug, not breeze.

Her fault.

Sweat trickled from the corner of one eye and down the line of her temple. She raised a hand and wiped it away.

Old gods—this feeling. Not since that long ago day in the sanctuary, since the morning she awakened with ash on her tongue and the looming horror of her mother's supposed death crushing breath from her lungs, had she burned inside like this.

A tremor coursed her spine. Guilt. Terror. Few options existed but to dwell within the despair such states of mind engendered.

No.

She sat up, looked over at Teska where the healer lay asleep on the other side of their long-cold fire circle. For her, so much had been offered up, so much lost. So young, the other woman seemed, curled on the hard earth, dust in her hair and silting her clothing. So young for an entire land to spin around, to fracture over. And yet where did any break or change come, but from one heart, one mind, one thing that truly mattered? That much, at least, Gahree had seen instilled deep within Leiel.

Gahree.

The Draigon's name went through Leiel's mind like a prayer. Gahree, you promised Teska's worth outweighs us all, but oh, how am I to believe that when I taste your death in my throat each time I swallow?

No laughing, cryptic answer rang bell-like on the morning air, and Leiel found herself unable to dredge from her imagination even a hint of what response Gahree might make. Not when the only image that remained in Leiel's mind was of blood and brokenness and of the smoke-carried, copper scent of dying. It had been so much easier, when shock still held sway, to pretend distance and acceptance in the face of such loss.

With a sigh, Leiel pushed herself to her feet, dusted from her clothes the dirt of another night spent on bare earth, and moved away from the make-shift camp. A few steps carried her down a low embankment toward the slow trickle of the stream that had somehow managed to survive the weather she had set across the region. Brave brook, I'll see you named on a map one day. For your stubbornness alone you deserve recognition. That brought a faint smile to her lips. She bent to unlace her boots, then rolled up her pants, and waded into the shallow, tepid water.

Crouching on a flat rock in the middle of the flow, she dipped her hands, scrubbed off the accumulated dirt of travel. When they were as clean as she was going to get them without soap, she cupped her hands in the water and splashed it across her face, following the flow with her hands, throwing back the wild tangle of her hair in the same motion. Travel and grit had cracked the skin of her palms.

She opened her hands, studied their calloused surfaces, the welts and scars of life on the mountain, of hard work and learning and willingness to *try*. Flexing her fingers, she worked the small muscles, back and forth, then rolled her wrists, feeling the wrongness of her missing ring. Such a slight change to matter so much, to carry such weight.

Another loss. In the face of everything else, should it matter at all?

She pressed her lips together, as though the change of expression could shift the frame of her mood from sorrow to determination. But only intention could do that. She forced a grim nod. Will was never something she lacked. She flexed her fingers again, rolled her shoulders, measuring weariness and strength. Too long remained before she would be able to take the Great Shape and carry Teska north. North to Cyunant and the myriad questions sure to await in the wake of Gahree's death.

So much to be faced.

Unexplainable.

Unfathomable.

Hers to own, whatever the cost.

2

Cleod – 38 Years

BRUTAL HEAT BLURRED EVERY SENSE AS CLEOD MOVED THROUGH twisting dust. Not even Gweld could cut the violent energy generated by the whirling particulate. The Council building loomed out of the storm. Inside awaited a fearful gathering of men for whom the past days' events meant both terror and exhilaration—a chance to claim the power of which they had always and only dreamed. And he and Trayor were the steel-edged tools by which that dream would be carved into being. How many men across Arnan would feel that rush of power as the truth about the Draigon, the death of Shaa, spread throughout the land? If Cleod's belly twisted at the thought, well, that was the cost of changing the world.

The structure blocked the wind. Cleod shoved open the door to the Council chamber and stepped inside.

From across the room, Trayor glared. "Nothing?"

Cleod stood a moment with Kilras's determined expression and Sehina's stare filling his mind, then shook his head. He ran his hand through his dirty hair as he watched the Draighil pace the length of the Council chamber.

"Gone! How?" Confusion and rage warred in Trayor's expression as he looked at Cleod.

Cleod blinked as surprise backed realization—that *Trayor's* Gweld sense had somehow not discovered the women. Something tingled in the depths of Cleod's mind but vanished before he could focus on it.

"All of them, *gone*. Where are their families?" Trayor's emotion landed on fury.

"Gone as well," came the cracked voice of the old man Cleod remembered from earlier meetings.

Trayor rounded on the Councilman. "Where?"

Where indeed? *Sehina leading the women into the swirling dust.* Somewhere beyond her, the others—Nae, Rimm, Jordin, must have gathered the loved ones. And somewhere on the trail they fled for safety. Where would they go? South most likely. Toward the coast and boats that could lead to escape.

Pulled like the tacky candy sold at fairs, the connection between Cleod and his caravan life thinned and thinned again, drawn brittle in the tempest-dimmed light of morning.

Escape. *Escape from him.*

The thought pierced, burned. Yet the boil in his gut was not regret, but deep anger. He acknowledged it even as he shoved aside any intention to examine the depth of it, the tangled ball of its roots.

"*Where?*" Trayor demanded again, eyes bright, jaw trembling.

Before anyone else could respond, Cleod spoke, "It doesn't matter." He met Trayor's vicious glare as it turned on him.

"Doesn't—?"

Cleod cut the pale man off again. "What do you want to do, send out search parties and chase them through this storm? Wherever they've gone, they'll carry the message of what happened here with them. They, and anyone else moving away from Melbis this day. If warning is what you want to spread, they will do it for you."

"I want them to carry more than a story of what happened here."

In the back of Cleod's mind, a heavy sigh, but he held his body still. "What more?"

Trayor crossed the room to stand before Cleod. "Obedience. They need to pay for their years of lies and murder."

Old gods he was out of patience with Trayor's arrogance. He was so like the elders who trained them. Nose to nose with the furious Draighil, Cleod shook his head. "Those women and their families aren't Draigon, Tray."

"How do you know? Draigon are women. *How do you know?*"

"Because if these women were Draigon, why in the names of all the old gods would they be living in Melbis?"

Silence dropped over the room.

"Yes," an old man said. "For years, we've kept a list of women who meet the needs of a Sacrifice. It's never been secret. They were told the truth of it—they were never to leave here, as one day their death might be required for the good of all."

At those words, Trayor's jaw dropped open a fraction and he turned to face the speaker.

Nausea rolled through Cleod. "These women have known all their lives that you meant to kill them one day?"

"It never mattered what they knew."

Three strides carried Cleod past Trayor to reach out and crush the front of the Councilman's tunic in a twisting grip and yank the man to his feet. "You idiot. It's *always* mattered. Or haven't you yet figured out what the Sacrifice has been about all these centuries?"

Behind Cleod, Trayor swore.

Cleod, glanced over his shoulder at the Draighil. "You finally understand." With a shove that sent the Councilman stumbling, Cleod released the shaking man.

"What?" he gasped, as he staggered to a halt, staring between the two swordsmen.

"Recruitment," Trayor snapped. "All these years—the more you hated a girl, the more likely the Draigon had found one worth bringing into their ranks." He stared at Cleod. "Your old friend. The one you nearly died for on the Spur." The gleam in Trayor's eyes shifted from anger to glee.

Cleod met that torturous gaze. "Are you satisfied?" he said.

"What greater punishment could you hope for, but that I was betrayed by one I trusted? That she tricked me into betraying the Ehlewer?"

"It's time you learned how that feels." Trayor's lips twisted. "Your precious Leiel *is one of them.*"

Fierce streaks of light slivered outward at the edges of Cleod's vision and the room swam as his senses expanded like the dust kicked up by the storm outside. Every speck of grit that coated his skin sat as a point of awareness; the voices around him echoed and rebounded inside his skull. Memories spilled through the gap in his control—a barking dog, feckless laughter, pages turning, the gleam of a crystal reflecting blazing firelight—Leiel—all things that had been and might have been Leiel—and the thing that she now was. Cleod swayed, braced will, and closed his eyes. He reeled, fought back Gweld even as the trance tugged and threatened to overwhelm him. Pain flared through his skull, a signal that the Overlash he could no longer hold off would soon drop him to his knees.

"A bronze monster," he said lowly, and opened his eyes to glare at Trayor. This pointless meeting needed to be over. *Leiel! No!* The thought screamed through his mind, whether plea or demand he could not say. Shaking, he turned for the door and offered angry words as though to solidify his emotion. "One I mean to deal with as you dealt with Shaa."

3

Cleod

*W*E'LL NOT CHASE THOSE WHO RAN. *P*LENTY MORE TO ROUND UP HERE. *Plenty more everywhere as the news spreads. Let the Draigon try to draw new numbers from the deepest dungeons of Arnan.* Trayor's final words to the Council bit deep into Cleod's mind, stripping all possibility of a restful night. He sat at the narrow desk by the window and shook, fighting Overlash until the inevitable desire to shut it all out overcame will.

The ercew consumed to stem trembling and induce sleep held sway for only hours before nightmare dragged him awake. The dreams lingered on the edge of consciousness in flickers of flame and suffering, unclear, yet hot across his senses.

He lay with one arm bent over the top of his head, staring at the shadowed ceiling. Every part of him ached, and he breathed hard into the discomfort, into the cramping in his gut that spoke of rising need. Drowning partly in Overlash and partly in unrelenting physical longing, his mind skipped and shuddered between waves of pain and vile emotions he could not name. Sweat broke a scattered line across his forehead. He closed his eyes as the shaking began again, and gritted his teeth, not quite able to contain a moan.

Old gods, after so many years, to have ended up here. With a gasp he rolled onto his side, eased his legs over the bedside and put his bare feet on the floor planks. Through the wall came Trayor's snoring. How quickly their tent camp had been abandoned for the comfort of the Nest once no one remained in Melbis to confront Cleod with choice. How lucky now, to have what he needed close at hand.

He pushed himself to his feet and staggered toward the door. Down the hall and the narrow stairs he moved, a hand pressed flat to the wall to hold balance and stay upright. The sweat thickened, slicked over his whole body, drawn by more than the heat.

On the ground floor, a single lamp burned, bright in the welded, metal lantern affixed to the registration counter. Cleod turned from it and staggered toward the storage room beside the kitchen.

Enough bottles of ercew had filled his grasp in years past that he knew the correct container by feel. A twist and pull of the cork and he raised the bottle to his lips and drank deep as tears mingled with sweat and ran down his face. He buried confusion in the pressure rising through his chest.

Yesterday, before consequence upended him in agony, his purpose seemed clear. In the Council house, confronting men who both feared him and held him in awe, the correctness of his choice loomed stark and certain. He ran a hand through his hair. Was it only yesterday that he walked away from Kilras? *Kilras. Sehina. Rimm and Nae and home.* Cracks laced their way through the foundation of a self built through years and by striving. How could everything that, just days ago, held Cleod's world together shatter so completely? *How had he let it?*

Green-gold eyes glinted in memory, bright and dangerous, warm and deepened by concern. Flames lit his mind, searing. He gagged and bent double, but managed to hold back the bile rising in his throat. An act of will forced him upright. Those eyes. Those vibrant, damning eyes. Would Leiel's eyes look like that, over time, as she aged and changed? Rage whipped through him. *No.* He would see her dead before he would witness her so marked by the creatures who had claimed her. *See her dead and see her eyes then...* Another shudder racked him. Dead like the woman on the hill outside Melbis. *Take Teska and go...no malice* or regret had carried with that thought, only something he could not bring himself to recognize.

The fight. Leiel and Teska. Shaa—and whatever, whoever, Shaa had become before she died. Smoke and fire and cuila and blood. So much blood.

He took another long, desperate pull on the bottle, drank until the shaking in his limbs subsided. The hill. The battle. Death. A bright gleam in the smoke. He had to know. Leiel. *He had to know.*

Bottle in hand, he made his way back upstairs to dress in the sweltering darkness.

Through the ongoing storm, the first hint of daylight lightened the air as Kicce walked across the rolling plain to the low hill where Shaa had died. The blocky suggestions of buildings slipped behind, and Cleod's stomach churned when he passed the now-vacant caravan camp. Hot wind swirled and buffeted, and he bent his head to let the brim of his hat catch the fiercest gusts. Between bursts, the bitter air settled, revealing the stark, burned landscape.

The land sloped upward, and the lingering scent of smoke and cuila filled his nose. The latter should have eased tension from his body, but instead his stomach turned again.

Ash and blown dust littered the torn earth. Scorch marks smeared between the scars made by great claws, the soil raked as though by a mad plowman. He turned slowly, his gaze sweeping the ground, measuring, seeking... What? Some evidence that he had been wrong? That the woman murdered here had not, after all, been Shaa, and so Leiel could not be what he feared, what he hated?

Not Leiel.

Not Leiel.

He dismounted, fighting cramps that swarmed up his legs into his belly. He swayed a moment, then drew a deep breath and surveyed the brutalized earth, tried to pick out the spot where the woman had fallen. But no clear indication remained. How was that possible? Blood had coated Trayor's sword, sprayed and pooled over the ground. For the flicker of an instant, memory flared of a wide, shimmering swath that marked annihilation, glittering impossibly in the starlight. So much spilled blood should have stained this ground for days. And yet nothing remained. Impossible. And impossible was proof. The woman had been other than human.

A shaking started in his hands and worked through his entire body. He sucked in air, turned away – from what? His belly boiled, hot acid and foam. Rage at—Leiel? Trayor? Himself?

Wind gusted, and the world tilted before him as the air cleared briefly. He found himself looking at the post where Teska Healer had been tied. A flash of pale light blinked from the soil a few steps past the post. The glint in the swirling sand, faint though it was, stopped all thought as recognition dawned.

Slowly, as though too-fast movement would somehow cause the item lying twisted in the dirt to vanish or even flee, he took a step, another. Each pace forward hovered over a void opened by shock. At last he crouched and reached out a hand, the action made hesitant by disbelief. Yet under his fingers it was solid and real. He jerked his hand back.

How many hours had he searched across the Spur, all those years ago, seeking hidden clusters, half-collapsed holes, outcrops of rock, until he found a place where the crystals were both large enough and pure enough to warrant choosing? Not only for himself—he reached up to touch the stone mounted atop his sword hilt—but, more importantly, for a gift meant to last and hold memory.

He scrambled downward, slipping and sliding with the shower of earth under his boots—sand and granite, the stumblingly mystifying combination that made up the soil of this mountain. Rattling stone, half-skidding, he landed at the bottom of the old pit. Just a bit deeper than he was tall, the hole was filled with enough sunlight that what he sought would not be difficult to spot as he dug.

The old books in Adfen's library offered only the vaguest clues about the best quality gemstones found in the Spur. The locations of those deposits were even harder to figure out. But figure it out he had. And now the digging of the Wild Stones would be easier than the finding of the mine.

A happy pressure built in his chest as he looked around, caught glimpses of shiny, fractured pieces of crystal protruding from the earth. Nothing large. Nothing whole. To find those, he would have to dig and dig and dig. But now that he knew where, he could come back, take the time he needed to find just the right stone for the sword he would own one day. And the right stone to give to Leiel—something to always remind her that they were friends.

Cleod gasped as his mind dropped back into his body and he folded onto his knees, the charred scent of the ground rising up to meet him. His head fell back and he closed his eyes, breathed, just breathed, for several heartbeats, until the hammering in his chest eased and the spiral of his mind slowed. Face raw from the dry blowing of sand and the bite of the wind, he cracked his eyes open and stared up at the whirling clouds.

He slid the stone across the table, heart in his throat as he lifted his hand away so she could see what lay on the dark wood, see what he offered. Something so she would know for sure he would keep his promise to her, and become what he needed to become to make everything right for both of them. Keep their friendship. Fight to keep her safe.

At last, he dropped his chin and stared at the torn circle of metal half-buried in the dirt. To either side of him huge, heavy dents scarred the ground. And beyond them the ash had flattened and flared wide. Leiel. Leiel had changed. Here on this spot, she had... The thought stumbled, stopped, and again he saw her standing small and fierce in flickering light and billowing smoke. Leiel... changed...and shattered the ring in doing so. And left it here—a token of the ruin that their friendship had become.

A flash in the moonlight. A ring, wrapped around her finger as she raised it to gently touch his cheek. So light. So gentle. Like a whisper of memory. Impossible. True.

And yet... All these years she had kept it until... Until he and Trayor had cut down Shaa and left the claiming of the Sacrifice to Leiel—*Bronze Draigon. Draigon in flight.*

The ercew had not been enough. He needed cuila. Needed so much. Overlash, too long denied, tore through him, laid claim. More cramps ripped into his thighs, seared upward until he doubled over, pressed into the ground. Every part of him shook, his thoughts tumbling and slamming into one another. What was he doing here? How had he come to this moment, this place where he lay in the dirt absolutely alone? He reached out, twisting his fingers through the soil to enclose the broken ring in his fist.

As pain pulled him under, his fractured cognition coalesced into a single realization backed by horror—his first thought upon arriving atop this hill had been that the woman who died here had been murdered.

4

Cleod

COUGHING IN THE GRITTY AIR, CLEOD PULLED HIMSELF ONTO KICCE'S back. Half the day he had lain with the heat beating over him and the storm covering him in sand. Kicce's worried nudging awakened him in early afternoon. The gelding, given his head, made straight for the livery across from the Nest. There, Cleod stripped Kicce's saddle and staggered through half-competent care of the horse before making his way to the inn.

He shoved open the door and met Lorrel's gaze across the dim-lit entryway. The innkeeper stared at Cleod a moment, then asked if he wanted the poit readied. Cleod's stomach lurched at the thought of the hot, dark space, and he shook his head. "No, just send extra rags to the room." The worst grime could be sponged off. Given the storm outside, no one in Melbis could claim cleanliness as a virtue.

Back in the familiar room, Cleod slung his sword harness onto the bed, then peeled out of his sand-packed clothing and let it drop to the floor. A clink sounded when his pants landed on the slate, and he paused, reached down and picked them up again. He fished into a pocket and pulled out the twisted remains of the gold ring. An indrawn breath hissed through his teeth. Instinct. Reflex. He had saved the ruined band without thought.

He turned it, stared again at the uncut stone mounted rough in the heavy setting. The stone intact. Unchanged. Unlike Leiel. Unlike himself. Unlike the dreams and promises they once shared. What had she held on to all these years?

A pounding started behind his eyes, and he closed his fist around the metal before crossing the room. He set the ring on the dresser beside the pitcher and basin, and just stood for a moment, trying to pretend he could not hear the howl of wind outside, or the rattle of grit on glass, or feel the heat pounding through even the Nest's thick walls. Then he ran a hand along the twisted flesh of his right hip, over the new-raised scab-over-scar formed when Trayor shoved him into the poit stove. Scars upon scars upon scars.

No. No time for such thoughts.

He ran a hand through his hair, knocking dirt loose. Tangled and filthy, his hair was too long for the role he was reclaiming. But cutting it... The idea rang false. The headache built, and a new cramping started in his belly. He gripped the edge of the dresser and bent his head, eyes closed. Breath flowed and, if the pain did not lessen, neither did it spiral him into helpless oblivion. Old gods—why so much pain? Not even the early days of learning Gweld had brought so much misery. Trayor seemed unaffected. Cleod shuddered. What had changed so much that he, the Draighil who so easily recovered from Gweld immersion that even the elders looked on him in awe, found himself plowed under despite cuila?

A few heartbeats passed, then he gathered will and straightened, reached for the pitcher and poured the basin full. He picked up one of the clean rags folded beside the bowl and soaked it in the tepid water. The dirt that he wiped from his body quickly tainted the bowl, and he tried to believe that he cleaned off more than dirt and heat—that he could wash away the weight of unrequited memory. The ring sat twisted beside the bowl, its ruined shape mimicking the churning of his unsettled mind. All these years, Leiel had kept the Wild Stone. Not just kept it, but worn it.

He wrung out the cloth, weeping water into the basin. Promises—made, kept, shattered. A lifetime of them. A lifetime that meant...what? He closed his eyes. Leiel. Vengeance. His purpose, chosen so long ago. The continuing imperative of his existence.

And the reason he, in the name of every old god, had ended up here like this.

At last, as clean as he could get under the circumstances, he turned and looked with distaste at the filthy clothing on the floor. Nothing for it but to shake it out as best he could. He carried the pants away from the bed and knocked free the worst of the encrusted sand and dirt.

A rap sounded on the door, and he had just time enough to yank on the pants before the handle turned and Trayor stalked into the room.

"Come on in," Cleod said. Long gone were the days when equal rank and skill demanded mutual respect. Well, time enough to correct that in the weeks to come. Cleod crossed to the dresser and picked up the rag to run over a particularly stubborn stain on his pants. It thinned under his scrubbing but did not come completely clean.

"You're alone?" The Draighil's gaze swept the space, measuring, then halted on Cleod. "You're returned from...where? The bottom of a filled-in well? Where's your vaunted pride?"

"Still in the well," Cleod said. "What did you expect to find here? A party of whores and me swimming in a barrel of ercew?" It was only half a joke. At this moment he would happily fling himself into just such a vat. He tossed the rag down beside the basin, stopped a flinch as it landed atop the damaged ring. Straightening his shoulders, he faced Trayor. "Why are you here? More words and quibbling from the Council?"

Trayor shook his head and gave a quick, dismissive wave of his hand. "What little purpose they ever served is no longer relevant. I'm here to discuss what comes next." He dropped himself into the chair by the window.

Cleod's chin came up, and he squinted through the headache. He studied Trayor, registering depth behind the other man's words that reached beyond the obvious. "You think you know what's next." Cleod tipped his head. "What? You believe that without the Draigon to claim as enemy, there won't be any need for those Councilmen either?"

Trayor laughed, low and with far more amusement than the moment warranted. "Petty fools. What have they ever been but tools of either the Enclaves or the Draigon?"

With a shake of his head, Cleod bent and picked up his shirt, shook dirt from it, and pulled it on. Of course Trayor wanted to see the Councils as only tools, but time had not been kind to the Enclaves. Of the six originally founded to train men to fight the Draigon, only three remained—and of those, only two still followed the full training regime and actually produced Draighil. But every town and city of any size had a Council. How could Trayor think that was irrelevant? The arrogance of that—Cleod formed a snide reply, then stopped, holding the pale man's gaze. "What do you know?" he demanded. All these years, the Ehlewer had kept the ruined uniform that Cleod had nearly died in on the Spur. Kept it and then repaired it. Trayor had traveled to Melbis with it. Trayor had come for Shaa knowing Cleod would also be here. A plan. Of course a plan. One long in the works and centered on Cleod and his knowledge. A plan that would affect far more than just the Enclaves. "What have you done?"

Trayor leaned back and laughed lightly. "Exactly what needed doing for years. Ensured Shaa would be the one to come for the Sacrifice in Melbis. Ensured you would help me kill the beast. With Shaa dead, what's to stop us and the King's best from marching north and destroying the rest of them?"

"You're telling me the King has his army waiting at the ready under the assumption you would succeed?"

The grin the spread across Trayor's face was all the reply Cleod needed. Old gods, could he ever have been so much a fool as to have believed the Enclaves ever *let a Draighil go*? All these years, all the trails and roads traveled, for what? To learn he was only ever a game piece on the board of Arnan? To learn how quickly the years of struggle for sobriety and purpose could be wiped away? To learn that the violent intent to which he had given himself long ago had ever and always been his destiny?

He turned his back on Trayor and stood staring for a moment into the dirty water in the basin. Beside it, the crumpled rag hid the ring. Hid the past. All of this had always been for Leiel. *He* had always been for Leiel. The headache expanded and he pressed a hand to his temple. Need creased his gut.

Behind Cleod, the chair creaked as Trayor rose to his feet. "Meet me downstairs. I'll tell you what comes next, over as much ercew and boiled meat as you can keep down." The door whispered open, then closed with a click.

For a few breaths, Cleod stood still, then he slipped his hand under the rag and gathered the ring in a tight fist, metal pressing into his palm until it pierced skin. With a curse, he stuffed it into his pocket and bent to pull on his boots.

The dining room buzzed with speculation and uneasy chatter as the wind rattled the windows, and blowing sand etched at the glass. Seated across from Trayor at a corner table, Cleod half-listened as the Draighil recounted, with growing embellishment, the tale of Shaa's killing for every curious citizen who approached with questions or praise.

Cleod wrapped one hand around a crockery mug, and stuffed the other into his pocket and turned the broken ring over in his fingers. Every line of the metal band, every angle of the uneven surface of the stone, etched its way into memory as he rolled it this way and that. The ache in his head expanded, and he closed his eyes. Leiel. The purpose chosen long ago. The continuing imperative of his existence.

"Not a word is reaching through your throbbing skull." The shove of Gweld power backing Trayor's words pierced with a sharpness all their own.

Cleod's fingers stopped their movement, and he opened his eyes to glare at the Draighil. "Are any of them important? This story you spin as though it were truth?" Cleod raised his drink and let the ercew burn its fated way into his belly. It landed like flaming coals, and he held still to be certain it stayed down.

Something dark and frantic flared in Trayor's eyes, something that did not match the words that followed. "We've a war ahead. Only you would think that what I've got to say about it is meaningless. So, by all means, tell me what *you* have planned."

The Draighil's tone tripped a fleeting flash of memory—*a moonlit night, a field of damp grass*—gone as fast as it came. "Is that what you've been rattling on about? The King's army and the coming war? I thought you were regaling your admirers with tales of blood and glory." *No blood. Why had there been no blood?*

Trayor laughed, and the note that had caught Cleod's attention was gone. "That too. Better get used to it. I'm the man who killed Shaa. Whatever you make of my re-tellings, that remains *truth*, as though such is of concern to anyone." He grinned, bending the scar on his face. "If the King isn't wise and wary, perhaps, before this is over, I'll be *more* than the greatest Draighil who ever lived."

Cleod's thoughts skittered, then leaped. "*You* want to be *King*?" For a moment, the idea spun terrible possibility through his mind. Then the absurdity of it crested like a building wave and broke against deeper held knowledge. Cleod laughed, full out and from the gut for the first time since Leiel had stepped from the shadows. "The King sits too far from daily admiration for your needs."

Trayor's jaw tightened and his eyes narrowed. Then his lips curled into a shape something between a smile and a sneer and the scar moved like a fang. "You think you know me."

All laughter in Cleod died, and he met Trayor's chill gaze. "I've always known you," Cleod said. Young laughter and ego and skill and hard-earned pride. Fear and grief and jealous fury.

All the things he and Trayor shared—past and present—now mattered only so much as it commanded action over the next days or weeks or months. Honor. The Enclaves. Pride. To what end, any of it, if not to finally *end* what had so long ago begun? To destroy the Draigon. Whatever treason came after, mattered little to him. "What are we riding into when we leave Melbis?"

Trayor leaned back, lowered his voice. "A kingdom primed for war. An army ready to ride north and wipe out the Draigon. An army led by the Ehlewer."

"You mean led by you."

Trayor simply smiled.

With a shake of his head, Cleod braced his elbows on the table. "By the time we reach Sibora, it will be the heart of winter. No army will march across Spur country, much less to the Great Northern Range before spring."

Trayor laughed, certainty brimming his words. "But it's *Draigon* we face. And what is their greatest power? Look outside. *Draigon Weather*. Heat and fire. Even before we learned their greatest weakness, winter was the *only* time to strike. The very things that make this time of year dangerous for armies will be negated. To stop us, they have to stop winter as well. No blizzards. No thigh deep snow. No broken supply chains. No chance of freezing to death. In all the centuries of record—only a handful of Draigon remain." He laughed, reached for his own mug and took a deep drink. "*And Shaa is dead.* Their leader. The only one really worth fearing. And when I march north with the greatest Farlan army ever assembled, with every Draigre from every Enclave," He paused. "With you." Another drink, another widening grin. "We'll destroy the monsters forever. And then, if you think I will be unable to demand whatever I want as tribute—well, you say you know me. I look forward to watching your face when you realize your latest mistake."

Cleod's voice held ice. "Generous of you to assume I'll make none between now and then." They had underestimated the

Draigon for centuries...and yet Trayor's words made uncomfortable sense. The Draigon were few. Even if every girl and woman they had taken through the centuries still lived and was one of them now, that was how many? A few hundred? That might matter if all were capable of becoming the monsters he knew...but were they? No evidence of that existed. How many Draigon did the histories record as claiming Sacrifice? Two dozen? And how many of those had fallen to a Draighil blade? More than half. And the only new beast anyone had seen in decades was the one that had taken flight from here.

The ache in his skull expanded, violent and ringing. He raised the mug and forced down a long drink, and his next words slurred. "And that you'll make no mistakes yourself."

"Damned drunk." Trayor waved his hand for a serving boy to replenish their drinks. "If nothing else, it saves on my cuila."

Rage slipped between the pulses of pain in Cleod's skull, and he bent his head, squeezed closed his eyes. Some understanding slipped vague and half-acknowledged through his mind before pain overwhelmed it. Cuila. Trayor. A plan to destroy the Draigon. Why not? In all the unfolding madness, why not?

The pounding in his skull demanded comfort and the click of crockery settling on the table rang like a bell. He reached for the fresh offering and downed it with something akin to desperation.

5

Kilras – 46 Years

STEP AFTER STEP, THE MARE CARRIED KILRAS NORTH THROUGH THE desperate dust and dryness of each merciless day. Despite the endurance of years spent on the trail, the unbroken hours of days in the saddle brought a steady ache to his knees. Every part of him creaked through the coating of dust and grime that pressed into the fine lines around his eyes and each seam of his clothing. Not even the tight-woven brekko kept it all from his lungs. Twice this night he had stopped to change the cloth he had woven through the mare's bridle to protect her from the worst of the particulate grit. Riding head bent against the wind, did nothing to ease the worry in his mind or the anger twisting his heart. Only reaching into his bag and gripping the crystal of Draigon blood helped, though he did not understand the instinct that pressed him to reach for it at all. His fingers itched for it now, but instead he reached for the canteen slung from the pommel. The water was tepid against his lips, but he welcomed every drop.

Well supplied though he had been at the start, scarcity of the precious liquid threatened more each day. After the second, he found shelter to sleep through the boiling daytimes and traveled only at night. Did Leiel consider that this violent deepening of Draigon Weather would harm her potential allies as much as it held off her enemies? Unlikely, burdened as she must be with the weight of the events that unfolded in Melbis. And if she thought of such things, what would she do differently? What would he do in her place? Pointless consideration. His own choices lay stark over his thoughts. Could *he* have acted, somehow, differently or sooner, to disrupt the pattern that led to such loss as they all now carried? And did it matter at all that he could look back and say, yes, perhaps? Because there existed no chance to affect those moments where the possibility of change had dwelt. Too late, ever and always, to look back and wish for alternate action, or the wisdom to guess future consequence.

Behind, traveling south with what he hoped was all purposeful speed, Sehina and Rimm and Nae led the caravan to Giddor and safety. What would become of them, his friends, his chosen and created family? Despite what he had told them, how much did they understand about events unfolding across Arnan? Would the knowledge he had imparted, and their own steady natures, be enough to keep them safe? Were they far enough ahead of the news of Shaa's death and the truth about the Draigon to not be connected with the events that now marked Melbis? If the old gods were anything more than mortal women ensconced atop a distant mountain, Kilras might have prayed.

He sighed and swung out of the saddle to give the mare a break. One of Sehina's best trained, he trusted the horse over any terrain, day or dark, but the relentless heat and limited water worked against both of them. What rest he could offer her while still maintaining steady progress, he would give. Ahead, somewhere, Leiel and the healer, Teska, worked their way across the rolling plains. Another day might see them into light forest and rolling, broken hills. Far from the main trade road, their cross-country route discouraged pursuit. Little good it would do them if Cleod and Trayor organized to pick up the trail. More than luck made that unlikely—the storm Leiel had set served both to cover her tracks and punish those tempted to pursuance. A benefit to her and her charge, but torment to Kilras and his mare.

Kilras offered up sincere words of gratitude to Kinra and Aweir and Gahree and all their training in survival and way-finding. Though useful through his years of travel, those hard-learned skills mattered more than ever as he followed in the wake of a Draigon determined to not be caught.

The mare snorted and shook her head, rattling bit and reins. "Easy," he said. "We'll stop with the dawn. There's ground to cover yet." As though she understood his words, she settled, walking steadily beside him.

Then, for a moment, the wind abated, and as the dust slowly settled out of the air, the moon washed him in silver light. With a sigh, he reached up and pulled down the brekko, breathed in mostly-clear air for the first time in days. Would it last? Had Leiel's rage and pain eased enough that she would lift the storm, if not the heat of Draigon Weather? Doing so would make her journey easier as well. Unless—he scanned ahead—unless he was close enough to be sharing in clear air she positioned over herself and her companion. Was it possible that he had gained ground on them? Only one way to tell.

He stood still, measuring the risk of detection by hostile parties and the potential force of his own banked fury. Limits marred choice. He surrendered to the first true need he had encountered in years, and opened his senses to the full awareness of Gweld.

Like a golden flood, it washed outward from where he stood, a rolling wave of brilliance and delicate connection that pulled together pieces of his mind and spirit long held separate. For the sake of peace and Cleod's sanity, for Kilras's own protection and that of those in his charge, decades had passed since he allowed himself to unfurl the entirety of his connection to the world around him, to feed the full depths of his soul. He swayed where he stood, rocked by the return of something he, until this moment, refused to acknowledge that he missed with a desperation that bordered on agony.

Wind on high! Was this what kind of unanswered need that Cleod felt when he craved the ercew, the cuila? If so, then the other man's decade-long-abstinence was nothing short of miraculous. But no...Gweld did not possess, did not carve out dark depths of spirit, did not shatter conscience, or render friendship and will and choice irrelevant. Only the Enclave's madness-inducing drug-plant could warp this dazzling experience into something that demanded pain and brutality to wield. Had Cleod ever experienced Gweld without Overlash—Gweld like *this*, natural, essential, sublime, *unifying*—would Trayor have been able to lay claim to the darkest parts of Cleod's soul?

Standing still in the brief respite of moonlight, something important, shadowed and as yet unformed, *almost* moved into view of Kilras's senses. But before he could grasp it, a flicker of something far distant, at the very edge of his expanded perception snared his attention. Another Gweld-touched awareness, hot and bright and relentless. A consciousness that burned with determination and a heat not unlike that sweltering the air around him.

He drew a breath and loosed a needle-thin arrow of intention across the leagues separating that mind from his own. And waited. Like a star being born in velvet night, he witnessed the moment that deliberate message connected across the void. For several seconds, nothing happened, and around him nothing stirred, not even the mare. Then the wind kicked up again, but this time, not in a battering swirl of storm, but in a sharing, cooling breeze that pushed away the dust that remained in the air and opened a clear sky above him. It swept the sky clean and moved on, left the night cooler, and the landscape visible all the way to the starlit horizon.

Tension slid from his shoulders like water. "Many thanks," he offered to the distant entity, and shuttered the glowing sense that edged all the world in gold. Best to contain it, not yet get lost in it. Because need dictated that he relearn to make full use of the skill in the days to come.

Leiel

DAYS CRAWLED INTO NIGHTS AS LEIEL AND TESKA MADE THEIR WAY
north, each one harder and hotter and more wearing than
the last. And while the wisdom of Gahree's long years of teaching might linger in Leiel's heart, reaching it was, at least for now, marked by pain all but too brutal to bear. Only time would change that, and this morning marked not yet time enough.

"Leiel—?" Teska's voice carried on the morning air.

Leiel raised her head to see the healer standing on the top of the low bank. The light had brightened enough that the tired lines on the other woman's face showed clearly. Soon the sun would break into view, and with it would come the first taste of truly brutal heat, unlifted despite Gahree's death. Unlifted because Leiel held the weather, like her sorrow and her anger, close and tight. The energy of the storm she perfectly measured to last until a reason for dismissal could be found and wielded like mercy. Such seemed unimaginable this moment.

Then the worried excitement in Teska's expression registered, and Gweld sparked a rainbow fervor of lines and swirls across Leiel's vision. "He's in sight?"

"No, but he's closer. Much. I can almost see him without seeing him."

Leiel nodded, straightened from filling their canteens and came up from the scraggling creek to join Teska. And if Leiel was nearly ready again to claim the Great Shape and fly them north, one thing remained to be confronted—the man who followed them, unerring, at the border of her senses. Whether because she recognized the imprint of his presence, or because she had spent the last days more alert than she had ever been, she felt him in the distance though she had yet to catch sight of him. Kilras Dorn, following them north.

The unsubtle impact of his Gweld-backed message rocked her. Whatever had happened in Melbis after the Sacrifice had driven him from the life he had built over three decades. Where were the rest of his people? Where was Cleod?

Leiel's stomach churned and she blinked hard, set her jaw. Her thoughts swirled, threatening to tumble her mind into chaos and her heart into a spiral of guilt. She sucked breath, and shook herself. No time for any of that. No time for self-pity. She knew too little about the events unfolding behind her. Kilras would have that information. And he would understand her grief in a way Teska never could.

"Gather your things," Leiel said. "We make for higher ground."

Flat on her stomach, ignoring the pebbles and roots that dug into her hip bones and forearms, Leiel gazed out over the landscape. The week since she and Teska had walked away from Melbis seemed an eternity, edged by a fog of grief and anger.

Movement shivered out of the heat-cast mirage at the edge of the horizon. From her vantage on the tree-broken ridgeline she watched him cross the long valley that marked the end of the plains. Head bent, leading his mount in the high light of the mid-day sun, he moved with steady, purposeful strides. He stopped near where she and Teska had camped last night, walked down into the ragged trees to water his horse and fill his canteens, then moved toward them again.

Sprawled on her belly beside Leiel in the narrow patch of

shade cast by a stand of stunted, wind-bent firs, Teska stirred, impatient. "That's him? The caravan leader?"

Leiel flicked a glance at the other woman. "Yes."

The healer raised up a little on her elbows and squinted down at the man. The air thickened in a way Leiel had come to recognize as signaling a level of attention that tapped Teska's instinctive access to Gweld. Wind and wings! What would she be able to do with that skill if she gained the Great Shape?

In the valley, Kilras slowed, stopped. He raised his head and scanned the mountains before him until at last he fixed his gaze in Teska's direction.

The healer drew a sharp breath, and when Leiel glanced at her, the younger woman's expression was pinched with something more than surprise. "How?"

"Gweld," Leiel said.

"The word you use to describe how I can see enai?" Teska looked at Leiel.

"It's the word most use to name such skill, yes." She lifted her chin a fraction toward Kilras. "And he has known how to use it for almost as long as either of us has been alive. And how to sense it in use."

"But—" Teska began, looking back toward the figure in the distance. She frowned as though considering something, then shook her head. "He knows we're here."

Below, Kilras started walking again, his mare trailing behind him, moving directly toward them. The narrow notch that breached the ridge several dozen paces from where they crouched was not the easiest route into this range. To have selected it meant that his pause and fixation of attention in their direction were not at all random.

"He knows." Leiel pushed her self back onto her knees and brushed crushed leaf bits from her shirt. "What do you see in him?"

Again, Teska shook her head. "Distance muddies my skill."

"Yet, you reached out anyway."

The healer smiled faintly. "Since I've no longer any need to hold back what I can do, I might as well test the limits of it."

Despite the weight in her heart, Leiel's lips twitched upward. She remembered feeling the same way, once she gained her freedom, though her realization had not come quite as swiftly as Teska's. Was that because Teska had been raised with more freedom of mind and action than Leiel had ever dreamed to know? Or was it simply part of who Teska was, that she adapted so quickly to the idea? Perhaps it was simply easier to expand on what she was already comfortable with, than to dwell on the events that had led them to this point. The thought crushed Leiel's grin. She swallowed, her throat thick. Time would be the test, for both of them. She looked down on the man walking toward the mountains. The test for all of them.

Leiel got to her feet and offered a hand to Teska. "We might as well set camp. He'll be most of the afternoon crossing that valley, and in need of what hospitality we can provide once he arrives."

7

Leiel

SHE MET HIM WHERE THE TRAIL BEGAN TO FLATTEN TOWARD THE CREST of the notch. He moved slowly over the rocky terrain, letting the mare behind him pick her way with care, his gaze sweeping ahead with sharp attention. When it found hers across the arid, empty space, he paused, then crossed the remaining distance between them. The mare's shoes rang on the stone and echoed off the ridgeline behind her.

He stopped before Leiel and lifted off his burgundy hat to run a hand back through his hair with the same calm control that she remembered from their brief encounter in Melbis.

"Kilras Dorn."

He shook his head. "Kilras *Hantyn*."

Her breath hitched. If he had chosen to reclaim the name he was known by among the Draigon, then the situation he had left behind must be darker than she imagined. What had happened? How many more had been hurt or endangered by her actions, by the events unfolding because of her choices? Shivering despite the warm air and the Draigon heat deep in her spine, she pressed her lips together, trying to contain the tug of tears in the back of her throat. She managed quiet words. "So bad?" What was coming? What had she set in motion?

He nodded, returned his hat to his head. The mare beside him nudged her nose into his shoulder, and he slipped his arm under her chin to scratch her far cheek. "You've found water up here?" He flicked his gaze over the stark terrain.

That simple, practical concern shook her attention back to the moment. "Yes. A healthy spring. Come." She turned and led the way over the stone toward a scraggly stand of trees near a granite outcrop.

The mare snuffled her nose into the low depression among the stones, sighed as she found the water and settled to quenching her thirst. Kilras held her reins, made sure she did not over-indulge.

Silence hung in the air as Leiel studied him. Dirty, trail weary, he stood with a contained poise that reflected hard-earned confidence. Every word she had read of his, every story she had dragged from Delhar *and...Wynt...and Gahree...* She shook herself from clutching memory. Every line scribed by Kilras's hand had been carved by a self-aware honesty that could cut to the bone. How many years had she wondered about this man? Despite having read his book-length letters to Delhar, despite dozens of conversations with those who had known him in his youth, Leiel's curiosity about the person who had taken it upon himself to save Cleod's life had grown year by year. A thousand questions unfolded in her mind. As many as she was certain he had for her. And something more important. "I finally get to thank you."

He returned the slightest flicker of a smile. "You're welcome."

Leiel nodded. "But you never did it for me."

"I did it for Gahree," he said. "At least at first. Then for me. And for him. Cleod is worth saving."

"Even now?" she asked. *Gahree's body draining crystalline blood into the brittle grasses and cracked soil of the plains...*

Kilras looked at her. "Cleod is Cleod."

When I am grown, I will be a Draighil. "Stubborn."

"Loyal."

Her heart dropped like a tossed stone. "To all the wrong things."

"It often seems that way."

She gazed back, swallowed pride. "You've spent years with him. Tell me what I don't know, that I need to now." It burned to her core—that the horror of Melbis had cracked the certainty that had driven her to confront Cleod, had shadowed her assurance of self and vision and deed. And yet she *knew Cleod*. Knew him still. The way she knew the beat of her heart and her breath and the heat that lived along her spine. She believed it. She had to. Because in that belief lay what sustained her, always—what Gahree died to protect—hope.

The mare shook her head hard, rattling tack, then snorted and dipped her nose back into the water. The faintest breeze whispered the air, unexpected, and was gone. Another few heartbeats passed, then Kilras said, "Not loyal to the wrong things. To whatever he cares about enough to allow it to give him purpose—especially to protect."

She considered, felt the truth of his words, said, "For a long time, that has been you and your caravan and his friends among you. Before that, the Ehlewer."

Kilras nodded. "And that was for your sake."

She shook her head. "I spoke with him then. It was more than that. The Ehlewer *became* the purpose you spoke of. Look what they have been able to shift him to once again."

Again, silence fell between them. "And yet, when he fought Shaa on the Spur *for you*, it took only that encounter with the truth to crack his connection to the Enclaves."

Leiel shifted, took a step closer, and held his gaze. "You are saying I should have done more—told him more then."

Kilras shook his head. "No. When he was fully Draighil? It took Shaa to reach him, and then it was only in Gweld."

Now, how had he known that? She blinked, then shook herself, reminded herself of what she had told Teska only hours before. Kilras had known the Draigon, known Gweld, since before she was born. "Are you playing at being Gahree—telling me things I already know?"

A low laugh came from the man. "I'm nothing like Gahree," he said. "But I learned from her. Just as you did. "

Hot and bitter, a weight pressed through Leiel's throat and into her chest. It was hard to swallow, hard to breathe. Gahree was gone. Her knowledge and her singular way of sharing it, through story and humor and wit, lost. Could the Draigon recover from that? Would they survive the coming war to even try? And what could Leiel do to save either legacy?

He added, "But neither of us will ever be her."

Were her thoughts so obvious? "Never."

"It's not judgment. No one should try to be." His words held a touch of self-recrimination.

She smiled, raised her eyebrows.

With a wry shrug, he said, "I've gotten used to being right."

Between them, unasked, hung the question that weighted every word spoken. Soft, but firm, she said, "I went to him because I felt it in him—the same thing that drove him to seek the Enclaves, to face Shaa the first time in Adfen. That anger—that need to *make things right*. He *wanted* what happened in Melbis—perhaps not as it happened—but he wanted—Shaa...." Her words twisted into silence. But she remembered—what it was like for desired revenge to take hold, to rip her soul from purpose. Then she shook herself and continued. "He would have sought the battle, Kilras Dorn, whether I showed myself or not."

"Given Trayor Draighil's presence in Melbis, I cannot disagree," he said, but something hard marred the words, and his gaze shifted inward for a heartbeat as he spoke.

"*Used to being right.*" She repeated his words. "And in charge."

He grunted, brought full attention back to her. "That too. " He patted the mare's neck. "Though that might be useful, going forward."

Her shoulders stiffened. Had he been so long away from Cyunant that he had forgotten how Draigon society worked? But then she thought of the list Gahree had left her, dozens of names of those who had never lived among Draigon, yet were still considered allies. Among them, Kilras was not only known by his reputation and his years of travel, but likely to connect and communicate better with them than any of the Draigon ever could. That truth saddened her, even as she accepted it. And allowed with it a thought that might matter even more. "Can we reach him?"

His reply came without hesitation. "We'll damn well try."

So poised, with the same kind of certainty she had possessed just days ago, when she sought out Cleod. Oh, to share in it now. And yet... She looked at Kilras. Different, somehow than when she met him in Melbis, his expression less balanced, darker. She shook herself internally. What else could be expected, after what had happened? Then something deep in her stomach flipped, flipped again. *They would try.* "Yes," she agreed. "Though the question of how might take more than the two of us to answer."

With Kilras's horse cared for and left with easy access to the spring, Leiel led the way around the jumble of boulders and along the ridgeline to the hollow of land she had chosen as their campsite. Purposefully heavy footed, she kicked pebbles over the rocky ground, offering Teska fair warning of their approach.

The healer looked up from the pile of rocks she was arranging into a fire pit, then rose to her feet when she saw Kilras, wariness in her stance. Her hand went to the narrow cut on her neck.

Leiel smiled in reassurance, and after a heartbeat Teska came forward. She stopped a few paces from them and looked at Kilras, and the air between them shifted with the intentional pressure of Gweld sense, seeking and measuring.

Kilras stiffened, straightened, and his eyes widened. "Storms and starlight! I see why Gahree came for you herself." He looked at Leiel. "Untrained?"

"Trained by my grandmother, Nortu," Teska said.

He returned his attention to Teska, studied her for a few seconds, and nodded. "Teska Healer, I'm Kilras Hantyn. Most know me as Kilras Dorn. Your grandmother was known for her skill, but I never knew this was part of it."

Teska glanced at Leiel. "I never knew what I do is so special." She paused. "Or so threatening."

Kilras's expression shifted, became partly puzzled, and Leiel answered with what little she understood of Teska's gift. "She can see—see the weight people carry—the tones of it. Their pain. Their confusion. She can use that to measure when something helps heal them."

Teska hesitated a heartbeat, then spoke. "Grandmother always told me what we could do could make others fear us. I never understood why, until now."

Leiel's jaw tightened. So many things held the possibility of multiple action and outcome. Beginnings were endings. Wisdom so often paired with pain. "I learned, when I came to live with the Draigon, that when something is dangerous, it is also often many other things. Like fire. It warms. It cooks. It kills."

"Fire?" Teska shook her head, a slight smile on her lips. "I think my grandmother would have liked that idea." She gestured toward the circle of stones she had constructed. "If it weren't for the comfort of a hot meal, I wouldn't bother in this heat."

Tears gathered in Leiel's eyes as the man beside her nodded. She had witnessed, from careful distance, the small, crackling fire he built for Cleod on the plains outside of Melbis. Nothing dictated need for that blaze. Nothing but familiarity and the offer of such comfort as hand-build heat could offer.

"Fire, in Arnan, is never far from our hearts," he said.

"For best moments, or for sorrow," Leiel agreed, blinking back the moisture in her eyes. "You have enough wood?"

Teska nodded, and returned to the work their arrival had interrupted.

"I've enough provisions in my saddle packs to feed us all for a couple more days," Kilras said. "I know you didn't plan to be on the ground this long."

"No," Leiel agreed. Not this long. Not long enough for Gahree to die and for them to have to flee. Not this long for Leiel to be alone with her thoughts and her fears and her anger. "But Gahree, being Gahree, left us well supplied. And I don't need much."

Kilras tipped his head to acknowledge her words. "Food's like fire."

Memories blossomed—Gahree carefully spacing bright peppers on a blanket as though they were jewels on display, offering Leiel crisp snap peas on a hot day, digging through rich dirt in the greenhouse. "Comfort," she whispered, then blinked and looked at Kilras. "Tell me you have fresh peppers."

He offered a short laugh, and something darkly thoughtful flickered in his eyes before he shook his head. "No. But I've some dried pepper flakes, if that will suffice. I never had Gahree's talent for growing things, especially on the trail."

"Or in a drought."

"Yes."

Through the heaviness in her heart, Leiel smiled the slightest bit. "Break out what you've got. We have a lot to talk about and I have a feeling we're going to need much comfort."

Sunset slid toward night in layers of silted grey and deep blue. Plate in her lap, seated cross-legged beside Teska, Leiel looked across the fire at Kilras as he picked up his tin tea cup. His fingers flexed and tapped against it as though seeking something more substantial. Other than that, his calm spoke of a spirit so self-contained and confident that it took her little effort to understand the passion and loyalty of those who followed him. Unsurprising that, molded as he had been from childhood within the framework of Draigon integrity. Like Kinra and Dahlie and Gydron, he faced the world with an unflinching stoicism. No wonder Cleod, and so many others, had found a place with this man. What happened in Melbis? What had he left behind? "Where is your caravan?"

"Heading south at all speed." He sipped the drink, frowned.

"Apologies that it is not coffee," she said, and he offered a vague smile. She waited, but the silence held and at last she requested, "Tell me."

He drew his knees up and rested his forearms across them, cup loose between his fingers. "The Council declared themselves the law and dispensers of judgment. With Cleod and Trayor's help, they arrested as many women as the city jail could hold."

Leiel sucked air, and beside her Teska's gasp indicated as much fear as shock. "Who?" Teska demanded, her meal forgotten. "Are they alive? Did the Draighil hurt anyone?"

"No. Those women are well, and long gone from the city," Kilras said. "I saw to it before I left. I didn't get all their names, but I did get them all out. At least the ones they took the first night. Staying longer wasn't possible."

Leiel took in the meaning behind that simple statement. Wind on high! He had rescued women put in danger by events she had set in motion. Why had she ever believed she could—? She cut the thought short. *No.* Too late for blame and self-deprecation. There was no such thing as *undoing.* And what had been done had, regardless, only partly been done by her. Cleod's bitter determination. Trayor's furtive scheming. The Council's arrogant rage. All were part of the same events, and where causation began, where blame ended, could not be measured in any place beyond her own conscience. "You were seen."

"By Cleod."

Her heart turned to lead in her chest. She met his gaze, held it, and waited, listened as he spoke in detail of his last meeting with Cleod and what had passed between them. Of his orders to his team and the risk they, too, had willingly accepted. Of his choice to abandon the life he had built and follow her north.

"You risk so much," Teska's words slipped between them, filled with sorrow, and an unspoken question—All this for me?

Leiel reached out and grasped the healer's hand.

"No more than either of you." Kilras's words landed gently.

Leiel nodded at his answer. "Change is upon us, Teska. And if you are at the center of it, then so are we. We take the blows as they fall, and we move forward. It's all anyone can do."

"Is change always pain?" she asked.

Aching with remembrance of just how young the other woman was, Leiel managed a smile. "Often."

Kilras made a noise of agreement.

"But not always?"

A thousand memories filled with hope and light and promise spilled through Leiel's thoughts. *Ilora's firm assurance on the steps of the Tower. Cleod sliding the Orast stone across their shared desk. Gahree seated on the wagon's tailgate, kicking her feet.* "No." *Leiel's first sight of Cyunant as Shaa banked over the mountain. The moment Gweld fully filled her senses. The Great Shape letting her claim the sky.* "Most definitely *not* always."

Silence fell, and the sky continued to darken with the slow approach of nightfall. Leiel reined in her thoughts, tried to simply breathe in the quiet.

Then Teska spoke again, quickly, as though expressing thoughts as they formed without any pause for evaluation. "If that's the way of it, then maybe the pain we've already been through is enough?"

Leiel blinked, raised her free hand to her face and closed her eyes to hide a smile that seemed not at all fitted to the moment. Then Kilras burst out laughing, the sound startling and yet *completely* appropriate. With a choked gasp, Leiel joined him, and Teska, as though she recognized the absurdity of her statement, surrendered to mirth as well.

When at last they regained composure, Leiel's sides and head ached. Nothing was truly funny, and that made the need for laughter all the greater. "Oh, if the world were so simple as that," she said. "Imagine—fairness. What lives we could have if such a thing were the heart of existence."

"I've a vivid sense of wonder, Leiel Draigon, and I can't conjure up what that world would look like," Kilras said.

The dream that sustained her, of a world where laughter and learning were denied to none, echoed through her. The dream Gahree and Ilora and all the other Draigon supported, encouraged, fed with wild ideas and endless passion. "*I* can," she answered, quiet, staring at the horizon as the last color slipped from the air. "At least in part."

Teska added wood to the fire, spiking flame that pulled Leiel's thoughts back to the moment. She held up a hand in the dying light. "No, let it set with the sun."

"Mood or practicality?" Kilras asked.

A smiled pulled briefly at her lips. "A bit of both. We don't need it, and we're camped high enough that the light might carry."

"I suspect you would know if anyone was out there to see it."

"Maybe. It would depend on who."

Teska shifted, resettled on the rocky ground and asked, "You mean others who see the way that you—that *we*—see?"

Leiel looked over at the other woman, fast becoming nothing more than a shape pressed to shadow in the growing darkness. No better time than now to begin sharing the knowledge that could lead Teska to the Great Shape. Her natural abilities were incomparable and priceless. The sooner insight granted the ability to expand them, the more they could potentially render healing through the world. "Not all of us see through Gweld in quite the same way. Or with the same clarity, or across great distance. So, since I don't know who might be out there, or what they can measure over long range, the less we offer them to find, the better."

Teska's silence held several seconds. "What do *you* see?" she asked at last.

"Color," Leiel said, and as she spoke, her words framed themselves in a prismatic sheen in her mind. "Like rainbows birthing rainbows. Until I need to know something, then color stabilizes, intensifies. I've come to understand what each tone means, at least much of the time." She laughed. "Or so I like to think. I've been wrong more than once."

"When it was important *not* to be wrong?"

Leiel shook her head, realized that Teska could not see the gesture and spoke instead. "No, not yet. Only my judgment about what to *do* with what I know has been badly enacted. Never the message itself—not the heart of it." She had not been wrong about Cleod. Not ever. But... *No.* Not even her choice of actions had been wrong, because, looking back, even had she chosen not to show herself to Cleod, Trayor still would have found him, would have turned the unquiet depths of Cleod's heart and wreaked havoc in the wake of that compromise. Whether that had been easier to accomplish because of her actions, she would never know. But nothing altered the fact that the brutal shift would have occurred with or without her.

"Trayor chose his moment," Kilras said, as though he could read her thoughts. Or, more likely, his followed a similar bent. If he, so close to Cleod all these years, had not seen this coming, how could she—blinded by distance and nostalgia?

Leiel sighed. "How did we miss it? All of us?" The Draigon roamed Arnan in many ways, watching, listening. And yet no word of the treachery that had killed Wynt, and now Gahree, had reached them until it was too late. Or rather, word of it had been *bait* for Shaa...and so for Cleod.

"The Enclaves aren't populated by fools. They hold their knowledge close." He frowned. "And Trayor knows things about Cleod that no one else ever will." Kilras's tone dropped lower as the darkness deepened. "We thought they'd let him go. We were wrong."

Leiel's blood ran with mountain snow melt. Wind and wings! And the Draigon thought *they* had plans for the world. Failure to consider that their enemies might have their own had created all this. "All these years," she said. "We never saw. Never suspected."

"*You* didn't. *I* didn't." Kilras made a chagrined noise. "I'd lay silver on Gahree's vision out-stripping ours."

The letter. The list of names—people and places and skills—Gahree had left for just such this eventuality. Leiel laughed, despite the ache in her gut and the crawling chill of realization. "Yes. It's likely that she suspected."

"Then why did she let this happen?" Teska's words fell into a silence that held onto unease.

Then Leiel blew out slow breath. "Gahree was never one for absolutes. Never one to take choice from anyone else. She'd let me stumble for weeks until I figured a problem out for myself. In her eyes, this must have been no different. Barring the stakes. Barring her own death."

Silence held for several heartbeats, then Kilras spoke again. "You sound certain she was unsurprised."

"She left me something. A letter. A list of people—human people all across Arnan—to contact." Now Leiel regretted letting the fire go out. Impossible to read the letter and list of names now. "It will have to wait for daylight to share."

"If Gahree knew enough to plan for her own death, then she can't be the only one who prepared for catastrophe."

"Gydron and Kinra."

"And, I suspect, others." Kilras's voice held a thoughtful note. "We're not so alone as we might think."

"We," Leiel said. Of course. This was why he had followed her. Not just to bring her news, or demand answers for his own sake, but to join them. "You're not just riding north to distract from your team. You're coming with us. Coming to Cyunant." That the purpose of his actions had not been obvious, spoke of Leiel's distraction and exhaustion.

"I wasn't sure of that choice. But now, if you'll carry me," he said. "I think I can be of help there, at least for a while. At length, I'll be more useful far from the mountain. But knowing whatever plans you'll be laying will make me more effective across Arnan."

She took a deep breath, let it out. "Yes." She considered for a moment, the coordination of action and care she must practice to carry both Kilras and Teska north. "Yes. And your mare? Will she be all right when you turn her loose?"

"She was born wild. Transitioning back to old habits won't be too difficult." His words ended in a smile she could almost feel.

She chuckled a little. "If any being would know about that, it would be you."

A whisper of breath in the darkness marked his half-laugh-half-grunt of assent. "We'll see," he said. "I've been a long time away. A long time among men and meanness—and perhaps a bit of madness."

"Madness?" Teska asked.

He sighed, and Leiel sensed the weight of his thoughts. His words carried into the dark space before them. "The hardest thing I've ever done was go from living in a world ruled by women to one ruled by men. Gahree, Hech, Gydron, Delhar—everyone who raised me always talked about choice and integrity. I discovered, when I left Cyunant, that I'd two options—drown in sorrow at everything I encountered while trying to remain grateful to the equality of the minds that raised me, or to turn my back on all I was taught and revel in having power I hardly comprehended."

Leiel caught her breath. For all she had read of his life and travels, she never imagined that such a conscious choice ever crossed his thoughts. But why would he not have considered it? Power and authority, offered with open hands. Unimaginable. And yet...was that not exactly what the Draigon had offered her all those years ago when they carried her to a life among them? A place where her words and ideas and skills were taken seri-ously? Where she was not relegated to silence, but rather had a voice in all matters, a voice that counted? Was it at all the same? Half Farlan. Half Arnani. With his skills, his expertise, he could have turned Arnan upside down, used power and knowledge to inform and disrupt, to control and manipulate. He had not. Instead, he had chosen quiet influence and motion, over power. And yet here he was, at the heart of change, more than just a part of what was coming—one of the fulcrums upon which it would pivot. Power and the option to abuse it so often fit hand to glove—but *she* had not chosen it. Neither had he. "You chose to be grateful. You didn't drown."

He shook his head. "Not completely."

Now what did that mean? She did not probe the issue, said instead, "This is what caring for Cleod has wrought the two of us. Or what his caring for us has wrought *him*."

"Or what Trayor Draighil's hate's brought us all," Kilras said.

Leiel looked across at the Dorn, just a shape in the darkness. A flash, old memory, long buried, of Klem's face twisted in a sneer. Hate. Blind hate. Built of fear and loss and shame, gilded in greed and the need for domination, to control as much as possible so he would never have to be afraid again. Hate. The colossal, bitter evil that destroyed so often, so many. "Then it's that we must counter, if we are to survive."

"Conquer hate?" Doubt laced Teska's words. "Hatred isn't a sword that can be shattered with the right blow."

"Not hatred as a force in the world," Leiel said. "Just that which twists Cleod."

"Changing the heart of one person is going to end a war?"

Spoken aloud, the idea seemed absurd. Hard truth, that success was unlikely. Deeper truth, that Cleod was...Cleod. Something tingled the back of Leiel's mind, something not clear, just starting to form. It slipped away when she tried to focus on it. Still...

Change a person to change the world.

She whispered, "What else ever has?"

8

Kilras

KILRAS TURNED FIRST IMPRESSIONS IN HIS MIND AS HE MADE HIS WAY around the boulders and braced a knee against the rock by the shallow spring. Teska and Leiel, a combination of energies so vital and compelling that he did not wonder at their place among Draigon. He slipped a bowl into the slow-filling depression and waited as water seeped in to fill it.

Whether because of the long ride in the heat, strange dreams that would not let him rest, the straining events of the last weeks, or his use of full Gweld awareness, every nerve in his body vibrated with unusual sensitivity. And the strength of the women's minds, in close concert with his own, weighted his thoughts and his heart anew.

Those things and the list Leiel had shared with him.

So many names that he knew—some of whom that he long considered friends—filled the pages that it nearly took his breath away. What had the Draigon shaped in the bright light of day while everyone watched and no one noticed? How many souls had they touched, held in quiet reserve?

He shook his head and considered his current companions. Teska was one such marked soul. Her scrutiny carved straight into him—the way she studied him with uncanny focus and the lines that formed between her brows when she gazed at him for more than a few seconds. What did she see in him to warrant such attention? How long had it been since that kind of intensity had been focused on him? The sound of crashing waves filled his memory. He shook his head.

Teska.

Healer.

Sacrifice.

More.

How many others were also more?

As she and Leiel explained the power and potential that brought the Draigon to Melbis to claim Sacrifice, something in their words tugged at Kilras, dug for something buried deep in his mind. A nagging tingle rose behind his eyes and refused to subside, as memory trembled, hidden just out of reach. What was it? Nothing he could force. But time alone and a few moments silence might succeed, where will could not, in inspiring recall.

Teska's gift, what little he yet understood of it—what would it become if she claimed the Great Shape? If she could measure where pain lay over the land the way she could see how it touched people...what would she see? What could she awaken in the way of healing? What would that skill allow her to witness, to understand, to effectuate?

What could attending the core need, the vivid heart of another being, call to action? How would seeing in such a way affect the decisions that followed?

Memory rose, of that blazing day in Adfen Square, the Tower looming above, the stench of sweat and eager fear like a living thing in the air. Of Cleod standing on the Tower balcony, bathed in a self-possessed amber glow unlike anything Kilras had ever seen. And unlike anything he had seen *since*. As Adfen's silver light warped around the Tower and grey shadow darkened those surrounding Cleod, his presence burned as a warm beacon against ancient stone. Of all the people Kilras had looked at while in Gweld, only Cleod, in that instant, had ever shown like that.

That day in the Square, that vision shifted Kilras's intention. Despite the years that separated that moment from his first confrontation with Cleod in the Rock Digger, the amber glow surrounding Cleod had marked something unique about the Draighil. Something Gahree had also seen? Something innate? Learned? Something that Leiel and Sacrifice had awakened? Something Kilras had never opened himself enough to search for since that day.

Kilras shook his head in slow amazement. Would that he had recognized the significance of *that* moment before this one.

Who was left to ask? Aweir was gone. As was the old traveling healer, Eirar. And Wynt. And now Gahree.

Gahree of all of them.

Now, who might hold answers?

Gydron would know. Gydron of the great library, who kept questions the way Gahree kept answers.

Gydron. Cyunant. His mother.

Home.

He drew in a breath and just waited for a moment with his hand and the pot immersed in the spring. He had followed Leiel from Melbis with no more certain plan in mind but to tell her what had unfolded behind her in the trading town, to warn her of the true depth of the bitter shift of Cleod's mind. Beyond that, Kilras had considered only the road to Adfen—the friends and contacts along the way north who needed warning. And Retta and Amhise who might need much more than only that. But now—now having met Teska, he needed to be more a part of what was coming. Needed knowledge that the Draigon had, and to share the things he understood of Arnan that they did not. If he was to help, he had to go to them. After all these years, the thing he never dared dream would come—a return to Cyunant. To the mountain and dreams and losses, old and new. And to a chance, in the shadow of looming disaster, to say proper goodbyes.

9

Kilras – 28 years

SEATED UNDER THE TREE IN THE DAPPLED SHADE, KILRAS CLOSED HIS eyes and cupped his head in his hands in an attempt to suppress the pounding in his skull and the weariness that accompanied it. Running a mountain with Wynt was less exhausting than an hour practicing control against Resor.

"Here." Something bumped against the back of his hand and he lifted his face. Seated cross-legged before him, the flame-haired Draigon held out a wooden cup.

He smelled herbs, and something darker, metallic and sharp. With a grateful nod, he reached for the offering. She only gave it to him when he reached the true limit of his strength. He took a long swallow and leaned back against rough bark as the tea washed through him, relief coming as soon as it hit his stomach. "Someday I hope you'll tell me what this is."

Resor smiled fiercely, shook a little with laughter. She pulled up her knees and draped her arms over them. "It won't matter. You can't make it."

He raised his eyebrows at her as he put the cup to his lips again.

"The herbs you can come by, but not the rest."

"The rest being?"

She chuckled. "You haven't guessed? It's blood, Hantyn. Draigon blood."

Almost, he choked, but then realized he was not surprised and took another drink. "Whose blood?"

"Not mine," she laughed. "I need all my strength to work with you." She leaned forward a little. "You are strong, Hantyn. And you are nearly ready to return to the life you have chosen."

A tingle traced down his back at the unexpected statement. Given that today's encounter with her Gweld had nearly left him blind, the side-ways praise was the last thing he expected. "Ready?"

She nodded, her wild curls bouncing. "Few could have withstood what I did to you today. Another day, maybe two, and it will be time for you to leave this ruined place."

He took in her words, then accepted the invitation within them, to satisfy the curiosity that had dwelt within him since he had first sighted Dinist through the fog. "You and the others here destroyed this Enclave. Why? How did you do this and live?"

She grinned at him. "Finally."

"Will you tell me?" If Draigon could destroy an entire Enclave full of those trained to slay them, why had they not done it to every Enclave? Why had they not done so years ago?

She nodded, got to her feet and came to sit with him, her back also against the tree. "It was luck as well as rage," she said. "The Dinist became suspicious of what we were, the women running all over the mountains, unafraid and barely trackable. They didn't think us Draigon, but they knew we were something dangerous.

"I used to sneak into the compound and watch their training, listen to their plans. And one day I heard them speaking of us, and their fears and worries. And I learned something—that they were planning to send all the Draighil to a gathering of the Enclaves, to discuss *us*. And to consult the oldest documents of the Enclave holdings, held somewhere hidden by the Elders. A vault of secrets. They hoped to learn what we might be, and how to either make use of us or destroy us."

"Secrets?" Kilras looked over at her as he rolled the last of the healing liquid in the cup, stirring it gently. "Elder secrets? The Elders and Draighil left here?"

She shook her head. "No. Just the Draighil."

He frowned. "If the secrets belong to the Elders, why would others be entrusted with viewing them?"

"I've wondered that." The slow smile that crossed Resor's face was filled with a knowing glee. "I've never learned why. But it was a mistake. With only old men and servants left here, we burned the place with natural fire, sent them fleeing."

He stared at her, tension around his eyes. "Why call such attention to yourselves?"

"Their thoughts were already fixed on us, we simply proved their fears correct."

He shifted to face her more directly, watched the breeze pick up her hair and twirl it across her face. If it were possible, she looked even more formidable than usual, with the softening impact of the locks across her face unbalanced by the steel in her eyes. "Resor, you said you burned this place with natural fire, but Draigon heat destroyed these buildings."

She nodded. "It did. The Elders fled with word of a terrible fire. And after they had spread that word, I took the Great Shape and let myself be seen over Ilris and Giddor. Then I flew here and created such damage that they would never rebuild."

He studied her. "If you can do this here, why haven't the Draigon done this with all the Enclaves?"

"Remember, this was long ago. I burned Dinist generations before you were born. Long enough ago that we Draigon were not as strong as we are now. And what I learned of the documents they so value also prevented us from acting further. We did not know where they were or how many guarded them. Only that they could be used to rebuild anything we destroyed, more dangerous than ever.

"Instead, we let them decline through the years. Until only Ehlewer and Bynkrol remain as a danger to us."

"What of Dilfan?"

"It's half what it was, and no Draighil has come from its

training in five generations. Ehlewer and Bynkrol are the last. They will fall in time as well."

He shook his head and drained the last of the blood tonic. His headache was gone, replaced by a fiery sense of well-being that soothed every part of him even as it seared him from the inside-out. "Before they find a way to destroy the Draigon? As they diminish, they'll become desperate."

She chuckled, got to her feet. "The time's coming where we'll find out," she said. "Maybe in your lifetime, Hantyn, if you've learned your lessons well enough here. Rest some. We've one more round, more intense than this one, for you to survive tomorrow."

He groaned in mock disgust and leaned back. "I can hope for one and wish against the other."

10

Kilras – 46 Years

UNDER THE SHADE OF A COPSE OF TREES MARKING A DEEP SPRING, Kilras slipped the bridle over the mare's head and patted her shoulder. Eager for the fresh fodder, she moved away, lowering her head to thick grass—a good space to have survived the drought and still be rich with food and water. And the trees stood dense enough to provide shelter. Perhaps she would even find other horses one day.

With a nod, he tucked the bridle under his saddle where it leaned against the base of a tree. Though it went against instinct to abandon it, he had no need of it where he was bound. If impossible luck held, one day he would be back for it. A final glance at the mare, busily grazing, and he moved away toward the open ground to the south.

In the distance, Teska waited with a small pile of packs and his saddle bags. Farther off, Leiel walked naked, a slender, dark shape stamped against the horizon as she gained space to make her transformation.

The irony did not escape him, that he traveled with Leiel while the woman of *his* childhood infatuation had died at the hands of the man who Cleod now followed north. Leiel, of all Draigon, would see him back to Cyunant. Leiel, who he knew not at all, beyond Cleod's stories and the painful conversations of the last few days. And Cleod, who they had both betrayed through secrecy and omission, to whom they both owed better, if they could find a way to offer such.

Leiel stopped, turned. Kilras's throat tightened as memory beckoned, of Wynt offering a grin over her shoulder before she unfurled power and knowledge and burned copper-bright into the Great Shape. But the woman now standing among pale grasses was far different from the one held dear in recollection. This woman, Kilras knew only from stories told around camp-fires, made warm and bright in the light of Cleod's nostalgia. What Kilras had learned of Leiel these last days justified Cleod's regard, but offered nothing to lessen the ache in Kilras's heart.

As he stepped from the shelter of the trees, energy pulsed, flared across all the planes of his senses. He caught his breath, froze in half-forgotten awe as the transformation claimed Leiel's potential and exploded it. Around her, dust and wind swirled, and he opened himself completely to Gweld, watched gold light refract and coalesce into a gleaming bronze creature born to shape legend.

The sight struck through to the core of him, for a heartbeat stopped thought. The longing that once accompanied such witnessed moments had long since faded away. The wonder of it never had. He stared, then remembered how to move again as Leiel turned her gaze on Teska, and he watched the healer quake and sink to her knees.

In a moment, he was beside Teska, offering her a hand to bring her back to her feet. She accepted the assistance and, as she stumbled upright, a feeling, almost voice-like, filled his mind and rocked his senses.

I remember the shock of it. Leiel's thought pressed into his.

Teska's eyes, wide and half-glazed, filled with tears. "The night of the Sacrifice, I didn't see, not really. I didn't really un-derstand. What I heard that night, was it like this? Not in my ears but in my mind?"

You hear me as your Gweld sense dictates.

"So much—" Teska murmured. She released his hand, still gazing at Leiel. "So much wonder. I did not imagine. Not this."

You remind me of my long-ago-self. Leiel raised her chin, gave her great head a shake that trembled her mighty frame. *The questions I hear behind your voice...so much the same as my own in this moment.*

Kilras looked between Leiel Draigon and the healer. "If this's meant to be a private conversation, it isn't."

Teska started, looked at him and laughed with a note of sadness. "No, I don't think anything among us is meant to be private." Her humor faded as she gazed at him. "Is this as strange for you as it is for me?"

He flicked his attention to Leiel, taking in the gleaming power of her giant form, brilliant and shining in the clear air. "Probably stranger," he said. "You've flown with a Draigon." A faint smile crossed his lips as he looked back at Teska. "I've never known that thrill."

Braced for the sadness that the expectation and memory brought to encounters with places once familiar, the emotion that rocked Kilras at his first glimpse of the mountain came not from disappointment, but instead from shock at how both comfort and awe still filled his chest at the sight. Perhaps the feelings were partly born of wonder. He approached from a vantage he once only dreamed of—on high—borne on the mighty wings of the Great Shape of Draigon. As Leiel broke through the clouds and the tallest peak of the Great Northern Range claimed dominance on the horizon, the fact that the wings carrying him were not his own, diminished none of the joy in his chest.

Teska pressed against him, one arm tight across his waist. She leaned on the other along the crest of Leiel Draigon's neck. As many times as his own, her gasps of wonder had filled the air on this journey. Sight of their destination set her trembling. At least he thought the tremor running through his muscles originated with her.

"Here?" she called over the rushing wind.

"The great ravine on the east side," he shouted back. "Cyunant sits below the scree field."

"You lived here? God's of old—it's so beautiful!"

"I was born here."

"And you left? How?"

Not how had he traveled from here, but how had he found the strength to leave a place as glorious as this.

"Necessity," he answered. "I've always been too human to truly belong here."

Just as you, Teska, are too Draigon to have remained in Melbis. Leiel's thought, skimmed his mind, unsettling in its clarity. So many years since he had connected this way with anyone in Gweld, since he had *allowed* such contact.

Take hold.

Teska's grip on him tightened. He relaxed his weight into the massive body beneath him and held on as Leiel banked and caught an updraft rising off the ridgeline, accelerating toward their destination. Home. At long last *home.* And yet so far from it. The distance between the heart of his youth and the caravan winding south from Melbis stretched and shimmered, a slender chain of separation and experience, each link forged by him, by longing and caring and grief. And by the inevitable connection between past and future, as certain and yet unpredictable as when the next gust of wind might buffet Leiel Draigon's wings.

Welcome home.

Uncertainty. Fear. Sorrow. The touch of the Draigon's mind seared with each emotion in turn, then tumbled them all together in a blazing wash of anger. Cyunant without Gahree. Could it ever truly be home again?

They clung to Leiel's back and to each other as she carved a hard final turn and dropped toward the mouth of the ravine. Buildings and forms, both familiar and strange rushed up to meet them, and when Leiel landed, the mountain rocked with the impact.

As dust settled to the earth, he raised his head and, before he could ignore instinct, searched the Draigon gathered across the clearing for faces as lost to him as Gahree. Grief dropped like a stone through his belly. Then his gaze fell on a slight figure at the front of the small crowd—strong built, dark hair streaked with grey, dye stains on her pants—and his breath hitched with his heart. Delhar—looking exactly as memory had deemed she would. Despite the emotions turning within him, he smiled. A Draigon advantage to ease the ache of homecoming—timelessness to make memory a comfort as well as a burden. He stared, watched as Delhar raised a hand to cover her mouth, as if by muffling her sob she could stop her tears altogether.

Teska shifted and dropped from the Draigon's back, seeking the solid feel of earth beneath her feet. Once she moved clear, he followed.

Scent claimed him—balsam and granite and ice, the smell of heavy moisture that foretold incoming snow, and the welcome bitterness of woodsmoke, thick and rich with cooking.

Then, before he could even move toward the gathered women, the small figure rushed to enfold him in her embrace and he was surrounded by the long forgotten odors of dyes and dark earth. Delhar was small against him, lean and almost fragile, and yet her grip was heat and iron and crushing tenderness. He closed his eyes and pulled her close and let himself reel.

11

Leiel

LEIEL BENT HER NECK, WATCHING AS GEMDA TOOK CHARGE OF TESKA and ushered her down into the village, just as Leiel had been led so many years ago. She remembered the concerned warmth of that touch, the gentle guidance of words and gestures that carried her to the moment when she could face her mother again.

Now, Ilora stood with Gydron and Kinra and Delhar waiting to greet her, as well as someone missed longer than she, by far. She watched the dye-maker race to embrace Kilras.

Leiel waited a moment, knowing that, *despite everything*, she would receive a similar welcome. But what to say? How to say it? At least she did not have to decide in this instant. With a huff of heated air, she lifted wings and took flight, left behind the welcome she saw in all their faces and retreated to the peak above to reclaim her human form.

On the rock dome, she let go the Great Shape, let the wind buffet her naked flesh and tear at her tangled hair. Before her, the Great Northern Range rolled toward the horizon, the first snow of the season dusted on stone and trees.

Her tears froze on her face for an instant before the Draigon heat that thrived at the core of her being melted them to stream down her face and off her chin. They splattered over her chest, and she shuddered, staring south toward Arnan.

There, in dark corners and bright streets, hard words filled the air, full of anger and fear and the need to act. There, armies might be gathering. There, her storm still raged. Heat and dust and suffering. She could not lift it, not for as long as it slowed what might be a gathering of enemies. Unless... She stared at the glimmering peaks stretching solid and powerful into the distance. Was it possible? Why should it not be?

Leiel wiped hard at her tear-stained cheeks and swallowed back a thickness lurking in her throat. Gahree would—She stopped the thought. No. *Gydron* would know. Leiel turned and started down the mountain in the fading light.

Well past dark, with the wind kicking up the ravine, Leiel crossed the snowy ground to stand before the women still gathered to meet her. No words flowed between them, just bright thoughts full of as much of understanding and caring as of shared grief. Just love blended with pain and rage and longing. Love that wrapped her in a warm, woven blanket, firm as her mother's arms. And when those closed around her, all the questions and need fled Leiel's mind and she let herself cry again as the story of the last weeks spilled forth in hard gasps.

They knew how her story ended. Her need to speak it, to stand in their judgment meant more than their need to hear all details. Between tears and hard-formed sentences, she managed the tale as well as stunned memory could recall it.

At last she finished, and the silence that followed in the wake of her telling vibrated with layers of emotion so deep and tangled there was no sorting one from the next. Leiel lifted her chin to speak again, but Gydron placed a firm hand on Leiel's shoulder.

"More can wait."

"But—"

Kinra said, "We aren't going to make any decisions tonight. We have too much to consider. Rest, Leiel. Tomorrow we will meet and plan."

Tomorrow seemed a thousand years beyond the night, and the urgency thrumming through her demanded action. Despite the fact that Kinra's tone left no room for argument, Leiel shook her head. "It cannot wait that long."

A firm arm went across her shoulders, and she looked over into her mother's eyes. "But it can wait a little longer," Ilora said. The pain and warmth of her gaze carried message enough.

Leiel nodded, and let herself be led home.

12

Kilras

A HUNDRED HUGS. A THOUSAND QUESTIONS. AND TEARS—MORE than could be counted—heavy with joy and grief. Unconsidered through all the years, came the realization that one expression of emotion could encompass so much of a moment. Old friends and new, old losses and new, old fear and old loves and old dreams, all wrapped around Kilras as he walked with Delhar through the fading light toward the cabin he once called home. Promises lingered in his ears of what tomorrow would bring— warm food and connection, pain and laughter. His chest ached, weariness and awkward happiness at war in the core of him.

Delhar held tight to his hand, the Draigon warmth of her radiating through the grip with the power he had always hoped she would gain. Satisfying and strange at once, he reveled in the firm heat of her fingers clasped around his. Draigon. The pressure in his chest increased and he found himself smiling.

She looked up at him, her gaze awed and measuring. How strange he must look to her, the marks of time and travel heavy upon him in a way she would never experience.

"What brings that smile?" she asked.

"You're Draigon," he said.

"That's been the case for decades."

He laughed. "But it's new to my experience of you."

She stopped, and he turned to face her, let her study him in the greying air. "All of *this you* is new to me," she said at last. Her voice went soft, but did not tremble. "My boy."

Was it loss he heard in the words? Or pride? Perhaps something of both.

He raised a hand and cupped her cheek, met her gaze. "Long a man," he said. The decades that marked her wholeness had aged him beyond her, with drawn lines around his eyes and streaks of grey painted into his hair. "Ever your son."

She nodded into his touch. "Come home."

They shared a silence as the sky darkened grey to indigo, then she shook herself and took as step down the trail. "We've much to talk about. I would see you properly welcomed before night fully falls."

"Your friend, he's the cause of all this?" Delhar poured soup from the cook pot into the serving bowl and returned the pot to the warming area at the back corner of the stove.

Kilras, hair still damp from the bath he had savored, finished setting the table and looked over at her. "No more than I am, or Leiel." He paused, considering. "Or Wynt, or Gahree."

"Oh Kilras—" Delhar turned and placed the serving bowl in the middle of the table.

"No." He shook his head. "There's no single cause. Just the decisions and actions that led us all here."

"Eat. We need to meet the others soon." Delhar pulled out a chair and settled into it. She sighed. "No single cause. But somehow he's at the center of this. He and Leiel."

Kilras sat across from her. Yes. Leiel and Cleod stood at the heart of everything unfolding across Arnan. But... Kilras considered the list Leiel had shared with him, Gahree's list, and the shock that coursed through him upon seeing it. Leiel and Cleod were not the only people around whom the future pivoted. The center was full of those with the power to choose and to change. But neither could he deny the path Gahree set him on so long ago. "Leiel and Cleod matter greatly," he agreed. "I'm not sure the center is a firm point. Years of travel taught me there're many ways to reach the same destination."

"My son, a philosopher?"

He blinked at the old joke arisen from the depths of time, then laughed. The old Dorn, Acyn, and Delhar would have liked each other. "It's been many years since anyone called me that."

"What've you been called most recently?"

His smile grew, thinking of the words Sehina whispered in his ear as she hugged him goodbye. "A madman."

She ladled soup into her bowl. "Only a true friend can get away with that. Who is she?"

Kilras said, "Sehina."

"The horse trainer."

"It's unnerving to hear you speak of people I haven't even mentioned."

"Draigon are well-read."

He chuckled, recalling a hard scowl and the frustrated turning of pages at this very table. "You hated braving my hand writing when I was a child."

"It's not improved," she said. "At least back then I had you here to tell me what it said. These last years..." Her words drifted into silence as she looked at him.

He returned her gaze, nodded. She was almost as he remembered. But for her—Was it stranger for her or for him, the changes time had worked upon him? Did anything remain, in her eyes, of the boy he had been? He scooped soup into his bowl, smelled the rich, vegetable steam as it rose. "I never thought I'd return."

"None of us thought you would either, once you left us behind."

He canted his head as he returned the ladle to the serving bowl. Left them behind? All his youth, the Draigon of Cyunant had prepared him to leave, prepared him to travel, prepared him to be anywhere but here. "I was never meant for this place."

With a shake of her head, Delhar said, "No. I know that. You didn't leave us behind when you walked over the ridge. You left us behind when you figured out who you were." She waved a hand in the air in a dismissive gesture. "Out there. On the wide roads. When you became...*you*."

He laughed. "I've always been *me*."

"No," she smiled and lifted her spoon to sip the soup. Her eyes crinkled. "I wasn't fully *me* until I became Draigon. You weren't fully *you* until you became Kilras Dorn—with all that implies."

Silence fell between them. He considered, raised his own spoon, tasted. The rich liquid filled his mouth with warm and gentle spice, pooled into his belly in comforting heat. When *had* he first felt whole? Confident and sure? Able to help others and take risks, secure in his own mind and skill? A certain day, even year, escaped noting—but at some point just such clarity had accumulated within him, until being *himself* seemed the only thing he had ever been.

Did that happen to everyone? That slow, silent becoming that claimed heart and soul and marked purpose? Perhaps. But so many people he had met in his travels lived lost lives. Only the rare few displayed the empathy and self-assurance that marked wholeness and satisfaction. What made the difference? What allowed humility and understanding to take hold and render a life full and satisfying?

"Cleod," he said, his friend's name slipping into the air without thought.

"What about him?"

"I thought he'd reconciled all of himself. Or at least enough to know..." Kilras shook his head. "I was wrong."

"If we're lucky, that's what's happening now," Delhar said. "Maybe all the pieces of him are finally coming together. For good or for ill."

He stared at her, then found himself smiling again. A mother's wisdom, long missed. "I'm glad I came back."

She reached out and grasped his wrist. Again the heat and strength of her touch pulsed through him. "Whatever comes, I am glad to have this time with you. I know you'll go soon, and I don't dare dream that we'll ever see each other again. Because you've a friend out there in need of help. And for all the ones you couldn't help through the years, you'll do what it takes to save this one. You and Leiel."

Wynt. Hech. Gahree. Tylen. "We intend to try."

"Yes," Delhar said, with a firmness in her words that spoke of more change he could not measure. "*We* do."

Shock entered his voice, unfiltered. "The Draigon are planning to *help* Cleod?"

"The Draigon are planning to end a war before it begins, if we can. Gydron and Kinra think the key to doing that is your friend. And Leiel."

"And why do they think that?"

She smiled. "Because Gahree thought it."

"She said this?"

"She didn't need to say it. You forget, there're no secrets among Draigon. Leiel's heart lives partly with that man. We've always known it. A Draighil loved by a Draigon? And the other way, as well, perhaps? You'd know that better than we. Gydron says such a thing's never been. What's more powerful than something that's never before been true?"

13

Cleod – 16 Years

CLEOD WATCHED AS LEIEL'S WAGON DISAPPEARED DOWN THE tree-shrouded lane. For a strange, strangled moment the desire to run after her almost overcame him. But what would he do here in Adfen? Return to the life of a woodcutter? Give up the education and honor the Enclaves bestowed on him? He shook his head that such an idea even crossed his thoughts, and turned to enter his father's house.

"Was that Leiel?" Ellan asked as he pushed the door shut behind Cleod.

He turned to face his father, so thin and grizzled, dry-skinned and wasted even in the dim light of the single lamp burning on the table in the center of the cabin. Only two years had passed since Cleod had last been home. *Only two years.* When had he come to think of that length of time as short? Or was it just that he faced so many new things, from day to day, that time was the least of his considerations? But it should not have been, based on what it had done to his father. He shook himself and answered Ellan's question. "Yes. Leiel."

Ellan smiled. "She's grown up strong." He walked to the table, eyeing Cleod as he passed. "I look as bad as that, do I?"

"I—"

"It's all right to say it, son. I've had a hard few months after catching that leg injury. But I'm better every day. I'm just sorry to be in such a state when welcoming you home."

Cleod stared for a few seconds, then straightened. "I apologize for seeming so shocked. I just—"

"We never expect our parents to grow old. Just as I admit to having trouble looking at you and not wondering when my lanky boy grew into this height and this strength."

With a blink of surprise, Cleod glanced down at his calloused hands and the lean muscle that layered his arms. He smiled faintly. Yes. He, too, was different than the last time he and Ellan had been together. Different enough that he should probably be grateful that his father was not looking at him with the same astonished wonder that filled Leiel's expression when she first saw him in the shop in the city. Cleod nodded. "We've both changed more than a little."

"Sit down, Cleod," Ellan gestured toward the chair across from him. "Tell me what you think I should see when I look at you."

Cleod blinked, laughed. "Your son."

"No." Ellan shook his head. "You want to be seen as what you're trying to become—a man of the Enclaves. Your back's so stiff that I'm not certain you can claim that seat."

For several seconds, Cleod stood looking at his father, at the vague sadness in his father's eyes. How dare the old man—! Cleod stopped the thought with an indrawn breath, the white heat of shame flooding his chest. "I'm sorry," he said, and forced his shoulders to loosen. He moved the three steps to the table, grasped the wooden back of the seat, and pulled it out to settle across from Ellan. "Among the Ehlewer, a certain stance is expected. Along with—"

"A worthy level of arrogance?"

"A—What?"

Ellan chuckled, and if a low rattle accompanied the laugh, the wry humor in his voice masked it when he spoke. "It's nothing I didn't expect when you joined them. It's part of what I knew you'd learn." He folded his arms atop the table and leaned forward a little. "You just remember you never learned it in this house. Now, tell me—Leiel, how is she? It's been far too long since I've seen her."

Cleod frowned. "Is that not appropriate, given her status as Draigfen?"

Ellan's gaze hardened in the way Cleod recalled from his childhood, the look that hinted his father hung on the verge of being disappointed.

But why should he be, when Cleod spoke only the truth? The casual defiance of some of Leiel's words on the wagon ride from the city prickled the back of his mind. Too easily could such utterings, if overheard by someone less understanding than himself, lead her into trouble and perhaps even true danger. And she was just stubborn enough not to see that. He shook his head. Nothing for it but to hope she came to sense before perilous circumstance overtook her.

"Do you hesitate, now, to be seen with her?" Ellan asked. "You seemed comfortable enough on that wagon."

"I do not live here anymore. And I am of the Ehlewer now. We are trained to resist any such taint. A moment being seen with a Draigfen will not mark me as it might you."

"*Mark* me?" Ellan's eyes widened and he laughed. But the humor in his gaze went flat as amusement turned to violent coughing.

Cleod reached out and grabbed his father's arm. "What do you need?"

Ellan shook his head, bent a little over the table and heaved in a breath. "No—Noth—Will—" He coughed again, not as hard, wheezed in more air. "Just need—" another breath deeper and cleaner than the last. "A moment." He met Cleod's gaze. "Happens now, from time to time. Just—" He forced in another long pull of air. "Just don't make me laugh *too* hard."

Tension stiffened Cleod's face as he watched Ellan struggle to breathe, but he released his grip on the older man's arm and sat back in his chair.

Ellan patted the edge of his mouth with the sleeve of his shirt, then nodded, the shocks racking his body coming back under control. "Now what were you saying? About me being *marked*? What nonsense are they teaching up on that mountain? It's only women who can be Draigfen." He narrowed his gaze at Cleod. "Or did you take to heart the ridiculous notion that her father threw out the last time you were home—that a woman can somehow corrupt a worthy man just by being in his presence?"

"No. Not that at all." Cleod shook his head. "It's more that—" He stopped. How to say it? Even after all these years of training, how to express the *difference* he still felt from the other Draigre, the oddness he dealt with every day as he moved among pale men and boys who never quite saw him as an equal even when he bested both them and their expectations.

"That I'm your father and you're worried, since you're not Farlan, that those Enclave aristocrats would use any excuse to see you as less than you are." He paused. "Do they still call you cefreid?"

Cleod smiled faintly, glad for his father's understanding. "Every day."

"And yet *you* are easy in your mind, being seen with her."

Cleod hesitated, turning over his conversation with Leiel. *I don't want to miss you anymore than I already do.* "I do not fear being seen with her, but some of her words worry me."

"Because you chose this path on her behalf."

"I chose this path for *me*."

Ellan smiled the slightest bit. "And to mark your friendship with Leiel Sower."

Cleod sighed. "Yes. Yes, her pain gave me purpose. Do you think I wouldn't have joined the Enclaves if her mother hadn't died the way she did?"

"I think it's pointless to wonder what might have been if different events drove us. You were always going to be something other than a Woodcutter."

A conscious swallow held down the confusion Ellan's words

awakened. It tangled with Leiel's question: *How do we hang on to our friendship in all this?* Was his position endangered? *Would the Elders think less of him for sharing time and conversation with her?* For his acceptance of her vibrant nature? For loving the very aspect of her that made her different and dangerous to others and herself? "Can we?" he whispered.

"Can we what?"

Cleod brought his attention back to the moment. "Can we be friends, Leiel and I, when everything has so changed for both of us?"

"People always change. We age and run into new ideas and new ways of doing things. But you only grow apart from a friend if the things you both value become incompatible. Or you get so caught up in your own desires that you no longer try to understand each other."

With a frown, Cleod nodded. "Friendship is work."

"Sometimes," Ellan agreed. "Most things worth keeping require some." He pushed back from the table and got to his feet. "Are you hungry? What did you bring in that supply box that might be good for late meal?"

"Plenty. Let me get it." Cleod glanced at the woodbox which stood half empty—shameful, in a Woodcutter's home. As was the two-thirds empty lean-to against the house. "Then I'll fill that woodbox and start to work on restocking your shed."

Ellan pressed his lips together and nodded, as though he knew how much those empty spaces said about the real state of his health.

Cleod rose and met the older man's gaze. "There's a room in the Old City, right off the Square."

Ellan shook his head. "I'm not a city man."

"A hand here, then," Cleod said. "My old room is plenty of space for anyone." Something had to change here. Something must be offered and accepted.

Ellan hesitated, then gave a single nod. He pushed his chair back and got to his feet. "Perhaps. But food first." For a moment his gaze went soft and distant. "Hard talks are best shared over good meals." He refocused on Cleod. "Do you still remember how to wield an axe, or have they trained that out of you along with common thinking?"

The fact that Ellan did not argue further about accepting help spoke more of the state he was really in than any words. But the weight gripping Cleod's chest eased a little at the humor behind the statement and he managed a laugh. "I remember," he said. "I'll have the bin filled in ten minutes and half the shed by dark."

Ellan grunted as he turned away to cross the room and add logs to the stove. "Such arrogance you never learned from me."

14

Leiel

SOFT-WOVEN CLOTHES, CLEANER THAN ANY SHE HAD WORN IN WEEKS, signaled to Leiel's body, if not her heart, that she was home. Wind rattled the windows of the common cabin, blowing particles of ice and snow as though to temper the glass. Inside, the fire held off the worst chill, though Teska stayed close to the hearth and close to Gemda.

In the center of the room, Leiel helped Dahlie unroll a huge map over the largest table and weight it with heavy mugs at each corner.

"This is the most current version I have of the entire continent. I've been working on it for two years, at Gahree's request." Dahlie's voice stumbled a little as she spoke the ancient Draigon's name.

How long before any of them would be able to talk about Gahree without breaking? Leiel placed a hand against Dahlie's back.

The mapmaker swallowed and continued. "I drew from every old source and all the new reports. This shows all the current roads and byways, as well as a few mostly forgotten ones. Some might still be useful."

"You speak as though our part in what is coming will be a ground war." Ilora's tone was puzzled.

"No," Kinra said. "Not us. At least not most of us. But our allies, and their allies—the ones on Gahree's list and all those they might have gathered through the years—this is information they will need."

"Need to do what exactly?" Leiel asked.

Gydron leaned in, pushing her long, dark hair back over her shoulder out of the way. "To direct the fighting north, toward us. To stop a greater war before it starts."

Kinra nodded. "That was the hope Gahree left us with." She spread the last pages of Gahree's letter along the bottom edge of the map, then, one by one, placed each page atop a different city or region. The sheet with Torrin's name on it settled just below Sibora.

A chill unrelated to the icy weather outside traveled Leiel's spine. Wind on high, how long had Gahree planned all this? How long had she known such a day as this would come? Or had she in some way hoped for it? Tears gathered in Leiel's eyes. And hoped to be here to see it? Leiel blinked rapidly and shook her head. "You think the people on this list can stop a war?"

"No," Kinra's voice was firm. "But they can help save the population from itself."

The women. Realization struck Leiel just as Teska spoke those exact words aloud. "The women. What happened in Melbis—the taking of the women."

Gydron nodded as she glanced over her shoulder at the healer. "Just that. The people on this list are the best defense of Arnan among its own people. They are the ones set to resist what might otherwise be the destruction of women, and others seen as too different, across all Arnan."

Leiel parted her lips to speak but Kinra stopped her with a look and fierce words. "*Never* another word of guilt from you."

With a hard swallow, Leiel nodded. Kinra was as sharp as the weapons she taught others to use, and she was now their best hope at forming a defense. The Draighil would come, backed by the Farlan, led by Trayor, and—Leiel's heart jerked in her chest—by Cleod. She battered down the words she wanted to blunder into the air. What good would speaking do? More important things lay before them now.

"Our greatest enemy," Ilora said. "The rage and fear of so many."

"The rage of men. The fear of women's power." Kilras's voice was low and strange in the room.

Leiel looked to where he leaned with folded arms against the wall near the door. "What a powerful fear that has always been."

He nodded, his expression grim yet thoughtful.

She held his gaze a moment, then turned back to the map. "Do we know what's happening? How far word has spread?" She pressed her palms into the tabletop as she bent over it, studied the dark lines that marked the roads and trails leaving Melbis. She measured distance, counted riding days, tried to guess how need and anger might drive the speed of dire news.

"Impossible to say yet," Kinra reached out and tapped a finger to the hash marks that denoted the tiniest villages and hamlets along the main trade routes out of Melbis. "It's likely these people know. And these." She paused. "Likely that they've sent riders north and south along the back trails. The smaller towns will hear before Ilris and Giddor. But I'd say we have several weeks until the cities rally against us."

Leiel looked again at Kilras. "You sent your people south."

He nodded. "They'll arrive just ahead of the news. And in time to contain at least some of it."

Kinra jerked her head up. "You asked that of them?"

He nodded. "I offered them Dinist, should they choose that path."

Breath hissed from Kinra's lungs and a murmur went through the room. Leiel stared. He had not mentioned this before, but then, on the trip here, so many other things had held priority. Still... "Would that not require that you told them the truth?"

Without hesitation he nodded again. "Earned trust makes even hard truth easier to take." He shrugged. "And even lack of trust can't change facts. They listened. They questioned. They rode south. What they decide to do with what they know is up to them."

Silence held for a long moment. Trust and the truth. The power of both of those. Leiel nodded slowly, "You trust them in return."

"Yes."

"Then we will add your people to our list of allies," Kinra said. "And hope they can do well by the people of Arnan." She flattened her hands on the map and spread her fingers wide. "Still, we've much planning to do now, much to decide about how to approach these people and what exactly to ask of them."

"In the morning, I'll gather everyone in the library," Gydron said. "It will require all that each of us knows of Arnan."

15

Leiel

IN THE WARM DEPTH OF THE LIBRARY CAVE, ILORA STOOD ON ONE SIDE of Leiel, Teska on the other. Kilras, across the room beside Delhar, nodded as Leiel met his gaze. Along the perimeter of the cavern room the rest of the Draigon gathered. With luck, their shared knowledge, examined and considered, could lead to a plan to limit the violence set to spread throughout Arnan.

"We have a greater part to play once these tasks are done. All of us must claim the Great Shape and stand to fight if we are to save what we hold dear."

"Fight?" Gemda trembled. "A siege we might withstand. But we can't fight a war." She folded her arms and sat deeper into her chair. "Even if we wanted to, we don't know how."

"Enough of us do," Kinra said. "Though that does not mean we have any wish to do so."

"War. Siege. Does it matter?" Delhar said. "We have choices. Stay and fight the best we can. But if we must, we can leave and find a new home elsewhere."

"We cannot abandon those we ask to stand with us and for each other. Not across Arnan." Gydron's voice was firm. "And we can't leave the library. Gahree would say the same."

"She's right." Ilora paced across the space. "We must do what Draigon have always done—defend the knowledge we protect."

Kinra raised a hand. "There are plans to defend an attack on Cyunant. The uncertainty lies in coping with our loss of advantage. The Enclaves know the truth of what we are now. They will take strength from that knowledge. Unless we are willing to stay forever in the Great Shape, we are vulnerable." She studied the map of Arnan spread over the rug-layered floor, paced and paused, crouched and examined, as though the parchment would come to life and spill secrets of landscape and subtle shifts in terrain. "And with the Enclaves joining the Farlan with our closest held truths in hand, perhaps not even then.

"But there are other options to consider." She placed stones, marking towns and road crossings and narrowing points of contact. "What we might face—where forces might gather, and supplies might be drawn from. Potential strongholds or vulnerabilities of enemies and armies, which cities and towns would harbor the most anger and fear, and therefore, the greatest threats. Where our allies will most need our help."

Never had Leiel asked Kinra where she gained her knowledge of weapons and battle, but watching her it was obvious that it came from more than books. A small wedge of hope cracked Leiel's heart, despite the grief and worry that filled her. Whatever came, strength and knowledge and unity would guide their response. But could they find a way to face what was coming, a way to save not only themselves but the most vulnerable people of Arnan?

Kinra raised her gaze and met Leiel's. "You believe Kilras is correct? That the Enclaves planned this for longer than we have imagined?"

Leiel nodded. "Yes." That statement should have been simple, but the implications that overlaid it trembled Leiel to the core. If what they suspected was true, then the Enclaves had never let Cleod go. They had simply bided time, watched his path unfold, until they imagined a way to use him, to get what they really wanted—the destruction of Shaa. And with that accomplished, what would they want next but the annihilation of the Draigon? And the knowledge that the Draigon were human might awaken a confidence in the Farlan that was capable of birthing a threat unlike any the Draigon had faced in centuries.

"Trayor was not in Melbis on a whim. Wynt did not die the way she did for no reason." The Enclaves and their twisted plans.

For all the Draigon's knowledge, they had underestimated their enemies in a most unexpected way.

Gydron spoke. "I agree. The Enclaves are fading. Fewer candidates survive the training every year. And how many actually make it to full rank? If they don't destroy us soon—they never will. They have to do it now, while Trayor is still strong enough to lead the battle."

"If he planned all this to return Cleod to the fold, then he's made other plans as well. Plans to march north," Leiel said.

"Only north?" Ilora asked. "Can we know that for certain? What of the other settlements? Are they in danger?"

Leiel shook her head. "Trayor was not prepared for the truth of what we are. I cannot imagine he would know about the other villages. So many of the others spend most of their time in born form that I doubt the Enclaves could have suspected them."

"But that's no safety any longer. We agree they will suspect *all* women." Ilora's words fell hard in Leiel's ears. The very things that had protected so many for so long were now the greatest danger.

"What we have planned already today will help that. Word of Shaa's death will be warning enough to most." Gydron's voice broke, then firmed. "As we spread that throughout Arnan, those who might face danger will have time to prepare, and help where they can."

"Gahree's list is our greatest hope. And the people Kilras thinks will help." Leiel's gaze swept over the map, noting the vast distances between town and cities, and recalling the names on the list and their locations. So many. So wide-spread. "Was Gahree the keeper of all those names, or are there more?"

"Gahree knew most of them," Kinra said. "But there are others, known by leaders in other villages. And some of us know a few more."

Leiel drew breath, let it out. "And how many know what we are?"

"Few," Gydron said. "But most would accept the truth if it were offered to them."

"So many..." *What is an army, Leiel? A group of people organized to fight for a purpose.* "Do we think any will have the strength and skill to help?"

"You mean 'will they fight'?" Kinra said. "Some. But other things they might do are just as important."

"Can we really ask this of them? Do we have the right?" Gemda's voice fell soft.

"We do. We can. And they have the right to refuse, and we have to accept no if that is the answer. And we have to accept what that will mean for us and for this place," Kinra said. She turned to Kilras where he stood beside Delhar. "You know the rest of Arnan better than any of us. Show me what you think we have missed. Show me roads and trails we don't know. Show me their most likely route into the heart of the north. If our thoughts agree, then we can finalize a plan."

He nodded, but Leiel stepped forward before he could respond. "Wait." Leiel looked around. "Draigon Weather."

"Scorching all of Arnan will yield us nothing."

"No," Leiel said. "But wind without heat—swept south into the drought and storms that I have set. Northern winds and moisture... Is it possible?"

For a few heartbeats silence held, then Gydron laughed. "I don't see why it would not be nor why we have not thought of it until now. It will take many of us though. Acting together."

"Not all of us are fighters," Gemda said. "But this is something we can do. We can carry word. And we can focus a Wing Wind."

"We have other advantages." Kinra's words were measured, as though the hope she offered with them might be assumed to hold more power than was warranted. "How long has it been since the Farlan army faced a real foe? A generation at least. No matter their training, practice is not war. And the Enclaves... For all their skill, they are trained to fight *us*, in the Great Shape, not warriors on the ground. One-on-one, Draighil are deadly...but face to face with a determined host, will they know what to do?"

"But the numbers of a trained army..." Gemda's words trailed off.

"We don't have to defeat an entire army," Kinra said. "We only have to defeat enough of one to break the spirit of the rest."

Gemda pulled herself straight. "I'll begin Teska's lessons."

One by one, the other Draigon murmured their responses. Gydron organized them, arranging the Draigon by the regions where they had been born and raised, then drawing aside those most well-traveled. Leiel smiled. If Delhar did not fit well into that worldly group, she refused to leave Kilras's side. Well known was the fact that the dyer never expected to see her son again, much less have him with her. This all-too-brief reunion must suffice to ease the ache of a lifetime.

To each grouped region went a list of names and a request to speak of the customs of each area, and how they might impact how those named should be approached. Copies of the full list went to Kilras and Kinra and Gydron, and they balanced the recommendations of each smaller group with their wider knowledge of Arnan. Slowly, a plan formed, for contact, for inclusion.

Leiel claimed the duty of connecting the Draigon with many in Adfen—Brea the healer and Mother Harver among them. And one man in Sibora, though she knew the silver city not at all. But Torrin was there. And Torrin she needed to see and speak with most of all. Just as it had on the morning after Ilora's Sacrifice, and so many other times through the years, the thought of the smith's steadfast, direct presence filled Leiel with an odd comfort. In a time of increasing loss, that was not to be discounted. And where Torrin was, likely Elda was as well.

And Klem.

Leiel frowned. Was that a meeting she was destined to make as well? She could wish that such an encounter remain overdue forever. How unlikely that grace seemed now.

She glanced at Ilora whose face was drawn tense, the line of her jaw stark and hard in the warm light. Did similar thoughts fill her mind? Of the sons she had left behind? Of the anger they still carried? A question for a quieter time—and perhaps one they would be forced to confront eye-to-eye and far too soon.

One by one the other Draigon murmured their own responses, each taking on a task or piece of research with intention to protect home and future, settling into groups to work.

Leiel accepted hugs and whispers of support, and watched them scatter, determined expressions masking worry and grief. Ilora was the last to grip Leiel's hand before slipping away. Was it enough, their plan? Were their numbers enough?

"Mathematics were never your strength." Gydron's chiding voice brought Leiel around to face her.

"Are you reading my mind?"

"Your mood," Gydron said. "We're all wondering if we have assets enough to face these impossible choices."

Leiel forced a smile. "Gahree taught me that few things are impossible."

Gydron shook her head. "Not few enough."

16

Kilras

FROM WHERE HE SAT WITH DELHAR, KILRAS STUDIED LEIEL WHERE she huddled with Kinra and Dahlie. Seated crossed-legged at one end of the woolen rug that covered the center of the room, she gestured to the map spread out on the floor. Dahlie leaned toward her, and Leiel sat up a little, startled. Then Leiel's laughter rang big and wild, filling the cavernous reading room. Not a bell-like sound, as Gahree's had been, but more a clarion reverberation of unfettered joy. Every book, every scroll on the shelves seemed to rustle in response. In the midst of the sorrow and worry that hung over them all, hearing such a laugh was like awakening to a clear sunrise after days hunkered down in a storm.

Whatever Dahlie had said to elicit that response, Kilras was glad of it. They needed laughter as sorely as they needed whatever ideas might hatch themselves in clever minds. If the joke mattered, they would share. If not, just the sound of such carefree mirth seemed to lighten the air in the library.

Even Delhar smiled the slightest bit. "Leiel and her mother—both able to laugh even when the rest of us can barely draw a steady breath."

Kilras looked at Delhar. "Ilora Sower," he said. "She arrived here just after I left?"

"Yes. Within a few months."

He nodded toward the group now gesturing animatedly over the map. "How much like Ilora is her daughter?"

Delhar held quiet a moment, her lips pressed together as she considered. "Enough that you would not mistake their connection. But Leiel—" Delhar lifted her shoulders a little, opened her hands. "There's something in her—" She shook her head and fell silent.

"Something?" Kilras asked. What did Delhar see when she looked at Leiel?

"Something...insistent." The words came slowly, carefully chosen. "Something that demands she resist."

"Resist?" The word spun a tingle up the back of his neck.

"The expected," Delhar said. "Leiel dreams beyond the moment in a way few Draigon ever have. Except Gahree. She's of that same bright thread, woven to stand out in the fabric. She seeks justice. She's made of...possibility." Delhar's expression shifted into wistfulness. "In that way, she's often reminded me of you."

He reached out and took her hand, his now as scarred and calloused as hers, and even more marked by the small lines and discolorations of time.

She shook her head, squeezed his fingers.

They let silence fall between them, and he looked again at Leiel. Resistance. Possibility. Determination. All the things Cleod had spoken of through the years when her name came up, when memory dragged the former Draighil down dark sluices of guilt and regret, or carried him to heights of joyful recollection. Both extremes, by turns, had this woman awakened in Cleod through the years.

Kilras tipped his head, watching her expression as it shifted, the unflinching efficiency with which Leiel moved. It was not that she was unmarred by the events of past weeks. Far from it; he had witnessed her pain and indecision and guilt, heard her voice shake. But where she *was* sure, that certainty emerged with glowing potency. Such was true of the women born to the Draigon, and of the women who came to become them. Leiel did not have Wynt's unrelenting confidence. Who ever could? But the vibrant sincerity Leiel possessed was just as he remembered from his encounter with her at the Market stall in Adfen more than two decades ago.

Leiel glanced at him and smiled, half-sad, then pushed back her hair and returned to her conversation. Something deep within him shivered. Her spirited directness, the force of her intellect, the spark of irrepressible freshness that burned within her despite the way the world tried again and again to douse it—she reminded him of Tylen. Not completely. Not naïvely. But enough that the *why* of Cleod's obsession with her pierced Kilras to the core.

"What haunts you?" Delhar asked.

He blinked and returned his attention to her. "Are my thoughts so easily deciphered even after all this time?"

"You're my son," she said with a slight smile. "And Leiel and your friend, Cleod—well—I know *her*. And I've read what he's meant to you. You want to be sure she's worth what he's lost. Just as I want to know from you, if *he's* worth what the Draigon have surrendered on his behalf."

Kilras stared. Time had dulled his memory of his mother's intelligence, and he chided himself for the foolish simplicity of his recall. Delhar—he remembered her broken, or only partly healed. But the turning of seasons had done their work on them both, and respect was owed to the woman she had always been, even when pain had masked her strengths. "Forgive me." He spoke the words through an ache in his chest.

She squeezed his fingers again, for longer this time. "Kilras, there's nothing you need to apologize for."

"I've been too long among men." He shook his head. "Among so many *wrong* men."

"And do you count Cleod as one such?"

The question landed hard but took no thought to answer. Even now, twisted and riven of core self-awareness, Cleod was worth a hundred of most men Kilras had met through the years. "No," he said. "Not Cleod."

As though the Ruhelrn's name was a lit beacon, Kilras felt Leiel's gaze again. He held Delhar's eyes a heartbeat more, then looked back at Leiel. She had heard Cleod's name if nothing else.

"What is it?" she asked, and the unflinching curiosity in her expression, so reminiscent of Tylen that his heart skipped, sent a sliver of pain into his gut, red sparks edging his vision.

Only years of practiced control held Kilras's voice steady. "I'm discovering why he loves you."

He watched her draw a sharp breath. Then she got to her feet and beckoned for him to follow.

Leiel moved through the stacks, down winding passageways, led him deeper into the ancient cave. Once, he had known every twist and cubbyhole of the great library, every hiding place and private sanctuary. Some of those still existed, he was sure, but much had changed since his youth—additions and rearrangements blurring his memories.

At last they stopped in a small chamber where he once tried to hide from Gydron's lessons. Against one narrow wall now stood a new, wooden spiral staircase. They climbed it, rising until the dim light of the cave faded and they moved through absolute darkness. His grip on the handrail tightened and he slowed, feeling for the next tread. "Leiel—"

"You can see, Kilras," she answered from above him.

Almost, he laughed, at the now-pointless habits of half a lifetime that blinded him in the very place where his sight could be brightest. He shifted awareness, cracked his senses to Gweld, widening access until golden light filled his vision, almost blinding in its intensity. Rusty skills clattered awake, and the stone walls of the passage through which they climbed defined themselves in sheets and sparks of vivid detail. He stood still for a few seconds, taking in the vision, then resumed the climb.

At the top of the stairs, she waited for him in a room lined with the neatest shelves he had ever seen in the library. Each held a series of sixteen hand-bound books with numbered spines. Against one wall stood three copy desks, with fat volumes open on stands, and works-in-progress spread before them.

Leiel reached for a lamp on a shelf above the desks, lifted the chimney and lit the wick with a touch of her fingers. Lamp light blended with Gweld until the entire room glowed. He closed his mind to his golden lights and let the softer, flickering warmth suffice.

"What is this place?

"This is where your letters are copied."

"My—?" He stared at the books until the titles, in multiple languages, at last impressed themselves in his mind. He moved to the nearest shelf and ran a hand across the stiff leather that bound each tome. "They're being copied?" He bent his head, looked sideways at row after row of the books. "*Translated*?" The shock of it left him breathless. The letters Gydron had convinced him to write that day in Bajor had never been intended for any eyes but those of his old friends and family. He turned and met Leiel's gaze. "Why? And why'd you bring me here?"

"You said you were coming to understand why Cleod loved me." She gestured to the books. "This is how I learned why he trusts *you*. This is where you taught me what Arnan is *today*, and not just in histories and stories from centuries past. Not just the frightened words of women like me, carried here from terrible circumstances, afraid and angry. These letters taught us all. These letters will help us fight for more than survival."

He held her gaze. The intensity of her expression. The fire behind her words. The energy that pulsed into the space between them. All passion. All sharp thought and obstinate will. The force of her being echoed to the core of him. However she saw herself, between one breath and the next, understanding coalesced inside him—why Gahree had chosen her, from childhood, and for that moment on the hill in Melbis. Leiel would love, would fight, would *do*, no matter the cost. Because she clung to hope the way most parents clung to newborn children.

And it was for that she had brought him here. To Cyunant. To this room. To show him how she saw the world and what she would demand of herself for the chance to bend change to her will. And in that vision Cleod loomed. Always.

The *why* of *that* Kilras understood, just as she did. He nodded slowly. "He's the purest of us. What he wants. What he's always wanted—to keep those he loves safe. No matter how that's been twisted, that's the core of who Cleod is."

She nodded, reached out and pulled a book off the shelf. He recognized the hand-stitched papers. Not a copy, but an original. The letter in which he described his first meeting with Cleod. She opened it, turned pages, tracing her fingers over the scrawled writing as though she could absorb the words into her body and make them part of her. "Cleod has always been, for me, something out of the pages of lore. Hero and protector. Someone talked about around smoky fires and warm stoves." She closed the book and just looked at it for a moment, then raised her gaze and met Kilras's. "But he's also always been *my friend*. Real and solid and loyal. Myth made flesh as much as Gahree and the Draigon ever were." She smiled wryly. "As much, I suppose, as I am now. But once he was a boy, and I was a girl. Two proud, frightened children, witnesses to horror and pain. Children born, it seems, to *act*." She shook her head. "And Gahree told me there was no such thing as prophecy."

He studied her for a moment. "Not prophecy. Story." He shrugged. "All myths begin somewhere."

She met his gaze, and her lips twitched. "The witch in the wood."

He smiled. "Just so. The monster slayer."

"It is easier to appreciate the hero in the tale when you are not the monster."

Cold flashed up Kilras's spine. *Did you ever see a monster?* For a moment, no words came to express what filled him, then he said at last, "And all three of us have been both."

She stood silent for a long moment and the easy companionship in that quiet again offered him surprise. At last she drew a breath and said softly, "I must convince them that he is worth saving. I must convince them that he can *be* saved."

"They already believe that."

She looked at him, gaze sharpening. "What?"

He nodded. "Long ago, Gahree set me on a path to help him. I've yet to discover why. But this is the moment to find out. My mother says she told Gydron and Kinra as well."

"Gahree—?"

He shifted and leaned his hips against the edge of the desk, then let the story of his first meeting with Gahree in Adfen Square spill forth—all the Draigon's cryptic requests and the implied weight behind them.

"That was *you!*" Leiel gasped suddenly. "I remember you now—the silver you paid my father to save me from a beating!"

Again he shrugged. "I was raised by Draigon."

She laughed and tipped her head to study him. "So this has never been just about me."

"It's always been about you *and* Cleod."

She tilted her head slightly. "He felt me. On the trail to Melbis. I raised a hand—and it seemed he sensed it."

Kilras nodded. "I suspected you were what he sensed, once he told me he had seen you."

"You brought him back." Regret painted her words in red light. "If not for Trayor—"

"If not for so many people."

"And you, it seems." She shook her head, the puzzled twist to her lips offering evidence that she was discovering things she had almost known all along. "We should get back. I have a thousand more questions to ask now. It changes everything, knowing that Gahree believed all along that Cleod is vital to *all* our futures."

17

Leiel

TWO MUGS WAITED ON THE COUNTER BESIDE THE STOVE, AND LEIEL poured them full. The snug space of her cabin filled with the earthy scent of brewing tea. Leiel's thoughts spun, refusing to focus. So much still needed to be discussed, decided. That she could claim no exclusivity in that consideration came clear as Ilora spoke from where she sat waiting at the table. "I fear none of us is thinking clearly enough."

Leiel pressed her lips together, nodded slowly as she set the kettle on the back corner of the stove. "We can't afford all the time we want, to remember and grieve." She turned to face her mother.

Ilora shook her head.

A sad smile found Leiel's lips. Too well she understood that grief bowed to no power of will, no moment of necessity. She picked up the mugs and joined Ilora at the table. So like the very first evening spent in this cabin—good company, hot drinks, this table. So much joy and hope filled Leiel that night, despite the strangeness of the place and the confusion of emotions filling her. The warmth of that memory lingered—along with all the comfort and laughter she had found here in the years since. But tonight a seat stood empty, a favorite mug unused. A glance at Ilora told Leiel her mother was not heartened by the usually calming ritual either.

Silence thickened between them, wavered, deepened, until the words not being spoken glowed in Leiel's mind like coals.

Ashes on the wind.

The hot ache of unending grief, of impossible loss.

Gydron was right.

Leiel looked at Ilora. "I never thought I would feel this again. Not this." For a heartbeat she sat again as a child, unable to comprehend the complete obliteration of her world. Then she blinked, and the hollow horror of the moment settled into only simple devastation. She was no longer that girl. No longer so many things she had been—guiltless among them. She looked at Ilora.

The older woman's eyes, red-rimmed from her own tears, lifted and met Leiel's. "She was your mother, as much as I ever was. More so, in some ways." No resentment hung in the words. Years had eased old anger, and if regrets lingered, the shadow of more recent mistakes hung far darker.

Leiel lifted her mug and let the rising scents of earth and myth fill her nostrils. "She made me tea, the first day we met. She made me tea the last day." Leiel shook her head. "She was the only one who told stories as well as you do."

Ilora wrapped her fingers around her mug where it sat before her on the table. "She told better stories than I. She had a few more years of practice. A few more stories to share."

A short laugh escaped Leiel. "A few," she agreed. "A few for every joy, and more for every sorrow." She tried for another laugh but it emerged as a choking sob. A hand raised quickly to her mouth to suppress the sound. "Old gods—" The oath from her youth, unused for years, escaped her.

Ilora reached over and touched Leiel's wrist. The contact was warm—part Draigon energy, part the soothing kindness of loving touch. "What outcome are we seeking now? What is the best we can hope into being?"

Leiel drew in a few more ragged breaths. "Hope into being. That's exactly what she did, with everything." It was what Gahree had left them all to do—write the story of Arnan's future. Gahree's legacy was, ever and always, a story of possibility. "The way forward won't be any easier than what's come before."

Ilora shook her head. "All the hard choices we have made through the years—"

Leiel's lips lifted the slightest bit. "And why would the ones ahead be any easier?"

"Exactly."

Wiping her eyes, Leiel chuckled. "Gahree would appreciate what little humor there is in that."

"And that you saved Teska," Ilora said softly.

Silence draped itself over the room. "My heart says the cost was too great."

"There's not a heart in Cyunant that disagrees."

Leiel met her mother's gaze. "And yet we all agree that it was necessary." She pushed her hair back. "I've spent weeks with Teska, and seen some of what she is capable of, but tonight my heart cannot find a way to believe what my head knows."

"How could it?" Ilora asked, soft yet incisive. "No one but you was there. Leiel—Gahree chose *you* to be with her at the end. *You*, of all Draigon, old and young. *You*, because of all of us, you are tied closest to Arnan *as it is now*. You still love those who move through it, who live everyday under its oppressions and its whimsy. Torrin. Elda. You love them as you love us. You love them as family."

"And Cleod?" Leiel asked. His name slid into the space between them. Blood on her hands. Blood on his. "You're saying she knew—"

"Who could know that with certainty?"

"Then what *are* you saying?"

"The weight you're feeling isn't meant to be lifted. It's meant to be borne. Gahree chose you, because you would bear it for all the right reasons."

Logic and emotion split understanding yet again. What Leiel knew, and what lay claim to the anguish in her soul, stood separate. "That eases nothing in me."

"No," Ilora said.

Leiel collected her fraying emotions, the doubts and remorse splintering all she knew from all she felt, and forced thought from her exhausted mind. Her connection. Her understanding. Her inability to completely let go of the life she had led in Adfen. Her left thumb slid over her palm to the base of her ring finger, seeking the band of the ring lost on the plains outside Melbis. She flinched. Her inability to let *Cleod* go. How had Gahree counted any of those things to be assets? *Perhaps we have made a mistake, staying safe on our mountain and in our secret places.* Gahree's letter. Isolation. Safety. Desolation. Could any knowledge, held safe and secure, make up for the loss of connection to the rest of the world? Could it matter more than the people who lacked it, the societies that needed it, the loves denied because of it? What value did anything have with no one to love it? What was the value of any story left untold?

A whisper of thought rose, dredged like memory from the grief silting her mind. *My tale is over, wild daughter. What ending would you write for yourself?* Gahree might have whispered the words directly. Leiel's fingers tightened on the mug, let the heat seeping from the crockery flow into her skin and sinews and soul. "We need to gather the others again." She met her mother's gaze. "What we discussed—what we decided—is not enough."

Ilora's eyes crinkled in puzzlement. "The plan is solid. And Kinra is right. We need to know how the Farlan are organizing."

"We do. But we need to consider far more. What are we protecting here? Our secrets? We no longer have any. The library? This village? We've been secure here for so long...is that worth more than justice for the rest of Arnan? What did Wynt die for? What did Gahree die for, if we're not willing to risk all of this to give the rest of Arnan a better future?"

"What are you saying?"

"We have a plan to stop this war. What we don't have is a decision about what we are prepared to lose in doing that. Or what we want on the other side of the outcome."

18

Leiel

L EIEL PRESSED HER BACK AGAINST THE SPINES OF THE BOOKS LINED raggedly along the shelf. She was glad for the support as she spoke into the too-quiet space of the central cabin. The Draigon, gathered again in every corner, listened, attention fixed on her with intensity born of Gweld-centered awareness. The silence that followed sat deep and ominous in the room.

"How can we conceive of such a thing?" Gemda's voice trembled. "The library—"

"Because we must." Leiel kept her voice firm. "In order to face this threat at all, we must be willing to lose everything. Otherwise, why fight at all? Why not run? Why not seal the cave and fly far from this place?"

"All these centuries, we have protected the knowledge of Arnan," Gydron said. "The maps. The histories. The stories. Why would we abandon it?"

"And what good is any of it, if we never share it with the world?" Leiel scanned the faces arrayed through the room. Some Draigon sat, some glared, some paced. But all listened. "We have chosen to fight. Why? We *can* keep ourselves safe. We *can* keep our stories safe. But then what is our purpose in the world? How long have the Draigon archived and protected and recruited? To what end? Gahree was right—we have spent too much time secure in our secret places. *If we do not seek to share what we know, to rejoin the world, what are we doing?*

"This war *cannot* be simply about surviving. Not for us and not for those we are asking to support us throughout this land." She shook her head, looked at Ilora. "You know my dream—that no girl, no child at all, should have to grow up as I did, alone and threatened with beatings, or destruction, for wishing to *learn*. If that dream is worth fighting for, then we must fight *for that future*. We must fight knowing we might lose everything."

"The Enclave keeps secrets as well," Kilras said. "Almost as old as what's stored here. And as dangerous. They guard them well."

Leiel frowned at him, watched Kinra do the same. He gave a nod in indication that he would explain later, then said, "They'd never suspect that any such knowledge would be left vulnerable. They'll assume we've left a force here to rival any we send to fight them."

Silence hung for so long that Leiel thought it might never be broken. Then Kinra nodded. "This cannot just be about protecting ourselves. This war has claimed our oldest, our wisest—and what she loved best was walking in the world. Our strategy cannot only be about protection, or even just stopping this war. It must be about freedom. We have to fight for more than ourselves." She looked at Teska, seated with Delhar and Kilras. "We place a great burden on our newest arrival, but Teska is proof of what Leiel says. Of the truth Gahree wrote. Teska's presence is about more than preservation. It is about healing. In the Great Shape—what good could she spread through Arnan?"

Leiel watched the weight of those words settle on Teska, watched her curl inward, shrink...then straighten. She looked around, rose, and took a half step forward.

"I am new here. And I am afraid." Teska's words filled the room, trembling but unrelenting. "But I was raised under threat in Melbis, raised to fear those in power. I was raised knowing that only my skill in healing kept me from harm, and that even one day that might not be enough. I was raised to keep learning, no matter the cost." Teska shook her head. "I don't know this place, or what you protect. I only know what it cost me to come here. And I look around and see what it cost *you* to *have* me come. What is it all for, if the future holds only more of the same?"

"We don't know that it will come to this," Ilora said. "We don't know that the Farlan and the Draighil will make it this far. But we must plan as if they will."

"If we plan to stop them, why must we prepare to fail?" Dahlie asked.

"Because if we are not willing to risk everything, we will not fight with all we are. We will not give all, to save all." Kinra's words carried softly into the space, and something haunted the edges of them, something dark and private that Leiel had never heard before. "We've lost so much already. Teska is right. Leiel is right. It is all for nothing if we fear so much to lose more, that we come at anything with only half heart and half focus."

Leiel shook her head. "It is what I have wrought, by being among you. What my life and my will and my dreams have forged for us all. In my selfishness, I have led us to this. And in that same selfishness, I ask you to be willing to risk everything."

"Leiel, no—" Ilora stepped forward.

Leiel raised a hand. "No, mother. I am responsible. Not alone, but not incompletely either. Draigon among Draigon—one thing I have learned is not to shrink from who I am or from my mistakes. I will ask forgiveness, someday, from myself as well as from all of you. But today, we must decide. Are we willing to prepare for the worst outcome, in order to achieve what we best hope for?"

Silence held for a long moment, as they stared at her with eyes full of sorrow, or fear, or anger.

In the back of the room, seated close with Delhar, Kilras met her gaze, unmoving. Presence hung in the air. Gahree. Wynt. Cleod. Loss and love and possibility. Gweld pulsed with all of it, across time and along the chain of light that marked past and present, and whatever shone beyond life.

"Please," Leiel said, though to which souls she directed the request, she did not know.

For a few heartbeats silence held again.

Gydron's response fell soft into the quiet. "What else is there for us, if we're true to the hope we have always claimed to guard for the world?"

One by one, the women nodded, taking control, taking in the worst of all possible futures, alongside the best. Long ago, each of them had taken a chance and trusted and journeyed to this place in order to become *other*. To become what they all were now. As hard a choice, made for the future, as what unfolded now.

They would leave Cuynant undefended, to fight for what mattered in the wider world and for the unimpeded future they might offer it if hope prevailed.

Leiel opened herself, and Gweld pulsed, surged, powered by connection and caring and the wild knowledge so ancient and deep that it carried no name. Color and light and heat filled the room, struck outward, rang the mountains like a gong, as though the ripple of it could settle the world into something new. And was that not exactly what was coming? She stood witness as change, brutal and filled with grace, was born into the willing moment.

19

Cleod – 38 years

A DEEP CURSE CAME FROM TRAYOR AS HE PULLED HIS MOUNT TO A halt and stared at the expanse of half-cracked, half-muddied riverbed through which the Seebo normally flowed.

Cleod drew Kicce up beside him, stared at the brutal landscape through which he had passed only weeks before. "You must have come to Melbis from the south."

The Draighil nodded. "I rode through Glasvetal to Ilris with the King's messengers."

More information previously withheld. "You missed the joy of this then." Cleod paused. "How long has the Farlan army been mobilizing?"

Still staring ahead at the devastated landscape, Trayor held silent a few heartbeats before replying. "Since midsummer."

Midsummer. The caravan had left Bajor in the spring, moving steadily west. Cleod tried to recall if they had passed any obvious couriers on the road. No memory emerged as confirmation. How widespread was preparation for war? And the impact of the news he and Trayor carried? *What* would that be? Would it inspire? Empower? Enrage?

Bad luck that they arrived at this place late enough in the day that while they still had time to make the crossing, it was not enough to travel farther west before night fell.

Ahead lay the flat swath of land where the caravan had camped after the brutal crossing of what remained of the Seebo. Just upriver was the mud bar where Shaa's wings had marked the earth in wide lines. Did those impressions still mar the ground? He shuddered and pulled his glance away. No matter. The determination awakened inside him had not begun here. It began in the Square in Adfen, in flames atop the Spur. It began with promises in need of fulfilling. It began with understanding—the vile ways of the current world could not stand.

"Which way?" Trayor's word's splintered Cleod's thoughts.

"Follow me." He rode Kicce past Trayor and down into the valley, toward the ramp he helped build, and the weaving line of stakes that marked the safe route across the dying river.

The trail sloped gently to the riverbed, but he dismounted before leading Kicce to the bottom. Though drier than it had been, the sticking muck of the riverbed was still too hazardous for a mounted rider to cross. Behind him, Trayor swung down as well and for a moment they stood together staring again at what remained of the river.

"Is it this bad to the West?"

Cleod shook his head. "Not so bad as this. Though Sibora's gardens were in poor condition."

That neglect of the city's proudest feature spoke of the intensity of the impact. Sibora was weeks ride west of Melbis, and yet Draigon Weather reached the capitol. Trayor drew a sharp breath at that news. Cleod looked over at him. Shocking, in one way, the size of the damage, but then Shaa had been the Draigon they faced, and none more powerful existed. Of course the beast's—his thoughts stumbled—the *woman's* reach had been far. He frowned, looked around, lost for a moment in the memory of the dry, harsh weeks of travel just behind them. Of ravaging heat and dusty storms. Of Draigon Weather. And yet...Shaa was dead. Had Shaa *not* controlled this Draigon Weather? And if not Shaa...?

He drew a breath to speak, but another half-formed thought stopped him. Since midsummer, Trayor had said. Only so far back as that had Trayor involved the Farlan in his plans—though by his own admission, the plot to return Cleod to the Enclaves had been laid many years before that. Unease crawled with chill claws up Cleod's back, but a dusty cough from Trayor snapped Cleod's attention back to the stark scene before him.

"Lead on," Trayor said. "It'll be dark soon."

Cleod shoved aside his muddled musings, took a moment to study the ground, before leading the way onto the treacherous path.

Eyes on the battered ground before him, Cleod clenched his jaw and ignored the deep gouges in the mud, marks of the caravan's passing that not even weeks of heavy winds could erase. Each sucking step of man and horse echoed as memory. Cleod clenched his jaw and kept his gaze, as much as safely possible, on the western bank. They moved slowly, occasionally forced to backtrack or pick a blind route that proved better than the one previously marked.

The steady cussing of the man walking in his wake, under other circumstances, might have amused. But now it only served to emphasize the echoing strangeness of each passing moment, lived in unlikely reversal, grounded in the pain that dwelt as a steady companion, in the back of his skull.

Trayor let out another stream of foul language, and for a moment Nae's voice echoed through Cleod's mind. He bent his head and closed his eyes for the briefest instant, and when he opened them again, the burned-out ferry house filled his vision. Semmio and Ejor. Old friends, long fled—and unlikely to be encountered again. Like Nae and Jahmess. Like Rimm and Sehina. Like Kilras.

The Dorn's face, serious and open, flashed into focus in Cleod's thoughts, accompanied by a stark cold that cut like a blade and ran far deeper than a chill simply drawn from emotion. For the space of a dozen breaths, the air itself seemed laced with ice. Then new understanding swept the feeling aside— Trayor had not involved the Farlan sooner than this summer *because of Kilras*. Because of the Dorn's vast network of connections, and the fact that such actions as the King had set in motion would not long be kept hidden. But the secret held just long enough that Kilras, and therefore Cleod, had no warning of Trayor's intentions...

Cleod sucked a hard breath as anger flashed, spinning his vision toward Gweld frenzy. But before it spun him away from himself, Kicce's hooves rang on the hard stone of the old footings of the ferry pier, soil caked and partly fractured. The hollow sound jerked Cleod back into control.

Harsh self-awareness defeated rage—that it was unlikely any warning would have altered what unfolded in Melbis. Or the choices he made. The Draigon sign here in this riverbed had been a bright arrow pointing firmly to his path.

Underfoot, the slick foundation stones warned of broken utility. How long before anyone came to rebuild and repair this place, to take over work too long abandoned?

Much like his own.

He shook himself, slipped as he took the next step. Slipped as he had so long ago in his choices. How much would it truly take to right him from the mire of his life?

Abandon. He glanced over his shoulder at Trayor, gestured for the other man to move upstream where the footing was more solid. *Walk away.* The Draighil glared, waved off the direction and continued his struggle through the heavy mud. Cleod reached up and grasped Kicce's bridle, guided the big grey a few steps sideways to firmer ground. *Run.* The gelding whickered, and Cleod turned his full attention to climbing the looming embankment at the place where only weeks ago his team had descended to cross the Seebo. The frustration of that day hung distant and petty in his mind. So much change since then. So much reckoning met and so much more to come...

Run.

And Leiel ran. And he ran. Through heat and hate and loss. He gritted his teeth, scrambled the last arm-length to the level ground in the shadow of the burned-out ferry house. No wagons this day to help across. No friends. No purpose to this push along the trail but the completion of too many things long left undone. It all had to matter somehow. He had to make it matter.

He turned, spoke to Kicce, urging him, and the gelding gave a last lunge and topped the bank, hooves scrabbling, sides heaving.

Trayor flailed and slipped, landed hard on his knees with a shout of pain and frustration. Cleod stared, finding no humor in the moment and no words of either sarcasm or assistance for the man stuck in the way he had chosen. No familiar voices, wry with humor, broke the moment.

Cleod turned away and led Kicce toward the well beyond the ruins of the house. If water remained in its depth, there was camp to be set, and an angry Draighil to wash clean. Ignoring Trayor's furious shouts, he tied Kicce's reins to a bent post and went to test the pump beside the house.

By the time Trayor arrived, mud-covered and furious at the makeshift camp, Cleod had water drawn and a fire lit to cook their meager late meal. "No offer of help?" Trayor demanded.

Cleod looked up from stirring the pot hanging over the trembling flames. "I thought I'd give you another reason to curse me." He pointed toward the bucket beside the pump. "Sluice off," he said. And the words rang strange. Only weeks ago, Kilras offered the same easement on the opposite bank, only weeks ago—before the past bent to the will of the present and everything changed.

"At least you're of some use." Trayor tied off his own mount and stomped to the bucket, muttering stronger curses and kicking dust.

Despite himself, Cleod laughed. "You're smug for a man who spent years plotting because he needed my help to kill Shaa."

"And yet I killed the beast without you."

"You killed a woman." The words slipped out in a rush, before thought.

Trayor lifted his head and his voice. "You think too much."

"You've said that since we were boys."

"You think too much for a *drunk*."

"And you've said that since I knocked you down in an alley."

The expected vile response did not come. Instead, Trayor laughed, true amusement in the sound, and Cleod found a smile tugging over his own lips.

"At least you've always been able in a fight." Trayor stripped off the last of his clothing and dumped water over his head.

In spite of the easy reply that formed on Cleod's lips, his thoughts whirled, tangling, as nameless unease crawled over his shoulders. How many times, at the Enclave, had the two of them traded banter with the abandon of children chasing fireflies? If their friendship had descended into bitter rivalry, that was simply the expected result of their training, their purpose. One they still shared, despite the years and distance between them. Despite the anger and hatred that now laced most of their conversations. Despite the irony that reigned—that Trayor needed him. As he always had.

At the edges of Cleod's mind, realization woke. The violence with which the two of them had always engaged loomed like falling night, discomfiting in its familiarity. And rising to meet it, the terrifying knowledge that he knew *more and better* what friendship could mean. Beyond what he and Trayor were. Beyond the fact that they became the men the world commanded them to be.

Before the idea took deep enough hold to demand he actually examine it, he gave the food simmering over the fire another stir and forced a reply. "You can hate needing me, but need me you do."

"At this point," Trayor said with a laugh laced deep with satisfaction, "I'm the only one who does, even if it is just for the strength of your arm in a fight."

Shock ripped through Cleod, locked him motionless with a hand on the stirring spoon. Somewhere in the wilderness, Leiel and Teska Healer fled north. South on the trade road, the caravan probably moved at top speed. Kilras and Sehina and Rimm and anyone else who had ever needed Cleod—now sought only to put distance between themselves and him. Had he ever in his life been less needed than he was this moment?

He closed his eyes.

No matter. Such realization only sharpened hard truth—that he had been born to fulfill one objective—the eradication of the Draigon from Arnan. Nothing else remained. And what came after that, be it something better or oblivion, mattered not at all.

20

Kilras

IN THE EARLY MORNING LIGHT, KILRAS PULLED HIS COAT CLOSE AND made his way along the rocky trail away from the heart of Cyunant. Up through the ravine he moved, around boulders and wind-twisted trees. As he had a thousand times in his childhood, he climbed toward the waterfall, though this trip wended through memory in a way no other had.

At a level spot in the trail he paused, studied the snow at the edge of the path, then stepped into it up to his knees. Slow progress led around snow-bent trees and tumbled rocks. His breath crystallized in the air, shining clouds of vapor the briefest mark of his passing. At last he came to the place he sought, a tight grove of trees taller than most in the ravine, growing in an irregular oval with an open flat place in the center. He stepped into the small clearing.

On his last visit to this spot, the mossy ground had been littered with fallen leaves, and the crisp scent of stone and cold tree-bark had filled his nose.

And his body had found the Draigon heat of Wynt's embrace.

So long ago.

The sun shared warmth without reservation, but the granite domes of the surrounding peaks pushed cool air along the ridgelines. The breeze picked up mists from mountain streams and the melt of snowpack still lingering in the shadows and deepest hollows.

Beneath him, the rough wool of the blanket was cushioned by the time-packed pile of fallen fir needles and ancient mosses. Kilras tangled his fingers in Wynt's hair and smiled, watching clouds chase through the bright air.

She sighed and raised her head, tapped a finger against his chest. "We're getting better at this."

"Practice in all things."

"As sweaty as sword work."

"With half the footwork." She rolled onto her back, propped herself on her side with her head on her hand and met his gaze. "What if we make a child?"

"Draigon and human? Gydron says that's not possible."

"You asked her?"

"She told me."

"Ha!" Wynt blew a stray hair from her eyes, lay back, and looked up at the passing clouds, and her hair fell back across her gaze. "Just as well. I'm not the mothery kind."

He laughed. "What'll you do? If you decide you are mothery after all?" There were no male Draigon in Cyunant since Hech's death. As far as he knew, no male Draigon now existed anywhere.

Wynt grinned and sat up. She caught his hand and turned it palm up, traced her fingers down his. "I'll do what all the others do, I suppose. Go into the world and find a girl who does not belong out there. One who is smart enough, and brave enough, and strong enough to join us here. I'll care for her and teach her, as though she were my own. And, when it is time, if she chooses, and if I am skilled enough to survive the fight, I'll bring her here. I might find many girls. I might take them lots of places. There are as few pure Draigon as there are strange, pale humans among us. We'll all have to make do with what we are."

He freed his hand and flicked a finger at her nose. "I'm not pale."

"All right, paler than me."

Again he made a wry sound, shook his head. "Regardless, I'm the only male option you have at the moment."

She snorted and moved quickly, wrapped herself around him and toppled him onto his back. Crouched over him with her copper curls curtaining his face, she laughed. "I've seen paintings. You're a fine option. Enough talk. Let's practice."

Kilras shook his head and flicked his gaze to a bare pile of rocks stacked against the shelter of a birch. His fingers tingled. Sharp breath caught in his throat. Impossible. Why would a bark message be curled under a stone, awaiting him? Years had passed. Decades.

He moved closer, and already half-cursing the foolishness of the action, dropped to one knee and picked up a rock. Only bare dirt greeted his gaze. Drawing in a heavy breath, he shook his head. Whatever he had hoped to find, recollection would have to suffice, in this place and in many others on the mountain.

A last glance around and he rose and made his way back to the trail. Memory and loss followed as he traced the steep, winding way among rock and bare shrubbery. Eventually, the sound of crashing water guided him, and he stepped between the boulders that guarded the turn to the waterfall pool.

Along the edges of the pool, the first ice of winter laid claim to the water's surface. Kilras stared across the glimmering surface at the waterfall. Cyunant. Cyunant and all the memories that dwelt in the scree-filled ravine, the crags and notches of the mountains, the granite-washed scent of the air. Familiar yet foreign. Haunted yet home. His throat tightened.

Haunted because it was home.

He blinked and pulled in a long breath, allowed the deep ache to flow through him as cold wind tugged at his hair and worked the edges of his clothing.

So long away, shaped and motivated by so many things he could never have imagined in any of the moments spent splashing through this water, running these trails. Gahree, this moment, would have said wise things about time and change and choice. Wynt would have laughed—with or at him—laughed and spoken true, offered hurt and comfort that complicated his pain even as she eased it.

He wished for all of it.

For none of it.

Because what was past was done, and so was beyond altering. What lay ahead—Cleod and Leiel and Trayor and the Farlan, Delhar and the other Draigon, Sehina and his team—well, pain was coming to them all again. Coming for him. But what had been born here long ago, and reborn again and again on the trail, was understanding that change and hope were forever entwined, and that he, in however small a way, was part of both.

A footfall alerted him, pulled him back to the moment, and he glanced over his shoulder to see Teska Healer, bundled in layers against the bitter chill, moving toward him with a purpose. Below the thick brow of her hat, the intense focus of her gaze fixed on him, and he squared himself around to meet her.

She halted before him, dark eyes unblinking for several heartbeats, then she glanced past him toward the water, the cascade, and back again. "You're different," she said.

All these years and strangers still felt the need to tell him that he was odd. His lips twitched.

She smiled. "I say that as though you haven't always known it."

With a grunt, Kilras shook his head. "If you followed me to tell me that, you've hiked far to offer little."

"That's not what I came to tell you." She studied him for another few seconds. "I came to tell you why."

He went still to his very core. Why? How many years had it been since that question mattered to his life? Why, for him, ceased to be useful when Tylen died. It mattered only in as far as he needed to explain things to others.

Into the silence left by his lack of reply she said, "You access Gweld, but you cannot change as others can."

And that, too, was no revelation at all. With a sigh, he reached up and lifted his hat off, ran his fingers through his hair. "I've known that all my life."

"Yes, but not *this*."

He frowned, "Teska what—"

"It isn't in you." Teska's eyes flashed bright as she swept her gaze over him, measuring, assessing with even more intensity than she had at their first meeting.

"What isn't?"

"The...flash...the bit inside you that can light your enai and turn you into Draigon. I see Gweld in the lines of your knowledge, your thoughts, your breath...but it's not in your bones, Kilras Dorn. Not your muscles or your blood. It's surrounds all you are, but does not flow through your *body*."

His skin rose in gooseflesh and the back of his neck grew hot. Could Teska be offering the answer to the question that had haunted his youth? To the reason he had been forced to leave Cyunant so long ago? His fingers tightened on the hat, the leather, shaped and softened by wear, compressing deeply. "Explain what you mean."

Teska drew breath, let it out. "For everyone here, everyone but you, Gweld works from the inside, from the core of them. But not you. You, it surrounds. You...pull...pull it toward you, and shape it for your own use. It's not part of you until you make it be... No. Until you *ask* it to be."

Powerful understanding, offered too late. But still... He let her words settle inside him as she spoke, let them become part of his knowledge of self.

Until she shook her head and her last phrase struck like a blow. "Like the Draighil did."

He stared, every part of him pulled taut as spun wire. "Like the *Draighil*?"

She nodded. "The one who killed Shaa."

Kilras frowned, weighing the implications of her words.

"Teska Healer, are you telling me that I use Gweld as the men of the *Enclaves* use Gweld?"

She hesitated a heartbeat, shrugged deeper into her coat, then nodded again.

Kilras took a step back. No wonder she looked at him strangely, warily, when they first met. What she could see of his—what did she call it? Enai?—must look much like that of the men who had tried to destroy her. "The *same*?" Even though he was raised and taught by Draigon?

And yet that made sense, in a way. The men of the Enclaves could not claim the Great Shape. They could only wield Gweld through years of discipline and training—the same way he had learned. Once, Kinra or Gahree had explained to him how strange it was that he could share the vision and feelings of creatures other than Draigon—that he could know the desires of wolf and deer, and touch the minds of men as well. The Draigon could share only among each other, and those able to fully join them.

And Leiel—the connection she spoke of—the way Cleod sensed her presence on the trail. That was strange as well.

Kilras considered the stories Cleod had told him of Draighil training. How the Elders created visions in the minds of the Draigre. And of the day Cleod faced the Blayth hounds and the Hlewlion and how he shared their thoughts. Was *how* Gweld was accessed the difference that made those connections possible? Gweld attained from without rather than within?

And yet... The Draighil suffered for their knowledge. Kilras had witnessed enough of Cleod's screaming bouts of Overlash to know just how much. But he, Kilras, did not experience such pain. What was the difference?

He faced Teska again, found her gaze upon him, uneasy, as though she feared how he might respond to what she had shared. Unsurprising, that uncertainty, after what she had lived through in Melbis.

He offered a nod of understanding and kept his distance as he voiced the conflict her insight opened within him. "I don't know what to make of what you're telling me. Gweld is corrupted in the Enclaves. It pains the Draighil to use it. I've never experienced that."

She shifted her weight from foot to foot. "You know more of that than do I. Perhaps it's the hatred you spoke of before. The way the Draighil are taught to hate Draigon. Perhaps that's the difference."

Kilras stood a moment, then a wave of dark emotion unfolded as revelation. "Not hate," he whispered. "Poison. The *cuila*. The plant that molds obedience to the Enclaves."

"A plant?" Teska said, her eyes widening. "A poison?"

"I asked Gydron long ago. She said there is no cure for Cuila addiction." He shook his head. "That it was a miracle he broke free at all, back when I found him."

"Broke free? You mean your friend Cleod?"

"Yes."

"Did he really, if the other Draighil could bring him back to the Enclave way so easily?"

The acrid scent of burnt sage, the battered walls of the poit and the smear of burnt flesh on the edge of the stove. "It wasn't easily done."

Teska remained silent a moment, then looked past him at the icy waterfall, her stillness leaving him room to think.

The cuila. The damned cuila and all it had birthed within Cleod. "*A poison*. Teska—"

She returned her gaze to his, a question in her eyes.

"Can you cure poisons, Teska? Could you help Cleod?" Kilras held his voice even, unwilling to express too much of the emotion that surged through his chest as he asked the question.

"My grandmother taught me," she said. "How to burn out vile substances—how to clear a body and so the enai."

"With Gweld."

She nodded. "Yes, though she never called it that."

Was it possible? Could she cure Cleod? What would that entail? And how would they even get her close enough to him for long enough to try? How, when he traveled with Trayor and would soon have all the Enclaves and the entire Farlan army at his back?

"Does any of this matter?"

"It matters." Kilras spoke the certainty building in his chest. "I don't know why, but it does." He shook himself, then tipped his head toward the trail. "We need to share this with the others."

21

Leiel

IN THE WARM HEART OF THE LIBRARY, EVERY PART OF LEIEL HELD STILL—as still as Cleod at his calmest and most determined—as Kilras and Teska shared their new understanding. As they spoke, the pace of Leiel's heart changed, gathered fierce speed. Could it be true? She had to move.

"Gahree said there is no cure for cuila addiction. But if we can find a way to treat the damage to Cleod's body as though it is a direct poison—" She stalked the shelves, running shaking fingers over the uneven spines of books. Soft or ridged under her touch, the volumes seemed to shimmer when her Gweld sense traced them in conjunction with her need. At last she tugged one free and carried it back toward the center of the cavern. If what Teska believed was true—

"No, that's not an answer," Gydron's voice, soft and empirical, cut like a blade through the thrill rising in Leiel's heart.

Leiel froze with the volume open in her hands, "But Teska could simply—"

"When has anything ever been simple?" Gydron came around the table and crossed the room to meet Leiel's gaze. "We've spent centuries seeking a cure. Nothing has worked. If it was just a poison, something would have. Eirar tried using herb, Gweld heat, mental fire...all the things Teska is considering. None of them had any effect."

"Why?" Leiel demanded. She tapped a finger hard into the pages of the book. "If Gweld provides us the ability to resist poisons and Teska can expand that ability to—"

"Leiel, the question remains—if Gweld skill offers protection from cuila, how do the Draighil become addicted to it at all?"

All the energy Teska's news had awoken ran out of Leiel. "You're right," she said and dropped her gaze, her stomach suddenly churning. Wind on high, was she so desperate for some way, *any* way, to make even a small correction to the damage her actions had rent in the world that she would grasp at even the slimmest hope? Of course she would. She frowned. "Why, then, can *we* resist the drug's effect? It did not harm me or Gahree or Teska in Melbis. Trayor burned it all day and into the night, to control Cleod."

Kilras spoke from across the room. "It must have something to do with what Teska discovered—*how* the Enclaves use Gweld."

Trembling with barely suppressed energy, Leiel faced him. "But if that's true, why did Cuila not affect *you*?"

He shook his head, "I've never inhaled the smoke," he said. "Even that night at the poit where I discovered Cleod missing. I caught scent of it and I moved away. I'm no measure of how it works."

Leiel's shoulders slumped. The hope that had burst into being within her when Teska and Kilras arrived with their news, fluttered like a trapped bird in her chest, weakening by the moment. But, as it had before, some almost-understanding hung at the edges of her mind, just out of sight, just out of reach. Because it had to mean *something*, Teska's discovery. She frowned and looked at Gydron. "But this *difference* in Gweld. Why would it exist at all?" she murmured.

"Perhaps because Gweld is of Arnan." Gydron pulled out a chair and settled herself at the table.

"What?" Leiel shifted her attention to the older Draigon. "What do you mean?"

"Kilras sparked interest in me when he was a boy. He learned all we had to offer, mastered Gweld, and yet he could not claim the Great Shape." She looked over at him, and Teska, gestured to the chairs on the other side of the table, then glanced at Leiel with the same invitation in her eyes.

Leiel looked back as Kilras and Teska joined Gydron at the table, then sighed and settled herself into a chair beside the library keeper. "And what have you discovered?"

"Nothing certain."

Kilras laughed. "You didn't bring us all to the table to tell us you've nothing to share."

Gydron smiled. "I have much to share, but I am not certain any of it matters enough to be an actual explanation."

"Will anything explain enough to help us turn Cleod's mind?" Leiel asked.

"I do not know," Gydron laced her fingers and settled her hands on the table. "But I do know that I found no record of a Farlan—even the Draighil who learn Gweld—ever claiming the Great Shape. Not one."

"Well why would they?" Leiel asked. "If they could do so, they would have learned long ago what we are."

"But that's just it. They *never* have. Not once. And we know that the Great Shape is a natural outcome of those who come to understand and express the nuance of Gweld."

"Not for *all* who learn it." Kilras's voice held a cool amusement that tugged a twitch from Leiel's lips.

She looked over at him. Most men she had known would have layered that statement with resentment. "Not all," she agreed.

"And why would that be the case?" Gydron leaned forward, drawing all their attention. "Perhaps because the Far Landers are not native to the land where Gweld came into being."

"And my father was Farlan," Kilras said.

"You mean *only* those without Farlan heritage can become Draigon?" Teska asked.

"I don't know," Gydron said. "I have no understanding of why that would be true, only that it's one possible explanation."

Silence draped itself over the room. "I don't understand," Teska said. "Why would such a thing matter?"

Gydron shook her head. "I do not claim to know. It makes little sense. Unless there is something in the environment here that builds within those of this land for generations until we can take the Great Shape."

"But the Far Landers have been here more than a thousand years." Leiel closed the book she still held and placed it on the table. What sense did this strange idea of Gydron's make?

"The histories say that the Draigon took ten times as long as that to discover that secret of Gweld. And it was not until the first Shaa came to leadership after the Second War of Arnan that we learned we could make Draigon Weather. Who knows what power Gweld will open for us in another fifty centuries?"

"So is it being of this land, or time on the land itself that makes a difference?" Teska asked.

"Both," Kilras said. "The answer to questions like that is always 'both'."

"We may never know." Gydron leaned back and shook her head. "I am not sure any of this changes anything."

"It does," Leiel said softly, voicing the certainty that burned in her chest. The back of her mind tingled, as something half understood at the heart of their conversation pulsed and tugged deep in her thoughts, demanding attention. Gweld. Cuila. Cleod. Arnan. What was she missing? Something else important.

"What is it?" Teska asked. "Your enai—"

Enai. Leiel gasped and raised her gaze to the healer's. "You told me, the night of the Sacrifice in Melbis, that Cleod's enai was almost clear until Trayor burned more cuila. Why would that be true if the poison controlled him so completely?"

Teska drew a hissing breath, but shook her head to indicate that though she understood the implications of the question, no answer arose.

"Because it doesn't control him completely. Not anymore."

She looked to Kilras. "How did Cleod escape the cuila the first time?"

The Dorn narrowed his gaze, nodded slowly. "He became a drunk."

"He traded one addiction for another," Leiel said. "But what if it is more than that?"

"You cannot think that ercew is the cure for cuila!" The astonishment in Gydron's voice matched the building pressure in Leiel's chest. "That's not something Gahree or Eirar or any of the others would have missed through the years."

"But none of the Draighil has ever been *Cleod*." Leiel shook her head. "Kilras, you said Gahree told you that Cleod mattered. That he always has."

His expression turned thoughtful, and several seconds passed before he answered. "I've never doubted that. But I've never known how."

Leiel shook her head, her heart a dark, vibrating weight behind her ribs. Long ago, the Woodcutter's son had claimed part of her mind, her soul. Luck? Accident? Fate? Gahree had promised that destiny played no part in their friendship, and yet the shining threads of their lives had tangled early, tangled still.

She envisioned the shimmering embroidery of the tree on Gahree's pack, the strength of each strand, root to branch. The story of lives intertwined, supporting and shaping each other, twisted together and forged by the storms of life. As part of her, was Cleod any less a part of that tree than any of the women whose lives danced as the leaves? If she were anything more than a single sentence in the tale they were all now writing to bend Arnan's future, then how could he not matter? "If that question leads where I think it might," she said, "the answer could reshape this world."

22

Kilras

THE SCENT OF SALT HUNG STRANGE IN THE AIR, AND KILRAS TURNED, chilled and uneasy in the purple half-light. Leiel looked up from where she knelt studying the map laid out on the floor. "Here," she said. "Come see. The way. I've found it."

Kilras frowned was he walked toward her. The echo of his boots on stone rang *wrong* in his ears. Everything felt wrong. And found it? Found what? Her tone said she expected him to know what she meant. But he recalled nothing they might be looking for. He stopped beside her, looked down. A ragged coastline wound over the parchment. She laid a finger over the mark that denoted a town.

He stared. Why was she looking at Clyfsirth?

"I've found her," Leiel said.

"Her?" The skin on his arms prickled, and he shifted his attention from the map to Leiel's face.

A bright copper gaze returned his stare. He sucked in a harsh gasp of air. "Wynt?"

Her hair, windblown and more curly than usual, shifted in a breeze that could not possibly have filled the library.

"Is grim a normal state for you that I've just been lucky enough not to have experienced so far?" she asked.

He stared, his heart suddenly pounding within his chest like crashing surf. "Who are you?" he demanded as she laughed and looked away.

Shaking, he reached for her and she raised her head and

looked at him, the street around them darkening as the sun slid toward the far horizon. He stiffened in shock and she vanished like smoke.

In the next breath, exhaustion weighted him like a thousand stones. Worn, wrung through though he was, the thought of missing any time with Tylen was unbearable. Someone must know where she could be found. Had someone not just said they found her?

He walked past the shop and looked down at the docks, scanning for anyone he might ask. For a moment, his vision blurred and it seemed as though his eyes were not his own. Then there she was, working her way along the far dock, walking toward the narrow walkway that wrapped around the cliffs, sloping gradually down to narrow beach in the distance. Tiredness forgotten, he moved quickly after her. By the time he caught up, she was descending toward the sand.

"Tylen!" he called.

She turned, one hand catching back her hair to hold it out of her eyes in the breeze. And her expression opened, unfolding with joy. He caught his breath and just stared. Never had anyone looked at him like that. That such a look was possible at all locked his heart in shock. He smiled, raised a hand in greeting... and she was gone.

He froze, gaze sweeping the beach. There. A hundred paces further down the shore, she walked toward the surf.

"Tylen!"

She turned, lifted a hand to hold her blowing hair from her face. He took a step toward her, and she waved.

Again he reached out and the beach cracked open, shuddering and trembling, split as though by the blow of an ax. Before he could even shout, the landscape bathed itself in red, crystalline and gleaming, then everything before him shattered into a mist that cut like glass as it blew over him with whirlwind force and he came awake with a jerk that left him gasping.

He heaved breath, wide-eyed and stunned. How long since he had dreamed so deeply, so darkly? He lay on the narrow bed he remembered so well from his childhood and shook as he had not done since those long-ago nights when his dreams had torn into his mother and left them both filled with horror.

Heart leaping, he sat up to push aside the curtain. He listened, but the only sound from the other bed was his mother's even breathing. Tension slumped from his shoulders and he reached up with both hands to push his hair from his face. He had not hurt her, not pushed uncontained Gweld vision into her mind. And yet...

He closed his eyes. Something remained at the edge of his mind, some sense of unmeasured connection unlike anything he had felt in decades. *Tylen.* He had dreamed of Tylen, tangled her up with Wynt and Leiel, with the sense of lost love and longing that permeated his every thought of Leiel and Cleod. Small wonder that all three women had formed at the center of a nightmare.

He shivered a little and got to his feet. The floor was chill and no warmth radiated from the stove. Kilras sighed. His mother, as Draigon, had lost the habit of maintaining warmth in the home for human comfort. He crossed the room and knelt to open the stove door, used the once-familiar poker to stir the ashes. A few coals glowed orange amid the grey, and he carefully added sticks, then logs, until flames tickled upward and warmth spread into the air.

Delhar turned in her bed, but did not wake, and he stayed for several moments, feeding the fire and soaking in its dancing warmth. He considered returning to the comfort of quilted mattress and woven blankets, but instead he sat in the quiet darkness and listened to Delhar's breathing. The farewell he and his mother were soon to share would be difficult.

Another few days and he would leave this place to take up his part in the coming battle. In the quiet, he admitted to himself that he longed for that separation. He was not, any longer, of Cyunant. And he would find no peace here as long as his world and all those he loved within it stood at risk. With luck, distance would ease the tangled ache in his heart and keep dark dreams at bay.

Hard dreams. Connection. The chill that whispered through him had little to do with the temperature of the room. If *his* thoughts and nights were so muddled by dark memory, what must Cleod be feeling? Or was he willing, any longer, to let himself feel at all? Considering the years that Cleod had spent drowning the past in a bottle, a return to that habit of drinking, of denial, remained more than likely.

Kilras frowned. But Cleod was not the young, broken, drunkard Kilras had found at the Rock Digger. More than a decade together on the trail had built trust. Cleod's will to be more, to make a difference, had forged solid change.

For several heartbeats, Kilras found himself back in the wind-silted alley in Melbis, sword in hand, facing his friend. Then the moment broke, like the dream, and wearying truth laid claim to his thoughts—that moment, face to face in the raging storm might have done damage beyond measure.

And yet that worst possibility refused to settle within Kilras. At heart, Cleod was a protector, driven by the need to better the lives of those around him. And their years together had only solidified those traits. Given enough time, enough conversation, enough shared pain, they could once again reach an understanding, regain mutual respect.

The wind rattled the shutters.

If that chance ever came.

Kilras shook his head. Time and words. Words to move Cleod. How many of those had always been needed. He bent his head.

Careful not to wake Delhar, he rose and made his way back to the bed, pulled his pack from beneath it. Moments later, he was settled at the table by a low-burning lamp, with a bottle of uncorked ink, and quill in hand. How many letters had he written through the years? Thousands. And the books in the library proved how much those stories, those personal truths, could come to matter to people beyond himself. Once, such a thought might have filled him with embarrassment, that anything he said or did could have such impact. But stories mattered. Truth mattered. Always. And both, offered from the heart, could change the world.

So what could he offer Cleod, in absentia, that could reshape the entire history of their association? Could recolor and remold it into, not a series of lies, but a more solid and brighter foundation for a greater truth?

He sat for a long, long while, as the lamp burned and the storm carved against the cabin walls. He had shared what he knew of Enclave secrets with the Draigon. Now it was time to share his own in the hope that someday his keeping of them could be forgiven. He dipped the quill and etched purposeful words across the page before him.

23

Cleod

HE DREAMED HE WOKE AFIRE. HE DREAMED HE WOKE IN BLOOD. HE dreamed in splintered visions of promises broken and suffering unfurled. And when the dawn finally yanked him to full consciousness, he lay shaking under the scratchy wool blanket, afraid to open his eyes. Around him, the walls of the tent flapped and whistled in the gusting wind. Gasping for breath as images, only half-remembered, faded from his mind, his senses slowly replaced fear with recognition of where he was. The poles rattled, battered by the storm which grew worse each day they moved north. And a storm lived inside him as well.

Yesterday's crossing of the Seebo had stripped his nerves raw, the memory of Shaa's wing marks in the muddy riverbed dragging his mind, until the suck of them threatened to pull him under. Only the cuila Trayor burned with their cookfire had calmed Cleod enough to allow even nightmare-burdened sleep.

Canvas walls pushed at him, and he sat up, tossed aside the blanket, then started as goosebumps rose along his arms and across his bare shoulders. The blazing heat in which he had fallen asleep was gone, replaced by a chill truly in line with the season.

He reached for his shirt, tugged it on over his head, thrusting his arms into the sleeves as though he could stab confusion from his mind with action. The room swam a little as he bent to pull on his boots. He ignored the dizziness and finished dressing.

From Draigon Weather to rising cold in only hours? Not the usual pattern of the world. But what was usual now? Swearing under his breath, he got to his feet and crossed the room. He pushed aside the flap and stepped out into a frigid, swirling whiteness.

Cleod stopped, blinking, cold penetrating his flesh like an army of needles. *Snow?* When had snow ever arrived so soon on the heels of Draigon Weather? He choked back laughter. So much for Trayor's plans. Chill flakes melted against his face and he closed his eyes, shivering. The Draigon had abandoned their most powerful weapon. Were the monsters wise to Trayor's intentions?

Not monsters.

Women.

The small, dark body sprawled in dirt and blood.

Leiel. A gentle touch on his cheek. Her crisp voice in his ears. *Just Draigon, Cleod. You are not the writer of my story.*

Shaa, a burning vital presence in his mind shouting, warning—*I leave them nothing!*

Cleod closed his eyes, shaking. Kilras's voice. *The Draigon are what they have always been.*

Leiel.

The broken ring.

No.

Damn whatever dreams had woken him! Heaving in another breath, he raised his face to the sky. It was close enough to dawn that he made out individual flakes in the swirl around him, could see the fine mist marking his exhale as the air lightened, moment by moment. He pulled in a long breath, watching delicate, white beauty stream out of the sky. The wind kicked up and the surprise of the changed weather shifted into harsh reality. The dangers of brutal cold awakened as a blast of wind slashed, cutting through the thin comfort of his summer-weight clothing.

Shivering, he took a step back toward shelter. His belly cramped as need surged through him. Old gods, too well he knew this feeling, the frantic clawing at the back of his skull, snaking down his spine and into his gut—the need for heat in the face of harsh winter weather—a need met in Gweld trance backed by cuila... Every inch of his skin prickled. Every hair rose as some vital understanding *almost* unfolded across his mind.

Then the wind pushed again, and clarity fled, driven aside by a hunger that, once filled, would banish red-edged thoughts into the rising dawn. He turned and stumbled back into the tent, toward the flask of ercew stuffed in his pack.

"By all the lords of Arnan, what new suffering are we awakened to?" Trayor glared from his bedroll.

Cleod staggered a step, then righted himself and replied with equal venom. "Winter." He folded his legs and settled to the floor, plucked the flask from its hiding place and took a long pull of the bitter liquid it contained. When he looked again, the expression on Trayor's face had shifted, but the burn of ercew was enough distraction that Cleod could not read the subtle message in the change.

"Winter?"

"Snow and wind. The heat of the Draigon has not just faded, it's been replaced by a full blizzard."

Trayor cursed a stream that brought back too many memories for Cleod to inventory, which raised an unreasonable amusement.

"You haven't discovered anymore creative phrases in all these years?" Cleod recapped the flask as the ercew steadied the shaking in his limbs. "I'll check the horses. I hope you packed more clothing than what you've been wearing."

"Did you?" Trayor demanded.

"Are you actually hoping I freeze to death before we reach the next town?"

Trayor's reply improved on his previous invectives. Without bothering to respond, Cleod yanked on his second shirt, and made his way out into the storm.

Kicce and Trayor's mount stood huddled on the lee side of the tent. The past months of Draigon Weather had not allowed them to grow the thick coats needed to truly protect them from such sudden plummet of temperature. Thankfully, if they got moving and reached safety by nightfall, it was not yet cold enough to do the animals harm. He and Trayor, however, faced a brutal ride. If not for the needs of the horses, staying here until the storm abated held far more appeal than a day in the open under these conditions.

Old gods, to think just yesterday he complained of heat and sweat and the weight of his clothing under the dusty sky. The memory of warmth filled him, not comforting, but burning like the dream that had awakened him. Settle, he pleaded to himself. Settle and just get on with it.

The snow swirled, patting like small hands against his face, the world wrapped in silence by the drifting flakes. The world, as ever, was disinclined to bend to equanimity. Far from comfort, he reached up and tangled his fingers in Kicce's mane. "Old friend," he said. "We've come to a hard ride. I'm sorry." He shook his head. "I'm sorry." For a heartbeat he acknowledged the words were not meant for the grey gelding alone, then he straightened and made his way back around the tent. A harsh day lay between them and real shelter, and that reality left no room for sorting discordant thoughts.

24

Cleod

FETLOCK DEEP, THE SNOW ON THE ROAD SQUEAKED UNDER KICCE'S hooves. Cleod hunched in the saddle. An ache pounded through his skull, and the frigid air filling his nostrils only added to the pressure. All day in this bitter chill, and now a new storm was blowing up. His hands curled like claws on the reins, and ice crusted the edges of his shirt where his breath froze as it blew over the cloth. He had ridden away from the caravan in Melbis with only his sword, the clothing on his back, and his bedroll—and the Draighil uniform Trayor had returned to him.

His stomach cramped again, part response to the desperate weather, part unflinching demand for the relief cuila could bring. He trembled, raised his gaze to search ahead, seeking something, anything to relieve the frantic need of his body and the pounding of his unwelcome thoughts. The brutal change in weather. Fear. Loss. Pain.

He forced attention back to their desperate situation. They were close. They had to be. He peered into the storm, but it was several moments before grey shapes pushed out of the blowing snow, and relief slumped Cleod's shoulders. *At last.*

"Old god's be damned. Is *this* what you call a town?" Trayor's voice shoved between the snowflakes, as cold and biting as the wind that frisked every seam of Cleod's clothes. The Draighil rode up beside Kicce, offered a glare to match his tone.

No map declared Hengbaith even a hamlet. The settlement, built all of stone, stood as old as anything in Arnan, yet a blacksmith's forge, a small inn, and a half dozen farms were all the mark it made in the world. A speck of human habitation with an ancient, and thankfully reliable well, a way-stop on the long trade road between Seebo Ferry and Adfen, the village waited, unchanged in all the years Cleod had traveled through it. But the only thing that mattered today was the fact it existed at all. Even if Trayor decided to cut Cleod down for stubbornness, he would ride no further.

"I call it Hengbaith. The inn is Little Peace," Cleod replied, voice hoarse and shaking. Damn this chill and the weakness it awoke in him. Belly cramping again, he all but snarled his next words. "Does it matter if it's a proper town if it means shelter and a chance for supplies?"

Trayor scowled, but offered no reply as they rode the last few paces into what, at best, could be called a wide stop on the trade road.

In the yard of the tiny inn, only a few strides from the road, Cleod reined Kicce to a halt and glanced over at Trayor as the man snorted in disgust. The building was single story with a pair of steps leading to the door, and no porch. But it was tightly built and the door freshly painted.

"Here?" Trayor demanded, as though their previous exchange had not even occurred.

Cleod flicked his gaze from Trayor to the inn, and then up into the clouds rolling deep grey in a darkening sky. Then at the mounds of snow shoveled aside to clear the inn yard. Cleod found words despite the ache of cold in his throat. "Or another night in your blasted tent. You're welcome to it. I'll find my rest here." He dismounted, slipping Kicce's reins over his head.

"We could make Reerdon by nightfall."

"And find every inn there packed full with everyone escaping the weather, adding strain on their water and their wood supply." Who prepared for an early winter in the middle of Draigon Weather? And how in all damnation were they to survive a ride of those hours? "You've been asking for my secrets since Melbis. You'd do well to take advantage of what I've learned in ten years of riding these trails. You can hate what I know and how I know it, but don't be fool enough to ignore it."

Before Trayor managed a response, the inn door shoved open and a child of eleven or twelve, wearing work pants and too-large boots, burst into the yard at a run, arms outstretched. "Cleod! Cleod! What are you doing here? You and Sere Kilras came only two months back! Mother says—" Spotting Trayor, the girl skittered to a halt. The smile froze on her face. Snow swirled, and she crossed her arms as she stared at the Draighil. Then she looked around at the otherwise empty yard before her gaze settled back on Cleod. Her teeth worried her lower lip. Then her eyes widened, and she flashed another look at Trayor, as though realizing that her lack of skirts might be a problem in the eyes of a Farlan man.

Confusion rose in her expression. "Where's Sere Kilras?" she asked, soft and slow, as she met Cleod's gaze. "Where's Sehina and all?" She stared at him, and her unspoken query seemed to fill his thoughts. *What are you doing here without them? Why are you riding with a Farlan?* Her face scrunched, then shifted again, a message of *wrongness* etched across her changing expression. Wrong. So much wrong—Cleod shuddered as he looked at the child.

A woman with dark, wildly curly hair appeared in the inn's doorway, tugging a shawl tight around her shoulders. "Ain, what are you doing racing out in this weather? You know—" Her words broke off as she caught sight of the two men. Immediately, she stepped into the snowy yard, reaching out a hand to gather the girl back toward her. "Ain, come here. You know better— Cleod?" Staring at him, she stopped before her fingers touched Ain's shoulder.

"Hello, Leys," he said, watched the worry on her face move to relaxed recognition, then back to tension as she glanced from him to Trayor.

A fresh thudding took up residence in the back of his head as her expression closed into too-careful neutrality.

"Cleod's here with—" Ain began, but Leys interrupted.

"I see he is. Well, you know what to do. Kicce needs care, and the other Sere's horse as well."

"Yes, mamah," the girl said. She approached Cleod first, staring at him, eyes wide and expectant. He looked back, torn between offering his customary greeting of a hug, and the knowledge that Draighil never showed such affection. *Draighil. He was Draighil.* Had he ever been otherwise? If not...what did that mean for his every interaction since the day he abandoned the Enclave? He swallowed down the lump in his throat, and handed Kicce's reins to Ain. The small hand that took them from him trembled, and the rest of her form joined in that shaking as she turned from him to take the lead to Trayor's horse. Cleod refused to let instinct claim him, to gather her close and promise her all was well. Because it was not. Nothing might ever be well again.

He met Trayor's gaze, and the Draighil's scowl slashed through the blowing snow like a blade aflame.

"Come in out of the storm, Seres." Leys drew their attention as she gestured toward the stout building.

"Is your roof sound, woman, or will you need to direct me to a seat out of the drip and chill?" Trayor demanded as he stalked through the blowing cold and past her into the tiny inn.

As Cleod watched, Leys, so warm and easy-smiling through all the years he had known her, held her flat expression, as closed as a stuck flue on a stove. The gaze she flicked at him before she turned and followed Trayor inside held no emotion at all.

More than just the wind blasting into the seams of Cleod's too-thin clothing chased a chill across his shoulders. The snow scritched under his boots as he crossed the yard and entered the building.

Across the narrow common room, Trayor already occupied the seat nearest the hearth, boots propped up and dripping on the rug. His wet coat draped over the back of the next closest chair, adding to the puddle on the waxed wooden floor. At the desk, Leys pulled the register book out and opened it to an empty page, as though having her two newest guests scrawl their names on the old sheet would somehow contaminate the memory of the other guests.

Cleod stood shivering just inside the door and watched her deliberate actions. His name was on a previous sheet. His and Kilras's and the merchants of the caravan that stopped this way only weeks past. *Sehina glared at him over Kilras's shoulder, her eyes bright and furious through the swirling sand.* While Leys's controlled expression carried no anger, it lurked in her every move, in her uncharacteristic silence, her willingness to leave him standing, unattended at the entry. Had he arrived here any other stormy evening, she would be rushing him toward the fire, peeling him out of wet clothes, and forcing hot drinks into his hands while she sent Ain in search of dry garments. He stood dripping and so deeply chilled that his heart seemed edged with ice. A ragged series of emotions twisted up from his gut and into his chest until the only thought he could manage was a curse, and the only action he found himself capable of was to turn his back on Leys and half-stagger toward the warmth of the fire.

Turn his back. Turn toward. His thoughts tumbled. All he had done for weeks was reel from one determined extreme to the next, until neither his mind nor his body remembered equilibrium, much less how to attain it.

Half-way across the space, a touch landed on his elbow. He jerked around, looked into Leys's eyes where she stood beside him, worry and confusion flashing behind the anger in her gaze. "You're half frozen," she said. "Cleod, what brings you here with...?" She flicked a glance at Trayor where he leaned close to the blazing hearth, lowered her voice. "...like this?"

Her hand on his arm was like fire. He pulled away, shook his head. "We make for Adfen."

"Cleod—"

Trayor's voice cracked through the room. "Have you rooms ready for travelers, woman, or is that a chore you should be attending?"

Leys straightened her shoulders and turned to the Draighil. "We're always ready, here, to receive guests as needed. Can I bring you a meal, Sere, while you find warmth?"

Trayor looked from her to Cleod and back, his lips drawn in a stiff line that echoed the scar across his face. "Do that," he said. The wave of one hand matched the dismissal in his voice. "We *Draighil* have ridden far. Do your best for us."

"All these weeks you refuse me my title, and *now* you decide to declare it? How charming," Cleod snapped.

"Draighil," Leys gasped, the shock of indrawn breath like a startled shout to Cleod's ears.

"Please, Leys," he said, as her expression went stricken. "This is Trayor Draighil."

She stared at Cleod for a heartbeat, then turned and crossed the room to enter the kitchen. He watched as she disappeared through the doorway, then made his way the rest of the distance to the fire. Shoving Trayor's coat to the floor, he claimed the seat it occupied.

"You'd do well to treat your host with more respect."

Trayor scoffed. "A place like this—"

"Holds all the warmth you'll receive today," Cleod said as he tugged off his gloves, freeing stiff fingers. Trembling, he breathed deep and pulled off his hat, hung it over the ear of the chair. He shoved back his hair, then worked off his soaked outer shirt, and the one beneath that, both wet through. At least the inner one was thin wool, otherwise he would have frozen to death on the trails. He closed his eyes and leaned closer to the fire.

"Oh is that why you wanted to stop here? *Warmth.* And does this Leys you seem to know so well offer *that* up as well as a meal?"

For an instant, Cleod's consciousness expanded, leaped, Gweld opening in response to the burst of pure rage that fired through his gut. But Trayor's own Gweld sense snarled up to meet it. Seconds roiled as they locked, fierce and brutal, a poised clash of awarenesses on the verge of battle, a transfixed moment of pure violence held in check only by the exhaustion gripping both their bodies. Cleod yanked back the rising power of trance as his eyes snapped open and he pushed himself to his feet, forced words through a cloud of rage. "You'll leave her be. Her and the child."

Trayor glared. "You press too hard, traitor."

Cleod tipped his head, wet hair dripping into his eyes. "No more a traitor. You just declared me Draighil again. Remember that you need me, far more than I need anything at all."

For the briefest instant, something faltered in Trayor's eyes. "You're just a fool finding his way back to himself. *Sit down before you fall down.*"

Words like a kick to the gut. *Finding his way back to himself.* Was that what he was doing? *Cleod...Stay!* Kilras's voice like an offered hand.

Cleod's gut jerked as though someone yanked a string through from his spine as he continued to meet Trayor's gaze. "This endeavor will see us both dead," Cleod whispered, unwilling to measure whether the words held prophecy or plea.

The inn door opened, ushering in a blast of chill air and a swirl of icy flakes, along with Ain's slight, wide-eyed figure. Her presence snapped Cleod's thoughts from melancholy to practical. Chill was death. He glanced at the child, buried the spike of emotion that crossed his chest at her uncertain expression.

"Slam closed that door, girl!" Trayor snapped. "Did your father not teach you to honor the comfort of your guests?"

Ain stared even as she pulled the heavy door closed against the rising storm and failing light. "My father, Sere—"

"Is trapped in Adfen by this weather, I suppose," Cleod said, before thought, trapped by the fiction of the words even as he uttered them. Bandits had claimed Ain's father years ago. But to reveal such to Trayor was to offer up the establishment, and the women who ran it, to Farlan scrutiny. Cleod stiffened, jaw clenching. How had he ignored, all these years, the unorthodox company that Kilras so often led the caravan into? Women, did not, on their own, run inns, much less own them completely.

Cleod frowned. Why did he care? And why should that matter at all? What business of his was the fate of these people? Yes, they had housed and fed him through the years, but so had many others.

And yet as he watched Ain's face twist in bafflement, his throat went dry. He watched her take a breath to reply, and his heart leaped as his scattered thoughts sought a way to forestall disaster. Trayor, half frozen and half enraged, was unlikely to pretend indifference to understanding of the inn's true status.

Just as Ain's lips parted, Leys's voice came from the kitchen doorway. "Indeed he is—held over in Adfen by this storm—more's the terrible luck this week. But good for you Seres. I've clothes you can borrow against this cold."

"But—Mam—Sere Cleod—You—"

"I know you miss your pappa, girl. He'll be back as time and snow allow. No foisting off missing his hugs on our company. Come now and help me fix up warm bowls for the guests."

Ain looked at her mother for a heartbeat, then smoothed her expression into calm as understanding came to her. *So like Leiel at that age, that subtle shift...* Cleod's breath caught hard, and he ripped his attention back to the business of removing his soaked outer garments as the girl made for the kitchen.

"What was that?" Trayor demanded, his eyes fierce on the retreating child. Too much to hope that chill and exhaustion had dulled his attention. As reckless as Trayor's actions had often been, he had never been a fool.

Cleod grunted and hunched closer to the fire. Blood burned its way back into his hands as he held them toward the blaze, used the action to cover his search for an answer. "An unsubtle reminder that these women belong to someone. In case our intentions are less than honorable."

"Weren't you just ready to fight me for implying just that as an option?" Trayor's face twisted into a smirk. "Given your suggestion, I suspect you've learned from rough experience that the mother, at least, is not to be tried." He glanced toward the kitchen and shook his head. "If you've dragged us here anyway, the food must be the thing that keeps you coming back. It can't be the place itself."

"A solid roof in this weather is nothing to scoff at."

"This weather." Trayor mumbled a curse, shifted in his seat to face Cleod.

Cleod stared into the flames. "What's to be considered normal anymore?" he asked at last. Draigons. Women. Draigfen. Draigon women. More than a slur—a fact hidden in plain sight. All these years. Not even in his bitterest nightmares had imagination drawn such creatures out of shadow. Kill a Draigon. Kill a woman. *Murder.* The word whispered through him, adding a new shiver that his battered state easily masked. He swallowed, shut his eyes, need cramping his belly.

"What indeed?" Trayor asked. "Blood on enough blades and it won't matter anymore."

The tap of footsteps over the floor signaled the arrival of Leys with their meals. The stew she offered was as tasty and comforting as it was warm, but he found himself struggling to swallow. He forced down the food, let its warmth fill him.

When Leys led them to their rooms down the hall and beyond the hearth, he barely managed to remove his boots before collapsing under the blankets, every thought blurring into nightmare.

25

Cleod

"Is grim a normal state for you that I've just been lucky enough not to have experienced so far?" the stranger with curly hair asked, gazing up at Cleod with patient amusement.

He looked back at her, bafflement furrowing his brow. Where was he? The sound of heavy surf rolling up a shoreline pounded his ears.

"Would you at least take off your shoes?"

Salt spray filled the air, spilled along the ocean breeze in the fading light of day, and he looked down to see his dark boots covered in pale sand. Wind tugged at his too-long hair.

He raised his gaze and met Leiel's dark eyes. She turned away. He stood frozen at the window of the old inn as she started across the street, her back fully to him. A wagon passed between them, kicking up dust, and he spun for the door, hurtling out into the warm-lit room lined with shelves and books.

Leiel looked up from where she knelt studying the map laid out on the floor. "Here," she said. "Come see. The *way*. I've found it."

He stared, every part of him stretched thin and brittle like cold taffy, his heart a frantic beast trying to escape his chest. "Found it?" The words escaped his lips even as he reached over his shoulder to grasp for his sword. His fingers found only air, and the scene bathed itself in a blazing red that refracted all light. Then the world shattered into a glassy mist that blistered as it blew over him with whirlwind force and he came awake gasping for air.

Need rippled through him until he doubled over, snagged in twisted blankets. He struggled free of the snarl and stumbled to his feet. Out into the common room with its fire banked in the hearth he staggered, then to the kitchen, following the only light he could see...seeking...seeking... Nothing. What had he dreamed? *The sea. A map. Dancing eyes that changed and changed again...* Darkness, but for that single frail flame. Silence, but for the whisper of snow against the kitchen's only window. *The dream...* He shuddered and what remained of the images guttered like the light of the squat lantern on the tray on the table.

The scent of the mutton served for dinner lingered. The peace of the space, the emanating warmth of the big stove, warded off the aching chill. In the shadowed room, Leys sat at the table watching him with clear eyes, her face a stiff mask, her fingers gripped around the quill in her hand.

"Cleod?" His name was more than a question on her lips. How many nights had he and Kilras and Sehina and the others crowded around this table, shared good food and greater laughter? He shoved the thought aside.

"What are you writing?" Cleod demanded, the words pressed out hard through his clenched teeth.

"Tasks." She spoke softly. "What needs doing tomorrow, to make ready, if this weather holds."

"Now? In the night?"

"Worry wakes me," she said, meeting his gaze. "Worry over this and so many other things. You saw the ferry house? What happened to Semmio and Ejor? I heard they survived, but the loss..."

He stared at her, a vague recollection of concern flickering in his chest. Ejor and Semmio. Evenings spent at *their* welcoming table. The fear that had coursed through him as he gazed at the burned-out house by the dying river, as he worried for their fate. Only weeks, only a lifetime, ago. He drew a ragged breath.

Leys looked him up and down. "What wakes *you*?"

Draigon wing prints in the mud. The glint of the ring on Leiel's finger. Bright blood on Trayor's sword. Cleod put a hand to his head, pressed the palm against his temple. He needed—Did the Little Peace serve ercew? No. "Wine," he said. "Where is your wine?"

"Wine?" Her gasped question drew his full attention. "But—" She stopped, pulled herself the slightest bit straighter in her chair, then tipped her head toward a cabinet mounted on the wall to his right.

Without a word, he stepped to it, yanked open the door and grasped the first bottle on which his hand landed. Mostly full. And more lined the shelves behind it. And an open bottle was easy. He yanked free the stopper and tilted the bottle to his lips. Like silver knives, the liquid sluiced into him, smoothed the quaking edges of his mind, drowned confusion and rising panic. He finished what remained, reached for another bottle, and half-drained that as well. Gods...gods of old...Not cuila. Not what cuila could do. But, for now, enough.

A touch on his shoulder.

He jerked around, checked the blow that instinct demanded he land as Leys lurched back, raising her hands to ward him off. A useless gesture. Gods had he really almost struck her? He drew away a step. "Don't," he said. "Don't ever." Even as memory tumbled him, the scent of clean hair in his nostrils, the warmth of soft skin against his...*bright laughter carried on sea air...* He shuddered. "No." He spoke the word to her, to himself, lost for a moment in a swirl of bent memory and wine.

"Why?" she asked, whispered, voice shaking. "Cleod Ruhel-rn, what is happening?"

He started, his heart twisting in his chest at her use of the name he had carried for so long, so familiar and yet so suddenly strange in his ears. He locked down emotion, spoke with a coldness dredged from the depths of his soul. "Shaa is dead. The world is changed. Step back, Innkeeper. My purpose is not yours to question."

She stared at him, eyes bright. But even as she backed away, one pace, then another, she spoke, through fear that rattled her words, into the space that friendship had once occupied. "What purpose do you have in this world, Cleod, that you question anyone's right to wonder over it? Shaa dead..."

Raising the bottle, he slugged down another drink. "More than dead—a *woman*. The damned Draigon *are women* and Shaa died as one. Died small and broken and her body hangs on a spike in Melbis for all to see—"

Horror bathed Leys expression, jerked every muscle of her body into tension. "A woman," she said as her voice broke and tears shimmered onto her lower lashes. "What have you done?" she asked. "*What have you done?*" She stared and stared, then something shifted over her, something he sensed as much as saw, a need, a dignity, a *fierceness* that sliced straight through him. "No," she said and turned and fled the room.

For a heartbeat he stood—until he heard the slam of a door—then he pushed to his feet and followed her. The common area, dark and chill, was empty when he entered. On the floor before the front door, a scattering of snow spoke of an exit quickly made. Cursing, he dodged around the scattered chairs, yanked open the door and followed her out into the frigid night.

Cold blasted over him as he searched the darkness, bare feet instantly scalded by the new-fallen snow. Across the packed yard, a flicker of light came from the window of the blacksmith shop. A shadow crossed it. He staggered forward, fell, cursing, then shoved back to his feet. Heedless of the storm, he stumbled and tripped into a snowbank. Cold impact shocked him to the core. As he extricated himself and made it back onto the path, an indistinct shape moved, at speed, away from the heavy block of the smithy; a horse and rider, at full run, moved onto the road and were gone into the storm before he could even shout.

He gained the doorway of the building seconds later to find Leys and Sandin, the old smith, standing defiant in the center of the shop.

"Who was that?" he demanded, head pounding, need or fury cramping his stomach. "What message have you sent and to where?"

"You say Shaa is dead." Challenge laced Leys words. "Yet you *killed a woman, Cleod.*"

That stopped him like a dropped stone as a chill raised by more than the weather rippled up his back. He recovered. "Who left here?"

"If you wish more women to kill, you won't have my daughter." Fear lit her eyes, but she took a step toward him.

His stomach flipped. "What?" At the edges of his senses, light flared, hot as the anger surging through his core. "You think I— That Ain—" He stared into her eyes, and the swirl of light and scent and energy that expanding Gweld trance snared around her. And understood. The girl not in her own bed, but instead sent to sleep the night in the smithy. Leys awake in the darkness. Waiting. On watch. Alert. Because she feared what had entered her home. Not just Trayor. But Cleod as well—she feared *him.*

Every part of him shook, cold and shock and anger tearing at his senses and his self-control. Gweld sense slipped free, rang like a bell in the humble space as his senses exploded outward, searching, seeking, even as his gaze hazed with anger. Two steps brought him close and he grabbed Leys's arm, dragged her toward him. Every muscle hummed, taut with a frustrated need that marked imminent violence.

Before thought, he drew back his hand.

And Leys stepped forward to accept the blow.

Memory struck like thunder, *the crack of a slap that welted Leiel's cheek under Addor's hand.* Kilras's voice, calm and certain *He'd already made the choice to control himself when I met him—even if that choice was killing him.* In the back of his mind, Trayor stirred. In a flash Cleod *saw* what would come if Gweld woke the other Draighil. A half breath and the other man's rage would join Cleod's own, fuel on the fire of turmoil rampaging in the back of his skull. Then pain and blood would rule the night.

In a fractured instant, pure will lashed wine-burned awareness into fragile control. With a gasp, Cleod slammed closed the expanding demand of his senses and released Leys's arm. Shaking, he stepped back, bare feet bruising on the cold stone floor. Old gods—! Trayor's enmity flashed, dreamlike, then faded. Cleod turned his back to the innocents in the line of his wrath and shouted his fury into the night in a scream that echoed through every part of his being, glad of the storm that muffled his howl.

In the silence and Gweld lit-vibration that followed, he stood for a long moment, hearing everything, feeling more, the scent of sudden winter and charred coal filling his head. From behind him, the hammering hearts of Leys and Sandin pounded like drums in his skull. Without moving, he forced words from a raw throat. "I'm sorry."

The scent of fear, tangier than the copper scent of blood, but just as intense, sang into the air, but Leys's voice, heedless of her terror, filled the space as well. "I counted you a friend."

He turned at that, her words burning in his ears. "I kill Draigon," he snapped. "I don't harm *people*." Was she insane? The Draigon ravaged the land and threatened the lives of thousands. Brought fear and panic. *Stole women and turned them into monsters.* And yet—the look in Leys's eyes was like a glimpse into the past, into Leiel's dark gaze as she looked back at him in the Tower. Leiel's stubborn certainty as she had faced him, always. Wasn't that why he...? He shook the thought away. "How can you think I would ever—?"

She shook her head, looking back at him. "You tell me the Draigon are *women*, Cleod Ruhelrn. And if you kill Draigon, whom do you kill?"

Cleod's heart leaped in his chest as she spoke of the beasts. Spoke the truth he had spilled to her just moments before, as though the idea shocked her not at all. As though secrets were not just the realm of the Ehlewer and the Farlan and their allies.

Beside her, Sandin turned his head to gaze at her in shock, and his stunned amazement mirrored Cleod's own.

Leiel's broken ring glinted from the torn earth. Pressure built in Cleod's skull and he turned away again. No answers. None that made sense. Monstrous lies and misdeeds. He stepped back, fury and snarled thoughts making him sway. No reasoning with this kind of madness, then or now or ever.

Ain. He needed to go after her, stop her, stop...what? His gut churned, the desire to *act* colliding with the drink that fogged his mind. Stubborn girl. Foolish. Like her mother. Like Leiel at that age. His thoughts tumbled. Who was he to worry for fools? "Enough. Enough of your insanity. Find what rest you can this night. And, come morning, follow where I lead. For the sake of your past kindnesses, I'll let the girl run tonight. In this weather, you've likely sent her to her death."

Leys's face went grey, and she stepped back.

Cleod met her gaze. "Feed us well at dawn if you want us gone come morning. In the meantime, sleep with your guilt." Jaw clenched, he stalked back through the open door.

He counted as he walked, struggling across the snow-swathed dooryard toward the entrance of the inn. Counted each step, each breath, each ragged thought that swirled and dragged at him. Ain riding into the white-churning night.

By the time he gained the front door of the inn, dark against dark, and still open in the square of the building, he was chilled through, and even entering the space brought little comfort. Half reeling, he shoved the door closed behind him and leaned back against it. Nothing stirred. How had Trayor slept through the commotion? Leys's words clattered in his mind. He shook his head. What did it matter? Her madness was not his problem.

Unless it was shared by others. He considered the thought. Dismissed it with a shake of his fogged head.

Across the dark and lonely space, the rest of the wine awaited. It was not ercew, and it certainly was not cuila, but it would have to do. Feet prickling with pain of returning blood, he made his way back to all the kinds of warmth waiting in the kitchen.

26

Cleod

DESPITE THE WINE, EVEN THE IDEA OF SLEEP ELUDED HIM. IN THE long hours before the sun rose, he sat and stared at the notes Leys had been making before he entered the room. Her written words—ordinary. Dull and practical. Lists and notations of what needed doing and when. So simple and easy—survival, daily achieved—so easily upended by his arrival and his words.

As dawn slanted through the kitchen's single window into gradations of grey, he sat alone at the table, a cluster of open bottles before him. He shifted, and a sharp pinch of metal jabbed his upper thigh. He went still, then fished an unsteady hand into his pocket and pulled out the twisted remains of Leiel's ring.

Anger flared. He closed his fist around the ruined token. Old gods, what was he doing here? The emotion slid into nausea, then toward a shaking rage that had no outlet. With a snarl he swept the empty bottles off the table into an explosion of glass and alcohol fumes.

Shutting his eyes, he breathed deep, seeking equilibrium amid thoughts ensnared each by the other, racing and pattern-less. Lost in a wilderness of disjointed memory and confusion, only the rattling sound of a broom sweeping glass fragments brought him back to himself. He opened his eyes to Leys care-fully whisking bright-edged shards into a pile.

She glanced at him as he stirred, but said nothing, every-thing about her contained and unemotional.

"Leys—"

"I'll have breakfast on, once I've cleaned this up," she said, her tone too careful. "Watch your step. You're still barefoot if you don't recall."

He blinked, ground his teeth and pushed his chair back from the table. As he got to his feet, Trayor's voice boomed into the room, part amusement, part satisfaction. "Better the bottles than your head, woman." He looked Cleod up and down and grinned more widely than the situation could possibly warrant. "Is all this your doing?"

"I was in no mood to share," Cleod said, the smith-hammer effect of hours spent drowning his emotions settling into a steady rhythm inside his skull.

"Or to dress yourself." Trayor shifted his attention to Leys. "Have your daughter do that and start cooking. We've got a long journey ahead, if this fool can find his clothes."

"She's not about, Sere," Leys said without looking up from her work. "I won't be late with the food if you want to have a seat before the fire."

"Not about?" Trayor took another step into the room. "*Not about*? Where is she?"

"She rode out in the night," Cleod said.

Trayor went dead still, then shifted his gaze to Cleod. "Rode out." The words fell hard and deliberate. "And you didn't wake me, or," he dropped his gaze to Cleod's bootless feet, "go after her yourself."

With a grunt, Cleod crossed the room to stand in front of the Draighil. "She's a girl-child in a blizzard, Tray. She's dead in a drift somewhere, and we're here, warm and rested, and soon-to-be well fed by her soon-to-be-sobbing mother. Who's got the best end of this icy stick? You'll still get all the glory of the kill and of carrying the news to Sibora. So, either help the cook or get out of her way."

Their gazes locked, and the thudding in Cleod's skull picked up pace. Damn the man. Damn them both.

"If you keep looking for a fight, you'll find it, cefreid," Trayor, leaned in, as ever, unintimidated by Cleod's greater height. "I don't need you as badly as you might think."

Cleod grinned. "No, you need me far, far more. I'm the one who knows this land. The one who knows every town and every byway. Every short-trail and back alley of every city. And I've known the enemy since we were children. I'm an asset even the King himself would kill to have on his side. So threaten me all you want. You've been my better, and my inferior, but right now you're simply in my *way*."

"You've got much to pay for," Trayor said. "It's your luck that this morning I prefer breakfast to your blood." He walked out of the kitchen.

Cleod stood still, drawing steadying breaths.

"You—" Leys began.

He looked over at her and for a split instant let himself consider the impact of what he had said to Trayor about Ain. Then he shook himself and snarled his response. "*Don't*. Just do what you have to if you want us gone." He turned away.

"Cleod!" Soft urgency stopped him, and he looked back. "What's happened to you?"

He stared, shook his head. "You should consider your actions carefully from here forward, Leys."

She held his gaze, heartbeat on heartbeat, then something in her shifted, and he watched anger replace the fear in her expression. For a moment she reminded him so much of Leiel that his heart skipped. Her next words, firm and fierce, did nothing to dispel the similarity. "And what should *you* have considered, before you came here like this?"

The room swam, the edges of his vision shifting in waves of fluctuating light. Cleod took a step toward her, then another, hands curling into fists at his sides, fingers flexing. Leys moved back, and all resemblance to Leiel fled at the retreat. He froze. "Leys, I—"

She held his gaze, still and steady. "I'll have breakfast soon, Sere." Her tone stripped the statement of all emotion.

Cleod stared back, locked down all thought in refusal of dark implication—that he stood harrowingly far from all he had ever meant to be. Quiet desperation demanded action. He pivoted and stormed from the room.

27

Leiel

THE WIND BLUSTERED OVER THE MOUNTAIN CREST, PUSHING ICY particles of snow. Spaced along the ridge, the line of naked women stood in the rushing air, looking out along the sweep of the range. The setting sun etched them against the sky, and Leiel stared, speechless, as she crossed the last few paces of the trail to join Gydron and Ilora.

"In all my imaginings of what it would look like to have Draigon return to the world, this is not one of the visions in my mind." Gyrdron's voice held both sadness and wonder.

"How long have they been here?" Leiel asked. When they had chosen this evening for her and Kilras and Kinra to fly south and begin preparations for the fight to come, they had not expected others to join them. Not yet. It seemed too soon to ask so much...and yet the future of all of them turned on what each achieved in the next months. Why wait to step toward what lay ahead? Change circled overhead with the flight of clouds and the rotation of the stars. What use delay, now that the choice had been made?

Ilora lifted her shoulders, let them ease in a slow shrug. "They began arriving after late meal, saying their goodbyes and readying for long journeys."

Leiel smiled at the sing-song tone of the words. She clasped her mother's hand, as she tried to imagine what the next hours would be like, the Draigon together in flight across the gleaming northern sky, a loose formation of knowledge and strength declaring their unity. Something to savor. Too soon they would bank off toward their separate destinations and assignments, then the fight would truly begin. But for this moment...her heart was too full of wonder and awe for the unknown future to cast shadow for long. "You'll tell the story of this day for centuries."

Ilora murmured, "Cast against autumn sky on a winter night, they stood silhouetted along the shining ridge, brave in the last light of a passing day, ready to fly into the imminent unknown."

A sigh whispered from Leiel, and she closed her eyes, let Ilora's words etch the moment deeper into her soul. How many of her mother's stories had shaped the core of her? So deeply had they written themselves within Leiel that she could not measure who she would have been without them. And now the power of story would be laid out again, telling the truths of *this* time, carrying *now* into *becoming*. When she opened her eyes again, Ilora and Gydron were both watching her with a mix of pride and fear that exactly mirrored the painful, twin tensions within her. "Mark down those words, Gydron. They may be the start of a new age of Arnan."

The library keeper nodded. "Would that Gahree could witness this moment."

Leiel's ribs tightened as though great hands grasped her chest and slowly twisted it in counter motion. She forced air from her lungs, took it in again as she closed her eyes.

"Whatever the energy that was Gahree is now engaged in, is as powerful as what we do now," Ilora said with a certainty that startled the ache from Leiel's chest. She glanced at her mother.

Ilora answered the look. "Or do you really think that wherever she is, she is sitting idle waiting to see what we poor mortals decide to do next?"

Gydron smiled at that, true amusement crossing her features.

Despite the power and pain of the moment, a laugh came from deep within Leiel. "No. I cannot imagine that."

She returned her attention to the women waiting in the goldening light to take wing, and just let herself bask in the bravery and power stamped against the glowing sky. Then the scrunch of footsteps on the trail behind her creased the image. She turned to see Kilras and Kinra crossing the empty ground between the treeline and their small group. Something in the shared tension of their movement stripped the peace from Leiel's mind. "What is it?"

Kinra, in the lead, shook her head. Then she caught her breath as she saw the vision arrayed across the peak. "Wind on high," she breathed. "Everyone?"

"Nearly," Gydron agreed. "A sight to mark the times."

Kinra reached out and took Gydron's hand and Leiel turned away, let them share the moment. She looked to Kilras, watched him draw a long breath. Then he met her gaze and something shifted in his eyes. Whatever had been spoken between him and Kinra on the climb up from Cyunant, it hung heavy.

Leiel shook her head. She would not ask. She shifted to face Ilora again, but Kilras spoke her name and she turned back to him, to the intensity of his gaze.

"What is it?" she asked again.

He reached into the pocket of his coat, pulled out a thick envelope and handed it to her. "You'll see Cleod."

A frown bent her brow as she accepted the packet. The weight and thickness of it gave her pause. She knew his tight scrawl, the density with which he could fill pages. "What—?" she started. But she knew. Of course she knew.

He nodded. "He deserves to know. And it's not for you to give him explanations of why I did what I did."

"Kilras—you don't know that you won't see him again."

"I don't," he said. "But I won't take that chance. You *will* see him. You'll speak to him."

"We know how well that went last time."

He smiled, and it reached his eyes, bent the skin around

them into laughing lines. "This time he'll face all you are, and you'll face all he is."

She stared at him. "I still don't understand how you managed to keep all *you* are from him."

"I kept it from far more than him. For far longer."

"And it's easier to see things when you know they are there," Ilora said.

Leiel glanced at her mother. "Sometimes even the obvious answer isn't the easiest to accept." Had she met Kilras without knowing his history, would she have guessed he was anything more than he seemed to be? Had anyone ever guessed that *she* was more than a passing traveler or, in her most daring disguise, an envoy of the Draigon? "And this time I'll have Teska."

Kilras's smiled grew, became edged with a determined sadness. "If the two of you succeed, give it to him after."

"You could be there."

"Maybe."

Leiel studied him, then tucked the envelope into the bag at her hip. Somewhere between that first destination and the possibility of a return to Cyunant, she would find Cleod. Perhaps, *truly* find him. And when she did, there would be no more room for half-truths between them. "This could not have been an easy letter to write."

He returned her gaze for a moment, then turned his attention down the mountain, back the way he had come. She looked as well. Below, at the distant bottom of the ravine, a small, straight-backed figure in brilliant blue stood still and alone. "No harder than other words I've had to share today."

Delhar. "She did not wish to see you off?"

"If she made the climb, she would fly with us." He paused. "With me. For me." A shake of his head. "But she is not that kind of warrior."

"True," Kinra said. "She is a stronger kind."

"High praise." Leiel smiled slightly.

The weapons teacher studied them with the same earnestness she had the women waiting along the ridgeline. "The highest," Kinra agreed. "Like Teska. Like you."

Leiel flinched. Had she been a true fighter, Gahree might be alive. Had she been something different, something more... But she was not. And *different and more* was not what Gahree had chosen when she came to Leiel at the pond, in the Market, on the Spur. *Different and more* had not been accepted into the heart of the Draigon. Because, when placed against the actual power of *what she was,* different and more were only words given power by doubt and by fear. If time with Gahree had taught Leiel only one thing, it was that *she mattered for who she was,* regardless of what lack others found in her, or she feared within herself.

She straightened, uncurled shoulders that had collapsed toward her heart, and found all eyes of the small group upon her. "Like me," she agreed. "For the value that holds."

Ilora folded her into a hug. "Power and peace," she whispered.

Leiel nodded into her mother's shoulder. The weight of Kilras's words in her bag. The weight of Ilora's arms around her. The weight of responsibility, unfolding, expanding. For a long moment they just stood holding each other. Then Leiel drew a breath and pulled away.

She raised her gaze and swept it over the waiting women until it landed on a slender, clothed figure standing wind-whipped at the far end of the ridge. Teska Healer. "Let us take wing," she said. "It is time that Arnan again experiences the significance of Draigon."

28

Leiel

THE KING'S CAPITAL POKED UP LIKE A BROKEN TOOTH AGAINST THE horizon of the northern grasslands. West of the Spur, between the main east-west trade road and the Sarn, the city's unavoidable presence occupied the minds and imaginations of all who considered it. And who, in all of Arnan, failed to consider Sibora? Built by Arnan's conquerors in the heart of the land as the seat of wealth and power, the ringing of Sibora's stone streets drove home the message to all who entered: Here is majesty. Here is beauty. Here is that to which all allegiance is owed.

If the rich scent of flowers and vibrance of elegant gardens usually masked the arrogant demand of the place, the controlling intention of the city's design had never been lost on Leiel. She had called Adfen home for too long to not recognize what the Farlan attempted to achieve when they built Sibora—a repudiation of the *first* stone city. And now in stark winter, the difference between this city and Desga Hiage's was chillingly obvious—Sibora's stones were heartless in their precision, and the marble of the streets rang cold on even the warmest day.

And today was far from warm. Sheltered by Draigon heat, Leiel made her way through the trade quarter's cluttered alleys. The scent of unease filled the air, along with an undercurrent buzz of nervous chatter. Had word of Shaa's death reached the city even before Trayor and Cleod? Was that possible?

Leiel shook her head. No matter. Purpose beyond curiosity moved her through the frozen streets. The clang of steel on steel, so familiar from her childhood, signaled arrival at her destination. Without hesitation, she stepped into the gritty dimness of the blacksmith's shop.

Working the bellows with his back half-turned to her, the smith glanced over his shoulder as her shadow fell across him from the entrance. He froze. Stared while she did the same. So very long since their last meeting...

Neither moved for several seconds while the roaring of the forge filled the air. Then Torrin wiped the back of his wrist along his temple and turned to face her. "I'd hoped to have seen you before this."

She blew out breath and laughed at his complete lack of surprise. "Before this moment, or before these events?"

"Either," he said, and smiled. Lines on his face that had not been present when they were last face-to-face, deepened as his expression changed. Silver peppered his tight-curled hair. Labor had etched fresh scars on his arms and built thicker callouses on his hands, but the easy strength of him was unchanged, and his voice held the same honest good humor that she remembered. "Time must pass differently where you are."

"Oh, Torrin." How many times she had come to him for the simple comfort of his company? Yet she had not offered any in all these years. And she was not here to do so now. Tears gathered in her eyes, and all the reasons she had stayed away, and all the new ones she had now come, melded into this single moment of reunion.

His smile widened, and there was not, anymore than there ever had been, judgment in his expression. "Come here, Li," he said, and opened his arms.

With a laugh, she stepped into them, pressed her face against his sooty shirt. The familiar creosote smell of the cloth and the sweat of hard work filled her nose.

This forge was different.

She was no longer a girl.

But something about Torrin's arms around her eased the deepest part of her. It came to her, as she closed her eyes and hugged him harder, that she had come to him now after terrible loss, just as she had so many years ago on the morning after Ilora's Sacrifice. She pulled back a little and looked up at him through eyes suddenly blurred by tears.

"I know, Li," he said, nodded once. "Like old times. Tell me what you need."

He knew? What did he know? How could he? Her stomach twisted and she swallowed.

"Shaa is dead," she said lowly.

His expression shifted from shock to confusion to resignation all in the space of a breath. "Dead?"

Blinking back moisture, she stepped away and looked up at him. He nodded toward the wall by the entrance. She followed the gesture with her glance, then pulled the stool by the door closer to the forge and sat. Torrin leaned back against the wall, met her gaze.

Old times. Him waiting patiently for whatever she had to say, as though the words she would speak were the most important ones he would ever hear. She thought of all the questions she should have asked him in her youth, and all the new ones that had cropped up in her mind in the years since she had last seen him. So many things she wanted to know. But she had wasted the time she had then, and there was none to spare now for anything but the need that had driven her to seek him out.

Almost, she asked his forgiveness for her selfishness. But he was Torrin, and he had never wasted time with guilt.

"I was given a list of names. A list with notes beside each name."

He nodded again, sad and slow.

"Swords and spears," she said. "How long have you been—"

"Since before you were born. Since before I knew your mother."

She stared. Since before she was born. What events had shaped Torrin so that he held such knowledge and so many secrets? How did he know the Draigon? Had he actually known *Gahree*? A flash of memory—Wynt wrapping the tang of a sword, the glimpse of the makers mark on the metal—how had she missed it? She took mental grip of her purpose. "All the things you've been making in secret through the years. We need them now."

Torrin gave a light sigh. "I hoped they would never be needed."

"We hope so too." She smiled a little. "We've plans to blunt the edge of potential violence, but we won't stop it all. We can't."

He nodded.

She hesitated. "You never told me."

"Hard to explain why I made them," he said.

Leiel shook her head. When had she ever thought to ask him about anything but the obvious? Even when he hinted at more... When would it ever have even occurred to her that Torrin may have skills she knew nothing about? All the nights she had fallen asleep to the sound of his hammers working late into the night... How naive she had been, for all her thinking that she knew so much more than everyone else. Torrin, of all people, should be the last she was surprised to find she knew not at all. "Where did you hide them, back on the farm?"

"Do you think your family really needed a fresh privy dug every other season?" he asked.

"You don't mean to tell me—"

"Never in the waste, Li. But digging new holes in the back field was never questioned."

She laughed. "No, I suppose it would not be." She frowned. "Where do you keep such weapons now?" Could he possibly have brought them with him when he left the farm for his new position? She glanced around the forge, so much larger and better equipped than the one to her old home outside Adfen, so much more suited to the range she now knew Torrin's skills encompassed. Sibora, too, suited him, filled as it was with skilled craftsmen and wealthy patrons. *Sibora...* She turned her gaze back to Torrin, measuring this time.

He did not seem to notice as he answered her question. "Hidden north of the city. Plenty of ruins of the old settlements from before the Farlan built the silver city."

She nodded, still studying him, thought back to the little he had ever told her of his past. "This is it," she said. "This forge is where you learned your trade. Where your mother apprenticed you when you were a boy."

He flashed a grin, looked around the space and nodded as he brought his gaze back to hers. "It is. When Old Mawr died, he left it to me. His house too."

"I was wondering how you were able to leave the farm. I was so worried when I left. You seemed resigned to staying there forever."

"I had been. I'd probably be there still, but Mawr always wanted me here in Sibora. I suppose he thought enough time had passed that people would have forgotten me."

Leiel tipped her head. "Forgotten?"

Torrin straightened away from the wall. "A story for another day, Li."

"You didn't just happen to meet my mother and come to work for my family."

Another smile and he shook his head again. "No." He turned and pulled open a drawer on the workbench beside him, dug out a few loose sheets of paper and a worn quill. "Tell me what you need."

What she needed. So much. To turn back time, change her decision to show herself to Cleod. To fight on the high plains outside Melbis, instead of allowing herself to become party to the death of the oldest and wisest of the Draigon. And she needed a friend, true and clear minded. She needed Torrin as he had always been—solid and nonjudgmental and unflappable. She pushed to her feet and came to join him. "Come with me," she said. "You would be welcome among us. Your skills and your good advice."

He shook his head. "I'll do you more good here."

She studied him. "Elda?"

A few heartbeats of silence, then he acknowledged. "She's here in the capital. Moved with Klem when he became representative for the Spur on the King's Council."

How many years had it been since anyone spoke her brother's name? Even Ilora rarely uttered it. Though the fierce pain of recollection had lost much of its sting through the years, a chill still crossed Leiel's shoulders at the sound of Torrin's familiar voice speaking that one word—Klem. But the unease only briefly claimed her attention. Warmth tingled up from Leiel's toes and spread through her until it lifted her lips in the first true smile she had offered anyone since Trayor's sword had fallen. "You found a way."

"I told you not to worry about us, Li."

She met his gaze. The years she had spent fretting for him had been wasted. Torrin knew, better than she ever could, how to live in Arnan. His dreams were simple and solid. He had always worked hard, with a steady hand and an unflinching eye on the goal before him. He chose to want little, and he worked until he got what he needed.

"Is she well?"

He nodded. "Still cooking for Klem, evenings. Though she doesn't live in the house anymore, and he's got others to do the rest of the work there."

"And how much does she know?"

Torrin chuckled. "Since you told her what you did before you left? Everything I do." He nodded. "She's for the fight. Whatever it brings."

Leiel's chest expanded, full and warm. Elda, who had raised her. Torrin who had formed her. Both still shaping the world in their quiet, powerful ways. Suddenly insufficient, the purpose that brought her to Sibora unfurled like flower petals in the sun. Her teeth caught the edge of her lip. She held the idea, turning it over as she let out a long breath and said, "Tell me of your blades, Torrin."

His gaze lifted, swept the shop quickly. "I started making them here. Mawr taught me a little, knives and hatchets and such, before the trouble started." Something must have shifted in her expression because he shrugged. "There's always trouble when someone fearful notices you're different."

"Torrin, I had no—"

"It's past," he said.

She nodded. Another tale for someday, should it ever come. "How many spears and swords?"

"Nine thousand twenty-three," he said.

Her jaw fell open. "*What?*"

He nodded. "Long. Short. Small hands and large. Well balanced, all of them."

"How?" she asked. "How could you possibly—?" Where had he gotten the steel? How had he made so many, unnoticed? How had he possibly hidden them all?

He shrugged. "Friends."

Friends. *Friends.* Nine thousand twenty-three weapons. Nine thousand and twenty-three. So many times more than there were Draigon alive in all of Arnan. She envisioned the list Gahree had left her. Pages and pages of names. Pages of people who might side with the Draigon—just the ones she knew about. What about the ones she was not aware of? The ones the people *on* the list knew of who might help? Just as the Draigon hoped when they laid their plans back in Cyunant. Relief flooded her belly, that they had not overestimated this resource. "Friends."

Torrin smiled faintly, as if she was still a little farm girl and in need of quiet time to figure important things out for herself.

Leiel laughed. "All right, Torrin Mastersmith, tell me, how

do I figure out who to give all these weapons to? There aren't that many trained fighters among those who might join us."

"Just as there aren't weapon makers?" he asked wryly.

"You're reminding me just how little I know."

"Seems that the Farlan and their followers might know even less than you. You have a list? She said you would."

She said. Leiel held his gaze. So he *had* known Gahree? Or did he mean another. Did it matter? Stable hands. Horse trainers. Squires and farmers and shopkeeps. Who knew what *else* all of them were? Who knew where they had been and what they had learned and seen? As much forbidden knowledge as Leiel had been able to acquire in her youth, why could others, with years more to seek it, not know far more than she could ever dream?

"You mean all of them—?"

"Seems unlikely. But many," he said. "I'm not the only smith on that list, am I? My work alone isn't enough for this fight."

"No," she agreed. Among the names and notes—a few old guards and scouts, scattered across the continent. A few warriors and mercenaries, some retired, some young. If Torrin spent a lifetime creating weapons, why would others not have done the same? As Gahree scoured the land in search of girls and women to educate and help, what had others been sharing and building? Kinra—with her deadly knowledge and her discerning eye for talent. Kinra who traveled Cyunant as often as Gahree, yet never claimed a Sacrifice.

"You know the ones here, in Sibora. Or you know who will know."

Torrin nodded.

Pressure built behind her eyes, a pulsing intensity she had not felt since the day she faced the council in Melbis. She had wondered if she would ever feel it again, the determined certainty that had carried her that day. The moment Cleod had drawn his sword against her, something deep within her had shaken loose, rattled and shivered as though it would never again find true mooring. And then Gahree—Leiel shuddered, but the feeling remained, hard behind her eyes, wired through to her gut and wrapping through her hips until she was drawn tight like a drum, ready to thunder if struck. "I don't want to place you in danger."

"Not the first time," he said.

"It will be the first time that I am the cause." Brutal truth. To bring more harm to someone so dear—She swallowed. Not the first time for her either. His choice. She could only make sure that this time she led no one in blind, that the consequences shown clear and stark.

"There's no reason needed," he said, "for someone who wants to hurt another."

Torrin always found the simplest way to speak hard facts. That much had not changed.

Leiel shook her head. "But this is different. This is the King, the Farlan Army, the Enclaves, all against us. All bent to destroy—and not just the Draigon. You spoke of old trouble. This will be so much more than that, Torrin."

"In its way," he agreed. "Li, I haven't spent all these decades forming killing metal so I can sit on the sidelines when it's time for blood to soak it. The King's had the army drilling south of the city for months."

She blinked. "Months?"

He nodded. "It's been clear for a while that something is coming. And now that Shaa is dead... How much time do we have?"

"Trayor Draighil and Cleod are still weeks away on the road. I doubt the army will make a move before they arrive. But once word reaches the city, what the King's men or the Council will order within the city before that—You'll have to be careful of every action you make."

He studied her. "Cleod Woodcutter."

"Not anymore," she whispered.

"Li—Don't give up on him."

Her brow furrowed. "What do you know of it?"

"Nothing. Except what I know of you." He shrugged shoulders roped with hard-earned muscle. "You've always dreamed of impossible things. Don't change that now."

"Shaa dying was supposed to be impossible."

"So, it seems it's true that nothing is."

A sad smile tugged across her lips, and she offered a small nod as the half-idea that sprouted when he spoke of Elda now rippled into bloom. "I've a message for you to carry to Elda. A possibility. A hope. But a dangerous one." She quelled a tremor in her belly and did not say *A chance so faint and frail that even dreaming it tempted fortune toward destruction.* "Will you carry it? Will she hear it?"

No hesitation accompanied his nod. "Whatever is needed."

"I have not even asked."

"Li, we're here. We always have been."

Again the pinch at the edges of her eyes that signaled the rise of tears. She pressed her lips together a moment, pulled a breath in through her nose. Never should she have expected less. "Tell me what you know of any others willing to fight. And I'll tell you of the Draigon coming here to help you."

His eyes widened at her words, then a grin of pure determination split his face. "That's something to look forward to."

Kilras

Wary and guided by strategic forethought, Kinra winged him toward Bajor mostly by night. But what Kilras did see of the land he thought he knew so well took his breath. From the air, every creek and grotto, every canyon and river and peak seemed part of a great etching, carefully carved and wildly painted, streaked with golds and reds, and the stark ivory of new snowfall. Even at night, moonlight delineated high points and shadowed valleys, while the flickering lights of towns and cities sparkled like earthbound stars. Soaring over a living map of the land he knew so well, he finally gave up trying to fit the scenery into a shape he already understood, and simply surrendered to the awe of each moment and vision as it passed.

At dawn on the third day of travel, Kinra burst through a wall of clouds and banked hard through the chill air. Dropping through grey light, she made for a small meadow deep within dense forest, a swampy place now frozen over, where no trees could grow. Space enough to hide a Great Shape, and resource enough to shelter one human man.

You're even quieter today.

The thought pulsed through his mind as Kinra touched down and folded her brilliant wings closed.

"It's much to take in."

Do you still dream of it? Kinra turned her head on her great neck and gazed at him with quicksilver eyes.

Not surprising that she asked. The dream of his youth—to

be what Hech had been. One of them. To be Draigdyn. And though Gahree had honored him with the title the last time they spoke, the fact of it was never meant to be who he was. "Not the way I once did. Not of becoming something I am not. But of flight?" He laughed a little as he stretched and twisted to slide from her back. "I'll dream of it forever now." His feet landed on frozen ground and he grunted at the impact.

Beats of hearty laughter filled his mind. *Good dreams at least.*

Even the amusement in that thought was pointed. So she knew, or sensed, that his return to Cyunant had awakened old connections, old habits, old weakness. "In part."

He shouldered his pack and moved away from the warm shelter of her presence, seeking higher ground for a fire. That and potable water, and the camp he created would be enough for one night. "You might as well ask, Kinra."

Very well. The weight of her thoughts followed him as she settled into the tight space of the clearing, hidden from sight and sheltered within herself. *Ragged or restrained, old friend? After all these years, has circumstance damaged your control, or is this something else?*

He stopped and faced her, turning her question, seeking the answer. "I don't know what it is. What I'm dreaming, I've always dreamed. But it's widened now. No longer my own. Whether that's because I met Leiel or returned to the mountain, I don't know." He paused, met her gaze again, held it, and answered the question she really asked. "I'm in control. That hasn't changed. These dreams are something new." No clear way presented itself to determine whether being among the Draigon or the hard strain of the last weeks had wakened the imaginative connections that haunted his nights. The why of it hardly mattered, as long as the dark emotions the dreams awakened remained contained. And enough years of practice lay behind him that possible loss of that control did not top his list of worries. "If I come to understand, I'll share what I learn."

Very well, Kilras Hantyn. But even my dreams are no safe haven. I see some of your images in the night. At its worst, your slipped control never before impacted me.

He stared at her. Kinra shared his dreams? Kinra of all Draigon? The one whose defenses not even his most determine attempts could ever breach, with either sword or Gweld? "You've shared my nightmares?" Even waking beside her the last two nights he had not sensed that.

Glimpses only. Faces in haze. Words I can hear but not understand. Do you wish to share more than that?

Again he shook his head. "No." He understood too little of what he saw before he woke. He frowned. Perhaps Kinra shared the ethereal visions *because* of the form she wore. As soon as the thought touched his mind, he dismissed it. No. Based on what he now knew of how he used Gweld, she shared his dreams because *he* could share them. Still, the thought deserved exploration.

"How does the Great Shape enhance the use of Gweld? Or the ability to be touched by it?" Gahree's willingness to sacrifice herself in Melbis to save Teska indicated that increased power was a vital benefit of claiming the winged form.

For several heartbeats Kinra did not respond, then her pointed thoughts pulsed into his mind. *Yes. In a way. Using it takes no less practice than anything else we learn. Being impacted by another... that depends upon the nature of the other.*

So Gahree had given up her life for a goal and a dream that might be decades or even centuries in the making—a Draigon healer who, in the Great Shape, could wield curative energy the way the Draigon now wielded heat and cold. "Your hopes for Teska extend beyond lifetimes."

Yes. But first we must survive this one. Your sword skills, you've kept them as you kept the weapon I made you?

Kilras turned away and continued toward the sheltered hollow at the edge of the trees. "Even if we don't all live to see the outcome of this war, I agree that such a dream's worth dying for.

As for my skills, I've done my best to keep them honed. Only a real fight'll tell if it's been enough."

That's well. Kinra's thought pulsed bright and golden at the edge of his vision. *Because some of us will surely make that sacrifice before this struggle finds an end.*

A statement *that* true required no response. He set about making camp. The weight of potential loss could plow them all under if they let it. Better to take these times moment to moment. And tonight the best he could hope for was to sleep without dreams.

Another week of flying eased nothing. Flat darkness held sway, the new moon offering anonymity to the Great Shape that settled to earth with vibrating impact and a shudder of mighty wings. The spot was carefully chosen—far enough from the city that even that strike of Kinra's landing would not be noticed, yet close enough that Kilras would be in Bajor before the sun rose over his back.

You're certain you'll find the support you seek? He heard the extended questions behind her thought. How much do you trust these people? Will they think you mad? Will they turn on you when they learn the truth? And beyond those queries, the unspoken offer—that she would find cover and wait, fight for him or carry him away as needed.

Kilras considered as he slid to the ground and moved clear. If he had not spent all these days of flight turning the same questions in his mind, hesitation might have claimed him at the thought of standing alone against what lay ahead. But he had considered, had worried over and scrutinized dozens of possible responses and outcomes to the news he carried and the requests he meant to make. Not all unfurled in his favor. But many would. With luck, most. And as for facing all those possibilities alone, this time was far from the first. Nor was it likely it would be the last—if he lived through the next weeks.

"Certain enough," he said as he turned to look back at her. A dark shape only slightly more dense than the night itself, she waited, massive and firm and radiating vibrant heat. If he could not see the vivid shimmer of her gaze, he felt its intensity. "I'll see you in a few months."

Silence. Then she shifted away, put more space between them. Air moved with the lifting of her mighty wings, and he braced himself against the rushing blast of wind that pushed outward as she lifted into the sky. For a second, two, ten, his ears filled with the sound of rising motion, then she was gone and he stood alone in the stillness and the witch-hour-dark of the night.

Kilras closed his eyes and breathed deep. Even this far from the coast, the breeze held a faint hint of salt and sea. Though the night was cold, winter had not yet laid claim to this region, and around him night sounds returned, the whisper of insect and animal easing the edges of the quiet.

He waited a moment more, gathering focus, then opened his eyes to Gweld. The world glowed golden, the gloomy nature of the night overwhelmed by unbound vision. He turned and walked toward Bajor, open, for the first time, to take in the city with all his skill and knowledge.

30

Kilras

BAJOR SHIMMERED IN THE GREYING LIGHT. **A** FEW LAMPS LIT windows in the upper city, while the docks already swarmed with motion and rebounded the sounds of steady labor. Kilras slowed his steps, took in the nuance that Gweld vision added to his knowledge of the city he had called home for more than two decades. For a moment, fear trembled his gut—that the purely human intuition and perception on which he had relied for so long held deep flaws. But, though some spaces below him offered shifts in reflection that informed him anew, nothing grievous threatened his hard earned understanding of the place.

He stopped at the top of the road leading down into the city, and shuttered his Gweld senses, though only so far as to not be distracted by the range of information now available to him. Just knowing the skill need no longer be suppressed solidified confidence. Whatever came of his planned encounters this day, he had nothing left to hide. That alone unfolded a freedom he had not known, until this moment, that he lacked. He smiled and made his way along the cliff-top trail toward the caravan quarters.

Kilras rapped his knuckles against the door frame of Whels Ritt's office.

"C'min!" The invitation boomed through the still morning air.

"Morning," Kilras said as he stepped inside.

Whels froze at his desk, quill in hand. He raised his head, welcome recognition and confusion warring in his expression. "Kilras? What in the name of every dead god—? You were wintering in the east." His brow furrowed hard. "How did you get here?" His tone shifted. "What's happened?"

Kilras pulled the door closed behind him. "More than you can imagine." He slid the lock and faced his old friend.

Whels sat back in his chair, the dusty early light flowing through the room's single window brightening his face in contrast to his wary expression. "What news requires a locked door?"

No point in preamble. Whels was as forthright a man as Kilras had ever met. For him, only simple truth would do. "Shaa is dead."

Whels's jaw dropped open and silence expanded as though the room itself had caught its breath.

Kilras waited, attention steady on the other man. Gweld, held carefully in reserve, danced at the edges of Kilras's mind. In this moment, the Ritt's reaction, measured in human layers of shock, told Kilras enough. Around them, the quiet deepened, stretched, until at last Whels pushed to his feet, chair scraping over the floor, and paced across the small space.

"You're certain?"

"I was there. In Melbis. Shaa is dead."

"You saw it happen?"

"I saw the Draighil return from battle alive and well."

Whels crossed the room again, pivoted and returned. Back and forth the big man's measured stride carried him until he stopped almost in mid-step, and looked hard at Kilras. "In *Melbis*?"

Kilras straightened away from the door and nodded, watched Whel's expression shift and shift again as the real questions that would rule this meeting unfolded in his mind.

The Ritt's eyes narrowed. "How did you get here from Melbis? There's been no bell signaling a caravan arrival, no new ships in the harbor. Where are the rest of your people?"

Kilras shook his head. "My people are on their way to Giddor. Except Cleod, who's traveling to Sibora in the company of Trayor Draighil."

Whels stared. "Are you telling me that *Cleod killed Shaa*?"

Kilras shook his head. "Trayor Draighil killed Shaa, but he had Cleod's help in doing it."

"Shaa...is dead." Whels spoke the words as though only repetition would make him believe them. "What happened, Kil?"

"We ran into Draigon Weather starting in Sibora. When we reached the Seebo, it was all but dry. We found Draigon sign in the riverbed. Cleod...reacted badly. When we arrived in Melbis, the Council was preparing for Sacrifice. Then Trayor Draighil arrived."

"You're only telling a quarter of this story."

"I am. For the details, you'll want to sit down." Kilras gestured toward the chair behind the desk as he crossed to settle in the room's only other seat. He set his pack down, flipped back the cover flap, tugged the bag open and pulled out a clear bottle of pale brown liquor.

Whels's eyes widened as he walked back around his desk and sat. "Is that...Nyscot? Old gods and glory, its barely past dawn." But he reached to the shelf behind him and picked up two glasses. "What in all that breathes is going on?"

Kilras tugged the cork from the bottle and poured three fingers into Whels's glass and another three into his own. "All those answers you've spent years asking me for?" He set the bottle in the middle of the desk and picked up his glass, gestured for Whels to do the same. "Sit back. It's time for me to share them."

Whels's stare held both rising fury and denial, as though the two warred within him and he could completely shift into either with any word Kilras spoke.

Kilras lifted his glass and took a deliberate swallow, left space in the conversation for any words Whels might not be able to hold back. They came quickly, flat with anger.

"You're telling me your mother is a *Draigon*? And when you said you were raised in the north you meant—"

"I'm telling you just that. All of that."

"By all the old dead gods—"

"They're not dead. I was raised by them, taught all the skills I had the day you met me. The skills that saved your life more than once. And I've never been a danger to anyone who didn't earn it from me. That's something I also learned from the women who raised me."

Whels shoved back his chair, rose, and paced away again, shaking his head. "Draigon—*Women*? Kilras how can you sit there and expect me to—" Fury clouded the big man's face and he turned. He raised the hand that held the glass, and pointed at Kilras. "You're telling me that the monsters that've terrorized this continent for centuries are not only some kind of *teachers* but *also women*? What kind of a fool do you take me for? Why would you tell me a *bullshit infested* story like this? Are you on a bet? What's at stake? Who do you owe money to, trying to get me riled up?"

Kilras shook his head slowly. Of all the things Whels could have decided about the news he was receiving, this was one that Kilras had not anticipated, that the painful facts might be thought to be a purposeful untruth. "All the years we've been friends, and when've I ever lied to you?"

"A dozen times by omission," Whels snapped.

"So my correction of those omissions is a lie?"

"Whatever your game, Kil, even Nyscot isn't going to put me in the mood to play it." He stalked back to the desk and set his glass down hard enough to splash the drink over the rim and onto the papers strewn across the surface. Whels planted both hands on top of the desk and leaned toward Kilras. "*What is going on?*"

"Shaa's born name was Gahree," Kilras said. "She was wise, and kind, and she taught me a thousand things that I can measure and another thousand that I'll never be able to." He met Whels's gaze, kept his tone even. One chance, in this moment to convince the Ritt of the truth of the tale. One chance for the serious tone of Kilras's words to penetrate, to open the space in Whels's mind for belief. Belief had to come first, if understanding was ever to be a possibility. And if Kilras could not convince this old friend of the truth, what chance did he have with anyone else? What chance to help the Draigon prevent vile destruction across the breadth of Arnan? "She was more than a thousand years old. She led the Draigon for five centuries, and she died in human form in Melbis, cut down by Trayor Draighil. With the help of the man I've called friend for years.

"You want to know what's going on? I'm here to ask for your help. Because I can't stop the coming war, but I plan to do everything I'm able to prevent the deaths of innocent people. And I can't do that alone."

Whels's expression flashed and changed as each word struck him. If this meeting did not end in battle, much would bear repeating. How much could a man absorb at once, make sense of? Kilras's could almost see his old friend's thoughts tumbling over each other.

At last the Ritt managed words. "Innocent people?"

Bless the protective nature of caravan leaders that Whels found focus on that of all things. "Women, and girls, and supporters of the Draigon. Because Draigon are human, at least in part. And that news'll spread. And once it does, what's to stop those in power from taking their fear out on anyone they dislike? What's to stop you from being part of that violence? Unless you decide to trust me enough to understand things you don't want to believe. When've I ever given you a reason not to trust me?"

"Damn you, Kilras," Whels stared, then pushed away from the desk. "Does nothing ever rock you?"

Tylen's hair blowing in the ocean breeze. Wynt's hand warm on his in the chill morning air. The copper patches across the hip of Cleod's fireleather uniform. Gahree's blood gleaming crystalline against scorched earth. Kilras took a chance, closed his eyes and bowed his head, trusting the length of friendship he shared with the big Ritt would stay any violent intention in the man. "More things than you can imagine."

Silence fell and held.

Kilras opened his eyes and met Whels's gaze.

The creases around the Ritt's eyes loosened a fraction.

"Fire and damnation, you're infuriating," Whels said lowly, but he shook his head and picked up the glass of Nyscot. "Keep talking. If nothing else, it's a grand tale you're spinning. If you get me drunk enough, I might even start to believe you."

That brought a small smile to Kilras's lips. Less than he had hoped for, but probably more than he deserved, the reprieve in Whels's anger at least offered a chance that something useful would arise from this encounter.

The half-empty bottle stood lonely in the light piercing the window, and the air in the room held the weight of boulders.

Gweld-touched senses primed to back action, Kilras watched Whels as he absorbed yet another piece of information bent to tear down the world he knew. His fingers, stiff with tension, wrapped his glass as though he wanted to crush it. His free hand, curled into a fist, lifted and fell over and over, thudding the table in a slow, deliberate rhythm.

Kilras drew a breath, let it out. The Nyscot had either been a brilliant idea or a violent mistake. Though Whels had listened with as willing a mind as Kilras could have hoped, asked questions, taken his time to absorb the answers, the outcome of this meeting was far from certain. If Whels, who had so benefited from the accepted patterns of Arnan, unaware all these years of its deeper secrets, could be swayed toward understanding, then the plan conceived in Cyunant might be viable. If not, it was unlikely that either of them would leave this room unscathed.

The sword at Kilras's hip seemed suddenly heated. He held still, waiting. What happened was Whels's choice.

The room fell silent as the Ritt's hand ceased its steady action and rested solid against the table. "I don't know whether to thank you for sharing the truth or rip out your throat."

Kilras met Whels's gaze and allowed himself a faint smile. "So nothing's changed."

Several seconds passed, then Whels gave a disgusted grunt and shook his head. "Old gods but you've always been unbearable." Anger boiled under his words, dancing red and bitter along the edges of Kilras's Gweld sense.

"And yet you've borne me all these years." Kilras raised his glass. "Even bought me a drink more than once."

"Draigon-damned son of a Draigon," Whels whispered, his tone a tight rasp. "I wish it didn't explain so much—then I wouldn't have to believe you." He glared at Kilras. "And you told me all this why? Because you need my help to protect the monsters who've terrorized this whole continent since before my great grand parents where born?"

"No," Kilras said. "I don't expect you to care at all about the Draigon, or about me, come to that. I need your help to save the people *you* care about from being caught up in a war that has nothing to do with them. I need your help to save as many lives as we can."

"As *we* can?" Whels sat back hard in his chair, took a deep drink. "I'm not sure there's a *we*, Kilras Dorn—Ritt—Draigon son—Huh! I'm back to not knowing what to call you. Old times?" He drank again.

Kilras leaned forward and set his glass on the desk. No use claiming even the truth, that he was the man Whel's had always known. That he, like the Draigon, had always been exactly what he was, and new information about what that meant in the eyes of others did not change that central fact. "Your choice," he said and got to his feet, lifted his arms into a stretch that rolled down into his shoulders. He bore the risk in the action, that it might be seen as a threat, but Whels just watched him with narrow eyes.

"You've always been a cock-certain bastard."

That pulled a grin across Kilras's lips. "Are you glad to finally know the reasons why?"

"Son of—"

"Draigons. I know." Kilras met the Ritt's gaze. "And you know. Everything. Secrets. Weaknesses. What I'm asking." He nodded. "Can you trust me enough to take the chance that I'm on the right side?"

"You've been a willful mystery since the day I met you, but this—"

"How many people have you known who've died from Draigon Weather?"

"What?"

"How many? Draigon are feared and hated. Why?"

"They take women—"

"The Councils *give* women to them."

"If I'm to believe you, that's the bargain the Draigon demanded to stop the war."

"But have you ever heard of a Council reluctant to make that trade? Who valued their women enough to refuse to make a Sacrifice?"

"They call in the Enclaves."

"Men abused and addicted and so lost in hate and violence that they don't even know why they're fighting." The bitter knot in Kilras's chest thrust hard edged into the words. Where was Cleod? How much closer to Sibora? What pain and rage burned in his mind this moment? "And not all Councils send for a Draighil. Not even most. What are women in this land, if not expendable in the minds of most men?"

"That's a dark statement," Whels's voice was broken stone.

"Tell me it's not true."

"I never—"

"We *all* have." Kilras cut him off. To admit such failure in himself cut deeply. "Even me. *Especially* me. Because I was raised to know better. Sehina aside, I've never done enough to change this world for the women around me. And I intend to correct that, no matter what it costs."

Whels shook his head. "You're telling me you're willing to die for this mess?"

Kilras raised his glass. "I hope not to, but yes."

Whels's shoulders slumped. "You really would."

"What better reason?" Kilras asked, and waited. On this moment, everything hinged, perhaps even his life. Were their years of friendship and shared work enough for Whels to accept a request to alter so much that he believed about the world? Dark truth lingered—such had not been enough with Cleod. Would the outcome have been different if *he* had been offered as much truth as Whels, as Sehina and Rimm, and the others, had been offered in an equal moment of need? Hours had made the difference, and the loss of that precious time had rendered damage to scar all their futures.

Whels stared a long time, then said tightly, "None."

"None?"

"I've known none who died from Draigon Weather." He heaved in a sigh. "Damn you, Kil. What is it you need from me?"

31

Cleod

ESPITE STOPS IN LARGER TOWNS WITH FINER INNS, EACH DAY TRAVELED wore harsher than the last. Of Ain and the horse she had ridden into the night, they found no sign. Likely, she had died in the snow, frozen and lost.

Because of him.

The thought refused dismissal and sat like a stone in Cleod's gut. He drowned it in ercew every chance that arose, drinking steadily enough that Trayor gave up on burning cuila, though neither substance subdued the nightmares that claimed Cleod night after night.

In the rolling fogs of pain and brutal recollection, flashing visions of his life formed quilt-like patches of new-risen fears and old hopes. Plagued by unrelenting nausea, his nights became just times to be survived. Clarity existed only as memory, a part of wakeful awareness that had died on that hot night in the poit in Melbis. The *where* of his existence, the *why*, endured as vague backdrop to his bodily craving and his inarticulate rage. If there existed such a thing as a soul, Draigon Weather had claimed his. Regardless of the winter landscape surrounding him, all that remained within was cracked earth and dust.

Dawn brought little comfort, but with it, at least, came motion, and in that he could pretend there lay a future when peace might again exist—on the other side of whatever battles remained to be fought.

As best as the churning in his gut would allow, he ignored

the fact that the warm coat protecting him from the elements belonged to Leys's dead husband, Phal, and that the rest of the winter clothing that graced him and Trayor had been pilfered from Sandin's wardrobe. Once friends, those hardy inhabitants of Hengbaith had stared after Cleod with eyes that marked him as a stranger, and dangerous. If Leys shed tears, she did not let him see. Just as well. He did not want the weight of that image sprawled across his dreams with all the rest.

Today, for the first time in more than a week, the clouds lifted, and the vivid, clean blue of the sky gleamed like crystal. Sunlight reflected off sparkling snow and forced a squint as narrow as that needed even in desert summer. Then, in the far, far distance a faint shadow of grey edged over the horizon and drew his gaze. Cleod caught his breath. The Spur.

The last time he put boots against the granite peak of that mountain had been when he faced Shaa in defense of Leiel. And Adfen, once his home—almost as much time had passed since he had walked its streets. In all the years the caravan had visited the ancient city, he had never entered, despite Kilras's offer to reveal the secret of his mysterious cake.

Cleod shook himself. Adfen was not their destination. They would pass south of the city on the way to Sibora and the King. The King. Trayor rode forth so eager to share the truth of the Draigon...had it occurred to him at all that passing on the secret of the beasts diminished the usefulness of the Enclaves in the coming fight? Might even render Draighil irrelevant? Impossible to tell. Since Hengbaith, Trayor spoke nothing of his plans. Was it fear or ignorance that founded his silence? What transpired when they arrived in the capital would answer more than just the question of the depth of Trayor's understanding of his own vulnerability.

Weakness. Frailty. Adfen was a reckoning long overdue. But not yet. Rocked in the saddle, Cleod stared at the grey haze of the mountain, and the old battle unfolded in his mind. Smoke and flame, screams and pain. So much pain. The scars over his hips seemed to pull tighter, deeper, as they always did when he entered Spur country. For so many years he had faced the past sober. But never had he faced it down. And today he could only feel grateful that ercew numbed deep thought.

"A fine sight on our first day of clear skies," Trayor said from where he rode beside Cleod.

Cleod turned his frayed attention to the other man. "Clear skies are their own reward." His breath frosted the air as he spoke. He inhaled, then blew out hard, watched the small cloud slowly dissipate. "Do you still believe that the Draigon will turn to heat as a defense? They seem disinclined to accommodate your plans."

Trayor scoffed. "When they see what is coming for them, what we plan to do with their favored ones, they'll have little choice."

Cleod raised his gaze to the horizon again. "And the rest of the Ehlewer, what do they think?"

Trayor's gaze flicked away. "Soibel thinks me overly ambitious, the others will meet us on the battlefield."

Cleod started. "Soibel's *alive*?" How was that possible? The man had been ancient when Cleod joined the Ehlewer more than twenty-five years before. The Elder's last words to Cleod rolled though his mind. *You leave me no choice but to count you as an enemy.*

Something real moved across Trayor's face, something that might have been grief. Before Cleod could fully register it, Trayor shook his head and the action swept away the expression. "He died three years ago. But he made clear to me his feelings about my plans. Rohl lives, as does Vessor, the old librarian."

Cleod studied Trayor for a moment before asking, "Three years ago you came up with this plan?"

"I've been planning how to destroy the Draigon since the day Shaa nearly killed you."

Shock locked every muscle in Cleod's body. Kicce shied beneath him before he recovered enough to rein the gelding to the stop. Hoyd and Trayor in the snowy alley. A moonlight-drenched field just a few day's ride from their present location. *They want you back.* They had never let him go. He studied Trayor. Or was it *they*? He let the thought linger, unvoiced.

Trayor halted his horse and turned the mount so he faced Cleod. "You thought this plan was a new one?"

All the years on the trail, every day a fight for his sanity and sobriety. Every slip. Every stumble. Had it not been for Kilras... The thought cut away, unfinished, as another rose, a dark realization that pushed all others aside. "*You killed Hoyd.* You killed him so you could convince the others you needed *me* to help you destroy Shaa."

Trayor tightened his jaw and returned his gaze to Cleod. "Hoyd never got over the shame of having you as his mentor. He trained hard, but he never fully believed you left him untainted. With doubt like that, he could never have killed Shaa—or been reliable enough to help me do it."

More than fifteen years had passed since Cleod last saw Hoyd. In Cleod's mind the Draigre remained young, a cadet just finishing his training and taking his first strides into adulthood, arrogant and self-assumed as were all the Ehlewer. A shudder ran through Cleod. How much had changed. And how little. Violence. Murder. "So you broke his back and left him to die."

"The Draigon must be *ended*." Trayor's voice cracked the chill air. "In three generations the Enclaves will not exist. Too many Draigre fail before Investiture. If the Draigon are not destroyed now, we will never have the strength to do it."

Cleod's shoulders stiffened and Kicce shifted again beneath him. So *some* awareness was there, that the Enclaves were not invulnerable. "And your answer to that was to murder one of your own?"

"My answer *was to kill Shaa*. In all our recorded history of the Sacrifices, only seventeen Draigon have come to fight for their prize. *Seventeen*. And we've killed half that number through the years. But Shaa—for hundreds of years Shaa was *the one*. The one who came most often. The one who killed the most of us. And now—Shaa is *dead*." Trayor's eyes gleamed, wide and fixed on Cleod's, and again something Cleod could not name shifted through them. "Hoyd could not have stood beside me for that. Only *you* had faced that monster and lived. Only *you knew*." He straightened in the saddle. "And I was right. Shaa is dead. Now is *our time*. It's now or it's never at all. So yes, I killed Hoyd. And I killed Shaa. And before winter is ended, the Draigon will be no more. No matter the cost, this war ends *now*."

Cleod's pulse quickened in his veins, suddenly heavy in his neck. The bright light of the moment, surrounded by crackling whiteness, only increased the cold that claimed his heart as he listened to Trayor. "Is this what the Enclaves have become?"

"Keep your righteous judgment, traitor. Had you not betrayed us, he would still be alive."

"No." Cleod urged Kicce forward until he and Trayor were eye to eye. "He would be alive *if you had not killed him. Why,* Tray? He was a fully trained Draighil. You can't be worried about how few of those exist if you're willing to destroy one just to have *me* by your side." He leaned in. "What was it? Was Hoyd starting to question your plans? Your need to bring me back to the fold? Or was he simply starting to question *you*?"

Trayor's hand twitched toward his sword, but he did not draw it. "Your time is coming."

"You said this is *our* time." Ain's trusting face filled Cleod's mind. Whether or not he ever put a name to the strange darkness he saw within Trayor, Cleod knew the name of the pain in that child's eyes. "So that's true for both of us." He put his heels to Kicce's flanks and sent the gelding down the road in a furious kick-up of snow.

32

Kilras

H E WAS WELL KNOWN ALONG THIS ROAD, AND SO FAR LUCK HAD HELD IN his mission. He smiled a little. Even Doland, the man Sehina had been besting in long distance horse races for years, declared his willingness to stand for justice should need arise. Perhaps it was all the years of being outclassed by Sehina that had given him a respect for women unusual among the men of Arnan. Kilras smiled. Should he ever see Sehina again, she would enjoy the news, that her impact on one man might have saved lives. How many such associations had immeasurable impact on the world every day, person to person, shifting fate, building change? More than he had imagined possible it seemed, based on the attention people had paid to his requests along the way, and on their stoic willingness to stand in the face of the unrest that loomed greater each day.

If distance from the events in the east had given him and the Draigon the advantage of time, that shrank with each passing day. Still, hope lay in that fading resource—and the resistant nature of the best people of Arnan.

The sun arced just a sliver over the cold horizon when an out-of-place sound alerted him. He dismounted and stood listening for only seconds before certainty demanded action. He sent up a whisper of gratitude that snow had yet to fall this far west. A boon from the Draigon, perhaps, to make his travel safer. It could not hold, but for now it was a gift.

Stepping quickly across the frozen ground, Kilras led his chestnut gelding off the road and into the boulder-lined ravine, a long-abandoned bed of the Sarn that now flowed to the south. Deep and twisting, the gulch wove a route roughly parallel to the main trail.

Time and again on this journey experience had saved him. Slim but of infinite value, was the advantage of his intimate knowledge of the lands traveled for decades. If he missed the saddle abandoned months ago along with his mare, at least the gelding was more than reliable. Behind him, the horse followed with steady trust. Though it was young and not as reliable as his mare, the gelding was Sehina trained, and he trusted it to remain calm and keep quiet.

The earth, stone hard from the deep cold, remained un-marred as he passed. No foot prints. No tracks. Another advantage. But the cold ground also kicked no distant dust into the air, making it more difficult to spot signs of approaching trouble. This close to the Bynkrol Enclave, he could not risk using Gweld. Too well he recalled the outcome of his last use of the skill in this territory. All he could rely on was carrying sound and his instinct. That and his solid familiarity with the land—where he might safely shortcut the route, where he might hide. Where others might lie in wait.

The Farlan Army was not subtle enough to stalk potential conscripts through rough terrain, but if they caught sight of him they might decide that obtaining his horse was alone worth their time and attention. Twice already he had dodged a column on the march, ready to snatch up any who they encountered to add, if not to their ranks, then to the aggregate of forced labor that trailed in support.

Luck held this time, a trick of wind and angles of rock bounced echoes over great distances. Ahead of him, or behind, he was not certain, but a small party, moving steadily. Passing under a dead tree bent over the gully by wind, he led the horse down into the narrow gulch. A dozen yards beyond the point where he could no longer see out of the draw, he tied the mount to a leafless shrub, and worked his way back toward the road, staying low, moving slowly, pausing often to listen.

Strange and clattering, an echo of motion on packed earth and stone drifted and faded among the rocks. Where the half-fallen tree loomed over the gulch, he stepped up onto a large rock. Atop it, he could just see over the lip of earth, the road visible through a scattering of dead and dormant plants. Kilras took off his hat and dropped it, then shifted into the shadow cast by the tree.

The sound of shod hooves clapped on hard earth. The group of riders that appeared moved at a sensible walk, the short column of a dozen men gathered in loose formation, not at all the formal organization of trained soldiers. Their rough laughter and practical clothing gave away their profession: hired warriors—mercenaries at best, paid bandits at the worst. Even more than if the group were soldiers, Kilras was glad of his decision to move off the road.

Only a half-day ride east was the turn to the great bridge that spanned the Sarn and began the winding road to his destination. If men like the ones now approaching felt comfortable riding so boldly through Bynkrol territory, it was likely that his guess was correct—the Enclave would be empty of its best warriors, all the Draighil and finest Draigre having marched toward Sibora to join the fight. The compound should be lightly guarded at best, an opportunity not to be found elsewhere, to gather information about battle plans and logistics. To discover whether the Enclaves most guarded secrets were housed within. At least he hoped so. It was worth the detour to discover if he was right.

He held his breath and held himself still as the riders drew near, drew parallel, moved past, their easy conversation masking the alert glances scanning the terrain. A too sudden movement from him would surely draw notice. As it was, though they traveled on seemingly unaware of his presence, a tingle rippled up the back of his neck, and he took soonest opportunity to step down into the ravine. Instinct warred with unease. Safest choice was to get back on the road quickly, to put distance between himself and the mercenaries should they make the unlikely choice to double back. But something held him in the gulch, led him to stroke the gelding's nose and wait in the chill air, breathing shallowly to reduce the puffs of mist formed by his breath.

Minutes slipped by, thickened by the impatient knowledge that staying in place could be as dangerous as risking motion. Then a single, slick *chink* sounded from the road—metal on rock with a rattle of loosened stone rolling. Kilras waited. Time condensed again, moved on with another whisper of the trailing scout, moving slowly, but moving on.

Still Kilras held position. Would there be another? In other times, in such dangerous territory, there might have been, but here it seemed unlikely. The building winter weather meant the back-rider likely remained more a habit than a ploy, as it would be easy for the mercenaries to assume any useful loners had already been swept up by passing soldiers.

Kilras retrieved and donned his hat, then led the gelding on through the narrow space between fallen rocks until a fresh slide of earth offered a passable angle back to the road. Heartbeats after the chestnut topped the embankment, he was back in the saddle. Luck had prevailed again, but for how long could that remain true? He urged the gelding on.

In all his years traveling the long road between Bajor and Kee's Ferry, he had never turned across the bridge that marked the road leading up the mountain. At first, the decision had been a conscious one, to avoid any chance of encountering the Bynkrol after the raid on Aycn's caravan. Then habit had taken over, something he rarely allowed to happen. He hoped, now, that such avoidance had not been a mistake. But if there was a chance the documents Resor had spoken of so long ago were housed at Bynkrol, he must venture inside.

The Sarn, partly edged with ice but still flowing, pushed chill air upward to surround him as he crossed the stiff planks. While years of practiced control let him contain Gweld with ease, the past weeks of freedom opened a longing for the knowledge and insight the skill offered, since the river could tell him much about who moved near it. But he simply marked the desire to reach out, and crossed the bridge without surrendering to temptation.

The road, hard pounded, twisted as it climbed. It offered sweeping views that opened around turns, and little place to set a defense against an assault from above. The next switchback opened to the northwest, back along the trade road. On it, figures moved east with purpose—a loose column of riders with one trailing far behind. Kilras pulled the chestnut to a halt and stared. Yes. It was the same group that passed him hours earlier. Had he left some slight sign that they noticed? Or were they simply scouts returning from a specific assignment? And if that were the case, where else was there to return to but the Enclave compound up the mountain? For a moment, his belly tightened, then he took a deep breath and forced tension away. They had passed him on the road just after dawn, and the idea of descending this trail in the dark was daunting at best. No. They had come from somewhere else, and the only reason for them to turn back was because something made them to reverse their travels. And if there was something besides him to find, it would be a coincidence too perfect to imagine. With an apology to the horse for the request, he urged the mount around the switchback and harder up the trail.

Another third of the way up the climb, another glimpse of the road below proved wary instinct correct. The riders were nowhere in sight, east or west. Somewhere below, they climbed in pursuit. Kilras uttered a series of curses as he put heels to the gelding and charged up the climb. Snow now clung to the edges of the road, and the wind sang fiercer over the rocks as he gained altitude.

The horse was heaving for breath when, mercifully, the angle of the road eased as the slope widened into a broad bowl. The main basin was a well-maintained meadow, the grass poking through the snow brown from the cold. At the far end, a cluster of buildings backed up against the rise of the mountain. Smoke rose from the chimneys of only two. It seemed he was right, and the place was mostly empty.

That advantage mattered little now. He swung down, and led the horse east along the edge of the snow, perpendicular to the road, away from buildings. A glance back showed him the tracks he and the animal left as they bent the dead grass.

Thankful for the lead he had over the mercenaries, he continued around the edge of the meadow, laying a wide trail, hoping the rest of his guesses would prove accurate. As the land sloped upward again, he went with it, until, two bow-shots from the compound wall, a voice called out in warning and he stopped. The tired horse came to a grateful halt behind him.

"What's your business on this mountain?" The winter-clothed guard who stepped forward, spear leveled and ready, was hardly more than a boy. If he had seen thirteen summers, Kilras would be surprised.

"My name is Kilras Dorn. I come to meet the Bynkrol elders."

The boy stared, then his eyes narrowed into a glare. "If that's so, then why didn't you ride straight to the Enclave? Why are you sneaking around the training field?"

Kilras held back a smile. This one was just quick enough. The Enclaves had only ever taken in the best young men that Arnan had to offer, but they would not have left the brightest of them behind. "I'm avoiding the interest of the group of mercenaries trailing me. I thought it best to make them wonder what I was up to."

The guard pulled himself a little straighter, flicked a glance behind Kilras at the obvious trail he had left. "Kilras...Dorn..."

The spear tip came up slightly and the boy's stance shifted, as though he was readying himself to back his next words with force. "Your name is taught. You took in the Ehlewer traitor."

Had the key to the main gate of the compound been laid at Kilras's feet, the opening could not have been more perfect. "If you know that, then you know why I am here. Or did you think my involvement with Cleod Draighil was not always part of Enclave plans?"

Something akin to astonishment opened the boy's tense face, then his brow furrowed again. "If you're saying you've been one of us all along—well, that'll be the first I'd heard spoken of you without spite."

Kilras shifted his tone to the firm one he used with arrogant merchants. "What would be the point of having one such as you think otherwise? There's a fight on the horizon. Do you think I'd ride for an Enclave after all these years if I were sided with the beasts?"

As hoped, that knocked the sureness out of the boy's stance. If he was not wise enough to wonder how Kilras had gotten from Melbis to this mountainside, well, that was luck not to be questioned. More luck followed as the clatter of hooves and deep voices announced the arrival of bandits at the top of the trail, and yanked the sentry's attention. His eyes widened, and he stared.

Then the boy's uncertainty fled and he righted his spear and beckoned to Kilras with one hand. "Quick then, spy. If they follow the trail you've left, we'll be inside with the alarm raised before they're half-way to the gates."

Kilras withheld the obvious comment—that if they followed his trail, they would not even make for the gates. He glanced back across the fields to where the riders milled. He smiled as they split the party, three following his trail and the rest heading up the main road. Smarter than the boy before him. A near-empty enclave. A convenient lie. Danger on swift approach. The rest of the day would not be boring.

33

Kilras

THROUGH A SIDE DOOR IN THE WALL, THEY ENTERED THE COMPOUND and slid a heavy lock snug behind them. Then the boy slipped between narrow buildings with practiced confidence. Kilras smiled, remembering Cleod's stories of late night escapes from the Ehlewer compound and the trouble he got into. Youth found rebellion where it could.

"Your name, Draigre?" Kilras asked.

"Vennan, Sere." The young man tossed his response over his shoulder as he rounded a corner that opened into the main courtyard. "Elder Machar is just this way, in the cookhouse."

They crossed the central open space, and Kilras took in the layout of the buildings—a ring of stone structures, ringed again by others, then surrounded by the tall wall. Quiet enhanced every sound of their motion, ring and squeak and clatter. The place rang with absence.

He flexed the fingers of his sword hand in the chill air. However few Bynkrol remained in the Enclave, the danger surrounding him was not lessened by the compound's reduced occupancy. Had the situation required anything less than his full attention, he might have smiled at the irony—that the distraction of the approaching mercenaries might be more luck than misfortune.

He tied the gelding's reins to a ring attached to the building. Vennan held open a dark wooden door and ushered Kilras into the cookhouse just as voices from the front gate raised in alarm.

At the cries, a stooped, white haired man turned from the stove. His eyes widened at the sight of Vennan and Kilras.

"What is this, Draigre?" He stopped and place a wrinkled hand on the knife at his belt. "Who is this stranger? What rouses the gate?"

"The Ehlewer spy, Elder!" Vennan stepped forward, face bright with urgency.

"Spy?" Wary confusion graced the old man's expression.

Kilras stepped into the breach. "Kilras Dorn." He tipped his head in greeting. "I've come to share my knowledge, and bring you warning."

"Kilras Dorn? What—?"

Behind them, the door banged open and they turned as another guard loomed in the entry. "Elder! Warriors approaching!"

"It's what we came to tell you, Elder," Vennan said. "Fighters followed him up the mountain."

The Elder stared, and Kilras suppressed a smile as he imagined the confusion of thoughts that must be warring within the man. Then he pointed at Kilras. "Attend him with arms. Take his weapons."

For too long an instant, no one moved—enough time that should advantage have been sought, Kilras could have taken it— then the Draigre snapped to obedience. They stripped Kilras of his sword and knife. If Vennan's gaze held a flicker of apology, it signaled no further hesitation. Kilras raised his hands and let them search him. In the seconds that took, Elder Machar moved to the doorway and looked out.

"Let us see what these visitors want of the Bynkrol." He turned his gaze back to Kilras. "And with this one. Bring him."

They did not quite dare shove him, but the two guards moved closer, herding Kilras toward the door. He smiled at Vennan. The boy's guts must be flipping in his belly at this turn of events. Too trusting by half and again for the role he had chosen, which was likely why he had been left behind when the rest of the Enclave marched. Or...Kilras studied the boy. Or Vennan was smarter than he seemed. That felt more likely.

Out the door and across the cobbled open square they walked, toward the gate where a small assemblage of guards clustered on the ramparts to either side. Two at a time, his nimbleness belying his bent frame, the Elder climbed stone steps to join them. Spear-points close at his back, Kilras followed. Wisdom or folly to have sought out the Bynkrol? The question gnawed, and the next moments would hold the answer.

He stepped to the edge of the wall and looked down at the group of mercenaries scattered just beyond bow shot, and smart enough not to cluster. He counted them, frowned. All present. Smart enough, as well, not to have taken the bait of his trail after all. At least he did not have to worry about them sneaking entry through Vennan's favored door. He studied the group. They had ridden straight to the gate, and though they waited at a distance, their affect lacked unease.

A warning tingle laced its way up Kilras's spine. Familiarity. That's what gathered beyond the wall. They knew this place. And that could bode well, or poorly, depending on the manner of that knowing.

The Elder's call of greeting confirmed dread thoughts. "The Wistin Raiders on a winter morn. What brings you up our mountain this time?"

The man who had trailed the column brought his mount to the front of the group and offered a fierce grin in reply. "Followed a rider. One clever enough to get off the road before we even laid eyes upon him directly. Wasn't for a fresh-chipped stone trailside, we might never have passed him a thought." His gaze swept along the ramparts, stopped on Kilras. "And I see he found his way to the only place 'round here there is to find."

"He's Kilras Dorn of Bajor," Kilras replied. "With business that brooked no delay by the likes of you."

"That's a name I've heard long over the trail." The man ran

rough fingers over his chin. "Never heard it near an Enclave though. You being the one who kept the drunkard Draighil."

Kilras held his gaze steady on the raider. "Because you're trusted with all Enclave business, are you?"

Elder Machar cut off further exchange. "What do you want, Stin?"

"Want him." The raider, pointed at Kilras. "Money in a man of that reputation. He'll fetch a weight of coin from the conscriptors at Kee's."

Quick, as advantage loomed, Kilras calculated risk—the men beyond the wall—the men upon it—the weapons trained at his back—and braced to the challenge. In the whisper of an instant, with the grace of flowing water, he cracked open long-contained skill and unfolded Gweld sense. Gold rippled around him, coated and measured the lifeless stone, the earth and the trees and the men all around. A few paces to his right, the Elder went stiff and pivoted to face Kilras. One by one, as recognition struck them, the Draigre's attention also shifted to the stranger in their midst.

"You!" Machar gasped. "You do *this*?"

Kilras smiled and turned fully to face him. "Do you think just anyone could be entrusted to guard Cleod Draighil until he could be returned to his purpose?"

"What's offered new?" Wistin called. "Whatever much, I'll see it doubled to hand him here."

Ignoring the bandit leader, Machar stared at Kilras. Then the impact of the Elder's Gweld blazed up in counterpoint to dance a leathered grey against Kilras's gleaming lights, testing, seeking.

"You know this power as we do, half-cefreid. Who taught you this?"

Kilras shook his head. "We've more important things to discuss, Elder." He glanced over the wall, let contempt etch his expression. "If we can be done with distractions."

The Elder hesitated just long enough for Kilras to be certain he had truly claimed advantage before giving a single sharp nod. He looked down over the wall again. "It is quite impossible that you could offer a tenth what this man is worth, Stin. Or did you think he made for the Enclave on a whim? This is Bynkrol business. We'll replenish your supplies, then you can return to conscripting fodder for the Farlan."

The bandit leader uttered a series of blistering curses, but the offer of provisions seemed to blunt his focus. "Least you can offer then is the warmth of your cookhouse. Cold to sit out here while goods are gathered."

Machar stared. "We'll grant no such thing," he said. "Should you wish true hospitality, you should not again arrive at our gates with brandished arms and demands. Wait where you are. The supplies will be lowered over the wall." With deliberate control, he shifted his attention back to Kilras and his Gweld surged, shoved, like hands lifted to deliver a blow.

In the fraction of a heartbeat that it took for Kilras to measure the strength behind Machar's push, he calculated option against consequence and let his Gweld sense *give* under the grey pressure. The older man was strong, trained and tempered by Enclave teachings and decades of practiced control, but Kilras could have matched him had necessity not demanded the appearance of lesser knowledge. He let the gold lights shrink under the assault, enough that the Elder straightened a little and some of the hostility faded from his stare.

Kilras nodded, let his gaze drop. From welcome to suspicion to haughty certainty that both demanded and dismissed—was this the kind of changeable aggression that had molded Cleod through his years with the Ehlewer? The idea reshaped the edges of Kilras's every interaction with his old friend. No wonder Cleod had spent the first several years of their association wary and disinclined to trust. And as misaligned as Cleod was now... how would he respond should he ever learn how much Kilras had not shared through the years? Time enough to consider that should they ever actually meet again. He could only hope that the letter he had given to Leiel would reach his old friend. And that it would blunt the dark potential of any future meeting. "I appreciate your assistance." Kilras gestured toward the men outside the fence who had dismounted and stood grumbling. With a controlled smile he looked directly at Machar again. "And your time."

The Elder tipped his chin in agreement. A few words to the Draigre set them scrambling, and the Elder led the way down the steps to the courtyard. Kilras followed, two paces behind, studying the compound with its high stone walls and step-smoothed walkways. The place smelled of chill limestone and old sweat, as though memories of the trials created in this place to test and train its inhabitants were soaked into the wood and walls and earth. And the Elder moved through it as though oblivious, like a man so used to the scent of warm bread that he smelled nothing upon entering a bakery.

"Kilras Dorn," Machar said. "Of all the men to work for the Enclaves all these years. Unexpected." He looked over his shoulder. "And yet somehow fitting. Trayor Elder has said for years that Cleod Draighil would return to Enclave ranks."

"Years of planning," Kilras acknowledged, "on Trayor's part. Years of waiting."

"And yet never a word to us." Machar stopped and turned to face Kilras.

Memory stirred even as Kilras laughed in response. Could he be so lucky? "Because so many secrets are shared between the Enclaves. Or do you think I don't know of the rivalries?"

"Rivalries exclude all that impacts our mutual goal."

Kilras raised his eyebrows. So Resor had been right, all those years ago. The territorial Enclaves shared keeping of the Elder's most dangerous secrets. Were they still here, the documents? "Clearly, not all." Kilras stepped passed the man to the door of the cookhouse and pushed it open. "I hope you've got hot food prepared. I've had a long journey, and we've much to discuss."

34

Kilras

EMPTY PLATTERS AND BOWLS FILLED THE TABLE BETWEEN THEM. IF the food had lacked flavor and variety, there had been more than enough of it. Belly full, and completely warm for the first time in months, Kilras reminded himself that the man he sat with was anything but a friend. Through the meal, Machar had remained cordial, his questions light and friendly. But polite gentility vanished with the last of the food.

"You have tested my patience," Machar said, patting his mouth with a cloth. "I would ask what brings you to the Bynkrol, but that answer is clear. If the story you spin is to be believed, this is a visitation you could make only now. Where did you learn Gweld skill, Kilras Dorn of Bajor?"

Kilras sat back, and offered Machar a slight smile along with quiet truth. "From a student of the Dilfan." If Kinra had been far from his only teacher, what he knew of her history would serve him well in this moment.

The stillness that dropped over Machar was absolute. He stared, unblinking, and Kilras held his gaze, awaiting the only possible reaction.

It rose like molten stone from the elder, glowing with a rage so intense that even without Gweld Kilras would have seen it on the air. "Impossible." The word snarled through the room.

The fury pulsed, gathered, but before Machar could shoot to his feet and back his emotion with action, Kilras raised a hand and shook his head. "Do you think any active Enclave could train someone like me and keep it a secret?"

"The Dilfan are two centuries gone." Anger twisted Machar's wrinkled face. "Even had your teacher been an infant when they were destroyed he could not be so old as to have lived among them, much less learned their ways." The threat behind the words carried into the stiffness of the old man's shoulders.

"If you didn't know about me, what else don't you know? My teacher was very old. And learned from the last of those taught by the Dilfan."

"And I am to believe that a student of a dead Enclave passed our most secret knowledge to a half-Arnani trader?"

"Who better? I travel freely and no one suspects me. I keep Cleod Draighil close. Or don't you think Elder Trayor's capable of thinking that creatively?"

The old man's jaw worked but, for several seconds, no words came forth. At last he muttered. "Trayor Draighil has always had unique ideas about how to destroy the Draigon."

Acceptance of Kilras's tale should have eased some of the tension knotting his shoulders, but instead it twisted tighter. For years he, Cleod, everyone, had made the mistake of dismissing Trayor Draighil as simply a well-indoctrinated warrior with no ambition beyond the adorations of the masses which could be achieved by killing a Draigon.

Kilras resisted the urge to frown. Had he been more alert to the fact that Trayor had once been as much of a partner to Cleod as Kilras had become, how much might be different now? Cleod had only ever chosen extraordinary compatriots. Trayor's patience and determination, as expressed by his more than a decade of waiting and planning, was, alone, reason to respect the threat he presented—whether or not he had ever managed to tempt Cleod back to the Ehlewer. That Trayor had succeeded in that, despite years of built trust and calm intervention by Kilras and so many others, raised a warning like an erupting mountain.

"Trayor Draighil is a singular danger to the existence of the Draigon. What he's attempting is unprecedented." Kilras picked up a fork and stabbed the remaining bit of meat from the edge of his plate. He chewed and swallowed before adding, "If not, would Bynkrol be empty?"

"You're here to make certain we met our commitment?" Machar's eyes narrowed. "The Ehlewer dare insult us so?"

"I'm not Ehlewer and I care nothing for your pride, Elder. I am simply here to inform you of my purpose through the years. When this is over, I do not want my loyalties to be mistaken."

Machar raised his cup and sipped cooling cider, his attention fully focused on Kilras. Gweld sense he held poised to punch, like a fighter at ready on a tournament platform, circling, seeking weakness. "And that reason alone brings you to the Bynkrol when the true battles lie far from here?"

"No." Kilras made a flashing check on the controls and barriers that marked the edges of his Gweld, held himself centered. As much as he needed to learn from Machar, nothing could be requested directly. To ask for information that the collaborator he claimed to be should already know, could cost him everything. "I am here because of the documents."

Grey-edge crimson light flared around him as Machar's once again startled Gweld blazed up against Kilras's mind. "The *documents.*"

Kilras tipped his head, placed his fork across the now empty plate. "I won't pretend to know the full meaning of what I've been sent here to ask. It was assumed you would know which ones."

Machar's glare faded, and he straightened in his chair. "Then you can tell Trayor Draighil, when you see him at Adfen, that the Bynkrol are more than ready to accept the return of them back into our safe keeping should the need arise."

Kilras held his expression neutral. How had he gotten so lucky as to have the answers to half his questions presented in a single sentence. Only a part of him acknowledged surprise that Trayor had focused on Adfen rather than on pushing north toward Cyunant. Despite all the Draigon's planning for an attack on the mountain homeplace, the Enclaves needed the Farlan in this fight. And the Farlan had always hated all that Adfen stood for—the last ancient city of Arnan, the place where for centuries only Shaa had come to claim the Sacrifice. And with that great Draigon dead, where else would they focus their long-repressed wrath? He smiled slowly. "I'm certain he's no doubt of that, Elder Machar. But a time of war requires that caution be exercised. I hope, not to the point of insult?"

Machar drew in a breath, gave a single shake of his head. "No. No insult. We are prepared to do all that is needed to ensure the final defeat of the beasts. But tell me, how will you make it to the Spur region in time to deliver this message?"

"You know my reputation yet you doubt what speed I can make without a caravan in tow?" Kilras shook his head, glanced toward the window where snow could now be seen falling. "If winter weather's this fierce here, what speed can legions make farther north? Or do the Bynkrol, like the Draigon, have a way to clear drifts for an entire army?"

Machar bristled as though *he* were a beast. "Do not compare us to those creatures, cefreid."

"The question stands." Kilras leaned forward. "The Enclaves are only as useful to the Farlan as the skills they provide."

"And the Farlan are only useful at all for the strength of their arms."

Kilras raised both eyebrows and sat back slowly. Now that was unexpected, if not completely unsurprising, information— the Enclaves had as much contempt for the Farlan as they did for everyone else. Why had Cleod never mentioned that? Or perhaps that had not always been the case—those of the Enclaves were, after all, almost exclusively of Farlan descent—which meant something had changed. He frowned slightly. After what

he had just allowed himself to recognize about Trayor Draighil...
"You speak as though you are no more Farlan than I am."

With a flourish, Machar rose to his feet and crossed the room to pick up a decanter of liquor from a small stand against the far wall. He poured a glass, raised it and took a long swallow. He looked to Kilras for a nod before filling a second glass. "The Enclaves have always been more than simply Farlan." He brought Kilras the drink and waited.

Kilras took a sip. Smooth yet biting, and clearly expensive, the liquor coursed through him, landed with a blaze of heat in his belly. Grateful for the distraction, he considered the statement as well as the quality of the liquid in his glass. Both spoke of a pride he recognized from Cleod's tales of the Ehlewer, but the words hid more layers. Were they worth examining? Too mush risk existed in avoiding the offered challenge. Kilras gave the Elder an appreciative nod, and the man returned to his seat.

"More than Farlan?" Kilras asked, sipping again. "In what way?"

"We have knowledge and skills that give us value beyond the obvious outcomes of our work." Machar lifted his shoulders as though the idea he was expressing had sprung from his own mind. The far-reaching clarity of it, however, struck Kilras as beyond the capacity of the man before him. "Why should they not be brought into the open and appreciated?"

So...Trayor's plan included machinations that would end far more than the Draigon's existence in Arnan. Could such split focus be turned to advantage? As quickly as possible, he needed to ride for Adfen. The necessity of the message he must spread along the way in order to protect Arnan's most vulnerable people could not be set aside, but on the days when he did not need to have those conversations, he must add urgency to the journey. "A new purpose for when the Draigon are no longer a threat?" Kilras said. "Then I am doubly glad to have made myself known to the Bynkrol. On the other side of this war, I don't want to be mistaken for someone I'm not." He paused. "The boy—Vennan?—he seems of age to have ridden west with the others."

"He is." Machar's expression folded shut. Whatever held Vennan here was not the simple fact the Enclave could not be abandoned completely. Regardless, the sudden death of Machar's openness was not an invitation for further inquiry.

Kilras simply nodded. He got to his feet and paced to the window, drink in hand, to gaze out at the falling snow. In the fading light, the drifting flakes shown starkly. "May I impose upon your hospitality until dawn?" Should he, as well, request an escort of official Bynkrol members down the mountain? The possibility existed that Wistin and his people might decide to stay close, reclaim a chance they felt they had missed. He dismissed the consideration as soon as it crossed through his mind. Even in this time, respect for—or fear of—the retribution of the Enclaves should be more than enough to hold the conscriptionists at bay.

"I will have a fire lit in one of the guest houses for you," Machar said. "Please gather what you need for the evening and meet me back here. We'll see you settled."

How different from Kilras's first encounter with both raiders and the Bynkrol today had been.

He smiled. "Many thanks." He downed the last of the drink in his hand and placed the glass on the table on his way out into the storm.

35

Kilras

*V*AGUENESS BEYOND JUST THE DARK BLURRED THE EDGES OF SIGHT AS *stiff steps carried him over frozen ground. The night-time scent of cold pine marked the air. Little stirred, and as the wind shifted woodsmoke overtook the milder notes of winter darkness. Gloom surrounded, nerves tingled, and the itch of a too-long beard ricocheted through his mind. The high wall loomed close and wrongness clung like sweat. Trailing footsteps redoubled the feeling.*

Thoughts greyed, skipped, and then the door ahead swung open, illuminated by the blaze of a torch and the familiar but too-clean face of Vennan. Everything swam and tilted, went soft at the sides, strange and tight with violence.

Vennan spoke, "Quickly, uncle. While they're focused on the stranger."

The words brought attention back to the moment. A step inside, a shift along the wall, the others following. Wrong. Dark torches passed into hands, as they moved between buildings that exactly matched the layout in the map lowered over the wall in a bundle of supplies.

He took it all in amid a series of whispers and a free moment that would never have been possible had the Bynkrol not been called to war. The scent of blood and fire filled his mind like craving. At last. At last the vengeance so long denied would find fulfillment.

They touched cold torches to the hot flame of Vennan's and spread out, each with one hand filled by a weapon meant to cut and kill, the other with the means to bring the Enclave eternally to its knees.

Kilras snapped awake to heat and screams, every inch of his body demanding action. *Terror. Violence. Rage.*

Choking, he rolled from the narrow cot and pressed himself to the floor even as his hand grabbed for his boots and his sword. He looked up. The narrow window above the cabin's door was lit with dancing orange and crossed by billowing smoke. Behind him, with a roar, the wall erupted into flames.

He scrabbled away, crawled for the door. Not a dream. Not *just* a dream. Wistin and his men inside the compound. Bynk-rol afire. Behind the shock and confusion littering his thoughts, some reason lingered, lost in sleep-fogged recollection, of Vennan, of long held rage and hatred. Kilras had no time to sort the information as he pulled his shirt sleeve over his hand and surged up onto his knees long enough to grasp the handle and yank open the door. A glance into smoking chaos offered fast assessment, then he rolled over the threshold and into the ash-filled night.

Shouts and screams echoed off walls and down narrow passages. Understanding pounded through his head even as he shook off the last of the dream—the old, dangerous connections he had always been capable of had slipped his control, re-awakened. The question of why, he left for future consideration. He crouched low, threw open Gweld sense, and moved quickly around the corner of the burning house. Death. All around him, death. Blood and pain rippled through Gweld. Machar, and the Draigre who had prodded Kilras toward the wall, and the young cook who had made then evening meal—not one of the Bynkrol he had encountered earlier remained alive. He shuddered and bent his head.

In the flame-lit lee of the cabin, he tugged on and laced his boots, stood and strapped on the sword, and let his mind follow gold lights through the blazing darkness.

Smoked rolled and shrieks rose and fell. Shadows of running men flashed past—Bynkrol or raider he could not discern. The cold violence of the all the men reflected darkly against his expanded senses. Fear and anger roared like the rush of ash down a volcanic slope. Kilras quashed emotion. Swift decision demanded action in the face of destruction.

He drew his blade and made for the stables. Through rising chaos, Gweld guided his steps, told him where to pause, and where to move quickly. Sweat slicked over his body as waves of heat pounded him, swept aside by chills as dangerous warmth collided with bursts of cold air. His eyes refused adjustment to the shifting shadows of the mayhem, but he moved onward, careful, watchful, and made it to the barn without drawing blood.

Though every building around it was in flames, the stable, separated from the main compound by a wide paddock yard, remained unlit. Even bandits knew better than to harm horses. To mercenaries, they were of far more value than were the lives of the Bynkrol.

Kilras slipped inside to the wild neighing of terrified horses. The gelding, in the stall nearest the door, was, by barest measure, the calmest of the lot. But the horse settled as Kilras spoke the words Sehina trained each of her charges to recognize. Without her care and foresight, this night would be even more dangerous. The thanks he owed her was boundless, should he ever see her again.

One by one he turned the horses loose, then led his mount into the barn aisle and saddled it quickly, his mind turning through the items lost in the by-now-engulfed guest cabin. Habit and circumstance had combined into foresight, and he retrieved the small bag he had tucked under the feed tub in the stall. Fire starter, coin, dried meat, brekko and gloves, a spare knife. He would miss his coat and hat, but he had enough to get by until the next farm big enough to allow resupply. His fingers moved swiftly, and within moments, he led the gelding out into the glowing night. Heat blazed over him, the whole world seemingly afire and roaring. He choked, pulled up his brekko, and led the horse around the back of the stable, away from the inferno.

Behind him, screams rose again and he almost tasted blood on the air. Gweld glistened like flames, gold against the darkness. He wove toward the back of the compound, let his lights lead him, even as they traced the misery and destruction behind him. The dark edges of his talent trembled, and he forced himself onward, the night pressing cold against him the farther he moved from the fires.

Vennan. Vennan opened the door, let death into the Enclave. Would he have done so had Kilras not given the raiders an excuse to climb the mountain? The remains of the dream flickered in his mind, and echo of the conflagration behind him.

He reached the far wall, followed it east, careful and steady at the edges of the destruction. A patch of darkness ahead marked the entry he had come through earlier. Slowing, he reached up to touch the horse's neck as the animal snorted and sidestepped. Gweld surged, sought, marked the way ahead as safe enough, given the death and turmoil surrounding them.

No option existed for him to alter the brutal events unfolding within the brimstone inundated run that Bynkrol had become. Shivering, he pulled open the door and stepped into the mountain air beyond the wall. Icy wind whipped around him as he led the gelding over the frozen, snowy earth, the calamitous annihilation of war slicing bitter through the night behind him.

36

Cleod

THE ARCH OPENED INTO A WIDE COURTYARD FRONTING A TALL NARROW building with intricately carved stonework bordering the front entry. Soft light flickered from the mansion's windows, scattering shadows across white-scrubbed cobbles. Trayor swung down from his mount and handed the reins to a boy who appeared like a ghost, pale and silent. He led the horse through yet another gate, even as a second child stepped up beside Cleod and waited with wide eyes for him to dismount.

Cleod eased his leg over the pommel and slid his hip along the saddle until his feet found firm ground. The small hands that took the leads from him were dark as his own, and he looked into the face of a girl almost exactly Ain's age. His heart skipped, but she quickly dropped her gaze and moved away, soundless and swift as her counterpart.

For a heartbeat, thoughts blocked and blank, he stared after her as she led Kicce away. Then Trayor spoke his name with familiar exasperation, and hesitation vanished like misty breath.

Shouldering his pack, Cleod followed the Draighil up the short flight of stairs to the door. It swung open before they reached the top step, and a lean woman with grey-streaked hair ushered them inside with smooth words of greeting. Something about her raised a tingle at the back of Cleod's neck, but it wasn't until she raised her gaze to his, and he watched her eyes widen, that he recognized her. Not her name, but her face. And she was so far from the place he had last seen her that even after realizing he should know her, the answer to why took several seconds to arrive.

When the knowledge unfolded within him, rage followed quick upon it. *Right at home. A cefreid High Councilman.* In another space, another city, he would have drawn his sword and come straight to blows with the man standing across from him, if only to slice the knowing smile from his pale, scarred face. Because if this woman was here, only one man could reside in this house. Only the woman between them, and the deeper knowledge that such a reaction would satisfy Trayor immensely, stayed Cleod's hand.

Cleod's stomach churned. He drew a long breath, barely able to contain the surge of emotion threatening to breach his already shaky control.

"Hello, Cleod Woodcutter," the woman murmured, then pressed her lips together as her expression tightened and her voice thinned. "Pardon, Sere. I know that's no longer your name. You are...Draighil...once again?"

"No, Elda Kitchener," Trayor said. "Please tell the Councilman we are here."

The woman flicked her attention to Trayor, then immediately back to Cleod. "He knows, Seres. The guard sent notice when you came through the city gates."

Elda. Cleod Woodcutter. Dragonflies flitting at the edges of a pond on a hot summer day. Cleod shook his head to clear his mind.

This house.

"Klem Councilman is expecting us then?" he asked, and folded down the anger that tightened his throat as Trayor laughed.

"Huh!" The Draighil shrugged from his coat and handed it to Elda. "That took you less time than I thought it might. Not exactly an old friend of yours—but perhaps more of one than the girl."

Cleod met the blond man's gaze. "You enjoy that betrayal with all you are," he fired back, but even as he spoke he watched Elda's expression shift into careful neutrality. A tremor waved along the edges of his mind but he shoved it aside as he took a step toward Trayor. The other man pulled himself straighter and shifted his weight.

For a few more seconds silence thickened in the entryway, then Cleod, his gaze still on Trayor, eased out of his own outer garment and gave it into Elda's waiting grasp.

"My favored guests." Pitched to demand attention, the Spur accented voice came from above them. Cleod looked up. The balcony above wrapped the entryway, curving into a staircase that descended toward the back of the hall. Elda moved away before the words faded on the air. Her shoulder brushed Cleod's arm in passing, but he held his attention on the man standing at the top of the stairs with one hand on the gleaming railing.

Klem offered a smile with no humor or welcome, and time contracted and spilled backward like a bright leaf down a cascade.

Searing, open air. The pounding of drums and the pulse of thousands of voices shouting in fear and demand.

"Cleod, isn't it?"

Turning, and dropping his gaze to meet the other man's eyes. "Klem Sower."

"Klem Councilman." The correction pointed as a blade.

Cleod stared up at Leiel's younger brother. Time had refined him, the cut of his clothing, the sharpness of his gaze. Gone was the half-needy man who reached for approval on the balcony of Adfen Tower. Klem stood now with a poise that spoke of one used to power and the confidence it engendered.

"We deserving ones find our way to rise above our provincial beginnings."

Breathing shallow and too fast, Cleod held himself still as Klem descended the stairs and Trayor walked, hand outstretched, to meet him at the bottom.

The familiarity that accompanied their greeting rocked Cleod like an echo in too small a space. Their words blurred to confusion in his ears. The formality of the moment shifted, bordered by banter that spoke of depths that might normally be revealed only in long conversation. However uninformed the King might have been all these years, Klem, clearly, had not faced that disadvantage.

Trayor and Klem Sower—Klem Councilman—the man who had sent his own sister into the Draigon's clutches. Sent her to become what she was today. Turned her from someone in need of saving into something that now needed to be destroyed. Cleod's throat burned as though any words he would utter would scorch both himself and any to whom he spoke.

Trayor pivoted to face Cleod, leaving space for Klem to descend the final step.

"Ahhh...the former Draighil turned mercenary guard." Klem's gaze swept Cleod from head to foot and back as he crossed the small distance between them. "The years have been...unkind to you. But it seems Elder Trayor was able to put you to use after all." He flicked a brief glance at Trayor before offering a hand to Cleod. "Congratulations on your destruction of Shaa. More than twenty years late, but a victory, still."

Somewhere in the fugue of the too-comfortable conversation, Trayor had shared news of that death. Cleod tipped his head to the side, unable to claim the offered hand, unable to speak for the bitterness straining his throat.

Klem laughed with a hearty joy beyond what the moment demanded, and lowered his hand as Trayor stepped up beside him.

"We have better news than even that, Councilman."

"Better than the death of Shaa?" Klem turned from Cleod to gesture down the hallway. "Then we should have a seat in my office."

He led the way, paused at the door and called toward the back of the house, "Elda!" When she stepped quickly into the hallway he demanded, "Warm drinks."

She nodded and stepped away, vanishing into a room beyond the staircase.

Klem glanced at Cleod, then entered his office, Trayor a pace behind.

Cleod drew a breath, then forced his feet to motion, and followed. The room was all he expected—dark paneled, thick rugged, with a desk like a throne that Klem settled behind—every detail unoriginal and designed for intimidation. Cleod's thoughts moved sluggishly, but recollection demanded attention—despite his pettiness, Leiel's brother had always been too ruthless and intentional to be disregarded.

"Sit." Klem's tone made the word an order, not a comfort offered to travel-weary guests.

Cleod stood just inside the doorway as Trayor stopped behind a straight backed chair but did not take it.

"As you please," Klem said after a few seconds, as though a subtle battle of slights and slight gestures was nothing more or less than expected.

With a deliberateness of his own, Trayor stepped around the chair and lowered himself into it, crossed his ankle over his knee, and leaned back. "Your hospitality is lacking, Councilman. But the news we bring will force you to remedy that."

"You've told me the beast is dead at last," Klem folded his hands atop the desk, shifted his gaze to Cleod. "Something I had hoped for, when we chose *you*, Cleod Woodcutter. After all, we asked for you with a purpose all those years ago. Your...relationship...with Leiel Sower assured that you would fight harder to kill Shaa than would any other. We were pleased to have you with us on the Tower that day."

Leiel's name on her brother's lips hung stiff and vile. And something else about Klem's choice of words curled tension through Cleod's belly. He narrowed his gaze. "Though, as you've made clear, you were not so pleased with my lack of achievement on the Spur."

Klem freed a hand to wave in dismissal. "You lived to finish the fight, even if you failed the girl."

"But he didn't," Trayor said, a slow grin spreading over his lips. "She failed him."

Klem snapped his attention to the Draighil. "Your news gives you no leave to play foolish games."

"Your sister lives." Trayor spoke with a relish that rippled the air in the room.

Klem's face went stiff, and his hands clenched as though in spasm. "Did you not hear my warning?"

Trayor leaned toward the other man just enough to emphasize his low-spoken reply. "Some games cannot be won until all the rules are disclosed. Brace yourself to receive the final key to long denied victory." He grinned, his pause full of satisfaction. "The Draigon are human."

Whatever reaction that statement dragged from Klem faded from Cleod's awareness as the words ricocheted in his skull, as pinging and brutal as they had been when he himself uttered them—a truth so vile as to be unfathomable.

Distantly, he heard Trayor continue. "Did you not hear? *The Draigon are as human and vulnerable as you.*" Then, behind Cleod, the rattle of crockery announced the arrival of Elda in the doorway. He looked over his shoulder to find her stiff-faced and motionless, but the look in her eyes was not shock or fear. It was fury.

"Explain yourself, Trayor Draighil!" Klem's voice cracked through the air, but Cleod kept his gaze on the motionless cook. A heartbeat more she stood, then she backed out of the room and returned the way she had come, the loaded tray clattering in her grasp.

As Trayor spoke forceful reply, Cleod obeyed frayed instinct and followed Elda out into the hall.

37

Cleod

SHE DISAPPEARED INTO THE KITCHEN BEHIND THE STAIRS AND HE moved after her. From the entry, he watched as she set the tray down on a table and planted her palms against the polished wood surface. The tension in her shoulders trembled the air even as she took several deep breaths. A moment passed, two, then she straightened and turned with a purpose. Her gaze found him where he stood in the doorway.

Pure bravery confronted him as she clenched her jaw and held his stare. And—old gods—so familiar, the look on her face.

He remembered that expression from his childhood, from Leiel—the look that announced she would outlast his every attempt to dissuade her from her position. He had assumed she learned it from her mother. But perhaps Leiel discovered it in working long hours in the kitchen with the woman before him.

"What do you know?" He narrowed his eyes. "What do you know of the Draigon?"

"Sere, I don't know what you mean."

The lie burned his ears. "You do." He stepped closer, shoulders squared so his height carried him into the room.

She trembled, but stared up into his face in pure refusal to be intimidated, the grey in her hair not weakness but armor. When confronted with false accusation, most people slid into either fear or ferocity. She offered neither, and that added depth to his suspicion. Before he could say more, she spoke.

"I remember you." Her voice was cracked a little by time, but warm as memory. "The boy who came with Ellan to stack wood beside the bulkhead. The one who made Leiel smile when nothing, and no one else, could." Unexpectedly, she raised a hand as though to touch him, but stopped before contact. "The man who tried to save her even when she begged him not to."

Never had he spoken of his final conversations with Leiel. Not even Kilras knew what had transpired in the Tower, how she had begged him not to face Shaa on the Spur. *Leiel, backlit in the low light of the window, a breeze moving her hair, sadness in her eyes.* An army of needles pierced his mind. "How did you...?"

"Because she told me she would," Elda said. "She told me she would try to save your life." She lowered her hand.

Pent and too-long-undirected fury erupted through him and he took a step forward before he could contain it.

Her expression clenched, but she said, "And she did it. And here you stand." Fear flickered in her gaze, but she repeated, "*Here you stand.*"

For a heartbeat, his entire body was afire with violent potential, then the anger went out of him like water draining from a battered bucket. *Here he stood.* He and *not Leiel.* The girl this woman raised had climbed a mountain to her doom, and all Elda likely knew about it was that Leiel had promised to see Cleod live through that terrible encounter that took her away. The truth was far, far worse. But *what was he doing*? How would hurting this women, hurting *anyone but the Draigon* change anything? Sudden heat burned his face.

With a harsh exhale, he stepped back. She just stood looking at him in as much confusion as distress.

Had Elda understood the implications of Trayor's announcement in the study? Or had she heard the idea of the humanity of the Draigon and dismissed it as another excuse for the Enclaves and Klem to practice their manipulations?

Even with proof bloody before them, the Council of Melbis had struggled to believe. Unreasonable to assume that a quiet cook would possess less skepticism than those men.

Cleod shook his head, watched some of the stiffness ease from Elda's shoulders. "You need to understand." Even as he spoke the words, his thoughts rebelled. Why must she acknowledge anything? What explanation did he owe her? His headache returned, a harsh, pulsing pain across his forehead, but he continued. "Trayor spoke the truth. The Draigon are *women*. And Leiel is alive. *She's one of them. A monster.*"

She stared up into his face, and her expression shifted into a glare that defined contempt, then to one of utter incredulity. "Only a fool would ever believe Leiel a monster. A fool or a brute looking to blame another for the ills of his life." She shook her head, paused, her eyes briefly distant, measuring some internal reckoning. "She loved you. She saved you. She was never the cause of—" she lifted a hand and swept it downward in full measure of his current state "—*this.*"

Astonishment sucked the moisture from his mouth, and he stared at her without blinking until the edges of his vision burned. The layered insult of her response slashed so sharp that he almost missed the heart of her response. Or rather what it lacked: shock. No surprise carried through her words, no wonder of revelation unfolded at his declaration. No horror. No delight.

She *did* know. Had she always? Old gods and fire, was he the only one who had been left to struggle in bitter darkness all these years? Anger flared again, bright and rippling as Gweld cracked him open like a lightning flash.

Deep inside his skull a shriek rose, sharp and desperate, and he stumbled back, rage checked by pure will. For a harsh drawn breath he stood trembling, struggling for control.

Alone in bitter darkness. In a violent tumble of recognition, his mind awakened to the *wrongness* of that thought. Because Leiel had *tried to tell him.* In her own way, in the hardest moment, with stone walls unyielding around them and a dry breeze struggling in the air, she had sought to move him just as that low wind strove against the heat—determined yet unsuccessful in the fire of that cruel moment's demands.

His belly cramped as need gripped him, a thirst to shut out all pain and all dark thoughts. How many understandings, how many promises, had he drowned in that all-consuming desire? How many times had it been easier to stare into a foul mug than into his heart?

Another stumble moved him farther from Elda. Inexplicably, she followed, and something shifted in her eyes as she reached again, and this time touched his arm. "Whatever you've made of yourself, her choices allowed you that freedom. And if your choice is now to destroy her, then you have her to thank for allowing you the option."

Easier to parry the strike of hard steel than the impact of those words. He stood silent for a moment that felt endless, then asked, "Have you always known?"

A few seconds of hesitation, then she shook her head. "Not until she told me, when Klem made it clear she would be chosen. And even then I didn't believe it. Not until they carried you, alive, from the Spur. I knew then that she'd kept her promise. That she'd been right about everything. Even the stories." She released him and stepped back. "Especially about those."

"Stories?" His thoughts stumbled as he tried to follow the change in subject. "What do stories have to do with Draigon?"

She stepped around the work table in the center of the room and began clearing the tea service from the tray. "Everything," she answered, lifting her gaze to meet his once again, before returning her full attention to her work. But the simple chore could not hold her focus and she stopped her hands, looked at him. "Haven't you believed all the tales the world has told you, about who you are and why? Or at least enough of them to think you're owed more than others in this life?"

For a moment he was back in Melbis, the heat of the poit soaking his bones and the fire of tears streaking his face as regret spilled from his pores like sweat. "What stories was Leiel right about, Elda?"

"The ones her mother told her. About the past when women were free." Shock must have etched itself into his face, because she smiled. "Did you think Ilora Sower was sent up the mountain for something less dire than the truth?"

Truth? What was that? Was anything he had ever cared about, put faith in, less than a lie? He shook his head to sweep away the unwelcome notion. "What stories, Elda?" he asked again.

She shook her head. "None for your ears. Not when you'll use them to kill her."

Frustration burned his throat and he shook his head vehemently. "A story can't kill anyone."

"It can if enough people believe it," she said so quietly that he had to lean toward her to hear. "There's power in lies. Why else do the greedy so love to tell them?"

He blinked, and the room came sharply into focus. The dim-lit kitchen with its spotless floor and organized shelves. The small, wiry woman with work-battered hands in the center of it. Klem's kitchen. Klem's home. And the defiant—no, the *dangerous*—honesty of Elda's words. Why was she so willing to speak? In this place of all places and to him of all people?

To him.

"You've seen her," he whispered.

The tension fled her face as it melted into sadness. "No."

He studied her, the subtle pain that marked every line of her face. The negative response was simple truth, and the ache of it went deep.

"I have," he said, and watched defiance return to her gaze as it held his.

"Then she's still trying to save you," Elda said. "I hope you're worthy of what that will cost."

"Cost?"

"You're here with *him*. He's never come to this house without leaving pain behind. Even Klem fears that Draighil, no matter the face he puts on."

Cleod's headache grew as he struggled to follow her through yet another shift in focus. From anger to confusion to crisp flashes of almost-understanding, since the moment he entered the kitchen, Elda's words twisted and jabbed. A thin line of sweat broke across his brow as he stared at her, trying to make sense of the growing strangeness of the encounter.

"You're thirsty," she said, and to his utter disbelief she reached under the table and retrieved two bottles of ercew.

He stared. Ercew? In this house? Unease turned in his chest. How had she possibly...? But the look she gave him as she slid the containers toward him, squelched his questions with pure intention. Louder than if she had spoken the words, her action said *If you're damn fool enough to take up with Trayor and Klem, you'll need to be drunk to live with that choice.*

38

Cleod

"YOU'VE A HABIT OF DISAPPEARING AT CRITICAL MOMENTS." TRAYOR stepped into the kitchen doorway, his gaze assessing the room.

"I wasn't needed for that conversation." Cleod looked over his shoulder as he put an empty bottle on the table, setting it aside, along with deeper consideration of Elda's words, especially her answer to his last question. *There was a girl, from Hengbaith—Ain? She fled in the snow. Fled me. Elda nodded, eyes sad. If she lives, I will find her.* He turned, newly opened replacement in hand, to face the Draighil. "I remember Klem Sower's tantrums from childhood." Too well. Too clearly. And the adult version of Klem's satisfied cruelty, he had experienced only once. That was beyond enough.

Darkness and damnation that all the long roads he had traveled brought him around to face that pettiness again. A small kindness from Elda, to offer him these choice beverages before she fled the house. The wisdom of *that* choice, in the wake of their conversation, warranted admiration.

And the intensity of her words still vibrated the kitchen air. *I hope you're worthy.* Had he ever been? Stories. Promises. Lies. He slammed the doubts away. *Finish it. Finish it all at last.* He tipped the bottle up and took a long swallow, let the burn of the bitter liquor snake through him. The room blurred around him.

With a snarl of disgust, Trayor half-pivoted in the doorway. "I suppose he remembers *you* as a drunk. Both living up to your reputations tonight." He scoffed. "Pull yourself together. We've got a King to wake."

"The King?" Cleod stared after Trayor, then followed him into the hallway. "You plan to awaken Rawden?" The audacity of the idea seemed beyond even Enclave arrogance. And in it was the answer to the question of whether Trayor recognized the potential danger in the knowledge he held.

"We do indeed, Woodcutter," Klem said as he descended the staircase once again, this time dressed in formal court clothes and a fine, ankle length coat of a lush red fabric Cleod could not identify. "News such as this cannot be held in silence, even for a night."

Whatever shock Trayor's revelation had awoken in Klem clearly sat buried under the thrill of being the one to bring the information to the highest power in the land. "You're certain of yourself. Such an intrusion won't possibly be welcomed."

"*Only* such an intrusion will be welcomed. This land has waited more than a thousand years for this day. No ruler of this land would be ungrateful to receive the solution to the problem of the Draigon."

Cleod tipped his head and raised both eyebrows, then tilted up the bottle and drained it to the dregs. Fools, the lot of them. Himself, perhaps most of all. "And you think he'll happily hear that from a pair of cefreid? One a drunk, at that?"

He released the bottle. The other men jumped as it shattered against the stone floor in a spray of glass and reeking liquid, and the roll of curses they both uttered pulled a laugh from the depths of Cleod's belly. He strode through the mess, past them, and pulled open the door to step into the night. "What are we waiting for, if he'll be so pleased to see us?"

Stomach churning against the unfamiliar sway, Cleod gazed out the window of the carriage, watched snow kick from beneath the wheels. He swallowed hard, tense on the padded bench, as jolts over cobbled streets forced him against Trayor. Seated opposite, Klem settled into the journey as though being rattled in such a manner was the height of elegance.

As they drew nearer to the center of the city, the streets emptied and everything grew quieter. The interruption of horse hooves and iron-wrapped wheels echoing on stone drew more than a few from bed to fling windows open, heads peeking forth to measure the passing disturbance.

At last the coach slowed, and Cleod lifted his thin attention to the castle that claimed the heart of Sibora. It did not loom over the city, but rather announced its stature by the height of a thick foundation that raised it a few stories over the surrounding buildings. In the icy moonlight, the castle gleamed, the glass in its casements reflecting stars as they dimmed under slowly gathering clouds.

In all his years visiting this city, no business had required that he approach the castle. It was not imposing, though the elegant lines and carved stonework clearly were meant to impress on a more subtle level. Odd that. He had never met a Farlan he considered much capable of great nuance. Perhaps such was still the province of royalty.

Few lights burned in the windows of the upper stories, but the courtyard where the carriage trundled to a halt glowed with blazing sconces. Footsteps approached, voices raised in concern and confusion as the driver climbed from his perch to fold down the step and open the door. Silence fell as Klem descended in all his finery, and questions filled the air anew when Trayor and Cleod followed. The chill air plucked at him, tugging him toward a sobriety he did not want.

"At this hour? You cannot actually intend that we wake His Grace!" Standing before a pair of tall, carved doors, a man in court livery, his face flush with indignation, faced Klem. Moonlight retreated behind overcast, and snow whispered down, reflecting lamplight.

"Do you think I enjoy traveling in the night in this weather?" Klem's words were crisp in the chill air, his breath puffing mist as though for emphasis. "Or that I would arrive here, like this, with these particular companions with a message of no importance? More the fool, you."

The Courtman flicked his attention to Trayor and Cleod, confusion shifting to shock across his face as recognition dawned. "Draighil!"

"We bring important word of the Draigon," Trayor said, with all the city-born haughtiness Cleod remembered from their youth. "For King Rawden's ears alone." Never less than purely refined, even Trayor's accent shifted to include the bite reserved for those he held absolutely inferior.

It had been decades since Cleod heard that supremely arrogant intonation, but the man at the door read the threat behind the controlled diction, and he gave a quick nod, and opened the door to usher them into a grand entry hall. What the building lacked in towering height it more than gained in interior glory.

Marble and tapestry and thick rugs, the gleam of impeccably clean surfaces, the scent of cut flowers and undeniable wealth—all the trappings of a nobility only ever witnessed by a privileged few. Head tilted back to take in the majesty of the building, Cleod walked through the echo of their footsteps into the depths of the palace. A glance at the man striding beside him brought the twitch of a smile to Cleod's lips. Try though he might to project surety, Trayor's jaw was loose in awe, his shoulders taut in a determined attempt to retain dignified control.

Cleod's thoughts cleared enough for an unexpected realization—whatever communication Trayor had shared with the King had not taken place in person. What did that mean for the plans the Draighil had assumed to be fully embraced?

Ahead, wide doors swung open to reveal a long, narrow room with no rugs on the white floor, and with a balcony at the far end. On it, a single, stark chair overlooked the space. Every few paces, men in formal uniforms with swords at their hips lined the walls. Two stood directly under the balcony, armed, also, with polished spears.

The Courtman led the way into the space, stopped a third of the distance from the chair. He raised a hand and, with a formal glare, indicated that they should wait. He stepped through a side door.

Klem said nothing, just waited. The dark echo of Cleod's breathing pulsed loud in a space that seemed to demand quiet. Even Trayor, always desperate for the final word, pressed his lips together in silence. Some rule of etiquette here before royalty? Perhaps Kilras would know.

Cleod blinked and caught his breath as the room swam a little before him *Probably the man does exist* as a strange voice rang in his thoughts. He shook it away. And Kilras was gone. That life was gone. What happened in this room would determine what remained.

A whisper of movement and the wall—no, heavy curtain—behind the chair shifted and a blue-dressed servant appeared. "His Grace, Rawden, High King of Arnan."

A slender young man wrapped in a gold brocade cloak slipped past the servant to stand beside the chair. Cleod stared at the Farlan King, a man to whom he had given so little thought through the years that until tonight he had rarely heard the royal's name spoken. What use had he ever had to know or care for nobility? Only the Ehlewer had mattered. And after that, only anything that was not the Ehlewer. But here he stood in the presence of a man able to, with a word, direct the wealth and power of Arnan. The thought should impress, but instead left Cleod simply amused—finally someone Trayor could not lord over. *Here you stand.* Gooseflesh crawled up Cleod's arms.

The slim newcomer gazed down at them with eyes half filled by sleep, then he moved a step sideways and eased into the chair. The very air in the room seemed to settle with him, as though he claimed it along with the high seat. From one to the other, his attention moved with careful intent, until at last it found focus on Klem.

"I'm told you've brought important word of the Draigon, Klem Councilman. What I want to know is why *you* bring it to me, instead of the Draighil with whom I had made private agreement. Or rather—" his words went brittle in the air, "why that Draighil brought such news to *you* before *me*."

Beside Cleod, tension pulled Trayor straighter, but Klem simply stepped forward and raised both hands in a gesture of supplication. "My apologies, Your Grace, it is simply that the hour of the Draighil's arrival was so late and—"

"And yet it is now later still." Rawden raised the first three fingers of his right hand and flicked them to the side.

For the briefest instant no one moved, then Klem fell silent and shifted a half step sideways leaving Cleod and Trayor in the fore. A night for the improbable—an audience with royalty and someone who could cow Klem. If the trend continued, Cleod might find himself, by morning, head of the Palace Guard. He smiled.

The man on the balcony glanced at Cleod, raised his eyebrows a fraction, then returned attention to Trayor. "Step forward, Draighil, and explain yourself."

Cleod

DRENCHED IN MORE FORMALITY THAN CLEOD HAD ENCOUNTERED FOR years, the explanation of the events in Melbis poured forth. Within Cleod, clear recognition of the danger inherent in that rose. But even had he possessed sober words to express warning, even had Trayor been willing to listen, it was too late. What came from this meeting would be earned by them all.

If the tale Trayor offered was the cleanest version that he had uttered since the fight, it woke less awe and consternation in the monarch than it had in the roughest drunk along the trail.

Bending his head slightly, Cleod listened as though from afar, as though the King's emotionless attentiveness flattened the memories roused by the retelling. Present on that hill though Cleod had been, some events surrounding that night defied explanation. Why had Shaa offered herself to Trayor's sword? How were monsters capable of selfless acts? What had happened to the blood that soaked the ground? What had held the weather in violent thrall despite the destruction of the Draigon? Unless Leiel—he stopped the thought, forced his attention back to the interplay of word and truth and destruction filling the air.

Just in time, that shift in focus, as the King leaned back slightly in his seat and looked to Cleod. "And you, Draighil—if so you might still be called. Do *you* so assess the situation? That the woman who died in Melbis was the...Queen...of Draigons? That all women taken to their deaths do not in fact receive them, but instead earn a place among the beasts?"

Cleod pulled himself as straight as the remainder of the er-cew swirling in his gut would allow, and stepped up beside Tray-or. The dismissal and skepticism in the King's words drove home the hard point—that disbelief might be Trayor's only true advantage. Strange that Trayor's words stood for little in this place. What did that mean for all his vaunted plans? Was it blessing or disaster that would be born from that distrust?

Elda's fearful yet determined glare. Ain's stunned face, crumpled with sadness. With a nod that echoed through his skull, Cleod answered, "I do not think it serves us any longer to think of the Draigon as simply beasts."

"You say?"

Beasts. Leiel. The abandoned caravan and Kilras and Sehina and Rimm. What more did he have to lose to the truth? It came forth without thought, strange to his ears but filled with a *rightness* he had not felt in weeks. "Unless we wish to insist that *women* have also only been nothing more." The words hung blazing in the air. Beside him, Trayor gave a hiss of warning.

The King smiled without a trace of amusement. "For a man set to kill such a creature even though once you called it friend—don't look so shocked I know who you are—you have a high opinion of the Draigon."

Did he? *The Draigon are what they have always been.* Kilras had been right. What would his old friend think of this meeting, this moment, the unmatched levels of power claimed in every word? Would he stare in rare awe, or simply shake his head? "A thousand years they have been a worthy enemy. That alone earns a level of respect."

Rawden offered a grin that made him appear even younger. "Indeed, on that we can agree." He slipped his glance to Trayor, then back to Cleod. "And you'll kill them?"

Smoke and fire and pain that seared from skull to hips. Kill Draigon. What else was there, anymore? "It is what I have worked for since my youth."

"Then let me rephrase, *Arnani*. If this is truth you bring me—will you kill *her*?"

Cleod fought the desire to step back. Then he stiffened his spine and nodded. "I must." The whisper of Leiel's finger across his lips. "For what she cost me." *A column of steam burning into the too-bright sky. Blood running over his hand from a cut on a woman's throat.* "For what she has become."

"Intimate...yes, that is best. That kind of anger is not easily swayed." Rawden looked at Trayor. "And yours is the same—with this one beside you." The King narrowed his gaze. "Or did you not think I knew how personal this fight is to *you*?" His smiled etched itself full but stiff across his face. "Or what you desire at the end of this war?"

Trayor did not flinch, but Cleod recognized the ripple of unease that seeped from the edges of the Draighil's smile. "Your Grace, what I desire is only an end to the beasts that have spent generations haunting our land. Nothing more."

"Nothing more? And what use are the Enclaves or the Draighil, in a world without Draigon to destroy? What use are you, at all, in fact, if the Draigon can be killed as simply as any woman?"

Never able to keep true emotion from his face for long, the way Trayor's expression stiffened spoke of more than shock—it marked a level of unwelcome self-realization that Cleod had never expected to witness in the other man.

Rawden held the Draighil's gaze. "Do not take me for the same level of fool that you take your friend. You will stay here with me and *explain* your plans for the future—what you intend to do with all your glory and the Enclaves' archived knowledge. Then, if I am satisfied with your intentions, you will escort myself, Klem Councilman, and a division of my army, north to Adfen. There, you will tear down the Old City, stone by stone, beginning with the Tower."

The words entered Cleod's skull as though they traveled through water, stretched and muffled. His body, long attuned to react ahead of thought, trembled, his heart skipping, before understanding reached his mind.

"Tear down Adfen? Your Grace—" Klem stepped forward, his face tight as his voice.

"It was your home. Your *sister's* home. If she is, as you say, a Draigon—and as strangely sentimental as her actions in Melbis imply—what better way to ensure you know where she will focus her forces than to destroy the place she called home?"

Adfen destroyed. The ancient Tower's stone broken and scattered. Cleod tried to imagine it—the city of his birth stark rubble, the Spur looming over nothing but burned farms and smoldering debris as wind and lightning further scarred the landscape. Because how else could a war with the Draigon end but with fire and storm?

Trayor took a step forward, ignoring the way the Spearmen tightened their grips on their swords. "Your Grace—this man with me is only recently returned to his work with the Enclaves. It is early yet to trust him with your—"

"He assisted you in killing Shaa, and you declare him unreliable?"

"He has long been out of—"

"And yet here he stands before *me*." The King's tone matched the walls of the palace. He dropped his chin and stared. "Should my guards *act*?" The men along the walls pulled straighter, blades slicking from scabbards, and the Spearmen leveled their weapons.

Threat awakened Gweld, the air shimmering as connection rolled forth, instinct encountering Trayor's also awakened response. That alone shocked Cleod back into the moment. He locked his jaw and slammed his expanded senses closed with a force that foamed his already churning stomach.

Beside him, a visible tremor rocked Trayor, and Cleod raised a hand to stop Klem's movement toward the Draighil. "Don't." For whom the warning was meant, Cleod was uncertain, but the situation demanded it be expressed for all. Not even Gweld would allow him and Trayor to stand unharmed against the number of armed men in the room. And not even the number of men in the room would save the King's life.

Cleod looked to Rawden. "A city in ruins."

"Better than many cities in ruins."

"Focus the fight." Even as he spoke, something tingled the back of Cleod's skull—the knowledge that Leiel was vital, somehow, to the Draigon—her presence beside Shaa in Melbis was alone enough to prove that. Somehow the King knew that. No wonder Trayor wanted to take this man's place. To do so would prove the Draighil as clever as he had long believed he was. "Force them to our choice of battleground." Was that what Trayor was doing as well? Cleod's head pounded.

Rawden smiled. "Being outcast seems to have done you little harm." He clenched a fist, then opened it, and the guards relaxed their aggressive stances. "Calm yourselves. We've much to discuss before dawn."

40

Kilras – 17 Years

KINRA OFFERED HIM A RARE SMILE OF APPROVAL AS THEY STEPPED away from each other on the practice platform. "You've been practicing with someone other than me."

He blinked. She was rarely so direct with her praise, so he simply offered a puzzled nod. "With Wynt. And Aweir."

Her smile slowly widened. "Ah. You've discovered our horse-master's secret skill." She dropped to the ground and headed for the storage building, offered him a glance over her shoulder, a question in her eyes. "How'd you convince Aweir to pick up a blade?"

He rolled a stiff shoulder then hopped down and followed her. "I caught her and Wynt practicing and accused her of teaching Wynt new ways to best me."

Kinra's reply was a satisfied grunt as she disappeared into the building. By the time he joined her, she had racked her weapon and vanished into the back room. He grabbed a towel and began to wipe down his practice blade.

"You don't seem surprised."

"I'm not. I assume she agreed to teach you as well so you and Wynt could learn new things from each other?" Kinra called.

He paused his work. How had she known that? "Yes. How—?"

"She did the same thing to me and Hech years ago." Kinra leaned part way out of the other room. "Don't leave yet."

She ducked away before he could respond so he sheathed the blade, returned it to its place on the wall, and waited. "More lessons?"

"Not as such," she replied.

Kilras pulled off his wet shirt, slung it across his shoulder and ran his hands up to push back his sweat-soaked hair. Even though the sun would soon set, the swimming hole beckoned. For a moment he let himself imagine the icy water closing over his head, then Kinra's words penetrated his tired mind. Aweir had—? "Wait, Aweir taught you and Hech?"

A low chuckle came from the back. "Do you think I was the first sword trainer here?"

He had honestly never considered anything else. But why not? Long lived as they were, why would they not be skilled in many things? Gahree was a thousand years old, and Gydron nearly that. And Kinra and Aweir and Hech—well he had never asked their ages at all. He shook his head at his own foolishness. "I never thought about it."

"Huh," Kinra grunted as she stepped into the main room with a long, oil-cloth-wrapped bundle in her hands. "Don't keep making that mistake. People are always more than what you see them doing in the moment. And always even more than what you see them do from day to day."

His face heated. Did the Draigon never stop teaching? He nodded. "I'll remember."

She smiled. "Don't think about it now. Think about this instead." She pulled away the oil-cloth to reveal a shining, black scabbard from which protruded the burgundy-leather wrapped hilt of a sword.

He stared at it a long moment as all thoughts of swimming fled. The skilled construction of the scabbard alone meant that the blade it contained was too fine to be a new practice sword.

"Take it out," Kinra said with a tip of her head. She handed it to him and took a step back.

Hardly daring to believe what she might be offering, he reached down and lifted the scabbard. It was light in his hand. And when he folded his fingers around the hilt and slid the sword free, the easy balance of the weapon took his breath. The steel gleamed with a subtle weaving pattern that spoke of metal folded more times than he could begin to count. The handle fit his hand to perfection, and as he drew it in a slow arc it was obvious that it had been designed to allow the wielder to fight in a variety of styles. After a long moment of examination, he pulled his attention from the weapon and looked at Kinra where she stood in the middle of the room, arms folded across her chest, a knowing grin on her face.

"Good. You like it."

"Kinra I—"

"It's yours." She nodded. "Take good care of it."

He shook his head in wonder. "When did you—"

"I've been working on it for weeks." She laughed a little. "Wynt picked out the color for the handle leather. You can blame her if it's not to your taste."

He looked down at the sword, tightened his grip on the hilt, feeling the grain and texture of the leather under his palm. "It's perfect," he said, then smiled and shook his head. "Or as close as I'll ever need to that."

She laughed again. "I'm glad. Go on. Take it out and move with it. I'll leave you alone to learn it." She turned away.

"Kinra—thank you." The belated gratitude seemed too little to offer in appreciation of such a gift.

She glanced over her shoulder and winked. "We'll put it to a true test tomorrow. Enjoy."

He stood for a long time after she left, just examining the sword in his hand, feeling its weight, easing into the belief that this stunning blade was his, had been crafted *specifically* for him. For Kinra to take the time and care to make him a weapon so unique and deadly—the message behind the gift was clear. She believed he learned enough to be worthy of it. She believed he understood the value of that knowledge.

His smile crept wider until his cheeks ached from grinning.

With a whoop of delight, he trotted back outside and hopped back onto the training platform. Excitement burned his veins and he forced himself to pause, take deep breaths until he settled into the rhythm of the tension and, balanced within it, moved slowly into the first pattern of movement Kinra had taught him so many years ago.

After only a moment, he moved the blade as though he had always wielded it. Driven by more than simple exertion, the pounding of his heart filled his ears, and his blood pushed through his body in elation. He let himself laugh, then stretched his focus and settled into a new series meant to lead him, one motion after the other, through the entirety of his skilled knowledge.

What a defense he could offer with this blade! As his breath came harder and his heart thudded in equal effort, more than his body flushed with energy. Sweat spilled down his back and arms, and he opened himself to Gweld until the air tasted of fine wine, and the sky overhead seemed to vibrate with a music born from the flux of billowing clouds.

Every step, every purposeful pause in the form, emphasized the perfection of the sword—as it worked for him. Another might wield it and find appreciation of its quality, the skill of the maker, but understanding grew with each motion, that this blade was *his*, as no other could ever be. Created with him in mind to meet his every strength and weakness, designed for his potential, what Kinra had given him this day was more than steel. The sword hummed in his hand, the confidence it inspired outmatching that logically born from all the years of his training. More than a bright edge. He pivoted, pulled balance taut within, and brought the sword to rest at his side. More than power.

Was this, perhaps, her way of showing him the way to merge all the pieces of himself—student and master, warrior and dancer, destroyer and seeker? From anger to poise, the sword was a compass needle meant to guide his very soul. So simple an implement to test every part of him, every day. All that remained was the daily struggle to remain worthy of the faith behind such a gift.

In this moment, it meant all that he hoped and dreamed it would, but clear honesty demanded acknowledgment—the sword was only a tool. Any more meaning came only from within. He smiled wryly. A thought worthy of Gahree.

At last he settled, a slowing of motion backed by pure satisfaction, and let himself simply breathe with the sword balanced in his hand. A beautiful tool to be treated as such and nothing more, no matter who or what he encountered with it in his hand.

41

Cleod

SLOW. SLOW TO GATHER—THE FIGHTERS, THE SUPPLY WAGONS, COOKS, horse minders, smiths, and scouts, and the several hundreds of other people needed to support an army on the move. The weeks it took—that forced Cleod to linger in Sibora in the company of Trayor and Klem—did nothing to curb his need for ercew. Planning sessions and training time drove a different pain through his body until he sweated the liquor from his very bones. Those things filled the daylight hours, but the nights allowed too much time for thought, especially since they were spent under Klem's roof. Each night, he drank again, pillaging the cupboards to meet his body's frantic demand.

Elda failed to return to the house and her duties, and a search through the city did not discover where she had gone. Klem's fury at her desertion was matched only by his shock that it had happened at all. The new cook, timid and not as skilled as Elda, drove him to roaring fury every time she failed to prepare a meal the way he expected. At that, Cleod smiled as he imagined the shock Klem would face at life on the trail and the food that accompanied it. Then the smile faded as he considered how many such tirades Leiel must have endured in Klem's house.

But now, at last, they traveled east and north through icy air and heavy snows. Slow still, over the trail toward Adfen, especially where it narrowed. Slow and loud and heavy with foul odor. It filled the air, rancid and clinging. Everything lingered too long, above all, Cleod's thoughts, and especially the strange emotions lodged in the back of his throat that he refused to name as grief and guilt.

And despite his years with the Caravan, the unrelenting noise of such a mass of humanity tore at Cleod's nerves and drove the already constant pounding in his head to a violent rhythm. Between that, and the churn of his gut, not even riding at the head of the column could calm him enough to allow him to sleep through the night.

The racket and gruff laughter and the worried half-heard conversations of the men invaded his dreams—brutal addition to the strangeness that tore through them night after night. If he remembered only a fraction of the images that permeated his mind in the loneliest hours, the feelings they awoke lingered well past dawn—the wonder, the confusion, the loss. Always loss. The noisy camp drove the shadows from his mind upon waking, but the feelings required ercew to force down.

And word had come of hundreds of people assembled on the road to Adfen. Not soldiers, but farmers and merchants and teachers, all armed. And the spies Rawden sent ahead brought word that the strange army was not gathered to assist the King and his fighters, but to stand against it. What madness filled them, to think such resistance was possible? And why would they choose it? He could think of no satisfactory answer.

Cleod rolled from the layers of fine-woven blankets that swathed him through the night, and stretched in the lamp-lit tent that he shared with no one. Pillowed, and rug-filled, and heated by its own small stove, the canvas structure that the King's servants erected each night to house him offered more amenities than his personal quarters at the caravan headquarters in Bajor.

Not even the ridiculous comfort afforded him and Trayor and Klem—even if all Klem did was complain—as part of King Rawden's chosen circle eased the ache of winter travel, the sleepless nights, or a mind bent toward over-consideration. Ahead of the army lay the city of his birth, and all those who had gathered to defend it. Rumors abounded, came daily by messenger, of Draigon sighted in flight, peasants assembling, fights among old neighbors in villages as word of the true nature of the Draigon spread. So much in motion. The Arnan through which they traveled was not the one he had crossed and recrossed with Kilras for so many years. It was now a place of chaos and fear. The very things he had joined the Enclaves to keep the world from being. In the night, half dreaming, half despairing, he wondered darkly at his failings. If Ercew drowned that along with a longing he forced himself not to recognize, it fell short more often than it offered any relief.

Cleod dressed, laced his boots, and reached for the bottle left for him every morning beside the wash basin, and took a long drink. Where was Kilras now? What had he made of the new truths, the changes sweeping over the land? How much did he understand of what it all meant? What it could mean for the future? A world without Draigon, without Draigon Weather, without fear of losing more mothers and sisters and daughters to the monsters? Without fear that they would *become* monsters... Was that not why they were offered up in the first place? The thought flashed sharp and unwelcome, and he snarled an oath. The last of the liquor flowed down his throat, and he shook his head to clear it.

Today's march would bring them within sight of the Spur. They were less than ten day's trek from Adfen if the weather did not worsen. But since Draigon controlled temperature and storm, what chance of that? He set aside the empty bottle and reached for his coat. The beasts...Leiel...could change what the army faced at any time.

Why hadn't she already? He frowned, raised a hand to his head. Why had the Draigon not destroyed all of Arnan long ago? *What the Draigon are, they have always been.* Had they been here all along? *Just Draigon, Cleod.* Before the Farlan? When had it all started? Unwelcome, the thought arose, that the war had begun long before he was even born.

Ask her. The thought trembled through him. He turned toward the tent entrance, as though doing so would turn him away from the simple idea that twisted like a spider spinning a web through his skull. Ask Leiel. He cursed again and shoved out into the glittering light of morning and the organized chaos of the waking war camp. The guards on either side of the entry snapped straighter. He had yet to decide whether they were assigned for his protection, or in some ill-considered attempt to watch and contain him.

Ankle deep snow, fresh-fallen in the night, clung to the bottom of his pant legs as he walked toward the cook tent. He needed food to settle the new turning in his belly, to focus his unruly mind. But one step inside and all illusion of relaxation died as Trayor's voice cracked the morning like a whip. "When Adfen falls, the rest of the old cities will not dare to disobey any orders imposed upon them. Giddor, Orlis—none will defy us."

Cleod stopped in the entry, swept his gaze over Trayor's assembled audience. Draigre, mostly. A few common soldiers. *Us.*

Trayor's arrogance knew no bounds if he felt safe using that word in the shadow of the King's tent. Us was the Enclaves and their followers. Us was Trayor's ever expanding self-righteousness.

For a moment Cleod saw the two of them, young again, laughing as they raced toward the training grounds determined to best every other Draigre, determined to best each other and go on to save Arnan. Then, pride and cock-certain surety had moved them like the air in their lungs fueled their breath. Now, it seemed part of a madness that had claimed not only the two of them, but the entire world. Conquer. Destroy. Rule. Was that all they fought to achieve now? What would a world without Draigon look like? A world without challenge to all the Farlan valued? One without dangerous women?

One without women like Leiel.

Before he could either thrust aside or examine the thought, a Draigre in Bynkrol colors rose from the seat nearest the door and greeted him with eyes and voice wide with awe. "Cleod Draighil! Join me please. It's an honor, Sere."

Cleod looked at the boy, then shifted his attention toward Trayor. What tales was he spinning now, to have carried the story of Cleod's years away from the Enclaves from that of traitor to one once again worthy of respect? Refusal was gentled by a smile as Cleod shook his head—how old was the candidate, perhaps fourteen summers?—and spoke, "Thank you, but I must consult with Trayor Draighil."

He moved away, stopped beside Trayor's table and stared at the man seated across from him until the other got up and efficiently relocated himself and his food to the spot the young Draigre had offered Cleod. They settled together, all head-bent murmurs and speculation.

Trayor grinned, the expression pressing a bend into his scar. "Do you appreciate my change in tone?"

Cleod sat, reached across and lifted a biscuit from Trayor's plate. "What will my being seen as a hero again do for your rise to power?"

"I suppose that depends on if you live through the war."

What other response should he have expected? Cleod offered a grunt and a shake of his head and took a bite of the bread. Still warm. He finished it, let it calm his belly. He waited as the chatter in the room resumed along with the click and clatter of eating and drinking.

Trayor shrugged, raised his mug and sipped whatever liquid steamed there. "You needed to consult with me?"

With another shake of his head, Cleod folded his arms atop the table. "No more than I need to consult Klem about his saddle sores." The squirming discomfort of Leiel's brother was the one amusement Cleod found each day. "Do you think the Draigon will let you destroy Adfen? We march into the shadow of the Spur today. The scouts say common folk are assembled between here and the city. You want power? Who will follow a man who encourages the murder of untrained farmers and tradesmen? And the destruction of the most beloved trade town in the north?"

Trayor set down his mug, but kept his hand wrapped around the handle. He leaned forward, met Cleod's gaze. "Do *you* really believe that so-called army has gathered to stand against the might of the King's soldiers, and the Bynkrol archers, and the Ehlewer, without something greater to back it?"

"The Draigon have no army." Cleod tapped the table with a finger. "Those people stand to defend their home. Who is more dangerous than that?"

"We've gathered our strength," Trayor said. "The Draigon will meet us here. It's that or allow us to destroy Adfen and to march north to kill them where they live."

"What makes you think they care about Adfen?"

"They always have. Remember the history the elders drove into us all those years ago. In the first war, the Draigon defended Adfen at the cost of a dozen of their kind. Only when they all fell did the Farlan claim the city. And the Farlan only left it standing as a sign that they truly ruled Arnan."

"And if you're wrong?" Cleod sat up straighter, considered. "I'm a killer of Draigon. Not a murderer of men and children." Of people like he had once been. Of people like his father.

Trayor's face tightened into a smooth mask more threatening than any sneer. "Tell that to the girl, Ain." He narrowed his gaze. "Whatever is required to rid Arnan of the Draigon is what will be done," he said softly. "I'll kill who I must."

Cleod stifled a flinch. Ain. What had happened to the child? Then the rest of Trayor's words expanded inside Cleod. *Kill who I must.*

Yes. Trayor would. And lie and betray and cheat to do it. He would tear apart the world to build one he wanted, where he was in control, unchallenged, unquestioned.

That was not the Trayor who Cleod remembered. The boy he had known, the man he had trained beside, had wanted to make

Arnan a safer place, bring pride to the Ehlewer, earn respect. Cleod took a breath. Or was it only *him* who wanted those things? He turned memory after memory in his mind. No...the time had existed when Trayor had been more than a shell of vengeance and greed.

Cleod frowned. Had it changed the Enclaves so much? His leaving? Had that choice corrupted what good they meant to do in the world in favor of finding a way to *use* him to annihilate the Draigon no matter the cost? If he had returned after his battle with Shaa on the Spur, how much would be different now? Would they be closer or farther from the goal of ending the Draigon? What would the cost have been of that? Hundreds of strangers? An entire city?

Simply his soul?

Where did any of that leave him now? His head pounded, both strangely clearer and more muddled than it had been in weeks. Proximity to Adfen always turned the depths of him. "And after? When we've wiped out the shop owners and the sowers and the innkeepers?"

Trayor's expression shifted into something more considered. "Think it through. Whatever those people fight for, they stand against our quest to destroy the Draigon. For that alone they must pay."

"With their lives?"

"They've made a choice." Trayor raised his mug and drank.

"So have you."

Trayor gave a low laugh that would have been chilling had anything about the man been able, anymore, to rattle Cleod. "And you haven't?"

With a disgusted shake of his head, Cleod pushed back his chair and got to his feet. "Only that I'm not hungry."

He stepped out of the cook tent into a camp now fully in action, packing to move. Feeling ill in a dozen ways, he headed for the picket line where Kicce was staked with the other horses. At least the gelding knew nothing of betrayal.

42

Leiel

FALLING DARKNESS ENFOLDED HER IN A CHILL DEEP ENOUGH THAT
Draigon heat flared along her spine. Warding warmth
spread through her whole body, until even the tips of her fingers
tingled. As a whisper of steam rose from her boots, she smiled
briefly in the moonlight, the gesture offering more mist into the
air. Rainbow shimmers rolled outward, fairy wisps of her essence colored by Gweld.

On the plains ahead, the lights of Sibora burned and winked,
and she let her energy flow outward, low against the ground,
glittering as it swept over the land. Never had she attempted to
seek with such breadth. But it seemed the time for new and impossible. And if Cleod were in the city, she needed to know.

Ahead, on the trail to Adfen, Kilras and Kinra would be waiting. Despite their plans, it remained to be discovered whether
they would be able to separate Cleod from those he traveled
with, whether that was Trayor or the entire Farlan army. Locat-
ing him was the first step.

If she could.

Though she had sensed him before, it had been through
short distance or in wide spaces, and through an openness that
they both offered the world.

The stain of loss marred her spirit like the brutal slash that
had struck down Gahree. Both wounded more than just her.
And if the disastrous events in Melbis had marked Cleod's spirit
the way they had hers, that damage alone could distort whatever

connection had lingered between them through the years.

She shook back doubt. Reaching out with such sweeping intent would alert any Gweld users within the city. How many there might be, she had no way of knowing. Draigre. Draighil. Draigon in their born forms. Others who, like Teska, touched Gweld as naturally as they breathed. Only *some* of those she brushed in passing would recognize the importance of such unfiltered contact. What message, if any, would they find within it? It might matter in the future, but this night, she would trust that any shock she offered through passing touch would be more an awakening of possibility than of fear.

Over frozen earth, along streets of stone and silence, through cracks in walls, the prismatic waves of her Gweld vision passed and penetrated. Awakenings skipped like stone across water over her skin and across her heart and mind, but none echoed with the familiar energy she sought. Her awareness passed to the far side of the city and she let it fade until the night was again just the night, icy and stark, with the steam of her breath the only thing that fogged the air.

Cleod had moved on, likely with Trayor, north, toward Adfen. In the next days she would know more of how many traveled with them. Risk loomed, that she would be unable to reach him, to get close again in any meaningful way. And if she could not, what alternative remained? The threat he presented was unprecedented.

In Melbis, she had told Kilras that she could not kill Cleod. But what if no other option remained? What if, in order to save the Draigon, save the possibility of the Arnan she hoped for and envisioned, Cleod and Trayor must *both* be destroyed? Who could do it, take on two Draighil, the strongest ever known? Kinra perhaps...but the two of them had killed Gahree. And even Kinra could not face them alone. Who else stood a chance? Draigon trained to fight at that level were rare, and with Gahree gone...

Integrity begged internal honesty. Leiel bent her head under the weight of simple fact. She did not have the skill—or the focused ruthlessness—to overcome Cleod in a physical confrontation. She could not kill him—and not just because with all her heart she did not wish to do so.

Leiel lifted her gaze to the brilliant points of light engraved, yet dancing, against the arc of fathomless darkness. The depth of the shadow between the points of light beckoned, offering peace in thoughtless emptiness. Tempting. And yet, the spaces between were never meant for nothingness. They were the edges that marked shape and depth, and journeying through them could never lead to liberation.

Even had she wished to flee, nowhere existed where she would ever escape the layered emotions that pounded through her, moment following moment, awash with fear and pain and longing. In the back of her mind, a burning simmered, demanding and constant, not always heavy for her attention, but all too often un-ignorable despite that. Part desire, part regret, the ache of it lived as an undying pressure behind her eyes—what could have been. What might be. Against all sense and possibility she hoped for a future worthy of the sacrifices made by so many for so long. Foolish. Dangerous.

And perhaps, she had grown to understand, the very reason Gahree had awaited her at the pond all those years ago.

So where did that leave Leiel this night, with impossible choices looming before her and only the barest confidence to face them, and no certainty of outcome? Her heart sat in a tight knot behind her ribs, and she stared at the stars in fierce need, as though they might hold answers to questions she could not keep herself from asking. And perhaps they did. But the answers were far too distant from the moment to matter.

She drew in a slow breath and turned away from the shining, distant city, and walked through the knee-high drifts toward Adfen, the snow parting before her self-contained heat.

43

Kilras – 46 Years

KILRAS PLACED THE LEATHER PAD ON THE BENCH OF SNOW THAT encircled the fire in the center of the pit. He shrugged deeper into his coat and rubbed his hands together before holding them over the blaze. Its warmth danced upward, caressing his palms and settling the chill tension that held his shoulders tight in the evening air. With the sun long gone below the horizon, the heat flickered vital and bright in the growing darkness. He was glad for the depth of the snow, that he had been able to pack it against the walls of his tent, adding insulation against the biting cold. Even the fire was little enough ward against the bitter temperatures. He shifted to let the fire cast its limited warmth into the open flap of the shelter set into the opening beside him.

If nothing had interfered with Gydron's travel, she should arrive in the night with news from the north. No sooner had he finished the thought than the sweep of wings sounded overhead and the air vibrated with motion and power. A smile crossed his lips, and he pulled his gloves from his waistband and tucked his warmed fingers into them. As he stood, he felt the trembling impact of the Draigon's landing. If he knew Gydron at all, she would hold her news, good or bad, until morning. She always preferred to work with alert minds, and after a day of flight, and after his own long trek, neither of them could be considered blade-sharp.

He climbed from the snow shelter and moved through the trees, careful among their dark lines and low branches. He had chosen this camp for the large clearing at the center of this wood, the remains of an old grain-weighing station. The town it served had been abandoned after wildfire swept it away a few years ago. Forgotten places could often be havens, especially for those who wished to be as unnoticed in the world as the spaces they chose to take shelter in.

The wind pulsed through the wood, erasing all other sound with its passing. A tingle swept over his skin, separate from the cold. Something unexpected waited ahead. *Someone* unexpected. With the beginnings of a smile forming on his face, he stepped forward. A few paces brought him into the open space. Ahead, shadow loomed against the more open darkness of the night. Another step and his Gweld sense sent recognition through him and stopped him as though he had walked into a wall. The Draigon in the clearing was not Gydron. And she was not alone.

For a shocked heartbeat he held silent, then the name of the creature before him rose in his mind and he smiled. "Resor." And if *she* was here... Could he be so lucky on this icy, lonely night?

Footsteps scrunched over the snow, then a shape hurtled toward him. Before thought, he recognized it. And so he was ready when Sehina threw herself into his waiting arms. Her embrace was warmth and strength and appreciative need all in one smothering grasp, and he laughed in delight as he returned it in kind.

Finally, she pulled back and looked into his face. "I left Rimm in charge." Her hair, escaped from both her braid and the wool hat she wore, haloed in unruly wisps around her face. "I figured you needed my help more."

She had climbed mountains, sought truth, believed, and risked all to return to his side. Friendship like that held value beyond measure. A shudder of pure gratitude went through him. Staunch loyalty despite his years of deception, was far more than he deserved. "You found Dinist."

She grinned at him and raised both eyebrows in wry judgment. "You knew I would." With a glance over her shoulder at the Draigon rippling heat over the snowy meadow, she said, "And made sense of *many* things with just a few conversations." Looking back at him, she shook her head. "You should have told me sooner."

"Yes," he agreed. "That would have saved us both a lot of trouble."

"I forgive you." She chuckled. "After all, I got to ride a Draigon."

The statement was so purely Sehina that he laughed. If Resor objected to the idea of being ridden, the Draigon made no response other than the single thought *She's an uncut gem.*

He smiled into the night in Resor's direction and nodded. "Thank you."

Sehina flicked a glance into the clearing then back to him. Even in the scarce light he saw her eyes widen. "You can communicate with her?"

Kilras gave a single, sharp nod. "Apparently I've still got more to tell you," he said.

She frowned, but slipped an arm through his. "All right then, time to talk. I saw a fire when we flew over. Take me too it." She shivered. "It's cold away from a Draigon's heat. And I'm hungry."

He ducked into the tent and came out with a blanket. As Sehina wrapped herself in it, he served her a plate of beans with salted meat, then reached to pour himself a tin cup of coffee.

"Wait."

He stopped and looked at her.

"In my pack," she said.

He raised his eyebrows, lifted her bag, and tugged it open.

She forked up the food, watching him. And when his hand encountered the familiar solidity of Tylen's mug, he froze, blinked back tears. "Thank you," he whispered as he pulled it out into the light cast by the fire.

With a grin, she nodded. "Rimm says hello." She handed him her plate in request for a second helping.

He laughed softly. "Thank you *both*." He spooned more food onto her plate and gave it back to her, then poured the mug full. It, and her presence, warmed him more than the fire. Sehina, at his side as she had been for so many years. Like a puzzle piece found under the corner of a rug, then set carefully into place, something snapped toward wholeness within him. The silence they shared as she ate held a comfort so familiar that it was almost surreal, and though icy night crowded around them, it was kept easily at bay by her steady company.

At last she put down the plate and looked at him. "Son of a Draigon."

He met her gaze and offered a slow shrug. "The curse you've always wanted for me?"

She pulled her hat down over her ears, eyed him. "I've got better."

He smiled. "Tell me what happened after you left Melbis."

"To the point as always." She wiped the corners of her mouth with the back of her hand. "I've missed you, too." She pulled her knees up and draped her wrists across them. "We made good distance out of Melbis on the first day. After that, things went slower once the storms kicked up. It took us weeks longer to reach Giddor than it would on a normal trip—mostly because we had to hunt up water. But we also did as you asked and took time to warn people what was coming. We asked our friends to protect the wise women, and healers, and the others not liked by the Farlan and their followers." She shook her head. Her braid flipped over her shoulder and she reached up and tossed it back. "I've never seen anything like those storms. But we made it, put the merchants on ships and settled the team for the winter. Then Rimm and I made for Dinist."

He sipped the coffee, nodded. "And how did they take those requests, our friends and contacts?"

She tipped her head to one side and looked at him for a long moment. "I'm about to tell you about my first meeting with *actual Draigon* and you want to know how my talks went at the inns and trading posts?"

"Given what you now know, this shocks you?"

Sehina raised her eyebrows and offered a little grunt. "Ha! You'd be asking me the same thing regardless of whether I knew you were raised by Draigon."

Something loosened in his chest, and he acknowledged how much he had missed her direct practicality. "Well?"

She sat back a little and spoke again, offered a day-by-day review of the caravan's journey south and their encounters along the way.

He took in each bit of news and measured the reality of his contacts' responses against unspoken expectations. Too much to hope for, that *all* would have taken the message into deep consideration, bent their will toward assistance and mitigation. But if his doubts encountered solid foundation in the actuality of their reactions, that was truer of far fewer of them than he had expected. Perhaps the plan concocted in Cyunant out of desperate optimism was not as ludicrous as they all feared it might be. The thought was, in equal measures, heartening and unsettling.

The night drew on as Sehina talked, and he added wood to the fire twice. As a silence finally fell, Resor's thoughts pressed into his mind. *Hello, Hantyn.*

"Hello, Resor," he said aloud. "Thank you." That she had left her mountain home, taken her Great Shape, and flown north with Sehina as passenger, spoke of more than the depth of danger that they all faced.

Had the Draigon been present with them at the fire, he could not have felt her stare more deeply. *You're welcome, Hantyn. It has been many years since you visited us.*

"Too many," he agreed.

Your friend is an unusual woman.

Kilras smiled and repeated the statement.

Sehina laughed. "Kilras only befriends the unusual."

"Yes." Kilras suppressed a grin of his own. Sehina awoke in people either a passionate rage, or an equally passionate desire for allegiance. Resor, it seemed, fell into the latter category. If time among strong women had taught him nothing else, it had given him the knowledge that they were often smarter than he, especially in unexpected interactions. They read new situations faster, and often judged the nature of them more competently. That those abilities were rooted more in trained need for survival than in their natures was a thought that had often sobered him.

You visited Bynkrol?

He stopped with the mug halfway to his mouth, glad of the warmth that the crockery radiated to his fingers. "The documents are no longer there."

No reply came. He remembered such silences from her, when she reached up and braided her long, flaming hair, combing the tangles from it with her fingers as she went.

Sehina did not ask what he meant.

Kilras smiled at the horse trainer. "She told you."

Of course I told her. You sent her to me for that story.

"She told me," Sehina agreed.

"Probably a dozen stories that I'll wish she hadn't," Kilras said with a shake of his head.

At least that many. Your friend is a better listener than most.

"You mean a better listener than me."

I do. Though you listened long enough to hear what you needed to. Again stillness, then. *Your control remains strong, Hantyn. The minds of most others are safe from you.*

The long ago months under Resor's tutelage rose as reminder of the Draigon's set-in-her-ways nature. "You're a good teacher. I've recalled many of your lessons over the last months. I hope enough of them."

"She *taught* you?" Sehina asked.

Kilras looked at her. "That, of all things, she didn't share?"

"You were raised under Gahree's tutelage and you didn't learn that some stories should only be told by those who own them?

Kilras grinned. "You became a part of that tale the moment you decided not to kill me in Dinist."

That doesn't mean it's mine to share.

He looked at Sehina. "Do you remember when I was sick, in Sibora, all those years ago?" At her nod, he leaned toward the fire and lifted the coffee pot to refill his mug.

The moment of his greatest weakness and shame lay before him, a hot spike in his memory. Time had allowed him to push it behind cold walls, to consider it only in the rare moments of the night when he assessed the truth of his nature and measured his actions in the world against dark possibility. He closed his eyes a moment, then opened them and met Sehina's curious gaze in the dancing light. Then he chose careful words and told her all of it—who Syon had been to him, what happened the night he nearly killed the man, the dangerous aftermath of his self-loathing-based failure of control. Then of his journey to Dinist and the strength that Resor helped him discover there. He paused where Sehina's questions filled spaces between breaths, let her amazement and curiosity rock the night air in equal measure.

That she took it all in without raging at him, without disgust or fear or anger was both unexpectedly welcome and purely Sehina.

"All that," she said as he finished, "you kept from everyone." She folded her arms to draw the blanket close around her, and studied him silently. At last she shrugged. "It doesn't explain you, but it fills in some gaps."

At that, he laughed. "Have you been looking for a way to explain me to someone?"

The look she offered in response told him that idea was beyond ridiculous, and he laughed again.

Turning his attention back to Resor, he said, "But Resor, you're not here for any of that. You came because of the vault."

Did you discover where they've moved it to, since the Bynkrol do not guard it?

He sat back, took another drink, let the warmth of the liquid spread down his chest and into his belly. "No. But I know that Trayor Draighil has the location. Protectorship of the documents passed to the Ehlewer when he was invested as leader." Kilras thought of the dark decision made in Cyunant, to risk all the history and knowledge that the Draigon had protected for centuries. Again, the almost-understanding he had felt on that day in the library bloomed in his mind before it blew away like smoke. He took a slow breath and stated the obvious, just to hear the truth actually spoken. "But Trayor is too smart to leave them at Ehlewer. If he failed with Cleod, his knowledge of the compound would leave them too vulnerable."

Then where?

"That's what we need to figure out." He sat back. Was this where hope and necessity collided? "Or need Cleod to."

Sehina started and her face brightened with surprise. "Cleod's back? Where?"

Kilras shook his head. "Not yet. But we hope to change that."

And you expect that if you can turn your friend's heart, he'll come with the knowledge we seek?

"And how do you plan to make that happen?" Sehina's tone was flat with frustration. How much had the events in Melbis shaken her faith in the life she had known, the friends she had trusted? And yet she was here—so clearly not as much as they had Cleod. Despite her trip to Dinist, and her seemingly easy acceptance of what he had just told her, she had to be rocked to her core. That she covered it so well was no less than he had come to expect, but the set of her jaw reflected a tension he had not seen in years.

And if she was so deeply impacted, how much worse must it be for Cleod, whose intrinsic image of himself had been shattered like frail crystal?

He ran a hand through his hair, met her gaze with a certainty that he did not completely feel. "With the help of a healer named Teska, and the woman Cleod's loved all his life."

You're trusting the future to the feelings of a man who's spent his whole life training to destroy us. A killer.

Kilras shook his head. "Cleod's no killer. He's a protector." At Sehina's puzzled look, he repeated Resor's dark statement. "Cleod's always been more than what others think he is. Or what they expect him to be." He tipped his head toward Sehina. "Or would you disagree?"

"No. Tell her that Cleod is my friend. I have too few of those to throw any of them away." She met Kilras's gaze, all demand and expectation. "Your next move had better be a good one."

He chuckled, shrugged. "The game is only as good as the players, and not all are here yet. I was expecting Gydron Draigon and Teska Healer. Not you and Resor." He met Sehina's gaze, judged her response as he added. "And Leiel."

She pulled her head back. "Leiel Sower? Coming here? So that's the 'we' you meant." She leaned sideways enough to grab a few pieces of wood from the pile just beyond the circle of firelight and added them to the flames. Flecked with snow and ice, they sizzled as they joined the blaze. "Leiel coming here."

"She's nearly as unexpected as you are."

Sehina flashed her gaze at him with such fierce intensity that for a moment it seemed she cast sparks across the distance between them. He drew breath at sudden insight; if the world turned as they hoped, she might someday train to Gweld. What a new dimension that would add to their friendship. If they survived the coming weeks, that was something to look forward to witnessing.

You thought I was Gydron. A ripple of something new entered the tone of her sending.

"Yes." He paused. "You know her."

The Draigon's resonance shifted so subtly that Kilras almost missed the expectation in it. *We knew each other well...long ago. Many decades have passed since we spoke. We'll have a lot to discuss when she arrives.*

Even being able to nearly taste the layers of implied meaning in that statement offered him no insight. Resor and Gydron—decades—such a connection, such distance, could mean anything. "Do you know Leiel?"

He almost felt her shake her great head. Kilras considered. Resor and her friends lived far removed from the other Draigon. If he had never quite discovered their purpose in doing so, he still knew that one existed. Perhaps, if time allowed, he would someday learn what it was.

He rolled his neck on his shoulders and closed his eyes, fatigue settling over him. Morning would be time enough for such questions, if the others did not arrive with more important things on which to focus. Gydron and Teska. Leiel. What had they discovered in the months since they laid the foundation of their hopes in Cyunant? With luck, things more beneficial than what he had learned. With luck, things that would hold back the rising tide of war and allow them to turn the heart of the man he had called friend for so long.

"Time to sleep," he said, and looked at Sehina who yawned as though his words were a signal fire calling in weariness. She nodded and stretched her way to her feet.

"Don't mind my snoring," she said as she crossed the few paces to the tent, pushed aside the door flap, and ducked inside.

"I never have," he called with a smile. He poured the cold remains of the coffee into the snow and got to his feet.

I'll keep watch.

Gratitude relaxed his shoulders. "Thank you, Resor."

Sleep well, Hantyn. Your strength will be tested soon.

Whatever she imagined lay ahead, he had no doubt of the truth of her statement. He turned away and slipped into the tent to claim what rest the remaining night might offer.

44

Leiel

BENEATH THE GRANITE EDGE OF WINTER, SHE SMELLED SMOKE. SNOW scritched, settling and melting under her weight as she paused to determine from which direction the scent drifted. On a night like this, still and frigid, it could not be far, a half hour's walk at most. She tested the air, tasted what she smelled, then turned south and continued.

The number of travelers on the road despite the weather and her need for caution had slowed her progress—so strange, after so many years of moving freely throughout Arnan, to need to take care in her words and actions—and she was two days late to the appointed rendezvous. A flicker of concern sent tension into her jaw.

Had all the others arrived ahead of her? What had they seen and learned in the last months? News to rival hers she hoped, vital and practical and useful. Despite all the people she had spoken with, the plans she had set in motion through the last months, the necessity of restraint bound her spirit like wire. What mattered most still lay ahead, stark and demanding. Facing it, at last, would come with a price she was more than willing to pay. The need to *act* raised gooseflesh over her body, an undying itch she was unable to assuage. It was past time for her to face the challenge that had been born on the day her mother's name had been called in the Square.

To the east, the sky greyed toward brightness, and the stark lines of bare trees sought definition in the dying darkness. Far off, a brave bird offered a song into icy air. She walked on, exertion pushing her breath into great pale puffs that rang like crystal and vanished in the rising dawn.

Low voices reached her, unslowed and undisturbed by the sound of her approach. She stepped from the trees to see a pit dug into the snow deep enough to block wind and to shelter the battered tent tucked near the fire burning at the center. A simple snow structure designed for basic protection. How many such had she dug under Kinra's patient instruction during her first years on the mountain? Winter survival was the first thing newcomers learned in Cyunant. Only the heads of the people seated in the protective pit poked above its edge.

She crunched through the snow, puzzling over the number of people seated around the fire. Even without Gydron—where was she? Waiting in her Great Shape beyond the far line of trees?—more souls awaited Leiel's arrival than she had counted on seeing this day. A person who she did not recognize at all.

No, that was not true. It was the female horse trainer from Kilras's caravan. Wind and wings, how had she gotten here? The answer to that question became clear as Leiel recognized a second presence in the woods with Gydron—another Draigon. No one she had ever met, but that was unsurprising—the needs of the times had called forth many who preferred seclusion. She sent a question into Gweld, received greeting and reply from Gydron. And a name: *Resor*.

She recalled what Kilras had told her of his team and the orders he had given them. The Draigon leader of Dinist. She send a sliver of thought to the unfamiliar Draigon, both question and greeting, and received in return a wry flicker of acknowledgment that brought a smile. Stranger though Resor was, something in that brief touch reminded Leiel of Gahree's wink. That alone made Leiel hope to get to know her better.

Leiel flicked her gaze to the horsetrainer. There was only one way she could have gotten here. What kind of woman must she be to have convinced a Draigon to carry her? Sehina. That was her name. The girl from the north who caught the imagination of a young Hantyn on his way south, and whose fierce spirit had helped guide him ever since. Who, apparently, had returned against the tide of probability to stand beside him still.

"Leiel!" Teska rose to her feet and gestured toward the seat beside her. "We've hot tea for you."

The most Draigon welcome of all. Leiel smiled and dropped into the pit to joyful greetings and powerful hugs. The hot mug slipped into her hands. She settled in among friends and chosen family, the long, bitter journey over the land forgotten for a few moments as she simply allowed herself to be, comfortable and loved among those who knew her.

"Luck in your travels?" Kilras asked.

Leiel nodded as she breathed in the hot steam lifting from the mug in her grasp. "Yes. Old friends greeted and knowledge gained." And she told them of her meetings with Torrin, and a dozen others throughout Sibora and the surrounding region— the weapons, the fighting skills, the secret knowledge that would allow for disruptions of supply chains, and the hiding of women and other potentially targeted individuals, the sharing of secrets and the passing of messages.

In return, they shared their own months throughout Arnan. Teska of her time learning in Cyunant, Gydron adding detail to those tales of training. Sehina, her discovery of the deeper truths of Arnan and its history. Resor a succinct and, Leiel suspected, purposefully vague desire to come north and join the main battle. Kilras, the good news of his success with old friends and contacts, and the tragedy of the burning of the Bynkrol.

"The entire Enclave?" Leiel asked. The thought stunned, that a place so ancient and powerful could be brought down so quickly. For a moment, fear curled in her belly like a startled kitten—could such happen to Cyunant? But she took a breath and dismissed the thought. The choice to fight as needed, no matter the cost, was already made. Her idea. And her strength was needed to back it. "Survivors?"

Kilras shook his head. "I don't know. Perhaps a few. Maybe the Draigre who helped the bandits enter."

Leiel sat back a little, considered the story he had just shared. A Draigre traitor. One who chose another path despite the conditioning, the training. How? Perhaps because he had never believed in what he was being taught, had joined the Enclaves with a purpose that did not match the Bynkrol's? Were there other such among the Enclaves? She drew another breath. Among the *Ehlewer*. With Bynkrol gone, there remained only one full Enclave. Only one. "We could destroy them forever." The words came in a stunned whisper.

We can. Resor put forth, and the tight focus in her tone drove home that *this* was the reason she had come north. *If we destroy the Elder Vault.*

"The Elder Vault? I've never heard that phrase." Leiel frowned, looked at Kilras. "The documents you spoke of in Cyunant."

Resor sent clarifying reply. *That is what I call the knowledge. I don't know that it has a name. But we learned of it long ago, when we destroyed Dinist. It's the collection of the Enclave's oldest teachings. The knowledge they horde the way Gydron hides books in her caverns.*

A mental chiming that might have been laughter came from the library keeper. *I find no fault in this logic.*

Leiel smiled, but the expression faded as she considered the weight of what Resor implied. "You and your companions destroyed Dinist." That was a story she would have to hear in full one day. "And learned of these secret documents—which is why the other Enclaves remain. No one knows where they are."

A trembling filled the air. *And the information is too dangerous to leave to the world, unattended. Even if all the Draighil died tomorrow, the Enclaves could be rebuilt. Reborn. We cannot have that.*

"And you came here, to make sure we remembered how important that knowledge is."

"And I came to make sure she didn't accidentally murder Kilras thinking he was some Farlan spy," Sehina said.

That drew a chuckle from Kilras. Leiel looked at him. "And this is why you went to Bynkrol. To see if the documents were there."

He nodded. "They weren't. I learned that much."

"That means that the Ehlewer have them."

"Trayor has them," Kilras said.

Leiel let air out of her lungs in a rush. "Of course he does. And he's smart enough not to have stored them anywhere obvious."

"Cleod might know, by now."

Sehina scoffed. "You think this Trayor trusts Cleod? Didn't you say he drugged Cleod to make him turn on us all?"

"The cuila only accounts for so much," Leiel said, speaking the truth that haunted her daily. "Cleod has desired to kill Draigon since he was a boy. Because of me. And now, again because of me, I think that part of him always will."

"We're right," Teska said. "About the ercew. About Cleod and the Ercew and the Cuila. I know we are. I know I can clear the poison from his body. And then, Leiel, you can clear it from his mind and heart."

"You've found a way, then? With Gweld?" Kilras asked the healer.

Teska nodded. "Yes. In combination with a strong course of specific herbs. I can cure his need for ercew. And if it has already weakened his dependence on the cuila...I can break loose the pathways in his mind."

"Reach...into his mind?" Kilras asked, and something in his voice spoke beyond simple curiosity.

"No." Teska looked at him. "But the remedy I have can break the need in him."

"He's moving north. With Trayor and the King and half the Farlan army," Leiel said. "We have to find a way to separate him."

Silence held a long moment, then Kilras spoke softly. "I have a way to do that."

The look on his face made Leiel sit up straighter. "Why do I think that none of us are going to like it?"

45

Leiel

L EIEL TOOK IN THE STRANGENESS OF THE MOMENT, CROUCHED ON Resor's back. Flight, for more than a decade had been Leiel's escape, her place of wonder. To partake in it now but not under her own power was beyond disconcerting. And the crimson Draigon who carried them was no more at ease than was Leiel. Every sweep of her wings was taut and precise, measured and attentive to the point of discomfort. Leiel held as still as possible, forced her muscles to loosen, to settle against the warmth of Resor's body.

Take note.

As they climbed over the building clouds, Resor's request pulsed through Leiel's head. A blink and she unfurled Gweld sight, used its rainbow iridescence to pierce the cover of the storm below, took in the strange organization of the people there, the citizens of Adfen gathered to defend their home. Amid the moving multitude, she picked out Kinra's indigo presence, as she guided and directed.

Leiel knew nothing of the shape and action of battle beyond what little she had taken in from books and stories. What Kinra organized below was based on a level of understanding of such things that Leiel hoped she would never need to possess. The gathered army was one created in sudden need, but backed by years of kind cultivation—Gahee's and so many unknown others. Old warriors, farmers, shopkeepers, mothers and daughters and brothers and fathers, old and young. And if they were for the most part, unskilled in battle, they were armed with spears and knives and even swords made by the finest smiths, and led by a mind that had spent more than a century focused on warfare and fighting. Kinra would do her best among them, and take the Great Shape if the need arose.

The technicalities of that coming battle, of Kinra's plans to engage and retreat, to distract and impact the greater force, Leiel left to a mind far sharper than her own.

Her task was Cleod. Getting him away from Trayor. If they could move his heart, move his mind, then his knowledge of the Farlan's war plan alone could change everything. And the depth of his understanding of the Enclaves, of Trayor, could be worth even more. But most of all, the strength of who he was at his core, if convinced to stand against the forces facing Adfen and the Draigon, could shift more than just battles to come. It could prove to all of Arnan that deep change was possible. That the Draigon could be seen as something other than the enemies of the entire land.

Leiel watched the prismatic pulse of the bodies below, then tense with determination, said into the icy air, "I understand, Resor. It's time." For the sake of those gathered on the ground, she must not fail.

And the Draigon shifted her wings and arced southward, toward the Farlan army and the terrible encounter that the day demanded.

"Stay here. You'll be safe," Leiel said. She and Teska paused just inside the treeline at the crest of the low rise. With Gydron gone to fight with Kinra, this was the best place for Teska to wait, close enough that she could join Leiel if they succeeded, distant enough from potential conflict to flee if necessary. The wind parted the clouds, and they saw the armed multitude arrayed on the frozen plain below. The King's army spread over road and field, a force designed for singular purpose—the destruction of all she and Teska were and might become. Leiel reached out to take Teska's gloved hand in her own.

Cold violence trembled the air as Leiel swept her gaze over those assembled on the plain. Most wore the dark uniforms of Farlan soldiers, armed with spears and bows and swords. Then, in smaller clusters, the men of the Enclaves gathered in ones and twos. In the center were bright banners that marked royalty.

She stared. Never had she heard of the King leaving his safe palace in Sibora. What faith he must have in the plans Trayor had laid. A thought to strike fear, if she had any fright left to spare.

Then, as they watched, the army moved, divided, separated. And the King's men and the largest portion of the Farlan soldiers and archers marched away north. Well more than half, moving straight for Adfen and Kinra and Gydron's forces. And the King's banner and most of the men of the Enclaves followed. Then the Draigre divided, some riding to the front of the departing column, some away to the east. The remainder of the men shifted west, moving swiftly on horseback. To what end, any of it, Leiel could not imagine. If only she had devoted as much time learning battle strategy as she had to working in Gahree's greenhouse. What unfolded below was beyond her understanding. No matter. What she needed was to determine which direction Trayor traveled, because of one thing only was she certain—that where Trayor was, Cleod would be as well.

Determination furrowed her brow, and she shifted her attention to the head of the nearest column, the one riding hard away from the arc of the rising sun. She held back Gweld, sought with plain sight alone until she saw him, pale hair uncovered and bright even in the swirling whiteness—Trayor Draighil.

The bolt of pure rage that went through her rocked her where she stood. Fire spiraled up her spine and through her chest until bursting into flame seemed the only option.

But she did not.

She held, still and silent among the sheltering trees, and swung her gaze from Gahree's murderer to the man on the grey horse behind him.

The thunderous rage flooding her chest and smothering her very heartbeat was already too close to bursting forth. For a moment, as she recognized him, fear took hold—that she would be unable to contain dark emotion. But she held again as Cleod's gelding drove long strides through the snow, kicking it up in chunks. Held as the horse drew up beside Trayor, tossing its head as though nearness to the Draighil was a cause of fury for it as well.

Her heart cracked, breath came hard, and every bright thought fled her mind as she stared at Cleod. All they were about to risk was for him—as Shaa had once risked all for Leiel and the woman who stood beside her.

And Gahree had let them *all* know that the man on the grey horse was worth the same.

The only way to honor that was to trust the hope the great Draigon had laid within them all. Her plans and Trayor's had collided in violent tragedy, but that did not mean the outcome of either was predetermined.

Leiel trembled, forced her breath in and out, until her heartbeat was only that and no longer a roar and hammer in her chest. She whispered to Teska, "If we fail, make your way south. Gydron will find you."

"You won't fail," Teska said with unnatural ease. "You didn't save me in Melbis to no good end. I'll see you soon."

Leiel almost smiled at that. Teska spoke as though the parting army on the plains were only pieces on a game board. Perhaps that was how she had to think of them, to keep harder feelings at bay. Perhaps that was the only way to face this day, by dismissing the stakes. Leiel understood that forced certainty, the need to believe that things would work out as she wanted, simply because it would be too unfair for that not to be the case. But the world cared nothing for fairness. And even hope, the brightest of all emotions, guaranteed only comfort, never success. "If luck holds," she said. If Leiel stayed a moment longer, she would sprint down the mountain and through the crowd to Cleod, and that she could not do. Not yet. Her mind raced again as she resisted the very idea. She released Teska's hand, hugged the other woman for a long moment, then retreated back through the forest.

At the far side of the woods, determined Resor waited with Kilras and Sehina, all of them tense and silent. What they were about to attempt would have only a single chance at success, and whether they would all survive, none of them considered aloud.

46

Cleod

THE WIND KICKED UP AS THEY MOVED NORTH, SLUNG ICE CRYSTALS into miniature whirlwinds, overcast the horizon, and blocked the view of the Spur he had expected to see. Out of the north came the blowing, and carried with it high clouds heavy with snow. He had spent his youth watching the sky, and never had he seen a storm quite like this. It reduced vision to only a few strides, but layered no drifts over the ground. A whiteout without accumulation. A blizzard wrapped in purpose.

Around him, riders moved, carrying messages, preparing the army for whatever hid within the suddenly rising weather. The distraction, if it were such, would not catch them unaware.

Klem and Trayor rode ahead of him, the latter wrapped in a red cloak so thick he seemed doubled in size. Cleod kneed Kicce closer to Trayor's mount and spoke over the wind. "Our waiting is over."

Trayor, his pale faced reddened by the wind and cold, smiled with a fierceness to match the weather. "A welcome day."

Around them, soldiers moved through vaporous whiteness, crunched and clattered as they made ready to face whatever lay beyond the icy mist. The army would face any common people aligned against them. The Enclaves would take on any Draigon who showed themselves. Or so they had planned. But plans often died in real moments, when threat and action collided with need and swept aside even the best trained intentions. Had that not been the case on the Spur all those years ago? And in Melbis, when Shaa stepped from the smoke and revealed herself, in a single heartbeat, as fragile and mortal? What plans had *she* laid, before that moment when choice and necessity met and forced surrender at ultimate cost?

"This won't be a battle alone on a hilltop. We won't face just one Draigon any more than Shaa faced only one Draighil."

Trayor's laughter hung like his misted breath. "Do you really think I can't take down a Draigon alone, now that Shaa is gone? You and the Draigre will handle the rest."

"I know you can. That we can," Cleod said. "*And so do they.* This is a distraction. They have something else planned."

"They are *women*," Klem said. "What do they know of war?"

"And what do you know of the mind of any woman?" Cleod flicked his attention to the Councilman. "What did you know of your sister that would allow her to become the very thing we must destroy?"

"No." Klem shook his head. "The question is what did *you* know, Cleod Woodcutter, that day on the mountain? What did you know that allowed her to survive outside the realm of Arnan where she might have been safely contained?"

At that, Cleod laughed. "You never contained Leiel. Not even in your own kitchen. If you had, her name would never have been called in the Square. And who is to blame for that, if not the brothers charged as her keeper?"

The fury on Klem's face pulsed heat through the frosty air. "You—"

"Yes," Cleod said. "*I* as well. I never contained her. Not once." Her voice echoed across the years, quiet and thoughtful *I was thinking I was also allowed to be myself*. No, he had never stopped her, and whatever he suffered to destroy what she had become because of that, would be nothing more than what he deserved.

The Draigon are what they have always been. He shook his head to clear it. If such were true of the Draigon, of Leiel, then it was also true of *him*.

"No matter now. We're here to rectify your errors of judgment and inaction," Trayor said, and urged his mount forward as though what awaited within the whirling whiteness was destined for him alone. Perhaps, Cleod considered as he urged Kicce after Trayor, that was no more than the truth.

Kilras

Resor descended in a arrow-straight dive, so direct that it seemed the ground cringed as she approached, met, and rocked it, kicking up wild layers of debris. Kilras slid quickly off her back, and his knees took the impact as he landed. Turning, he nodded to Sehina as she dropped down beside him. Leiel followed. She met his gaze a moment, before gesturing to Sehina and heading away into the whirling smoke and mist. Sehina gave him a look he had no time to fully take in, then she pivoted and sprinted after Leiel.

Towering over him, Resor lifted her wings and took flight, to circle back toward the rear of the column to take on the Draigre, keep them out of the fight. He bent away, arm over his eyes as a wave of heat passed above his head, blasting away the snow and ice covering the ground, roasting the earth. Steam thundered away from them, formed a rising wall between them and the small force waiting across the now scorched open ground. He raised his head, already sweating at the sudden change toward heat, and watched the pale mist rise into the grey sky.

Cover.

Deception.

He unsheathed his sword and sprinted through the smoke toward the Draighil waiting on the other side. Over the hard, rocky ground, strangely puddled from the newly burned away snow, he ran, Gweld sense at the ready, trusting it more than sight.

Cleod

A thunderous blast of air washed the clouds into roiling waves overhead, and a streak of crimson, huge and solid and scaled, swept by with a roar that shoved aside all other sound and raised terror deep inside. Then old rage chased the fear, crawled through the back of his skull and sent fury spiraling into expanded vision. It collided with Trayor's Gweld sense as he too responded to the sudden presence of Draigon.

If the color of the beast was unfamiliar, and the fact that it had appeared with no warning disturbed, both shocks fled as the ground shook with impact and a wave of heat crashed over them in a wild billowing of hot vapor and debris. Somewhere, just ahead, the creature had landed and used its dire power to steam the winter layers from the earth in a foaming wall of smoke and mist.

Horses panicked, rearing and shying hard enough to dump riders. Even Trayor's mount jerked like an unbroken yearling. Kicce, Sehina trained, held steady, even as Cleod dropped from the gelding's back, and drew his sword. A few fumbling heartbeats later and Trayor was at his side, blade in hand. Gweld wove light and color through the air, twisting where their two trance-driven skills collided.

The shouts of fleeing men surrounded them. Through the billowing chaos, came another roar, violent and demanding, echoing even as it scythed through heightened senses. And suddenly what lay ahead was the fate Trayor had sought, had compelled upon them all. If internal honesty demanded acknowledgment that the choice to follow was his own, Cleod faced the idea only briefly before the land ahead erupted again in a spray of steam and heat.

He raised a shielding arm against the onslaught, met Trayor's eyes through it as the Draighil did the same.

"Split!" Trayor shouted, and broke away to the right. Whatever other threats loomed for the army racing in confusion around them, one thing they understood completely was how to deal with the threat before them.

Cleod moved in opposition to Trayor, their separation doubling the threat to what lay beyond the wind-driven wall snow and ice.

Strange at the limit of his spiraling awareness, something bright-charged and familiar rang like a bell within him. Whatever beast moved beyond sight on the plains ahead, it was not alone. And whatever stood with it... He shoved the consideration away. But every part of him burned with far more now than anger. An inexplicable fear trembled deep within, brittle and crackling and unnerving in a way beyond clarifying thought.

He paused in the raging air, tried to focus, realized the storm was calming. Through the thinning swirl, he could see bare ground, still smoldering, rocks and crisped grasses streaming vapor into the clouds above. Distant beyond the open space, something moved, danced in shadow and ivory.

He flicked his gaze to where Trayor stood poised on the far side of the bared ground. The air between them settled, began to clear even more, and Trayor flashed his old, assured grin across the distance.

Shadow shifted at the edge of Cleod's vision, the unknown Draigon approaching. He reached out, mind searching, encountered power and presence...no...*presences*...at once strange and far, far too familiar.

His connected conscious stumbled, just as Trayor raised his voice, full of confident excitement. "Whatever you think you know about these creatures, Cleod—We know the only thing that matters—*how to kill them.*" He raised his sword, and Gweld expanded, set ablaze like a match touched to oil. It rushed over Cleod, buoyed him, demanded attention. Melded to Trayor's purpose, the need to action exploded through Cleod's muscles, even as a cry of anguish rose in his mind.

Because it was not a Draigon, but Kilras, blade in hand, who stepped through the smoke, to face Trayor.

Kilras

He emerged into chill grey light, to see only a small contingent of fighters. Most of those who had not fled were crouched and stunned from the impact of Resor's landing and the heated aftershock.

Most, but not all.

Trayor Draighil waited, gaze stark and unflinching, at the head of the ragged group of soldiers and Bynkrol who remained.

And a hundred paces to the right Cleod stood poised—until Kilras met his old friend's gaze, then the disbelief that rocked through Cleod echoed through Gweld-readied senses. Old friend. So pained. Still so lost. Still in need of understanding. Would another shock help with that, or only amplify the battle raging within him?

Not Kilras's to choose. Now or ever. He returned his attention to the man waiting across the rock-strewn clearing: Trayor, pale and hard-eyed, eagerness in his stance. Too eager, if Kilras was lucky. Or eager with good reason, if luck did *not* hold. No matter. The moments ahead would unfold the truth.

Cleod

Impossible. A blow that took breath and balance, that tumbled and scattered, as the Hewlion had once thrown him to the earth and torn into his flesh—the impact of shock that rocked Cleod made the old, scarring assault seem as nothing.

Kilras.

Kilras here.

Kilras with sword in hand to face *Trayor*.

How? Why? A thousand questions roared, raging monsters inside Cleod's skull, demanding answers which his gut already recognized would never be satisfied. But one truth loomed wide—Kilras was going to die. No matter their years of training together no way existed for the Dorn to defeat a Draighil of Trayor's skill.

Kilras

The roar of the wind died and in the falling silence, Kilras waited, sword held low in an easy grasp. *His* sword, made by Kinra's deft hand to allow him to change style, match any opponent across Arnan. Memory leaped like the fire of a forge, of her steady hand wielding the hammer to shape bright blades, the scent of hot metal and the harsh ring of steel-on-steel cracking through his ears. A weapon formed by Draigon hand for purely human use. A weapon to cross divides. Or hold them open.

Open for change.

Open for Cleod to walk through.

Trayor shouted into the winter air, his tone dripping with arrogance, the words meaningless to Kilras's ears.

He held still. If he succeeded in the next instant, no fight would be necessary, no blood need be spilled this day. Braced in mind and body, he focused and sent a sharp edged sliver of intention toward Trayor. But the Draighil Elder was not an un-aware civilian, and Trayor's Gweld sense deflected the assault as fast as Kilras released it.

Nothing for it then, except what he had planned all along. With the flash of a smile and a power-backed glance at Cleod, Kilras shifted his grip on the sword hilt, adjusted the angle of his wrist, locked eyes with Trayor, and stepped forward to engage.

Cleod

Kilras lifted his eyes across the smoking, rocky earth and met Cleod's gaze and something *snapped* between them, like a plucked string on a sharply tuned instrument, vibrating and singing.

Hello, old friend. Kilras's voice, the sharp bite of his mind touched Cleod's like the edge of a blade. Shock stilled breath and motion and thought.

The moment held.

Then splintered as Kilras's attention shifted back to Trayor.

And the world fell away from Cleod's feet as the Dorn shifted his grip on his sword hilt, took firm grasp in Ehlewer style, and moved forward to meet Trayor.

In the space of the three heartbeats that passed before their blades collided, realization poured through Cleod: time spent on the practice ground, blades flashing, laughter and fellowship—and never once in any of those moments had Kilras used Ehlewer style beyond what Cleod, in rare moments, offered to teach. Skilled as Kilras was, the more advanced work of the Ehlewer never seemed to interest him. And now the why of that came clear. *He knew it already.* Knew it to his core.

Memory erupted.

"If you're wishing for a good soaking, you're not alone." Kilras walked through the sweltering heat toward the low shrub where their shirts hung beside a pair of towels and their scabbards.

Cleod followed. "You keep telling me you don't read minds." He grabbed one of the cloths and ran it down the length of his sword before wiping his face. His sword slid into its home with a snap, then he hung it and the towel over the nearest branch.

"A day like this, even if I could, I wouldn't need to." Kilras cleaned his blade as well, its dark, patterned steel gleaming in the sun.

Cleod watched. Then the curiosity that had been growing since he and the Dorn started training together finally pushed forth a request. "May I?" Among the Draighil, such a question breached all decorum, and Cleod's skull tingled as he made it.

Kilras raised both eyebrows and looked at Cleod for a moment before lifting the blade on flat palms and offering it for inspection.

Cleod hesitated as instilled habit warred with desire, then he took the weapon. Surprise pierced through Cleod's chest. Light though Cleod's blade was, this one was even more so, with a shining edge both sharp and unblemished. He grasped the hilt.

Kilras stepped back and gestured toward the flat area they had just vacated. With a nod, Cleod moved into the space, and walked through a simple series of moments. The unexpectedly perfect balance, and matching comfort of the leather-wrapped hilt, made every flourish a joy. "Old gods and demons, Kil."

"The smith was one of a kind as well."

The past tense of the statement caught Cleod's mind. He slowly eased the blade's motion to a halt and laid it across the back of his hand, once again examining the elegance of the construction, the beauty of the layered twisted waves that patterned the steel. "I've never seen its like."

Kilras shook his head. "And you never will."

The finality of Kilras's tone could mean only one thing. Cleod frowned. "He must have been a great talent."

A faint smile crossed Kilras's lips but he did not reply.

Cleod carried the sword back to his friend, and watched Kilras slide it into its equally well-made scabbard. "You never speak of your past."

Kilras shrugged.

"Why?"

With a flick of his wrist, Kilras draped his towel over his shoulder. "Necessity. Habit. Lack of desire to do so."

Enough things haunted Cleod's own history for him to understand such sentiment. And yet, whatever weight Kilras carried seemed less based in pain than something else entirely, something that defied clear definition. "For your sake, or for ours?"

The Dorn offered another faint smile. "Both," he said as he met Cleod's gaze. "Is there ever another answer to such a question?"

Every story and belief Cleod had laid in his mind as foundation for Kilras's reticence imploded. Cleod choked on his breath even as he watched, half unseeing, the fight unfold before him.

Step and parry, a shift so subtle and swift it startled and caught Trayor off guard.

Cleod's heart surged too-large and demanding in his ribcage. Instinct jerked him forward a step. But the fight moved beyond interference in the same instant and all understanding fled his mind as Gweld bloomed from Kilras's being and exploded between the two swordsmen, hurling everything Cleod thought he understood about the Dorn into a void dark enough to drown night itself.

Cleod's every sense caught flame, reached, sought to ride the strange rising power that guided the battle between two men into the realm where heart and mind outmatched body. In desperation to understand what was taking place before him, he yanked back his own unfurling awareness as shock followed shock through every part of him.

Betrayal uncurled its bitter scales inside his belly, but beside it rose pure awe as he watched Kilras match and meet every action of craft and deceit that Trayor engaged.

Fast beyond the ability of normal sight to discern, the two men moved, a deadly dance of footwork and blade and cunning. If not for Gweld vision, Cleod would have witnessed only blurring motion, heard only grunts of effort and the clanging of metal. Instead, his hearing ricocheted with thunderous heartbeats, whispered curses, his sight burned with eyes narrowed and darkened, muscles that strained with flex and demand. A violent dance of power and knowledge unlike any he had ever imagined possible wove over the scarred earth, strange and beautiful and terrifying.

How well he knew Trayor's unrelenting skill, his speed and cunning with a blade. Always, it had taken every piece of training and treachery Cleod possessed to match it. And yet, in the mortal contest unfolding before him, Kilras's poise and knowledge not only countered Trayor's but, in some stunning seconds, outmatched it. Blood rose from cuts and nicks in the Draighil's shirt. And if the Dorn was not able to strike a deadly blow, there were moments where only luck rather than talent or training saved the pale Ehlewer.

Did Cleod truly know anything of either of these men? How had he ever imagined he did? What he discerned of each of them as he watched shattered everything he held certain.

And yet one thing he knew to his core, learned in his first vicious battle with Trayor so long ago—if Kilras's abilities continued to best Trayor's, *the Draighil would cheat to win*.

Even as Cleod completed the thought, a taut note of doom warned the air, and a single, earthy streak speared across the open space to pierce Kilras's back in a spurt of blood.

From the corner of his eyes, Cleod saw the Bynkrol bowman draw again, even as the Dorn stumbled and staggered away from Trayor's next blow. A scream rose in Cleod's mind as his body churned through a decision his mind could not make, to hurtle toward the archer or toward Kilras. Then a roar of violent wind came from behind Cleod, lifted them all and hurled them through boiling air, and impact knocked light from his mind.

Leiel

W ITH ALL HER STRENGTH, LEIEL GRABBED SEHINA AND HELD HER back as the sight of the arrow piercing Kilras's back drew a scream of rage from the other woman. The horsetrainer's ferocious lunge would have escaped the grasp of any but a Draigon.

Then a tremor touched Leiel's mind and she gasped. "Down!" and tumbled Sehina to the ground, pinning her. Seconds later a wing wind blasted over them, brush and stone assailing within it. Had they been standing, it would have swept them from their feet and into the rocks behind.

As the rushing air took her breath, Leiel closed her eyes and held against the impact of the debris carried with it. Her heart pounded, a thunder in her chest. And in the seconds it took to pass, she understood that the wind had been cast in an act of desperation. Resor, in defense of Kilras, of her, and Sehina—and Cleod, stood grounded and against more than two dozen Draigre. More than any Draigon could hope to face. The Dinist Draigon's wounds were many and deep, and she would not stand much longer against her foes.

As breath returned to her lungs, Leiel shouted, "Sehina! Now, quickly. We must go now!" She scrambled to her feet, pulling Sehina up with her. As the auburn-haired woman struggled for balance, Leiel placed hands on her shoulders and looked into her eyes. "Sehina. Can you call the horses? Cleod's horse? We need him. We need him to get Kilras and Cleod away."

Sehina blinked and nodded, determination filling her face at the sound of Kilras's name.

"Then hurry." The words snagged in Leiel's throat but she pushed them out. "Resor is dying." She took a breath, tried to slow her racing heart. "I'll find Cleod. And Kilras. Come!" She turned and sprinted toward where she had last seen the two men. If her knife found its way into her hand, and her gaze scanned the broken earth as much for Trayor Draighil as for those she cared for, it did not slow her purposeful charge.

Resor's roars and the shouts of armed men filled the air, and the earth was tossed and shattered, the sounds bouncing over boulders and fallen trees. She scrambled, Sehina behind her, and the horsetrainer's piercing whistles carried over it all. Distantly, she heard the answering cries of horses—Sehina's near-mythical connections to the animals proven true in the greatest moment of need.

Then, ahead Leiel saw a body sprawled, long, dark hair tossed over a dirty face, a shaft protruding starkly from his back. "There!" She stopped and pointed, heard Sehina gasp as she rushed toward Kilras.

Leiel turned and kept moving, reached with Gweld, seeking. Resor's frantic fury and desperation battered her mind and she gasped back a sob. The cost for this moment was already far too great. Faint at the edges of her mind a flicker of familiarity sparked. She moved toward it, Gweld speeding her strides.

Among a tangle of twisted trees, she found Cleod, cut and bruised, unconscious but alive. If she was no healer, she could at least measure physical damage. She tugged limbs off him, used Gweld to search for wounds beyond the obvious and found none. By the time he was free of the debris, Sehina was beside her astride Kicce, with Kilras clasped against her. His eyes were open, and he nodded to Leiel.

She drew every bit of Draigon-backed strength into her body, then lifted Cleod and draped him across Kicce's withers. "Can you hang on?" she asked Kilras. "Your gelding waits with Teska on the ridge."

The Dorn nodded weakly. "Resor—"

"I know," Leiel said, unable to prevent her voice from breaking.

Kilras roused as thought to speak or act, but then slumped in Sehina's arms.

"Leiel—" Sehina gasped.

"Ride!" Leiel shouted. "I'll follow." As Sehina kicked Kicce, with his triple burden, into action, Leiel turned to join Resor's in the fight. But even as she did so, pain erupted through her mind, seared her, descended into blinding light. The force of the horror weakened her knees and she dropped, heaving for air, tears burning her face as truth upended her—Resor was gone.

With a scream of rage, Leiel stared into the settling dust and blowing snow, but the only thing she saw was a dying glow and the ongoing flash of silver swords. She shuddered, desperate to act, to render similar pain on the vile men and end their annihilating frenzy. But as it had in Melbis, greater need laid demand upon her. With a howl of frustration, tears blinding her, she shoved to her feet and raced after Sehina.

Snow, packed by blowing wind even here among the overhanging trees, crunched under Leiel and Teska's boots and the hooves of the grey horse with its motionless burden. The memory of fear, of screams, of blood, echoed too fresh and merciless in her mind. And the tremors vibrating the woman beside her spoke to the healer's own pain and confusion.

Leiel pulled in a long breath and forced down back the horrors trying to claim her attention. What happened through the night and next days would determine whether Resor's sacrifice had helped forge a greater purpose.

Ahead along the overgrown lane, the place she sought stood half-tumbled and dark. The once sturdy barn, collapsed now to rubble, loomed as an ominous shape beside the remains of the smaller house. That structure had fared somewhat better through time, with the porch still attached and most of the roof intact. Still, as she and Teska drew close to the dilapidated remains, Leiel took in that the back corner of the cabin had succumbed to a fallen tree. So sad, to see this place in a disrepair that its former caretaker would never have allowed. How long did it take a home, unused and unloved, to fall to ruin? Had no one been lived here since Ellan's death? If not, why? Because his son still owned it, and had wanted it left alone? Or because of who that son was and what others feared in that association?

"Why here?" Teska asked. Through the deepening gloom, her voice rang loud, though her tone shivered uncertainty into the air.

Why indeed? A stark and purposeful question that Leiel had not allowed to cross her mind. Why here? Why not a secluded campsite? Or if familiarity mattered, why not the old mill at the pond? Why here, a place she had never really visited, knew hardly at all? Words formed and offered answer before thought led them. "Because if there is anything in Cleod to bring home to what he was, this is home. The last place he was himself before the Enclaves laid claim to his future." That felt right. But was it? The risk of this choice was unmitigated despite any justification she might offer. What did she know of Cleod's feelings for this place? Of the loss suffered here? He had, after all, abandoned the property with Ellan's death. Too late now to change destination. While the fire that lived at the base of her spine held her safe, darkness crept closer every moment, and within it, the ever-deepening cold that threatened Teska and Cleod.

Teska's silence told Leiel that the healer shared the uncertainty of the moment, and that the answer had not satisfied. "We are here," Leiel said. "At least for the night. In the morning-"

"By morning he'll be conscious." Teska's words held worry. "And in this place—"

"I don't know what being here will do to him," Leiel admitted. "Whether it will wound deeper, or help heal." She looked along her shoulder at the man tied across the gelding's saddle. His hair, far too long for a Draighil, curled across his slack face. Her fingers itched to push it back, and her heart warmed to the hope it represented, that he was not what he had been, that this small refusal of Enclave norms meant that her friend still dwelt within the stranger carried beside her.

"So this choice is based on instinct alone."

Leiel looked at Teska. "Yes."

The healer's gaze was sharp and steady and the air between them thickened. Measuring. Testing. At last Teska said, "Such will do. I couldn't save Resor." Blinking back tears, she raised a hand to her throat, touched the thin scar there, the mark etched by Cleod's sword. "I am a healer. And this man is in need. And if he is as important as you and Kilras believe—as it seems that Gahree believed—then part of the reason you saved me is also to save him."

Resor. Too familiar, the horrible feeling they once again shared. Leiel drew a breath that suppressed a broken sound. With all that she was, she hoped Teska was correct—and that the losses they suffered would lead to a better future for them all. "That is the hope that we all carry."

They halted at the edge of the porch, and Leiel handed Kicce's reins to Teska. "I'll make certain it's safe enough for the night."

At a nod from the healer, Leiel stepped into the low porch and crossed the too-soft planks to the front door, amazingly still solid in its frame. She turned the handle and pushed it open to reveal an interior strangely untouched by the ruin of the rest of the place. A table and four chairs stood where they had been abandoned; pots hung against the far wall beside a woodstove. Though the scent of must and mold filled the room and dust covered everything, little debris littered the floor, and the roof remained solid overhead. What lay beyond the door at the back of the main room, she did not want to discover. The bedrooms, it seemed, had received the brunt of the tree's impact. Unlikely that anything could be salvaged beyond this one area.

She crossed the room and knelt to open the stove. Old ash lingered, along with a long-abandoned mouse's nest. A blink and her Gweld vision bloomed, and she used it to trace the length of the stove pipe, both pleased and surprised to find no cracks or obstructions. A few moments work and the shelter would be more than adequate, whatever other burdens came with that. She pushed to her feet and returned to outside to help Teska.

Fire burned in the stove, its door left cracked to spill orange light into the room, a single, bright line slicing the darkness. Gweld vision meant it was not truly needed, but comfort was formed of small things, and such small things meant much in the shadows.

Seated at the table across from Leiel, Teska sipped the last of the soup they had consumed as late meal. On a pallet near the head of the table, closest to the heat, Cleod lay carefully trussed. Sweat beaded his forehead and he shook, groaning as though pain gripped him to his very bones. Perhaps it did.

"You can help him?"

Long seconds passed before Teska answered. "If he allows it."

Leiel looked at her. "Allows?"

"This is not the kind of healing that can be forced." Teska's gaze measured Cleod. "I wish you could see what I do. The cuila has poisoned his mind as deeply as his body."

The glint of moonlight on a blade. Blood welling from Teska's throat. "I don't see as you do, but I see enough."

Teska hesitated again. "The kind of healing that is required has to be *his choice*. In order to reach deep enough to ease the scars in his mind, his will must bend toward wholeness. Otherwise, I can strip the need from his body, but the hate that's been ingrained in him may lead him back to it."

Leiel tipped her head. "Can he choose? In pain as he is? In such need?"

"I don't know." Teska's fingers gripped on the bowl. "You said you were friends once. And you brought him here, to a place he knew when he was someone you trusted. Someone who made choices that *he* trusted. Perhaps he wants to be that person again."

Would that either of them retained that youthful caring and integrity. Such hope was vanity itself. But perhaps something new could be formed in its place. Something even more powerful, and far, far more necessary. The knot that had ridden in Leiel's chest all day pulled tighter. "I am no longer the person he became Draighil for." Her voice dropped to a whisper. "I am what he hates."

"Are you?"

Leiel shook her head. "I am Draigon."

"You are *Leiel*," Teska said. "None of this will mean anything unless he loves you more than he hates his idea of what you have become. Isn't that why you went to him in Melbis? Because you believed that?"

The words dropped like boulders into Leiel's mind, and blood rushed to her face. War. Pain. Loss. So much loss. Wynt. Gahree. Resor. Each death that bled across Arnan as armies and towns and families split and faced off, as years of suffering broke open like poorly bandaged wounds. None of the cost destined to be worth the pain unless one man could be salvaged. Unless they could find a way to help Cleod *salvage himself*.

He jerked hard against his bonds, lost in whatever pain and memory the Overlash of his choices had dragged him beneath.

"We won't know until he wakes from this." Leiel raised a hand toward him, and traced her finger through the air as though offering a soothing touch to his brow, as she had across impossible distance on the dusty plains outside Meblis. As she had in truth the night she stepped from the trees and set horrible change in motion. Her touch on his life had begot too much. What would it bring to him tomorrow?

"Leiel." Teska's voice held the same strange note it had when she had spoken of the way Kilras used Gweld. "He uses Gweld as he was trained to. But he does not have to. It need not pain him, if he learns to touch it as we do."

Leiel frowned. "What do you mean?"

The healer sighed and shook her head. "I am not sure it matters."

Leiel sighed. She dropped her hand into her lap, shook her head. "Get some rest, Teska. I'll watch him through the night."

48

Leiel

SHE SAT AWAKE UNTIL TESKA STIRRED ACROSS FROM HER AND WOKE TO take over watching Cleod. As exhaustion, more of heart and mind, muddled Leiel's senses, she agreed to rest and lay back, expecting only to stare into the shadows until dawn. But against those expectations, she slept, though her dreams twisted and tumbled and turned on themselves like rolling storm clouds, amorphous and dark.

When she woke, just before sunrise, she lay with her eyes closed, listening to the chill wind rattle the slats of the half-tumbled building, to her heartbeat, to her breath whispering in and out. She half-feared the events of the previous day had been only a wish-dream. But a sharp twist deep in her gut told her otherwise. She was not alone in this broken space.

And another mind struggled toward wakefulness in the pre-dawn darkness, bleeding waves of pain and panic into the night.

Cleod.

Leiel opened her eyes and rolled onto her side, stared through the shadows filling the room toward the bound figure bundled in blankets before the stove. What would this place mean to him, when he woke? Would he know it at all? Know her? Feel anything but hate? And what had happened with Kilras... How would that affect him? This risk taken was based on that response. If she were wrong... Should she have left Teska to care for the Dorn instead?

"He aches." Teska's voice came through the darkness.

Leiel sat up slowly, looked over to where the healer sat with her back to the wall, blanket wrapped tight around her.

"I'm glad you slept," Teska said. "I've watched his Enai." Her words fell flat, laced with an uncertainty that had not been present last night.

A chill crawled up Leiel's arms. "You learned something?"

Teska exhaled slowly. "Yes." Wonder filled her voice. "I've learned how much Cyunant has to offer me. What I've come to understand in only weeks with Gydron—" She stopped and her next words held only doubt. "I see a limit to what I can achieve here."

Several heartbeats passed as Leiel tried to make sense of that statement, then she took a heavy breath, understanding. "A limit because he knows how to fight with Gweld." At every turn a barrier, a battle. "You said he has to accept help. But it's more than that. He can stop you. He can hurt you."

As grey light brightened the cabin's only window, Teska answered softly, "Yes."

Reaching up, Leiel pushed loose hairs out of her eyes, her brow furrowing. Cleod's will had always been as sharp and hardened as a fine blade. Tempered by time and the heat of Draigon Weather, that will had sustained him through brutal adversity and driven him to sobriety despite all odds. As strong as Teska was in Gweld, the chance that she could match Cleod if he woke in a state of determined rage—Well, it was slim enough that Leiel saw only one alternative. "I'll have to convince him, then, to let you do what's needed."

"How?"

Leiel closed her eyes, then opened them slowly and allowed Gweld to flood her senses. Across the room, the tangled mind of her old friend jerked toward alertness, red-rimmed and churning. Old friend. Did the fate of Arnan really turn on the strength of a childhood bond? Was that possible?

Cleod

Through air so dry and dust-filled that it sapped the moisture from every pore, Cleod moved, head bent. In a parched throat, thirst to crack flesh begged slaking, but the thought of water turned his stomach. The desperate desire rippling through him was for nothing so wholesome. Head thick and legs uncertain with need, he took step after step through the storm.

Wind and dust. Where had winter fled? Draigon. Damned and damning Draigon. The curse slithered through his mind, sinister and ruinous, but it contained no rage. That flared only as afterthought, somehow distant from the moment, more instinct than actuality.

A heavy scent boiled through the air. Blood. So much blood. So much. Not enough. None. A figure loomed through the storm. Cleod's shoulders stiffened as Kilras turned, sword in hand, a familiar, knowing grin on his face. "What they've always been," he said with a wink, his words wafting almost visibly across the smoldering ground that lay, grey with ash and dust, between them.

"Always?" Cleod asked. The air tasted burnt. Scorched flesh overlaid the copper-bright scent of blood. And his voice sounded muffled and distant, as though his ears were stuffed with cotton. Confusion permeated him. Where were they? Why could he not hear properly? His spine tingled. Kilras, ready to fight? Where was the danger? Cleod started to reach for his blade, realized half way through the gesture that he was not wearing his sword harness, and looked in alarm to Kilras in time to see the Dorn jerk violently as a dark shaft pierced his side with a violent spray of blood.

"Kil!" Cleod lunged to assist, but a gust of wind blew a wall of dust between them, and when it cleared Kilras knelt on the ground under a patch of blue sky, and the scent of smoke no longer hung in the air, but only brushed the edges of Cleod's senses. Kilras's shirt and vest were unmarred, no arrow protruded from his back, no crimson stained him.

"Kilras?" Cleod took a step forward, then froze as he realized what the Dorn examined—a glittering pool the color of mountain garnet, gleaming in the thin light. Breath caught in Cleod's lungs and he half-choked on the exhale as he realized where he was.

His pulse roared into his ears as Kilras leaned forward and placed a reverent hand atop the crystalline puddle, smooth as polished glass, reflective as metal. Realization came—that the great smear of blood was *somehow solid*. Cleod's belly rippled and he tasted bile.

And at the edge of the battle site, a long slash of red-gold gleamed in the waste, bright metallic and startling on the earth, then pooling wider, a spilled, warped circle. Invisible amid the smoke and darkness on the night of the Sacrifice, the stain glittered like a trail of rubies across the ruined ground. Draigon blood. He bent to touch it with a finger.

Cleod jerked back, the feel of the crystal surface still vibrating against his skin. *How?* He stared at his hand, then raised wide eyes to look again at Kilras in time to see the Dorn grasp the edge of the impossible stain and watch it explode into vapor, fine as loss on the wind.

As though his boots were filled with stones, Cleod stood immobile.

Only a shard remained, held gently in Kilras's hand.

Cleod opened his mouth but no words came, and when Kilras looked over his shoulder and met Cleod's gaze, the Dorn's eyes gleamed green-gold in the pale air.

A scream rose from Cleod's belly, caught hard in his throat, and the moment blew apart with the same misting force that dispersed Shaa's heart-blood into the storm.

Leiel

With a groan, Cleod stirred.

She pushed to her feet and moved toward him. How to convince him? No answers came to Teska's question other than the ones to which Leiel had always clung. With friendship. And with hope. She could voice neither idea. What could she do in the face of a body poisoned by cuila and a heart twisted by long-tempered hatred? What could she do in the face of such anger?

An image cracked open in the back of her mind, soft as smoke—the flicker of a fluffy tail breaking the stillness of a forest canopy.

She froze in the darkness, the pressure of Cleod's waking mind and the howl of the wind outside trying to drive even the shadow of the idea from her head. Imagination. Shared hope mixed with sadness and fear. The dream of a hot summer day beside a half-stagnant pond. A simpler time when even shattered innocence still held value. Could it be that simple?

Why not? Had not her whole world changed through the power of simple truth? Of stories recalled and shared, of bitter humor touched with caring? But what story did not offer something powerful to those in need? Every tale, in the end, came to righteous fruition through a strength born of compassion and caring. Even the most ridiculous of fables were meant to touch and to change.

She stepped closer, seeking words to express, to impress. A hint of grey showed at the edges of the shutters, not enough to pierce the dark, but enough to mar it.

Something hissed through her senses, alive on every level and filled with violent intensity. Like the scream of a knife over slate, it rose and scraped and twisted, spiraling upward demanding every bit of her attention and intent. She stopped, feet planted slightly apart, one a half step before the other, and braced her mind as Cleod came awake with a mental roar designed to strip from her all certainty and stability. Years of focused training allowed her to not only weather the assault, but shield Teska as well. Cleod's rage and confusion pushed on and on, like a wing wind driving a wave, until it crashed into full consciousness with a cry of such viciousness that it seemed designed to blow the entire building apart.

The confident grace that had been his for so long disintegrated in a wrath of frenzied desperation. With a snarling groan, Cleod jerked and fought the bonds that held him. Dark sweeps of his Gweld talent battered her mind, washed swaths of burgundy and deep indigo across her vision, each impact of his fear and rage both a blow and a scream across her senses. He cursed her, vile streams of words that spoke of a depth of agony she barely found space to comprehend.

"Great gods," Teska said, trembling as she stepped up beside Leiel.

Without taking her gaze from Cleod, Leiel asked, "Can you do this?"

"Without you? No. So the question is, can *you*?"

Leiel took in a heavy breath. After everything, how could it be that a friendship built in distant childhood had become the fulcrum on which so much balanced? Could it outweigh the demands imposed by time and suffering? Could it bridge the chasm of violence opened between them in the last months?

Leiel's vision flared again, wild and turbid as Cleod tugged and twisted against the restraints, his gaze unfocused, sweat slick on his face. The tones in her Gweld-touched vision grew harsher, waves breaking against the shore of her perception.

She remembered his reaction to a hand raised to reach across distance on a blazing plain. But now—another burst of savage light slammed across her vision—rage or craving or both—did any logic, any caring have access to his mind in the moment? Nothing remained but to try.

She put a hand on Teska's forearm. "If I am able—"

"I'll know." Teska placed her hand over Leiel's, gave a squeeze.

Leiel returned the pressure then released her grasp and walked toward Cleod. Each step carried her deeper into the undulating arena of his violent need. How fast, his slide from controlled warrior into this struggling state. Only a day without access to cuila or ercew and already his mind shifted and splintered. Old gods—how had he ever survived his first break from the Ehlewer?

She stopped and threw up mental defenses to block a blow of Gweld-backed fury. It ricocheted away. Powerful as he was, the trials of the last months, the ercew, anger and fear had muddled his focus. "Cleod, you can't hurt me. Not like this. You can't hurt me no matter how much you want to."

He struck out again with his mind, but, forewarned, she swept that attack aside as well. Two more strides brought her to him. She dropped into a crouch and met his gaze in the grey light and held it. So bright, so wide, glazed with uncontained hunger. And yet... As had been the case when she stepped from the depths of the forest so many months ago, recognition sparked in his eyes. A shock reverberated into the air between them.

"Do you want to?" A small knot lodged in her throat, marking her fear that he did indeed desire to harm her. But what looked back at her out of his eyes held more depth, instant to instant, than any spoken answer could share. A sliver of hope laced its way through the lump of doubt.

Then, with an animal snarl, he surged toward her and would have tumbled her had she not been more prepared for that response than for easy victory. She pushed up and back, landed steps away from him as he rolled, struggled onto his knees. His glare held a heat to rival that a Draigon produced on her fiercest day.

"Idohben, Cleod!" Leiel pushed authority into her voice. Gahree had once startled him into distraction. Teska said the

Enclave Gweld training *bent* the skill. Leiel settled into her mind, then reached, twisting through dancing waves of cold to weave among amber streaks and crimson bands of power. She widened her thoughts, trying to understand how to connect, to share. True alliance eluded her, but the intensity of the link forged in their youth, before Gweld, before...everything...held true. Would it suffice? It would have to.

The past rose up to meet the moment, and for the space of a heartbeat wind rustled leaves overhead and the splash of a frog broke the surface of a pond. She spoke, quiet in the face of a rage that beat at her like the battering wings of an angry hawk. "I am but a chattering squirrel." *Remember.* "Your anger need not touch me. I am not worthy of your rage."

He jerked against his bonds again, then something turned deep behind his expression, something that pulled only at the edges of his determined glare. Something that might be enough. *Remember.*

"Do you know where you are?" she asked. "We've brought you home. Let us bring you further."

Cleod

Stiff and twisted, hands and arms half-numb and bunched behind him, he came to consciousness lying on a hard surface. Something wrapped over him, soft and clean—a blanket?—his hands were...bound? The realization swept the dream from his mind in a rush.

Something brushed the edges of his mind and Gweld bunched, then spiraled, his every sense amplified as it streamed outward like a series of battering waves. As though they struck a seawall, they impacted, reflected, swept back into his mind, tried to wash him away into a rolling sea of fear and confusion. A hiss of language followed as though it were foam on a wave *can't hurt me.*

Anger overwhelmed panic as he rolled, struggled upright into a space barely warm and barely bright enough for his eyes to focus in. Old smoke, damp wood, and something vague that stirred the deepest fiber of memory tangled in his nose. Where was he?

Do you want to?

...Leiel? *Charred earth and cinders and the spray of blood, precious, acidic, full of smoke. Kilras bleeding. Too much blood. Not enough.*

Cleod's gaze found focus. The shadow poised in the center of the room took shape, sharpened at the edges. Leiel. Yes, Leiel. Head thundering with a rush of blood, he surged forward, body and mind, and again met resistance. Then something about the space itself rippled awareness into attention.

"I am but a chattering squirrel," Leiel said.

He stared at her, let his gaze slip past her to the other woman standing in shadow, slip again over the vague forms and lines of the room, slowly growing distinct in the grey light, slip back to Leiel and her dark, intense expression. Where was he? Where...

"Do you know where you are? We've brought you home. Let us bring you further."

Dream tangled with recollection tangled with loss and he shuddered, strained against the bonds that wrapped his wrists, until skin tore and hot liquid slicked over his hands. "What have you done?" he demanded, voice thick. Thoughts warred with instinct, memory with the need to act, to destroy—but—Home. She had said *home.*

Images tumbled across Cleod's sight, each more vivid and uncanny than the last—this room, warm with love and laughter, Leiel's tears beneath an oak tree, Kilras holding a cup of coffee on a frosted morning.

And suddenly every part of Cleod ached, heart to head, wringing knots down his back. His belly churned and the back of his throat burned. "What have you done?" he repeated, the words quiet. Shock quashed fury in a way he would never have believed possible.

He drank and drank, then looked up at his father. "I never believed you. The stories."

"Most don't until they see."

He spread his fingers, tested the knot that bound his wrists, sick to his stomach as he stared at Leiel. "What have you become?"

"I could ask the same of you, old friend," she said, and sank to her knees to meet his gaze at level. "A vengeful brute? A drunk? A killer?"

He narrowed his eyes and glared. "Yes," he said, and the word was a promise. How many promises had he made? Of them, how many lay broken behind him? And yet here he made another, to be all of the things she proposed, if that was what it took to finally end this pain.

She shook her head without breaking his stare. "You've never been a liar." She blinked slowly. "That's for the rest of us."

He lunged again, realized only as his body stopped hard and jerked sideways that he was not only bound but tethered to something behind him. Frustration drew a snarl, and he rocked back, a vile reply forming on his lips when some part of him checked the impulse, some part that took in the word *we* and vivid memory crushed him beneath the weight of truth. *Kilras leveled his gaze at Trayor, shifted his wrist to change the angle of his grip on the sword, flicked his gaze past Trayor to meet Cleod's eyes, and smiled. Then his attention returned to the challenge before him and he stepped forward to meet it.*

"Old gods," Cleod whispered. "Old gods and damnation. Kilras." His head was suddenly on fire, and a pain built of need and loss ripped through his gut. *"Where's Kil?"*

Leiel

BEHIND HER, TESKA DREW A RAGGED BREATH. WHAT BLOOMED IN Cleod's enai? What intensity churned and flashed in the brightening dimness? To ask would be to shift the energy of the moment in the wrong way. Instead, Leiel answered, "Kilras is in Adfen."

She watched the shock go through him, the conflict unfold and unravel the parts of him that cuila and ercew had stripped raw and weakened.

Cleod lifted blazing eyes, and if will alone could ignite conflagration, she would have been the hot match struck by his violent determination, and the entire cabin would have burst into flames. His intensity swirled around him, rising like the rolling plumes of an erupting volcano, dark with sudden desperation. "He's alive?"

If secrets and half-truths had separated them for years, the remedy for that could now only be honesty, no matter the pain it brought. "I don't know. He was when Sehina took him toward the city." She watched his emotions collapse, like columns of smoke falling back into an unfathomable chasm, and ached for the pain of all he had witnessed, for a loss of faith and friendship that she understood all too well. If Kilras did not survive... She refused to finish the thought. "Sehina was with him. If there is help for him, she will make certain he receives it."

Cleod's shattering gaze shifted to look past her, landed hot and held too-steady on the woman behind her. "If he was alive, he would need a healer. A healer worth dying for. And yet *she* is here with you." Bitterness flooded his voice and something else that might be the beginnings of despair. His gaze drifted, and the tension in his body shifted inward.

"No," Leiel said, her tone firm and purposeful. "She is here with *you*."

As though the statement scalded, he flinched, and his attention snapped back to her. "With me?"

She needed to reach him. "Why do you think Kilras took the fight to Trayor?" Needed to cut him deeply with what mattered, what had sustained him for so long. If they were right about him, all of them right, then chance was like a feather on the wind, and if she were lucky enough to catch and hold it, they could change everything. If she could but grasp it, grasp the Cleod she had known and who, with all her soul, she believed still dwelt in the man before her—hope would bloom. "Out of some need to prove himself? Out of pride?"

The planks of the cabin floor were hard under her knees, as solid as her belief in their once-sustaining friendship. She held his gaze. "You know better than anyone that could never be the case. But to save someone he cared about? To offer a second chance to someone he believed in? Would he do it *then*? Would Kilras step into absolute danger for anything less?"

Every bit of him trembled, though whether from emotion or the simple shock of a body enduring deadly cravings, she could not discern. What turned in his thoughts? Or were they stunned, locked and muddled? Had she or Kilras or any of them been anything more than cruel in bringing him to this moment? Her heart burned, heavy in her chest, and her breath trembled as she drew in air. "The only person who has never understood how important you are to the future of Arnan, *is you*." She made herself relax, settled back on her heels as she softened the tension pulling at her jaw. "Let us help you," she said. "Teska is here with me, *for you*, because we believe she knows how."

His expression changed, warring, violent and desperate one instant to the next, until every part of him seemed ready to fly into a thousand shards of solid light.

"*Leiel...*" A whisper from behind her, wondering yet powerful. She hardly dared to hope for what it might mean. She did not move, just watched Cleod.

Teska stepped up beside her, pressed a flask of warm liquid into Leiel's hand, the herbal blend that could force the need for ercew from his body. "If he agrees, I may be to exhausted to see he drinks this."

Leiel nodded, tucked the warm bottle into her belt.

The healer stood watching, and her Gweld energy pushed into the air, unseen but vital and full of authority. It made no demands, just wrapped through room, enfolded and asked a simple question. Asked permission.

Long moments passed, and the space vibrated with struggle, with fear, and doubt and a bitter tang that could only be named as guilt. What unfolded inside Cleod, Leiel could not even imagine. Years of pain and poison, tangled with misguided honor and his desperate need to protect those he cared about. An internal war. A thunderous, brutal awakening. It showed in every line of his body, the clenching of his jaw, the desperate shaking. She ached for the suffering unfolding within him.

Beside her, Teska trembled, sank to her knees, arm outstretched as though her touch could ease the battle within him. Leiel braced an arm against the younger woman's back. Every bit of the room vibrated, a low shuddering pulse that pleaded comfort into the air.

Then something crumpled into the trembling void between the three of them. He trembled, strained against his bonds. Then with all that she was, Leiel felt Teska *reach*. The feeling pierced, consumed.

Leiel backed it with a whisper. "Kilras took on Trayor to give us the opportunity to reach you, Cleod Ruhelrn. Cleod Draighil.

Cleod Woodcutter." She shifted closer to him, let her hand slip from Teska's back as the healer nodded. "You are our friend, Cleod. We need you. We need you with us in this final fight."

She watched him shudder. Teska's energy surged forward. Then his eyes rolled back, drifted shut, and Leiel was close enough to catch him as he collapsed forward into her arms.

50

Kilras

DISTANT AND MUDDLED, VOICES ROSE AND FELL WITH THE PAIN. HEAT and cold warred in his body, flash points of ferocious discomfort that boiled nausea through his gut and left him dashed like a frail boat upon a rocky shore.

Through cracked eyelids, pale lines of light poured through narrow gaps above him, blocked occasionally by passing shadows that hovered and loomed. The dark shapes pounded with energy, the intense demands of fear and worry. People? The source of the voices?

His thoughts refused consolidation. Where? Why? Never had he burned so. His body denied all attempts to reach alertness, and the weight of helplessness wove panic through his jumbled consciousness.

From far off, a word repeated with steady urgency, filtered through rising fear. *Kilras.* Lost as a whisper in a storm. Remote and fleeting. Vital. *Kilras.* His name? Gold light flared against the darkness of his vision, and he *reached* with all the strength he could muster for the world beyond the cage of his mind. Slowly, focus returned, tentative and fragile, and he blinked open crusted eyes to see a familiar face bent close to his own.

Gold illuminated her, flickered and searched until a name filled his thoughts. *Retta.* He tried to speak but no words came.

"Kil? Old gods—yes!" Her voice lifted. "Amhise! He's awake." She held his gaze. "You're safe. In Adfen. In your library. Be still."

Gweld pushed at his mind, frantic in its fight to hold him conscious. Memory unwound the pain, and recollection bloomed. A fight. Trayor Draighil and flashing swords. The sudden, stunning bite of metal through flesh and the roar of rage that followed as strength faltered despite will. He remembered falling. Falling and fear and then nothing at all until anguish woke him.

Falling again, now in the struggling moment even as other figures surrounded him in a flurry of concern and caring words. Gweld marked his danger and his need. Fever and infection—something else. A lack of resource. A battle that raged outside this considered space.

He tried to speak, but no sound came from cracked lips and swollen tongue. A moment later, the tilt of something against his mouth brought welcome moisture. "*The blood,*" he whispered, even as exhausted agony pulled him under.

The edges of his senses trembled, red-rimmed and radiating violent heat. Fear woke in his core, a hard, deliberate knowledge that beyond the dancing light lay suffering. But from the other side of that warning glow came sounds, pulsing and heavy with distress. Vague awareness told him that the rising and falling noises had significance.

Voices.

Friends.

"Kil's deliberate. It has to mean *something.*"

"If you don't know, Sehina, no one will."

Words hung muffled, only sorted into meaning long seconds after his ears took them in. *Sehina*? Who was that? Where was he? The red light surrounding him flared brighter and every part of him cringed away. But the sonorous voices continued, broke through the safe darkness in which he lay.

"Retta, keep reading. There has to be something."

Reading? His library? Anxious thoughts speared through him, demanded attention, forced consciousness. The dangerous luminescence pursued them into his mind and he gasped awake, fire lancing his side and streaming though his body like lava coursed the interior of a volcano. If he cried out he did not know, but the spasm that jerked through his body drew the attention, drew contact, and focused caring and the touch of a wrinkled palm against his forehead.

"Kilras? Can you hear me?"

He forced open dry eyes. "Amhise?"

She stared down at him, worry lining every aspect of her expression. "Yes. Old gods—we thought we'd lost you. I've dosed you with draperoot. It's all I have. Do you remember what happened?"

Recollection shivered his overlapping thoughts. A field of snow. The sound of blades crossing. Blonde hair and callous laughter. The violating lance of metal through his back, searing and painted with fire.

"What hit me?" he whispered.

"An arrow," Sehina's face leaned into view. "I brought you here. We worked it out. Stopped the bleeding. But something's wrong. You're not healing."

"Infection?" Even as he spoke the word, he recognized it as the too-simple explanation for the pain racking him. "Poison."

"Likely," Amhise said. "And we've found nothing in all your books to help..." A film of desperation clung to her words.

"You said *blood*." Sehina closed warm fingers over his.

Had he? His skull tingled and his vision blurred. Blood? What blood? His? He frowned as the pain radiating from his side intensified. Not his blood... "My bag," he whispered. "With the fire flint. Wrapped up."

"Retta do you have his things?" Sehina pulled away, and the sound of her conversation with the baker slipped up and down in volume as he fought to stay awake.

"Here," Sehina returned to his side. "I have it. What is it?" She held up a flat sliver of crimson crystal. Her voice flattened. "Kil? Is this *blood*?"

He turned inward, opened to Gweld and with an act of will mustered his thoughts to attention. He met Sehina's gaze. Her face shimmered in gold light. "Shaa's blood," he managed.

Gasps rose, from Amhise, from Retta. But not Sehina. She looked down at him, focused and intense, as composed as he had ever known her. The hand holding the blood-shard did not shake. She grasped his hand again. "Tell us what to do."

Amhise's fingers trembled against his blazing skin and he shuddered as she peeled back the last, crusted bandage to reveal the weeping gash in his side. The stink of it filled his nose, told him more than if he could see it.

Sehina met his gaze where she crouched near his head. "You're certain?" she asked. "We could try to burn out the corruption."

Weakly, he shook his head. Honey and herbs and cauterization were no match for the pollution seeping through his body. Whatever had coated the barb and shaft of the arrow was virulent beyond measure. His only chance lay in the untried potential of an old friend's final gift, one hope, backed by his trained skill in Gweld and the vague instinct of the absent Draigfen healer. "This is all there is," he whispered.

Sehina held his gaze a long moment, then she brushed back his hair and slid a hard strip of leather between his teeth. He bit down on it, and she placed a hand on each of his shoulders, used her full body weight to press him back against the floor.

Similar restraint loaded his legs as Retta lent her strength to the task at hand.

"Do it," Sehina said, the words like a hammer fall.

Beside him, Amhise drew a shaking breath. Kilras focused the gold lights of Gweld vision on the wound and drove all his intention into a single thought—*shatter*—as Amhise used both hands to press the piece of Gahree's crystallized blood into the gash marring his side.

The explosion was dust and inferno, searing into his flesh to course a brutal path along every blood vessel and through every fiber of muscle and bone. His body arched against restraining hands, and his jaw locked teeth against hard leather. Not enough. Too much. Struggle unfolded, will and blood and the flame of ancient knowledge at war in his body and mind. Convulsing under his friends' desperate grasps, he struggled for control.

Deeper and deeper the Gweld-backed particles of Draigon essence pierced him, until his vision boiled in myriad color and foam gathered at the edges of his mouth.

Lost in unfathomable anguish, he fought against a scream and lost. A shriek of pure agony and terror ripped from his throat and rose like a breaking wave to echo against stone walls and back into his skull before slamming him into utter darkness.

51

Cleod

SEATED ON THE SAGGING STEPS OF THE CABIN, CLEOD PULLED THE blanket tight across his shoulders, closed his eyes, and raised his face to the sun. Warmth. Not the fiery calefaction of Draigon Weather or the consuming heat of rage, just comfort like an embrace, a caress, a caring whisper.

Old gods, how long had it been since warmth was just that— something that spread deep through his bones and into his belly? Something that demanded nothing, and simply encompassed every bit of him in gentle comfort.

His stomach rumbled, and he tensed, waited for the craven desire that for so many years took the place of true hunger. His mind remembered—the falling feeling of repressed yearning, the tearing violence of need long denied. But this time his body did not respond with the soul-gouging ache that required pure will to ignore. Instead, the growl from his gut was just a request for sustenance, only a signal that his last meal was too long past.

Wonder bled tension from his body. He opened tight-pressed eyes and drew a long breath, savoring...what? The answer came without conscious intent: *freedom*. Not since boyhood had his body held such stillness, such peace. If long experience informed fear—*it would not last*—the moment earned respect through rarity. Yet, second passing second, it held, and he soaked it in like the sunlight. Nothing interrupted, not the lowing of the winter wind through tree boughs, not Kicce's whicker from behind the house, not the footfall on the porch behind him.

"I brought you food." Leiel's voice, bright and strong in the crisp air.

He turned his head to look up at her, the core of his being steeled for violent reaction to her nearness.

It did not come.

Though a part of his mind flickered to dark alertness, the visceral rage that had dominated their last encounters did not awaken. Relief washed through him like water over smooth stones and he blinked at her, half-shocked, half-numbed by the calmness within. She held out a steaming bowl, and he stared at it, at her, unable, for a few seconds, to respond. Then he reached out and took it from her grasp, careful not to touch her as he did so. That far, he could not yet imagine trusting himself.

A shiver spiraled up his spine. Trust—here she stood, a half-pace from him, unafraid, despite all he had done and tried to do. So very Leiel, that bravery beyond sense. It settled him, somehow, to know that she was at least that much the person he remembered, the girl turned woman turned…Draigon…still as reckless in her determination as she had ever been.

"Thank you," he managed, the words strange in a raw throat. He cleared it, swallowed hard, and met her gaze.

She held his, measuring, then took a step forward and sat down on the steps as far from him as the space would allow. "Teska made it," she said with a wry smile. "So it should be edible."

"All these years and you still hate to cook?" He turned his attention to the soup, lifted the spoon and took a sip, then paused. Did she even have to cook? Did she eat, for that matter? What did a Draigon need to survive? The weight of uncertainty extinguished his appetite and he stared down into the bowl in his hand. How much did he want to know?

He trembled, questions darkening his thoughts. The soup shivered and rippled in the bowl. Before it could spill, he set it aside, onto the porch between them.

"You can ask," she said quietly.

He did not look at her. "And will you tell me?"

Silence held for a few breaths, then she answered with a certainty that spoke understanding of exactly what she offered—offered to him who only hours ago had called himself enemy of all she was. "I will tell you anything."

He faced her, pulled like a fractured star between the peace inside him and the opposing knowledge he had for so long held as dear truth. "No matter the cost?"

She nodded, her eyes shining at the corners. "What value is left in measuring cost against loss?"

He turned away, looked out across the snow-covered yard where he had played and worked as a child. Memory jumbled over memory, like kittens tangled in string. "You chose this place."

"It could do no harm to have Teska try to heal you here." Warm crockery brushed gently against his hand. "You need your strength."

He looked down, glanced at her, took the bowl from her once again. His stomach rumbled and he forced himself to eat despite the questions that wrecked his appetite. What did he need strength for now? What purpose, what life, stretched before him? Everything that had mattered lay false and meaningless as fallen trees across the trail of his past. If vile hunger had died within him, reborn liberty offered no new focus, no reason or direction to guide action beyond each breath. Who was he? *What was he?* Choking desperation rose to block his breath, and he closed his eyes again to force calm, used the time to flip the question, force it through stiff lips. "What are you?" He opened his eyes and looked at her again. "Tell me what it means to be... this...creature...that you have become. Tell me so that I can understand...why? What was it all worth?"

She tipped her head, measuring as she studied him. "Can you hear it?"

He frowned. The question marked sharp awareness, that despite the physical change that blunted training, habit might still rule his response.

She raised her chin a fraction. "Hate born in ambition might fade given expanded knowledge and enough time. But to receive the former will come with pain—and we have little of the latter to spare." She offered him an open palm. "But I share with you whatever you need to hear, that we might become something more than Draigon and Draighil."

"Friends of old?" Bitterness creased his tone despite best intention.

With the flicker of a sad smile on her lips, Leiel shook her head. "No," she said. "It is long past time that we become something more."

"Then tell me what you are," he repeated. "Tell me why I should not hate you."

52

Leiel

HIS REQUEST TURNED THROUGH HER, NEEDLE HOT AND SPIRALING. Where to begin? What to say? Truth. Only truth would do, unpolished and hard as tempered steel. Nothing else could exist between them now if any future could be forged for them in whatever Arnan would become.

And so desperate was the struggle inside him that she did not need Gweld to see it. Bent over the bowl, his lean shoulders rounded under the blanket, he emanated uncertainty in a way she had never witnessed even in the most dismal moments of their childhood. She spoke softly, let the words fill the space the cold ushering of air had claimed. Whether they would add any warmth was beyond her to judge.

"I remember following you up the Spur, the way the morning mist moved around us as we climbed, the scent of fallen leaves and granite and balsam in the air. I remember how strong you were, how you moved, how centered and determined was every stride you took. I remember wanting to tell you everything, and knowing that you would not listen.

"How strange that was, realizing that the person I once trusted with everything was no longer willing to truly hear me, because other things had come to matter more. Other dreams and visions of the future. Other priorities. My sadness had no boundaries in that moment.

"But I too had a new future, new hopes and dreams, and so I would not have begrudged you yours—had it not meant your potential destruction. And that I could not stop, because you had chosen it as much as I had chosen to be walked up that mountain."

Her voice dropped to a whisper, as though the ache of memory somehow meant the air in her lungs could not provide enough force for anything louder. "When you fell on the Spur..." She drew breath, forced it on and out before continuing. "I thought I was breaking apart, not knowing if you were dead or alive. Then heat and fire claimed everything and I lost track of even my own breath. When I woke I was far, far from where I had last seen you, and I did not know if I would ever see you again."

She wanted to reach out to him, cover his hand with hers, but it did not seem an option. Not yet. Would it ever? What changes had Teska worked within him? What did he want, need, on this new morning in this place he once called home? And yet he had asked the hardest of questions. And *that* was so like the boy she remembered, curious and daring, even in the face of the utter unknown. That was what she had hoped to encounter in him when she stepped from the shadow of the treeline back in Melbis, his unflinching willingness to experience new things, to learn and grow. It had to be there, deep inside him, or nothing Kilras Dorn had said or done could have pulled Cleod from his self-imposed exile and carried him for decades over the trails of Arnan.

But how to tell him what she was? What she had become and was still becoming? The question cut through her, a fierce, biting demand. What was she? Longing pulled through her, to just let the flood of emotion within her guide what came next. But she straightened her shoulders and forced herself to patience.

"What am I, Cleod? I am a creature born of Arnan—a woman able to claim her power and integrity and use it to reshape the world. I am what I want everyone to be—free."

So close to him, yet still as far as she had ever been, she held back the words that rose within her. She forced herself to consider each one, to measure it against the potential volatility of his response. What mutual understanding still existed that might bridge time and distance, overshadow lies and fear and rage? Care must be taken and she let it grace each phrase, every tone, as she spoke. Quietly she offered her story, from her awakening in the meadow after the battle on the Spur, to her flight to the wonderland that was the Great Northern Range. And Cyunant. Her mother. Her anger and her tears. The joy of sisterhood blooming, carrying her on strong shoulders and backs, through words and laughter and the speaking of hard truths.

She spoke of the wonders of freedom, of education, of learning to dance with her body and her mind. Of how much she had feared and doubted, and how much she had grown and discovered and discarded, until she understood that the entire world lay before her, filled with wonder and a thousand, thousand things she might now be able to explore, and open to, and understand.

"Can you see it?" she asked. Despite her intent to hold back awe, excitement skipped through her words like children turned loose in a wildwood. "Can you understand the power of it—the knowledge that nothing was beyond understanding, because no barriers remained to any of it except discipline and time? And that *time* no longer mattered? That no insight would, anymore, be denied me? The learning of...*anything*...became possible. To see or go anywhere...because suddenly I could learn and hold it all inside a form that gave me freedom and security and even flight—"

She gasped a little and fell silent. The careful control with which she had begun her tale had fallen away, swept aside by the passion of remembrance, and the joy that every bit of her felt at being *exactly who she was*. How many ever had that? How many had died because they were denied even a taste of it?

He stared at her, eyes clear in a face gone tense and stiff. Almost, she reached for Gweld, but stopped herself at the edge of expanded awareness. A tingle across her chest told her he struggled with the same restraint, fought to hold down the trance skill that empowered his ability to conquer Draigon. Conquer her.

Choice loomed, to hold to silence, or continue and risk all that he was and had been and might become. Balanced there, with unquickened Gweld reflecting energy between them, she measured chance and spoke vibrant truth into danger. "The fire that lives within me now is meant to burn the world. Not the heat that lives at the base of my spine and churns my will into the Great Shape of Draigon and can sear the land and set mountains alight—but the one *you* have always known, my friend. The one that makes me who I am, and seeks to free others who wish to be all that *they* were born to be in a world that would deny them any part of that."

She hesitated. What right had she to tell the rest, the story not her own? And yet he needed to know, to understand how the Draigon had shaped not only his deepest pain, but his fiercest loves as well. She studied him, the set of his jaw, the ache etched through every line of his body. So much to take in. Had even a fraction of her words reached him, much less the depth of the meaning behind them? All that, he struggled to absorb, and yet she held more knowledge that he needed. And no time remained to hold back, to offer it gently. He must know the truth of all that mattered if they were to move forward with the purpose and speed that necessity demanded. Armies moved and clashed, and what little peace held sway within this broken space must soon be abandoned.

"Kilras knows," she said. "The joys of that freedom, and the pain of its potential loss."

Confusion pushed aside the darkness riding Cleod's expression. He drew back, his shoulders pulling tight as he stared at her.

"Kilras?" His voice stumbled mid-word, as though some long-unrecognized knowledge bloomed within him—perhaps exactly that. He had spent long years shoulder to shoulder with the Dorn. Surely in that time questions had arisen, unanswered, curiosity had been piqued.

His gaze turned inward. What memories rose, like bubbling froth from the depths of his mind she could only guess, but his face shifted through a flashing series of emotions, some deep, some dark, some touched with awe.

Before anger took hold there, she spoke. "Kilras's mother was Sacrificed before he was born." She offered the rest slowly, information leaned to the facts and delivered with as little emotion as she could. "He was raised in Cyunant, among the Draigon. He left just before my mother was offered on the Spur. He has lived his life, ever since, as you know."

The shock went through him, and she opened herself to Gweld in order to see the sheen of it across the echoing lines of her vision as it rippled and expanded. It moved with him as he let go the bowl in his grasp. It clattered down the steps. He rose shakily, moved away from her and the truths that she offered, and truths that burned and unfastened, scarred and cut free. He stepped back, stumbled, and turned away to plant his hands against the wall behind him. Every part of him shook. "Damn it, Kil," he whispered, and the dark energy of his tone burned crimson into her vision. "Damn you and all your secrets." His words fell into a whirlpool pit of frothing grey.

She sat still, let his emotions churn the air, the light, the depth of both their souls. At last she asked, "Would you change him?"

For a long moment he stood braced and motionless, then he pivoted with a sudden determination that took her breath, and the direct ferocity of his gaze offered all the answer she needed.

53

Cleod

THE DORN'S FACE, LIT BY A WRY SMILE, FILLED CLEOD'S MIND. ALL the years riding side by side, the sparring, the laughter, the *trust*... Had Kilras used him, as had all the others, for some unspoken end?

"Tell me," Cleod whispered.

She released a soft breath. "Kilras Dorn was born among the Draigon. His mother was like me—taken and changed. He was raised in the Great Northern Range, shaped by brave women and the dangerous ideas of justice and integrity. And he left there more than thirty years ago to join the wider world. He's exactly what he's always seemed to be, Cleod. Just more as well."

"More?" Fiery warning raced upward into his skull, hot as the pull in the air before a lightning strike. He turned and stared at her. "Is *Kilras* a *Draigon?*"

She took in his expression, wonder sweeping her features. "No!" A firm shake of her head. "No, he never could be. Why do you think he left Cyunant? Kilras is a man. A rare one, but nothing else."

"He was exiled?"

"Far from it," Leiel said. "He made the only choice he could, to live a life that offered value to the world."

The gild of admiration that overlaid her words set Cleod back. He stared at her as quiet realization filled him. For all his years in Kilras's company, it suddenly seemed more than possible that Leiel knew the Dorn better than he ever had. Not just more about Kilras's past, but more about why he was who he was, what inspired and drove him. More about what turned in the depths of his heart.

It could have cut, twisted, that sudden understanding, but instead is simply settled inside Cleod, became part of prevailing knowledge. Kilras had always held secrets. Some Sehina knew. Some Rimm. Some Jahmess. But the core of who anyone was not dependent on what aspects of them others else knew.

Cleod closed his eyes. The anger that lived inside *him*, burning cold and as potentially devastating as his undying need for ercew or his brutal hunger for cuila—how many even guessed at that? It rose from an empty place he almost never allowed himself to contemplate—and was the reason he had taken Leiel's loss of her mother into his core and vowed to avenge it. So, was he any different from Kilras? Was anyone? Could the whole of a person ever be discerned by another? To gain such knowledge would require a dozen lifetimes.

He looked within, sought it now, the rage, the thing that heated his blood through the bitterest nights.

The only heat he found was that of the sun beating against his skin.

And the fiery presence across from him.

He opened his eyes and looked at Leiel. All that she was now, all that she had always been, the power within her, and still she had risked everything to free him from all the things that haunted him for so long. He thought of Leys, staring him down in her kitchen, compassion in her stance, Ain's bright gaze, unblinking despite the tears filling it, Elda's firm and knowing wisdom in the face of his potential violence. Strong women, willing to risk. For him. Why? Could he ever be worthy of that kind of strength and caring? Could he ever truly be what he had once been so certain he was?

Leiel waited, her attention fixed calmly upon him.

"You wish my help," he said. Strangeness should have enveloped those words, but instead they came with an ease he had not felt in years.

His help.

A promise made, now perhaps to be kept at last—to avenge what had been done to her mother, to all the women of Arnan. To care about what mattered to her. To be her friend.

In the sun, breath misting before him, he breathed in air that tasted of home.

Was it possible?

Was the fury really gone? Was he free?

54

Leiel

"YOU CANNOT KNOW," HE SAID, "THE WAY RAGE CAN OVERCOME everything—sense and caring and decency. What it feels like for hate to claim all that you believe you are."

She studied the lines around his eyes, the tension etched along his jaw. Like dappled sunlight through a swaying canopy, flashes of recollection tripped through her mind, his seriousness at the pond as they sat under the oak, the pride in his stance as he climbed the Spur ahead of her, the weighted sense of him along the trail, the flashing fury that overwhelmed every part of him when she confronted him in Melbis. And the twisted desperation as he watched Trayor and Kilras engage sword to sword. The thud of her heart vibrated against her ribs and up into her throat. She swallowed. "I might," she said. "Let me tell you of the first time I left the Great Northern Range after I claimed the Great Shape."

He frowned, his face a mask of skepticism. He trembled, but held silent. The *will* that took... A slow breath, then she spoke into the quiet, letting memory flow through her with the force of reliving.

She told of it, how on a moonless night, she left behind the mountain with its roiling skies and icy dawns, and winged south over lands where the trees were not yet beginning to offer up their autumn radiance. As it had on her first flight, wonder consumed her, a tremor that pulsed through her entire being. Every air current she rode, every sweep of her wings shocked through body and mind, awakening joy like a flower turning toward the rising sun.

"The thrill of it!" she whispered. "In a hundred years I'll never tire of the freedom of flight—I kept thinking how easy it would be to remain in the Great Shape, to skim the ridges and glide over the valleys, send wind rushing up city streets, gust wind over lakes and through river gorges...to see the whole world with new eyes and know the awe of those below..."

She remembered Gweld-sight firing the land and sky in ever-shifting prismatic color, sensing settlements below, large and small, inhabitants huddled in warmth or fear against the changing season. How strange it had seemed to her that some who lived this far north despised the icy months of winter. "But then I remembered being trapped in a place, with little hope of a future. Breaking free is never as simple as desire or courage imply."

He pulled his gaze from hers at that, lifted his eyes to the Spur where it loomed against the horizon. Grey clouds hugged the summit, feathery but brooding in the chill air, like her memories of the moments where revenge nearly laid claim to her soul.

Trapped. Pained. Despite joy, she too easily recalled desperation and despair. "That day, I wanted to change it all, no matter the cost. I was only two days' flight from Adfen. Adfen and the farm and Torrin, the house near the market and Elda and Klem... And the damnable Council in their red tunics and those painted priests..."

She placed a hand over his and waited until he looked at her. "Cleod, I—" Her chest thundered with it again—the temptation that arced through her like a lightning strike, the rage as she banked hard against a rising column of air, refocusing her intention. Reunion. Retribution. Revenge. The desire to rain such upon those who had wronged her, and to gather close the ones she missed, patterned the beat of her heart like a drum pounding rhythm.

As though she still lived in that moment, an unfamiliar rush of dark energy flooded her veins. "I never before had power to back my rage. Not until that day. Wind and heat. Strength and focused skill learned over hard years." She remembered it like breathing—the anger, long banked in her mind rushing awake, backed by vile memory and long-suffered recollections of layered injustices. "Adfen and vengeance lay at last within my reach. You know Gweld vision. In that instant, it blurred from rainbow brilliance into crimson until everything I saw was overlayed with the tint of spilled blood. I wanted to destroy it all. Everyone who had ever harmed me. Everything that reminded me of that hurt..."

Her words faltered and she blinked back tears, closed her eyes against them. Then with unexpected gentleness, his fingers curled over hers. She opened her eyes to find his gaze on her, filled with a scrutinizing curiosity that she had not encountered since their youth.

"What stopped you?"

A sharpness lanced her chest, memory unfolding, stark and bitter as the winter air.

'Do not stop.' Electric and forceful, Gahree's thought sheared across Leiel's own, broke through the rising shift in purpose. 'Fly on, wild daughter. The world is wider than the pain haunting your heart. Let the wind and your strength carry you and let yourself see the power of it.'

Mighty wings faltered and Leiel dropped like a tossed stone before focused effort again lifted her skyward. Stunned to her core by the speed with which old grievances had subverted the objective of her journey south, she turned hard to the southwest. How quickly rage had claimed her! How easily had she forgotten all the gentle goodwill in her soul! At last she understood why Ilora had not flown south and let it be known that she lived—if the pain and rage of her loss were half what tried to claim Leiel—olds gods! Nothing would have remained of Adfen but smoke and ruin.

Beat after beat of powerful wings added quick distance between herself and the city of her birth. Her thoughts still spun. Only focus on the steady rhythmic motion brought relief, began to bring the calm that picturing people as squirrels had once done. She settled her thoughts, reconsidered her planned route of exploration. If her journey across Arnan began with Orlis instead of Sibora, what matter?

The elation of flight returned as she arced away from the Spur country, but the memory lingered, of the willing anger and hunger for deliberate vengeance that lurked within easy reach inside her.

"Gahree." Leiel blinked back tears as she held Cleod's gaze. "Gahree stopped me, with heart and with logic and with the compassion that always guided her."

He flinched away, his expression suddenly drawn and heavy. He released her hand. Uncertainty and shame washed across his face, drew his shoulders down and in, putting space between them. "I took her from you."

Untrue, in more ways than one. Because *she* was as responsible for what had happened on that hill in Melbis as anyone else. "*Trayor* took her."

He pulled away, spoke words cloaked in bitterness. "Do not dismiss the harm I have done you." A shake of his head and he whispered. "It is counter to everything I promised you."

"No," she said, and though agony backed the statement, she offered the sad, ironic truth. "It is *exactly* what you promised me—the death of Shaa. If only either of us had understood then what that really meant."

Her words fell into a silence that lingered beyond discomfort.

At last he returned his gaze to hers, and the pain in his expression pierced her like a molten lance. "You *do* know," he said at last. "I would not wish that knowledge upon anyone." He straightened, drew a breath and let it out again, slow and controlled. "What now? Do the Draigon truly plan to face the Enclaves and the entire Farlan army?"

55

Leiel

SHE AND TESKA ANSWERED HIS QUESTIONS LATE INTO THE NIGHT. Halfway through, the understanding of how strange it was that she knew so much about his life, while he knew nothing of hers, added even more weight to the necessity of her honesty.

The silences between his questions grew longer with each answer she gave, until at last she filled the pauses with the story of the last months, of the great gathering of Draigons in Cyunant, of what it meant to have so many of them there, of watching Kilras reunite with his mother after decades of separation and what seeing them together had awakened in her heart.

Then she bent to instinct, and spoke of Gahree's list and the plans the Draigon put in place to try to save not only themselves, but the women of Arnan. As she spoke, he closed his eyes, and settled deeper and deeper into himself until she feared he could simply close himself off to her words, as he had done in the Tower, in Melbis. But he did not. Instead, a single tear slipped down his face, and he nodded.

"And now?" he asked.

"Now I need your help," she said quietly.

He blinked open his eyes and looked at her; his expression held no surprise. How many times had he heard those words? How many times *had* he helped those in need? Since his childhood, what else had he spent his life doing? She studied him, as he did the same in return.

"Tell me."

She held out her hands, palms up, "The Bynkrol Enclave is gone. Burned to the ground—" She shook her head quickly. "Not by Draigon. Kilras was there. A Draigre turned on them, let bandits inside the walls in the night. Kilras made it out, but there is nothing left of the compound."

He stared at her, and whatever he was thinking, it was not visible in his expression. Perhaps he was too exhausted to react. Or perhaps this was simply one shock too many for him to even feel. At last he asked, "Why was Kilras with the Byn?"

"He went in search of Enclave records. The oldest of them. Elder secrets." She folded her hands together, looked down at them, then back into his face. "It's not enough that the Draigon defeat the Enclaves now. We must do to them what they will do to us, if they have the chance. They would destroy not only those living, but all record of our existence, all our secrets and all of our stories. It's not just the armies marching on us that must be broken. It is their mythology and their legend, and all record of the training that would allow the Enclaves to be rebuilt and new Draighil trained."

Cleod trembled, actively containing some sudden response. "You seek a way to destroy that which has been built to destroy you."

She nodded, searching his face.

"And then what?" The earnestness of his question sent a little tug through her heart. "The Draigon are hated, feared."

A slow nod allowed her a few heartbeats to take in the unexpected control in his last statement. No rage flew through him, no hate as he spoke the word Draigon. She offered answer into that space of unexpected calm. "The stories of us must be re-written if fear is not to overtake any victory that we might claim." She hesitated, glanced at Teska. "That is why a healer unlike any this land has ever known matters so much. She can save Arnan, in time. She can teach us all how to save ourselves."

Cleod shifted his attention to Teska, and his features tightened, but she could not discern whether sadness or regret or something darker held primacy. Then simple understanding swept the rest away and he met her gaze again. "In order for that to happen, the Draigon must be able to live without threat of being killed off. That is why these documents matter."

Knowledge had always mattered in its own right. The library at Cyunant with its hundreds of thousands of books and maps and pieces of art, Kilras's letters, the small, secret books that had made her days trapped in her life before the mountain bearable—all held more worth than just what they meant to her alone. And so the idea of destroying histories, information, no matter how dangerous to her, turned a hard knot in her chest. It went against everything she had ever wanted for the world. But she pushed the feeling down and simply answered, "Yes."

"This is the final Sacrifice the Draigon would demand of Arnan," he said.

She sat back with a gasp, heard a similar sound from Teska as his words ripped through her like claws. Her thoughts fell into one another, careening like tossed stones. Sacrifice—had it always come down to that? Sacrifice of self worth, of knowledge, of understanding, of friendships and even lives—and for what? Was it anything but loss, no matter how it was measured? The kind of land that Arnan had long since become, tore and battered all who lived in it, regardless of gender, or occupation, or wealth. Klem's face filled her mind, angry and bitter and sad all at once. She blinked the image away and looked into the strained face across from her. "It seems so, yes."

Teska spoke into the silence that followed Leiel's admission. "And if the records we seek were not at Bynkrol, they must be at Ehlewer."

Cleod looked at her again and smiled the slightest bit. For an instant the incorrigible boy Leiel had grown up with sat before her, then he spoke with a hint of chagrin that washed that innocence away. "Or somewhere Trayor knows that others do not. Is it for myself that you brought me here and healed me, or is it because you need this information?"

With a shake of her head, Teska met his gaze. "I know of you only what I have been told, and what I have sensed. I have moved from fear of you to sympathy for you, and now I am simply uncertain. Leiel holds you dear. And that impacts my measure of you, but yes, it is more than just yourself that matters."

Cleod tipped his head and studied the healer, then his gaze found Leiel's again. "You are more than just my old friend."

She smiled at that. "And you are more than just mine. You always have been."

"You think I know what Trayor does."

"From what you have told me of him, he is not likely to have left the documents anywhere obvious. Perhaps not even in the Ehlewer compound."

He sat in silence for a long moment, then drew a deep breath and let it out again. "There are other places. Caches in the mountains." His expression grew thoughtful, and he narrowed his gaze.

"Places you can tell me how to find?"

"No." The shake of his head was emphatic. "In places only he or I could find." He hesitated, then met her gaze. "I'll go."

It was the statement that she had both hoped for and dreaded. She needed his help, but she no longer needed his protection. Always he had put himself in the path of danger on behalf of others. He would do no different now, but he no longer had to make such a stand alone. "*We'll* go," Leiel answered. "I am no longer the little girl in need of saving. I am Draigon, and this is my responsibility."

He looked into her face, spoke haltingly. "And the future of the Ehlewer is mine. The war will go on without us, but the future...for once, maybe we can shape it together." The struggle within him carried into his tone, but his determination outshown it, and his voice gained surety with each word. "Your Draigon friends will stand well against them. And it's likely even your untrained army can hold Adfen against the King's forces—

the Old City at least. Once the Draigon have dealt with the Enclaves, facing the Farlan will be much less difficult."

She thought of the way the northbound army had split into groups, separated. "Was dividing the army the King's idea, or Trayor's?"

He hesitated. "It was mine. I convinced them that such a large group was too obvious a target and that smaller columns would be able to move and react more quickly."

"And that might be true," Leiel said. Not for the first time, she wished she knew more of strategy and battle. And wished she knew the true depths of Cleod's heart. Had he moved for or against the Farlan and the Enclaves when he made the suggestion that led them to separate? Did *he* know, himself? Would he say if he did? For all that she spoke complete truth to him, could she expect the same in return from a man who had been betrayed so deeply and so often, and who could not help but desire to protect himself and whatever secrets he still held?

Cleod shook his head. "The Farlan have fought no true wars for decades," he said. "The Enclaves train to fight Draigon, not people. Not armies. What any of us know of warfare, we know from books and old stories. Is that any less true of...you?"

She shook her head. "Of most of us."

He sat back. "So there's a warrior among you."

Despite her unease, she smiled and offered information that could only startle. "Enclave trained, and studied in the ways of the lands beyond the Great Northern Range."

He started. "*Enclave* trained?" His jaw hung open a moment, then he asked hoarsely, "A male Draigon?"

Leiel rose and paced away, just to move. Kinra's story was not Leiel's to tell. But the memory of how it felt for her to truly learn about the world, to understand that the knowledge it held was beyond measure, ran through her. She looked over her shoulder at Cleod in time to see him take in that other unexpected shock. "No," she said, and watched amazement fill his face.

"How—"

"If our luck holds, you'll meet her."

He stared. "*Are there* male Draigon?"

"*Draigdyn.*" She shook her head. "Not for many generations."

"Why?" The question came from Cleod, but she saw it in Teska's eyes as well.

"I don't know." She shrugged. "Perhaps because most men don't need to be."

He sat in silence as a log popped in the stove. The wind tripped against the windows, and relief was a warm balm through her belly—that he took in her words without questioning them. Whether that meant that he accepted the idea, or had no energy to consider it deeply, she did not know. Both options held the necessity for more explanation at bay. "You know where the records are."

"I might." He nodded. "But we need to do more than just destroy those. We must burn Ehlewer, just as those raiders burned Bynkrol."

Leiel hissed in a breath. The smoke from such a fire alone... "Cleod—" She stopped as a terrible understanding filled her. They had risked lives, hers, Teska's, Kilras's, to bring Cleod here and try to heal him. And *this* was exactly why—to use his understanding and skills to win the war, no matter the cost. No matter what it cost any of them. No matter what it cost him. And he knew it. It was clear in his direct gaze and in the resigned tone of his voice. Silence tinkled the air like snowflakes patting on iced glass.

Teska spoke into the quiet. "I can help with—"

"No, please," Leiel said quickly. "You've risked too much already. You are far, far from taking the Great Shape. We'll go, Teska. You'll be so very needed whether we succeed or not. Even *more* if we do not." She reached out a hand and, as Teska took it in her own, pleaded. "Please, my friend. You'll be safe here. We'll need you so desperately on the other side of this." Months in Cyunant had been spent trying to convince Teska of the truth of her importance. How much of that had she truly absorbed?

With a furrowed brow, the healer nodded, if slowly. "Very well. But only because I know worrying about me would be a distraction." She blinked and her gaze took on new depth. "You shine. Both of you. Brighter together." She pulled herself up straighter. "That is an even more important reason for the two of you to go up the mountain."

Leiel took in a quick breath. Cleod grew tense beside her. Of course. She and Cleod on the Spur again, where their story had begun on a day of fire and ash and pain. Draighil and Draigon on a mountain top. What more fitting way to herald change in the world? "We'll travel with the dawn," she said.

56

Leiel

HALF THE DAY THEY HAD ASCENDED, THROUGH TIGHT FOREST AND over stark ground, until they found the path now beneath their feet and let it lead them along ridgelines and traverses. Moving north across snow-blasted high meadows and ice-coated granite balds, they walked land that reminded her too thoroughly of the Great Northern Range and her home at Cyunant.

She had grown up in the shadow of these mountains but never explored more than the slopes of the Spur itself. And her memory of the Sacrifice grounds atop that mountain demanded more of her will than she had expected in order for her to face. Was it just the place, or the fact that she and Cleod had stood on it together? If he trembled from more than cold, and her thoughts refused to focus on anything but the scent of smoke and the heart-speeding recollection of beating wings and searing heat, at least they did not linger. And though a thousand things still needed to be spoken between them, old pain and new grief wrapped her in a silence she found herself unwilling to break. From the set of his shoulders and the tension along his jaw, he seemed no more inclined to conversation than she.

He walked ahead of her over the hard frozen trail, moving gingerly but with a confidence that came only from being on familiar terrain. The sword harnessed to his back drew her attention time and again, turning new knots in her stomach with every glance. Only the Orast stone that topped the hilt held any beauty. And though she hated the sight of the weapon and the thought of touching it sent tingling pain up her arms, she was still careful to stay close enough that if he stumbled on uneven ground, she could steady him. Strange to think of him needing such assistance, but Teska's healing and his own revelations had wrung him through, body and mind. Though he still moved with uncanny grace, even that could not make up for sapped endurance.

They abandoned the trail a number of times to explore caches she would never have found without his help. None held what they sought. And the farther they traveled from the Spur proper and the old place of Sacrifice, the more unsteady his steps became, until she placed a hand on his arm and stopped him, turned him to face her in the chill afternoon air. "You need rest. Another night won't matter to our task."

The young Draighil who had faced Shaa for her sake would have argued, forced the issue with a stubborn pride that took precedent over wisdom and self-preservation. But the man before her was no longer that arrogant swordsman. Time and pain and friendship had done their work upon him, and he did not hesitate long before nodding.

He looked around, measuring, then pointed west toward a saddle in the next ridge. "Half an hour. I know a place."

She took in the weariness around his eyes. Nothing Teska had worked within him could completely dissipate the impact of hard choices or years of self-abuse. Nor could it erase the memory of violence done, or of pain both caused and earned. "How do you know it?"

He shook himself a little. "An old training shelter. The Elders used to send us out for days at a time to explore these mountains and build our strength. Sometimes we were lucky enough to be sent to an area with a dry place to sleep."

"You never wrote me of such a thing."

"By the time we were doing such things, there was much I did not share in my letters." He turned away, stepped off the trail, and moved through the trees.

She followed, ducking under low limbs, each step sinking her calf-deep in fresh snow. A flare of Draigon heat at the base of her spine and the drifts melted away around her. "Let me go first," she said. "Just tell me where to go."

The look he sent over his shoulder was full of wary amazement. He looked at the cleared earth beneath her feet and then met her gaze. "You trust me at your back?"

Her glanced flicked to the sword, then back to his eyes. Cleod. Still and always, Cleod. Her friend. Her first source of hope. The source of the same in this very moment. "Just as, somehow, you have trusted me all day." She stepped around him to take the lead, clearing the ground before her as she wove through the tangled wood. Snow melted with whispered hisses of steam that wafted past her, and, she hoped, offered Cleod some warmth.

"Leiel."

Her name was soft on the air, a quiet request.

She stopped and faced him. Well more than an arm length separated them but he stood with his hand open, palm up in silent offering. And cupped in his hand were the twisted remains of her ring.

The stone glinted faintly, its familiar rough shape dark against the warped gold band. She started to ask where he had found it, but bit back the words. Where else but that low hill in Melbis where Gahree had died so horribly? And that meant he had returned there.... Why? She brought her gaze to his, let a question fill her expression.

"I made a promise to you, long, long ago. Not that I would kill for you, or die for you, but that I would always be your friend. In that I failed. But you kept this..."

His words held the same question that had just entered her mind.

She drew in a breath and stepped forward, touched a finger to the broken ring. "For your strength. And how often you offered it to me. And for how much you still had for *yourself* to have survived all that you have." Folding her fingers around the ruined ring, she lifted it from his hand and looked at it, shaking her head. "You went back."

"I needed to know what happened. What really happened. But there was no blood... Then I dreamed—" He stopped, the vision of red crystal shattering to mist sweeping across his mind. "But I found that." He tipped his head toward the bent metal and stone in her hand. "And it's been with me since Melbis." He lifted his eyes to hers. "It's been calling to me to change since Melbis."

"It's Orast and metal, Cleod. It has no power to—"

He shook his head and closed his fingers around hers. "Knowing it mattered to you enough to keep...to wear.... That's what gave it power."

For a few heartbeats she just stared at him. Could they, all of them, have been even more right about him than they had dared to hope? Back at the cabin, Teska had done her work with much less effort than either of them expected. Cleod's relentless consumption of ercew had already begun to sever his need for the cuila. As he always had, he had been striving to help those in need...even himself. She took a breath to speak, but he released her and stepped back, so instead she nodded. "Come on," she said. "We need to get settled before nightfall."

Warmth spread slowly through the small, stone hut with its central fire pit and poorly fitting door. The gaps around the boards let in far too much cold, but limited the wind, and she shifted subtly to add Draigon heat to the air, and to warm the floor. Gradually the tension of cold left Cleod's face where he sat, hands outstretched toward the dancing flames.

She opened the bag on her hip and drew out the battered envelope that Kilras had entrusted to her months before. What it contained, whether the words there would help or harm, she did not know. But such was not hers to examine.

"I promised to give you this." She held it out, across the fire between them, and watched his face twist into puzzlement, then disbelief as he stared at the writing on the front of it.

The hand he lifted to take it shook, and for a moment she feared he would drop it into the flames. But his grasp steadied and he drew it toward him, staring all the while at his name scrawled in tight, brutal letters on the parchment.

"Do you know—"

"No," she answered. "It's for you alone."

He shook, the trembling claiming every part of him. For a moment she hesitated, torn by the desire to go around the fire and wrap him in her arms. But the moment called for both more and less than that, and instead she got to her feet and moved away toward the door.

As she stepped outside, she heard him open the letter, and she braced herself for whatever might be awakened by what Kilras had scrawled across the pages. In the failing light and rising cold she leaned against the wall of the shelter and closed her eyes, all too familiar with the impact of parting words etched purposefully on parchment.

Firelight danced, washing the stone walls in flickering light. Leiel stood at the doorway with her back to the rising stars and studied the man bundled in blankets, asleep beside the fire. Cold crept over the stone and up her back, and though she pushed it away with Draigon heat, she paused to acknowledge it. The temperature had dropped steadily since sunset.

As though the chill touched him as well, Cleod shifted in his sleep and pulled the blanket closer over his shoulders. How much had changed in just a few days. More, it seemed than in even the last months of planning for war, of the armies moving like stones scraping over swords, sharpening until they cut like the flick of a bitter glance. Songs of glory and sorrow, written and sung. Lives lost. Futures changed.

He had not told her what Kilras's letter contained, and she had not asked. If he had cried or raged, he had done it in silence. What Cleod and Kilras's friendship meant to each of them was no more within her right or ability to define than it would have been for either of them to claim to understand that which existed between herself and Gahree. Some things simply *were,* beyond word or name.

Heavy emotions draped her, worn and picked at as old sweaters gone to pill and nibbled through by moths. Too much. Too much to think about. She let out a slow breath and moved another step closer to the fire. Other things mattered more in this moment. She turned the broken ring in her hand, over and over. Other things like him bearing the stone back to her, the way he carried its mate on his sword. Through all the years he had borne her with him, and she had done the same. She slid the ring into her pocket.

For a few seconds she stood, stilling her thoughts, breathing in the fine balance of air where it mixed cold and warm. Then she took a step toward the fire, tipped her head. It was useless to think what might have been, but here, now, opportunity and chance collided. She cracked Gweld sense open.

The fine lines around Cleod's eyes and the thin hash of a scar just at his hairline held her attention: the minute creases that wrote his story in worry and in action and in years. Again he stirred and possibility spiraled, laid out before in her in foiled layers of color and connection, bodies in motion, and laughter and tears...

He jerked awake, and she felt it, front to back, a ricochet through her bones. His gaze met hers through the flickering flames.

She bent her mind, let the ever-present expansion of awareness that hovered at the edge of her consciousness flood into her, and prismatic light streamed into the space between them, ripped her open, reflected off walls within and without.

Through expanded senses she watched color and violence play around him, as for the first time since Teska healed him, the brutality of his embedded training pushed to the forefront by his sudden awakening, still a ward against her presence, and the transformative nature of the Great Shape Gweld afforded her. He shuddered, tension rippling over his skin until a line of sweat broke across his brow. Despite the past days' progress, how long would it be until he truly escaped instinct formed by fear and habit?

Slowly, he sat up and his eyes lost focus, glazed by the struggle within him. Then amber light blazed hot from his core, met the dichroic spectrum of her vision and awakened an almost sentient eruption through the entirety of her being.

Past and present, and everything that would come with the morning, washed away with the Gweld-born explosion of color vibrating between them. Could he see it? It did not matter. Warmth pulsed from her core. She crossed the hard-packed dirt.

He straightened, gaze fixed on her face, tension in his jaw and heat in his gaze as he raised a hand to hold her back.

She reached out and pressed her palm into his, firm and steady, asking nothing. The conflict within him vibrated the air, pulsed through her hand and down her body. A simple turn of thought, of fear or faith, could unravel the moment.

A heartbeat passed.

He twined his fingers though hers and drew her toward him.

Leiel

P AWN, FILTERING GREY AND SILENT THROUGH THE CRACKS AROUND the entrance, did nothing to alleviate the chill drifting into the shelter. Draigon heat and the activity of the night left them warm under a nest of blankets, but Leiel frowned at the idea of leading Cleod back into the icy weather. His physical state, while not as fragile as his battered mind, still demanded careful attention. His rough hand pressed in comforting weight along her hip, the touch both startling and welcome.

She lay listening to her heartbeat, feeling its power and its strength, remembering how it had leaped and raced in the night. Had she ever dared to dream of such time with Cleod, it would have been close to what they had shared—not perfect, but filled with caring and gentle uncertainty and laughter. Her heart counted a steady rhythm, alive with a contentment she had never before allowed herself the courage to imagine.

She rolled just slightly to face him. His hair, loose over his brow, would be easy to brush away, but she did not raise a hand. The stories of her youth told her that in this moment she should see a peace in him such as she had never witnessed before. But that was not true. Even as children he carried a level of worry— for his father, for her, for the injustices of the world—that never quite faded from his features. Why, in this time of pain and trouble, would that fact be any different?

Still—perhaps such would be true one day, as it had been for her the first morning she awakened in Cyunant, home for the first time in her life. Perhaps he could someday know the same peace. The deepest core of her held doubt, and the already shattered pieces of her heart slivered yet again.

After all, what had they both done under the guise of righteousness? One after another, she rolled through the past choices leading to this juncture. The pain in her chest thickened and pressed deeper—the knowledge that she would, for her part, change nothing. Not even the choice to show herself to Cleod in Melbis. Facts confirmed sad truth. No decision on her part would have saved Gahree.

"Old friend," A whisper, exhale soft to keep from waking him, left her lips, "I am so very sorry." She shifted closer against him, shut her eyes as his arms closed tighter around her. She would change nothing. Would he, given the choice, say the same?

"Don't be sorry," he murmured. "I did it all for you. Everything I became, every harm rendered and justified."

She pulled back, studied him, half-believing he had somehow heard her unspoken question. Then unease shifted through her and she narrowed her gaze, unwilling to accept perceived sacrifice along with blame. Not from him. Not when she knew better, and knew that he did as well. "None of it was for you?" she demanded. "None of it was your will?"

He blinked, the last sleep leaving his face. Then he smiled just slightly, sad and slow. "Of course it was," he said. "Who I am—my need for purpose. My desire to play the hero whether or not I ever was one—that is my own. That's always been my own."

"And I, ever the catalyst?" she asked.

"Not always." His gaze drifted inward.

She set her elbow on the folded blanket that served as a pillow and propped her head on her hand. "You're more self-aware than the last few months would have led me to expect."

He brought his attention back to her and offered a wry grin. "Spend a dozen years with Kilras and see how you fare in sustaining internalized ignorance." The expression faded to something darker, something backed by a confused mix of doubt, anger, and worry.

"He is a singular soul, your friend the Dorn," Leiel said. No way existed for her to measure the turmoil within the man before her. The only wise recourse was to assume it outmatched her own. "But no more than you." She paused. "Kilras will be well."

"Without your healer at his side, can you be sure?" Bitterness laced Cleod's words, and he sat up, pulled away from her. His shoulder muscles bunched under his skin, drawing tight the scars that crossed it. She remembered the letter in which he described receiving that injury, from the Hewlion, so long ago. One set of many scars that marred his body through the years. Her hands recalled the gnarled welts on his hip, cold and twisted beneath her touch. Nothing at all compared to the ones that dwelt inside him.

"I cannot be certain, no," she agreed. "But he is strong. And Teska is not the sole repository of healing knowledge in the world."

He dropped his head into his hands, and she fought the urge to rest a hand against his back in comfort.

Gweld rippled her sight to gentle prism waves, and she took measure of him within it. "Kilras was always what he seemed. Just also more."

He trembled, used calloused hands to shove back his hair and looked over his shoulder at her. "I cannot decide which lies hurt the most—the ones I was told all these years, or the ones I wove in my own mind."

"And where would you be if either of us had offered you truth before now? What would you be? Would you *be* at all?"

Anger whipped through his voice. "No answer exists to such questions. None of us will ever know because no truth was offered."

She sat up as well and met his gaze as her heartbeat kicked up pace in her chest. "Cleod." She spoke his name only, let the ache and agreement and sorrow within her spill forth like slow moving fog to surround him.

The fine lines around his eyes deepened as he sought control. Every part of him rippled waves of amber light through her refracted vision. At last he bent his head and turned away.

She waited. All that churned inside him could not be contained or expressed in a single response. Time alone might realign and repair shattered faiths and dreams and a self battered far too long by the brutal waves of circumstance and intention. Hope remained that time was something they might indeed have—to sort the past, to build beyond tomorrow. "You know the answers," she said at last.

He choked on a bitter laugh. "We've always brought out the best and worst of each other."

"Cleod." She spoke his name again, this time just so he could hear it on her lips. She pressed herself against his back, wrapped her arms around him and let heat rise from deep within her and wash into him. Seconds passed as he tensed in resistance, then, slowly, relaxed under her touch. A quiet joy filtered into her chest. "It's only just dawn," she whispered behind his ear, and smiled as he shook with bitter-sweet laughter.

She bent closer still, but before she could say more, dark images swept through her mind—blood and spears, armies in motion, flames searing farmland and once familiar buildings. The painted faces of priests, stark and twisted in rage. Men in red tunics gloating. Draigon in battle against greater odds than any should face. Kinra's thoughts, like hundreds of bells struck through Leiel's mind, in the whisper-not-whisper that should be impossible over such distance. *There's no more time. You must return. We need you.*

With a gasp, she sat up and away, raised a hand to calm Cleod as instinct claimed him and he whirled to his knees to face her, fingers grasped around the hilt of his sword where it lay beside the pallet.

Heat and moisture filled her eyes, and she shook her head. "Wind on high, we've no time after all."

"What is it?" His poised readiness did not ease.

"War," she whispered. "Adfen at war. So much fear and pain and anger..."

"How—?"

She blinked away the images in her mind even as she sent tight acknowledgment to Kinra. "Draigon can know of each other's experience, even over great distance, though specific images and thoughts are clearer with proximity. I am close enough to Adfen and the battles surrounding it to see and hear in detail." She took a breath and spoke of what Kinra had sent, let the storytelling skills she had learned from Ilora and Gahree add depth and detail to the events as she described them. And if he did not relax at her words, he released the sword, and simply took in the ache and danger of what she shared.

"We should go," he said when she finished.

For a long series of breaths she just held his gaze and did not try to make sense of the energy and emotion that passed between them. It was a moment simply to be felt and not measured. Then she raised her hand and gently touched his face, the fine lines there, the heat of him. "We should not," she replied. "But we must."

58

Cleod

GREY LIGHT AND STORM. THE SUN HAD NOT YET RISEN, THOUGH IT DID not matter in the battering cold and whiteness. They stood on the main trail, the snow around them melted by her heat, and the passing seconds churned between them, heavy with the weight of impending separation.

"I can go with you," she said. "We're only an hour from Ehlewer—"

"No," he said, his voice hoarse but steady. The King's army assaulted Adfen. And with it stood enough Draighil and well-trained Draigre to mute the might of the Draigon arrayed to defend the city. Though Leiel had told him the ones defending the city were the strongest, the fiercest...even they would struggle to survive that many Enclaved trained fighters. And the people, the proud citizens of Arnan steeled to fight or to simply survive that attack—they would not stand long if the Draigon fell. Certainty uncoiled along his spine: the thing he must do was remove the greatest threat to them from the field of battle. And free Leiel to do what she must to save the city and its people...and her people. "You risked everything because you trusted that I was still the friend I promised you I would be. Trust me now when I say this is where we must part."

She held his gaze for a long while, argument brewing in her eyes. But they were no longer children, able to be selfish and simply think of and demand only what *they* wanted. The fate and future of Arnan reached beyond their hopes and desires.

And no matter whether the future hinged upon their actions, it did not offer them in the moment any choice but to face it with all that they were.

Slowly, she nodded. "I'll clear the storm." Her tone was firm, made quiet by necessity and resignation. She laid a finger to his lips, the same hand, then crowned by the glint of her ring, that had touched him so in Melbis. If that stone and setting now sat crumpled in her pocket, he felt the weight and power of it nonetheless.

"I'll find them." The words were promise. One he meant to keep as he had not done the ones he had offered her before.

No doubt entered her gaze as it held his. At last she tipped her head in acknowledgment, then turned away.

He took a breath. He would not follow. Would not watch her become...become the rest of what she was. Despite all that had passed between them, the thought of watching her transform, change, become...*that*...burned bile into his throat. Then stories she had offered over the last days swept through him. The power in them, the *joy*, settled his trained instinct and let him truly consider all that she was. And all that *he* was. And what *all* truly meant for both of them, this moment, and for the future.

She took not three steps across the clearing before he heard, as though it was his own, her heart pounding hard enough to burst from her chest. His own leapt to speed, thunderous in the wrongness of the moment.

Thirty years. Thirty years of loss and suffering, of sacrifice and denial. Thirty years of unspoken words.

No more.

No more, whatever came next.

He would not let her leave until he testified to what he had known, unexpressed, for most of his life.

With a gasp, he moved after her.

She turned in the same heartbeat, and before he could reach out she stepped forward and placed her palms flat against his chest, fingers wide, touching the core of him. Her heartbeat pulsed through her fingers, found rhythm with his own.

She looked into his face. "I—"

He cut her off. "And I." Like flame, his breath burned through him. "We wasted it."

Her grip tightened, and he raised his hands to grasp hers. "We did *not* waste it," she countered. Fierce and warm, her eyes met his. "We reached *this moment*, despite everything."

Once, he would have known exactly what she was thinking by the crinkle at her left eye, or the pattern of her breathing. But too long had passed since he had taught her the trick of hiding her emotions by imagining people as squirrels. Clearly she had long since mastered that—and other ways of controlling her responses. He smiled with wry self-knowledge. Until a few months ago, he would have claimed the same maturity for himself, but old habit and dangerous need had proved how fragile his strength was. He wanted to shake his head, but her eyes held him, her warmth surging through him, over his skin, down his spine until it owned every part of him.

"Tomorrow," she said. "Tomorrow we start over. On the other side of all the blood and pain that's coming, *we will start over*."

Tangled emotion wrapped knots in his chest. "Leiel—if—"

"I cannot think it," she answered. "Not if I am to leave now. Not if we are to do what must be done."

He held still, stared into her face, then let go of her fingers to run his into her hair. She nodded in his hands, and he drew her close to kiss her. Hope burned between them—that this touch would not be the last, that tomorrow would come. If the truth echoed into his bones, he refused to acknowledge it, and instead let the moment sear itself into every fiber of his body, into his soul.

59

Cleod

THE LAST POSSIBILITY IN HIS SEARCH LAY IN THE OLD, STONE CISTERN on the west slope of the mountain beyond the upper practice field. He skirted the cleared ground and approached from the south, working his way carefully over icy shale to the heavy wooden door that guarded the entrance. The lock did not give easily, and the noise it made as it groaned free ran up his back like a clutter of spiders. He paused, wind whipping over him, listening carefully, but no cries of surprise or warning came. Releasing held breath, he pushed inside.

If possible, the cold deepened within, and Cleod blinked until Gweld sight revealed the depth of emptiness that echoed through the ancient chamber. The certainty with which he had approached the place fell away.

Long ago, from the slope above he had witnessed Draigon Weather rolling toward the Spur country, had planned his first fight and victory over a beast for which he held only bitter hatred. A creature he now understood to be so much more than a monster... Leiel's breath in his ear, his name spoken with kindness and with joy...

He forced the thought away.

The pride that had filled him so long ago lingered like a ghost in his mind. The arrogance of that day. The fight it led to that gave him unwarranted primacy over Trayor... Cleod frowned.

He had been so sure that this place would hold the secrets they sought. If not here...then he did not know where. Only

Trayor would. And he would have to get Trayor alone if there existed any chance of learning.

But, that he had known before he and Leiel had left Ellan's cabin... Weariness clung to every part of Cleod like deadly vines entwining a tree. His strength, measured against the Draighil, was outmatched.

"No." The frustration knotting his chest slipped into his voice. Only one thing would draw Trayor from his chosen battle—the blazing destruction of Ehlewer.

It was well that the war had called Leiel away. Always, she had valued knowledge and learning. For her to have reached the point where she acquiesced to the need to destroy the history and writings of others must have broken some part of her heart. But in her mind it would be a *very* different thing eradicate the darkest, most violent teachings of a people, than it would be to render into oblivion *all* of their existing works.

Yet what else was there?

Kilras's letter. Leiel's stories. The knowledge they had imparted left no doubt in Cleod—he could extract from Trayor the location of the Enclaves' deepest secrets. But more than that was needed if Arnan was to have a chance at true change. Ehlewer must fall to ruin, like Bynkrol. And it must happen now. If the deeper understanding of why was one he refused to acknowledge, he could not hide from it enough to control the tremor that ran through his body.

He turned and moved through the doorway, out into the chill morning. Back in the grey light, under swirling clouds, he climbed the treacherous slope to the practice field above. He stood, breath misting the air, heart dark with the knowledge of what came next.

They would let him in.

He crossed to the far side of the field to look down upon the compound below. Strangeness hugged him like a second skin as he stared across the terraced ground, strangeness that Ehlewer lay before him after so many years. His thoughts refused to sort themselves for several seconds, one tumbling into the next like birds in a murmuration. The sound of wind over the mountains, the smell of granite and cookfires on the air. Laughter was missing, and the boisterous shouting of trainees, and the scents of sweat and pain and fear. But this place had carved itself into his soul, into instinct that twisted and burned his nerves. Even determined will could not hold back his trembling as he took in the once familiar view. All of it stood *exactly* as he remembered it, unchanged since he walked away. How was that possible, that everything was the same? How had the years passed without affecting this place at all?

He shook his head. Ehlewer had always been molded by specific purpose. And so it clearly remained.

Through eyes enlightened by experience, he took in the truth of the place. What in youth had seemed storied and formidable, a bastion of knowledge and honor, now looked old and worn, intractable in a world of wider truths and expanded priorities. Years traveling Arnan had broadened his understanding of what it meant to live with purpose, and how varied purpose could be in the hearts of so many people. Not everywhere was Adfen, was the Spur. Not everyone valued what was taught and revered within the walls of an Enclave.

"I was so young." The thought whispered into the air on a sliver of mist. "How could I have thought this place knew anything of truth or honor? Or could teach it."

We only knew what we had been told. Leiel's quiet words lingered in his ears.

His thoughts stumbled again. Leiel had learned different things, even though everything she had been taught as a child should have told her that such was not possible. But she had always possessed a mind bent toward questions. And she had different teachers.

He nodded, closed his eyes a moment. One of those teachers

had been the woman he helped kill in Melbis. The idea still staggered him. Shaa. No. *Gahree*. And yet still Leiel believed he was in part the boy he had been. Believed it enough, despite everything, to trust the man he had become. A strange warmth slipped through his chest and caught his breath in his throat.

He opened his eyes and looked at the compound, this time using memory as measurement. Details of routines and schedules filtered back into his mind, recalled the same way childhood rhymes and songs returned easily when he heard a fragment of one. Ehlewer possessed a rhythm all its own—even the randomness of the training calls fit into a bizarre pattern that made sense the longer it was lived—and that normality was missing. The smoke was wrong. And the sounds too few. Even had he not known the place had been mostly emptied to provide fighters for Trayor's cause, he would have sensed the vacancy within it.

The seeds Trayor had planted about his plans for Cleod would give him access. He measured chance against fate, action against outcome. Through an ache that ran through every muscle in his body, he had turned away from her, let her go. He straightened and moved down the hill toward the place that laid the path of his life.

Too easily they let him in, the few that remained to guard Ehlewer. Too easily they trusted the weight of their pride and instilled honor. Regardless of his years away, years of *not* being one of them, the belief Trayor had drilled into them—that reclamation was not only possible, but inevitable—held sway. Word of Shaa's death could only have re-enforced it. As would have word that he traveled with Trayor, in uniform once more.

Inside the walls, they greeted him, offered food and comfort—two old men, beyond frail, who trembled in the chill despite warm clothing, and five boys no older than ten summers.

Truly, Trayor had called every man of strength and skill to join the army that now surrounded Adfen.

Despite Cleod's exhaustion, disarming them cost him no effort. And only when Cleod tied and led them to stand outside the gates and watch the ancient compound burn, did they understand the error of the their trust. They stared in shock at the destruction unfolding before them.

"You cannot do this," an old man whispered.

Though he reminded Cleod of Soibel, that Elder was long dead. "And yet—" Cleod gestured through the icy air at the thunderous pillar of smoke and ash rising into the air. He held the man's gaze. "The Enclaves are finished. If ever you had another home, it is time you return to it."

The old man glared, anger and fear and grief flooding his face along with shining tears. "You speak as though you have one."

The man's pain set Cleod back, rocked him, but he shook his head. "No," he said. "But I have remade one before. Go. I do not want to hurt any of you." He glanced at the boys, stunned and bundled against the cold. "Lead them away. Down the mountain. Find shelter and stay out of what is coming."

"You once valued learning," the other elder said. And Cleod recognized him as Vessor, the librarian from his youth.

"I am sorry," Cleod replied, even as old memories surged, of peace among the shelves, knowledge gained that was not earned through bruises and blood. Long hours hunched over books, questions asked that were answered with undying patience. Lighting the torch that fired that building had forced disconnection born of pure will, but looking into the old man's face now, Cleod's chest tightened with something akin to shame. He let true sorrow color his words. "But the long war of Draigon and Draighil must end. And I have always been the one destined to do it."

"Trayor will destroy you." The furious words were a promise.

Cleod shifted his attention from the Elder to the still thickening smoke. If the documents the Draigon sought were housed anywhere within Ehlewer, they would not survive the conflagration. But Trayor was too careful, had planned too well—for everything but the ercew—or Leiel's unwavering certainty that Cleod was still her friend. Trayor would come. "He already has," Cleod said. "But I will return the boon in kind before the day is past."

Cleod dropped a knife he had confiscated from the Elder into the snow before the burning gate. Then he turned and walked away. Let them cut themselves free and find their way off the mountain. If they took the fastest route down, they could reach the nearest village by dark. But his destined route lay back the way he had come, back to the Spur and the trail that Trayor would climb to meet him.

60

Cleod

LEGS TIGHT FROM THE HIKE BACK ACROSS RIDGES TO THE SPUR, CLEOD paused for breath in the frigid air. Adfen lay below. He stood and took it in—the far-off, rapid motion of men and women at war, the breathtaking sight of every Draigre alive engaged in battle against a half dozen Draigon, that flew, and dove, and shattered. They took wounds and shrieked pain and terror and anger to the sky. And in the heart of the city, atop the Tower—how could he or anyone have ever thought it was meant for anything but to host a Draigon?—wings fanned to drive stunning wind and squelch both fire and assault, perched the impossible creature that was Leiel, bronze and shining in the high light.

Every part of him ached as he watched her, made small by distance but shining in every shift of shadow into sun. *Leiel.* That creature *was Leiel*, complete and powerful and full of determined justice. It was her, and she was it, and *all* of her, the choices she had made, came clear to him as he gazed down upon her. Confusion fled and what remained was only the quiet pride once reserved for himself and the Enclaves, for the things he thought meant honor and truth, but now floated only as dust and embers all around him.

He straightened and turned away. In the frigid cold, he pulled the fireleather uniform from his bag, flinching at the sight of the brilliant copper patches, stark against the traditional black. Wynt. The woman she had been. What she had meant to Kilras. The Dorn's words from the letter tore through Cleod. *She gleamed. She was my friend, as you are my friend.*

With a shudder, he pulled the uniform on. It was no longer armor of any kind. It was grief personified. It was penance.

Once dressed, he pulled his blade, turned to the west again and watch as the battle raged below. Clear sky, gemstone blue above, framed the billowing column of smoke that rose as a beacon behind him. Orange and black, a roil like rage incarnate, the plume rose and tumbled into the air—a message none could ignore, not even the warriors arrayed far below, swarming the great stone city of his youth.

Cleod—8 years

The odor of smoke lingered heavy and bitter, carried on the air along with a powder-fine dusting of ash. How huge must the fire atop the Spur have been for so much of it to fall like snow here? Standing on the porch, watching it land in the dooryard, Cleod shuddered, because what covered the ground, so bitter and dark, was not just wood ash, but what was left of Leiel's mother.

Across the yard in the small barn, the horses and cow needed feeding. The idea of stepping from the covered safety of the porch flooded him with a strange feeling. If his stomach had been full of rocks and his skin covered in beetles, he could not have felt worse. How could he walk into the yard, onto that ash, have it cover his head and drift into his eyes? And if he felt like this, how must Leiel feel? What must her thoughts be as she watched this grey dust rain out of the sky?

The door creaked open behind him, and he looked up over his shoulder as his father stepped onto the porch. Every thought in Cleod's head must have shown on his face, because Ellan did not frown or ask why the animals remained untended. Instead, he simply rested a hand on Cleod's shoulder and stood with him to watch the gruesome fall.

"It's wrong." Cleod let the words slip from his mind to his lips. "She was Leiel's mother." He looked back out at the dry yard, now covered as though by a grey skin.

"Her Sacrifice will keep us all safe for years."

How was that supposed to help this sick feeling go away? And if knowing Draigon Weather would lift soon was not enough to help him, what would? Ellan's words from the day before, Keep being Leiel's friend. Not many will. *"It won't keep Leiel safe," he whispered.*

Ellan was silent for so long that Cleod glanced at him again.

The smile Ellan offered was sad. "It might. Just not in a way she'll enjoy."

"Then how is that safe?"

"She's alive. That's the thing that matters. And without her mother around to influence her, she'll follow the laws. So even if her life is hard—"

"Like our life without mother," Cleod interrupted before thought. Then his belly jerked in a new way at the expression that crossed his father's face. More shock than pain, the reaction fell into silence. "I'm sorry." Cleod said quickly.

Ellan shook his head and turned Cleod to face him completely. He dropped to one knee and held Cleod's gaze with a new seriousness. "Don't apologize, son. You're right. I wasn't thinking about this the way you are. It's easy to forget that what happened this morning was about more than what Adfen needs. It's about what a family lost." He shook his head, and his expression shifted again. "I never thought about that before. Before your mother and I had you, and then we lost her, I never would have been able to think about the Sacrifice this way."

"Is choosing always so hard?"

"Choosing?"

"To hurt someone to save someone else?"

"I've never had to do that, but yes. I think it would always be hard."

"And is a Sacrifice the way to help the most?"

"In times like this, it is the most important way."

The carefulness with which Ellan spoke made Cleod's head hurt. What had he learned yesterday in the Square? As a boy, he could never be chosen for Sacrifice, so he could never help that way. Could he become one of the men who did the choosing? He recalled the Council in their red tunics, the pleasure they seemed to take in Leiel's hurt as she ran to her mother. No, he did not want to be one of **them**. So how could he help? Would he have to give up something to do it? If so, what would that be?

On the steps leading to the Tower, Ilora Sower had stood so calm and so straight. Sacrifice was important, but...how could anyone be that brave? If he had to be brave like that one day, would he be able to do it? Brave enough to stand for a Sacrifice like she had, atop a mountain, alone and burning? He shuddered at the thought. "Are there other ways to help as much?"

Ellan nodded, tightened his grip until Cleod felt the pressure of each of his father's fingers against his shoulders. "Many ways. Big and small. And not many of them require that someone dies." He raised his gaze to take in the falling ash. "Bad luck, that your first lesson in this involves your friend."

But it was always someone's friend. Cleod trembled a little. Someone's mother, or sister, or daughter. If his mother were alive, could she have been chosen? Could it be her, burned to nothing but what floated on the air? Was the ash falling on Leiel's home too, or was the farm far enough way that the wind would not blow it there? His eyes were hot, and he blinked fast and raised a hand to wipe at them.

Ellan looked into Cleod's face again, gave one last squeeze, then released his grip. "It's right to be sad, seeing what you have seen these last few days. But come, we have animals to feed."

Cleod swallowed back thicker tears. "But the—"

"We have to walk through it. No matter how hard it is. Sometimes that's just the way of things." Ellan stood and held out a hand.

After a heartbeat, Cleod grasped it and turned to face the terrible air and the mess on the ground. It would blanket his shoes and his hair and his hands. It would fill his nose and he would taste it. And he feared, before he took the first step from the porch, that he would feel it covering him forever and forever. A thought half-formed, that this was also a Sacrifice of some kind, though he had no words to understand what exactly he was giving up this day.

He looked up at his father and Ellan nodded. Then together they
left the porch and walked through the grey foulness toward the barn.

Cleod—38 Years

Not on the exact ground where he had faced Shaa, but so close
that it did not matter, he stood and listened as the wind washed
toward him, through scrub trees and over the stony ridge. Carried upon it were far-away shouts and screams and the roar of
fire, and a boiling noise that marked a wing wind rolling forth
with annihilating force. Battles raging as he awaited his own,
one that had been coming for decades. Long, long ago he had
promised to destroy the need for Sacrifice, to end the practice
for women everywhere, make it unnecessary through wit and
strong arm and keen blade. If his boldness had bent that intention into something more destructive than salvatory, the moment lay before him now to redeem what he could. Had he ever
truly had a choice but to face it? What was destiny anyway? Fate
blended with choice? Soul with desire? Pride with intention?
Maybe it was only the patterns he carried inside, the things that
drove him and that he had never learned to forget or leave behind.

Too late now to think through any of it.

He raised his chin and focused full attention toward the man
cresting the trail from the city.

Pale face hovering starkly over the black uniform he wore,
everything about Trayor hung somewhere between focus and
rage, his sword, his expression, the swirling vibration of his
restrained connection to Gweld. A gust caught his hair and
whipped it back, a toss of drama to match the moment.

Across the icy, windswept expanse of granite, dotted with
mounded snow and tangled scrub plants, they stared at each
other until the space between vibrated with energy so warped
by violent potential that it seemed it could split open both air

and earth. For an instant Cleod wondered what Teska would see if she stood witness to this moment. Would it be more or less vile and hate filled than their shared encounter in Melbis? Time hung heavy and dangerous, suspended by history and hopes, losses and needs.

Then Trayor snarled as darkly as any beast, his voice a bitter whip through the thin air. "I thought you dead. But I should have known no Draigon can kill you. Are you one of them now?" He looked toward the still dark-burning plume that marked destruction. "What have you done?"

"What I should have done decades ago. Burned Ehlewer to the ground."

Though Trayor had clearly climbed the Spur in search of vengeance, actually hearing the words seemed to rock him, as though gut knowledge and confirmation collided and the jolt of actuality shook deeper than could ever have been anticipated.

His face closed and twisted. "And only you would dare such a thing. What remains, cefreid, of the home that shaped you?"

"With all luck, nothing," Cleod replied, even as more words from Kilras's letter burned through Cleod's mind. *All of it was real, old friend—the friendships, the trust, the love of the trail and of the work. My lies of omission were meant to prevent harm, not deepen it. Home was where I made it, all these years. And it's my hope that the same was true for you.*

Deep within Cleod, something that had broken loose settled and stilled. He tipped his head in acknowledgement. "Yes, I would dare. Just as you would dare shape the fate of all Arnan— and try to claim a throne never meant for the likes of us."

"What do you know of power and how it should be used?" Trayor drew his sword, striding closer over the treacherous ground.

Cleod shook his head, at both the oddity of the question and the words themselves. But the revelation it carried into him pulled him straighter. Was that what Trayor thought? That all of this, any of this was about power? Control? And then at a second shock—part of the reason that the two of them stood here was Cleod's failure, for so long, to consider how much both those things had always shaped the actions of the Ehlewer and all the men of Arnan. He formed words along with thought. "Enough to know that I would end your quest for it, here and now."

"And you think simply burning Ehlewer will end the Enclaves."

"With Bynkhol gone as well, yes," Cleod said, and the way Trayor stiffened and drew breath confirmed speculation—that word of the other Enclaves' destruction had not yet reached this far east. "It's all gone, Tray." Cleod stepped to the right, seeking more predictable footing. "Even if you manage to take Adfen, to kill a dozen Draigon, there's nothing left of the history and pride you hold so dear."

Trained to counteract surprise, Trayor shrugged back into himself, and Gweld flared, pushed outward, until Cleod allowed the trance to claim him as well, raised defense to counter impact. Still, it pressed him, but he reached as well, tugged the edges of Trayor's skill, pried for weakness and the knowledge he needed. That above all.

"There's nothing to rebuild, Tray. You won't live long enough to recreate what has been destroyed."

An answer came as satisfied laughter. "I've never been the fool you seem to think." Trayor paced closer, knees bent, muscles taut with strength and energy in need of release. "There has always been far more Enclave knowledge than a simple library holds."

Cleod parried in Gweld, a single spear of intention meant to chase the thought and deeper meaning behind the pale Draighil's words. And for an instant, image flared, a bright space shining like glass in the sun—then Trayor tore through the connection and slammed it away. The tricks of the Elders within Gweld were too familiar to them both for any to offer advantage.

"You won't twist my mind so easily."

The guarded maze of Trayor's thoughts was beyond access. Would even physical force yield the information needed? "I could not twist it more if I tried," Cleod replied with a frown.

Trayor took another step, and his lips parted as though he would speak again. But suddenly they moved beyond words—if such had ever mattered at all between them—and in paired furious response Cleod swept his blade to the ready to fend off Trayor's first strike.

Like a nightmare born of a dream of their first true dual, the clang of swords awoke fullest Gweld and blue sparks showered through Cleod's vision, seared his mind. Attack and parry, back away and seek opening—long since matched in skill and experience, they took on the fierce dance that their long conflict at last manifested in deadly finality.

Circling, steps over snowy ground that squeaked under their boots, they moved within a weary spiral of rage that sounded through Gweld like a series of hammer blows on steel. Rang like their blades when they connected. Burned like the touch and thrust of metal into flesh.

Cleod pivoted, moved back, breath hissing through clenched teeth as blood flowed down his side, slicking the Fireleather, spreading crimson over the bright copper along his hip. His Gweld sense flared with pain—*Her name was Wynt, the Draigon whose skin repaired your Fireleather. She was my friend from childhood. She was my lover. She was healing to my most wounded heart. Trayor killed her as he killed Gahree*—and he stumbled as the layered knowledge that now weighted him exploded through his awareness.

A whispered curse and he rejoined the fight.

Clash and dance, connect and parry. Wounds that should cause a falter, cause shock, drowned in the labyrinthian power of Gweld. He rode it, carried it, felt Trayor do the same, until their battle existed beyond their physical senses, beyond even their souls. It tore through and swept between them as though it erupted from the very earth.

Cleod took it in, drew it close and let it whirl through him, guide him into a strength and pattern of action that carried him beyond exhaustion, beyond will. Somewhere deep within, truth reared, demanded acknowledgment—time had not altered old fact, that Trayor was faster. And, in this vital moment, he was less worn, body and spirit. Less battered in every way, and far more filled with rage.

A dread creature clawed and fluttered at the back of Cleod's skull, manifested realization of the fact that *he could not win this fight*. And if Trayor defeated him, survived, he would find a way to keep the Ehlewer alive—and stop at nothing to destroy all the Draigon and all their works across the land.

Horror clenched his heart, nearly choked him, that he might end this way—all promises broken, all friendships lost. Through exhaustion and pain and a fear like none he had known, he sent up a silent scream that arced through Gweld like a falling star called into the night. And in the space of the next heartbeat enough heat speared his soul that he knew he could only have been heard. By who, by what, it did not matter. Somehow, in the darkest instant as he dodged and struck back through trained skill driven purely by instinct, he was *not alone*.

Leiel

A plea of pure desperation roared through Gweld, tore across boundaries into a frontier marked by impossibility made actual.

Leiel shrieked her frustration even as she swept thunderous winds to blast icy waves of air over the heart of the city. Behind her, atop the Spur, blade clashed with blade, equal in skill and knowledge—but not in strength. In her heart, Cleod's exhaustion bloomed as though it were her own, and a terror like none she had known even when Gahree stepped forward to face her death, rose from Leiel's core and ripped through her, sweeping aside all reason.

Almost, she took flight. Almost turned from her post, and the precious treasure that was Adfen, to sweep over the Spur and rain destruction upon the man who would destroy all she held dear.

But she had never been meant for that kind of battle.

And Cleod had never been meant for anything else.

Teska's words blazed through Leiel's mind: *He uses Gweld as he was trained to, Leiel. But he does not have to. It need not pain him, if he learns to touch it as we do.*

And even as she focused the fury of the winter storm to dump snow over the flames lapping at the Old City's wall, those words resounded deep within. Of course it mattered. Gahree had known it mattered. Possibility churned like the clouds around her, a dozen potential actions and outcomes born and discarded before she steeled her will and *reached*.

Not to the other Draigon. Not to the desperate man on the mountain. But to the one abed and racked by a pain so deep it burned white hot when she touched his mind.

Kilras—Kilras we can win this. All of us. Though his soul is torn, Cleod is of Arnan. I am Draigon. You are Hantyn.

Not a heartbeat passed before she felt him sweep aside shock, not simply at her presence in his thoughts, but at the clear implication of what she pressed into him. *You use Gweld as he does. You can access his mind in a way I never could.* Horror spilled through them both. She knew what the force of Kilras's ability to invade minds could do, what had happened the last time he had used it.

In the space left empty by that idea another flume of fire roared down stone streets and she shifted attention, focused icy weather and drove it back. Through that determined action Kilras's reply came.

It will break him, Leiel.

Denial marked first instinct, but integrity demanded she acknowledge that likelihood. Despite the miraculous gains of the last days, Cleod had been trained to hate, spent a lifetime consumed and driven by it. Could his mind withstand the truth that dwelt in his very bones? In a heartbeat, she weighed his strength of spirit against vile influence, and chose the best of him. *Or it will save us all.*

She sent terror. She sent grief. She sent hope.

I am the knowledge. You are the bridge. And it will be his choice, Kilras. Always his choice.

But she heard Kilras's thoughts, mirrored deep inside by her own, a well of doubt, darkly reflecting. In the heat of battle, of pain and loss and fear—was any choice freely made? Having choice...was that, in the end, enough if the options were all bad? *Ask Gahree.* In that final moment, had her decision been any *less* freely made for the fact that it meant death?

Ask him. Ask Cleod. It was all they could do. Asking could cost him everything. Not doing so could cost all of Arnan.

She hoped Teska had been right about Cleod, right about them all. Hoped that what they shared over the last few days had bred a level of acceptance within him that would allow for the most impossible of acts.

Though her heart screamed, she sent her query into the heart of Gweld, passed it to Kilras to share across void and churning violence with the man they both so loved.

As Draigdyn, you can defeat him, Cleod. As Draigdyn you can change the world. As Draigdyn. As Draigon.

Cleod

Blood slicked the sword hilt, forced expanded concentration in the face of uncertain grip. Pain racked him, speared down his arm, weakening control and awakening fear deep in his gut. Outmatched, by pain and by pure weariness, Cleod parried and shifted his weight to land a glancing blow across Trayor's forearm. The Draighil stepped back, not giving way, but opening space, Gweld vision expanding between them in a vibrating symphony of motion and expanded sound.

Draigdyn... The voice, the following words, exploded in Cleod's mind, sent him stumbling away from Trayor's blade. The precious distance gained could not separate Cleod from the terrifying depth of the word and the statement—the desperate *request*—that seared across his mind.

In the flash that no purely human mind could comprehend, a thousand images filled his awareness, scrolling like dream vision, shifting and impaling, offering an understanding he had never dreamed possible. *Kilras. Leiel.* Both of them dancing within his deepest consciousness, Kilras like a blade cutting into his soul, and knowledge, impossible knowledge, shared by Leiel, like a rising tide. The question lingered, a radiant spark demanding fuel and air, as *truth* poured through him.

The question.

Choice.

Promise.

Sacrifice.

Every heartbeat pressured blood he could not afford to lose. Every breath neared the last, ushered failure closer.

In terror and determination, he grasped what was offered.

Knowledge rived him, poured through every fiber of his body, fired his mind, speared his soul. And in the flame-rimmed edge of the instant it took understanding to claim him, awe filled him past brimming—that what he knew of Gweld was a flaming twig in a child's hand and what lay before and within him was all-consuming as the sun.

A scream tore through him as he *chose*, and *let go*, and the change took him, and rent his world apart.

In a smoldering instant, he sundered.

He broke.

He became.

Kilras

Ripped through by a physical and emotion conjoining that defied wildest expectation or imagining, every muscle in Kilras's body locked, bent him into twisting convulsion. As Cleod, guided by Leiel's experience, was borne onward by muscles that rippled and tore and reformed in a shredding instant, and the distant and inconceivable transformation exploded every bit of his being.

Kilras's mind could follow what his body could never match and the brutal dissociation of form from mind roared through him as anguish that could be expressed only in screams. But his throat clenched so tightly that he could not cry out. Instead, silent tears spilled toward his temples as he rode the uncoiling manifestation of change through Cleod's awareness.

Draigdyn.

All along, Cleod was Draigdyn.

And now the vital and consuming nature of *Draigon* burned them both through. Vision, changed, broadened, deepened. Strength flowed like crashing water. And wings, impossible wings rose in counterbalance to unfurling size and might. But the *mind*—the expanded consciousness that seemed poised to grasp the nature of even the sun and stars above—dwarfed the physical change. Awe unfolded in a falling pattern that had no end. Possibility was only the beginning of an understanding that could only be earned with a thousand lifetimes.

That, Kilras could have ridden into eternity, but his body fought, wrung itself through with a ferocity destined to snap his very bones. Around him, blurred and distant, echoed shouts and scrambling. Vaguely, hands grasped flesh that fought against heart and mind. Some small part of him acknowledged distress—Sehina and Amhise and Retta, in frenzied action around him.

Let go. Leiel's voice raged into his thoughts, frantic and heartbroken. Were the tears he felt hers or his own? Could Draigon cry? Memory failed as consciousness turned like a whirlwind. *Let go, Kilras Dorn, or Cleod's destruction will be ours as well.*

From deep inside came a tearing, as though a precious part of him was ripped from another. And Leiel's words came again, pressing, pleading. *Let go.*

"*Kilras!*" Hands gripped his face and Sehina's desperate cry slammed into him with the force of a physical blow.

Greater than he could ever accept or comprehend, expansive knowledge loomed, beckoned, offered infinity. But pain carved reality with the force of Sehina's plea.

Pure, bitter will grasped *self,* and *pulled*—back, away—peeled clear with a cleaving agony that, as his throat loosened, tore from him a scream broken like blood-shards through Gweld vision.

He fell. Back into himself, a place of being too small to ever contain what he now knew. And left Cleod alone.

Vaguely, as connection faded, truth sank in consuming grief.

Cleod was changed.

Truth loomed from the wounds suffered before transformation.

Cleod was dying.

61

Cleod

BETWEEN FRACTIONS OF THOUGHTS AND REALIZATIONS THAT DEFIED clear definition, he understood that danger still loomed. As every bit of him expanded and *changed* into a body at once infinitely unfamiliar and somehow inevitable, instinct dictated action, and he moved to avoid an incoming blow carried over from Trayor's forward motion.

Then the Draighil's screams, twisted between horror and rage, filled the air and blasted through the surreal sensitivity of Cleod's new hearing. Through vision layered in strange, amber-tinted prismatic clarity, he watched the black-clad figure stumble away, then straighten and flee with purpose.

Deep within, something tore free, then another awareness rose and threaded through his mind, solid and fierce and fiery with resolve. Different than the shearing disruption that had followed Kilras's words into the wildest part of him, this consciousness shared his being, a vivid presence shaped to guide and offer a wealth of understanding that, in the space of a breath, calmed his racing thoughts. Leiel. Leiel *within* him, even as his senses whirled beyond control, a balm to the madness rising with the realization of *what he was*.

Strange around him, the feel of the air, the wildness of the ground, the pull of *wings* arching over his back. He slashed them downward and raised wind to blast souls apart.

Then something moved with deadly speed at the expanded corner of his vision. Reaction erupted with a roar and his new, great body moved *impossibly* fast. No sword training mattered now, and yet this new form drew upon that instinct to counter. Motion became dance, became hypnotic violence, a call and response of death and survival.

Hot blood rushed along an amber scaled side, blew over the man who had inflicted new wounds—and who lifted on the blast of air to impact the row of boulders where too many women had stood chained.

Cleod staggered. Leiel's voice within him, rose frantic and supporting, and her strength poured through him. Her strength. Old gods had he ever really understood how much of it she possessed? Even as he countered, struck, awe claimed him again. What she was, *he was,* and that had *always been true.*

A thousand, thousand thoughts unfolded, and the mind of the form he now inhabited explored them all in the space of an instant. But no time existed for wonder. The wounds his human body had sustained remained, unvanquished by the change, and the man who had inflicted them flashed like deadly lightning to add to their count. Blood spilled, slicked the earth, glittered over stone and snow and skin and scale.

He recognized the danger, *that he had become because no other recourse remained* to gain the knowledge he needed, to destroy an unrelenting threat. From within rose desperate purpose. Gweld flung instinct into icy air, and backed by the Great Shape he now wore, Cleod separated body from mind, let one fight as the other *reached.*

Even as Trayor landed another strike, he screamed at the shock of Cleod's mind slamming into him, resolute and seeking. Through memories, crisp and jumbled, Cleod searched, sorting, focused and desperate to avoid distraction within Trayor's mind. The Draighil's life unfolded, awash with wild emotions, ambitions, and few regrets.

Nothing came clear. Images poured into Cleod, tangled and uncertain, yet he discovered value in the intensity of feeling behind them, and swept the weak ones aside.

Bitter understanding arose, unavoidable—he would not live to sort the knowledge. Would not live to see his friends again. Would not live to share the future with Leiel.

He struck out, again felt both Trayor's blade, and the battering assault of his hate-backed mind, as the Draighil struggled and slashed and denied.

Loss surged through Cleod, swept him down a torrent of despair... but through it came the vibrant warmth of the other presence within him. Leiel, close to his mind and heart and soul. Leiel who had given him a way to fulfill the promise he had made long ago—to end Draigon Weather and all need for Sacrifice. Into her, he poured all he drew from Trayor's mind, raw and savage. And he wondered at her acceptance even as his focus slipped, his strength faded.

A last rally rained violence upon Trayor, rent him and bled him and ended all the enmity between them. A kind of grief chased Cleod as he killed the Draighil, one that spoke of loss and pity and endless regret. The waste of it, of the mind and skills that backed it. The loss of the knowledge within it. The terrible necessity of the killing.

A scream filled him, inside, burst forth as a blinding roar, as every fiber within him became fully alive—in one blazing instant complete, empowered, beloved—and fell through darkness into the light of all he was always meant to be.

Leiel

Perched on high, surrounded by the city that raised her, spurned her, marked the starkest turnings of her early life, Leiel split her focus between the battle before her and one on the Spur. Kilras's skill had breached defenses, but now the unmatched unity of linked Draigon awareness held hers tight to Cleod's.

Draigon to Draigon.

She shook with awe.

Was this part of the reason they had lived connected despite distance? One aspect of why they had never let each other go? Why he had sensed her on the trail when such should have been impossible? Because he was as much Draigon as she had ever been?

Had Gahree known? In a flashing instant of conviction, Leiel dismissed the idea. Gahree had guessed at Cleod's importance, yes, but never would she have held back a truth such as this. But why had no one sensed it sooner? No answer illuminated Leiel's confusion.

And now it mattered not at all, because a more vital reality loomed. As Cleod's mind expanded, delved through Trayor's, she followed, joined and searching, opened herself to the outpouring of Cleod's ongoing discovery.

The entirety of his being opened to and overwhelmed her. His love of his friends and family outshone the sun. And his shame washed over her, for his weakness and fear, for his loss of a child named Ain. And then even that was drowned by regret: That he would never again speak with Kilras, to sort hard truths and rebuild friendship. That hatred had directed so much of his life. That he had made the wrong promises to the wrong people. That he would have no more time with *her*.

Tumbled within it all, she dismissed such darkness and bled the prismatic light of understanding into him. She unfolded forgiveness, even as she begged it of him, felt it surround and embrace him, and settled acceptance into the well of his being, and understood it was returned.

And when the last of his strength shifted to pour into her all that he had discerned within Trayor. She opened to it—thousands of scattered, jumbled images that would change Arnan forever. Unclear but vital, they filled her, and she retained them deep within. If, in the moment, they meant nothing, shadowed as they were by their cost, their value and the sacrifices made to gain them, were acknowledged deep within her.

And as the life behind them dimmed, sought release, she let go and tumbled, sobbing, into her own mind, forced in an instant to bury grief in rage and attend to the violent present.

Kilras

RAW AND BATTERED, EYES CLOSED IN UTTER SURRENDER, KILRAS LAY shaken to the point of numbness. The shredding agony that racked his body over the last hours had dulled in the wake of heartache so obliterating as to leave nothing else to even examine.

Beside him, Sehina sat bent by silent tears, her hand light in his, her forehead barely brushing his arm.

Gone. Gained and gone in the same heartbeat, the same breath, the full potential of the friend they so treasured. Loss flowed inward with each drawn breath and grief spilled through the room on every exhale.

Gone.

And the last words between them spoken in fear and anger. And all the things that released truth and might have at last allowed them to share it, had been ripped from possibility with the final stumble of a desperate heart. Retta's cake. Delhar's gentle laughter. The snowcapped Great Northern Range snaking into unending distance. The stunning Library of Cyunant. The truth of both their lives.

Had Cleod received the letter? Had he read it? Had he understood? Accepted? *Forgiven*? A thousand more things remained forever unsaid...

Tears slipped toward Kilras's temples, and his chest heaved.

Sehina's grip tightened around his fingers and her head came up. When he opened his eyes, she stared into them, her own sorrow rimming hers in red.

Tired. So tired that the word exhaustion was insufficient, he squeezed her fingers in return. "There're so many things I can explain to you now." His words barely claimed the term whisper. "You and Rimm and Nae." He shifted his gaze to look at Retta and Amhise where they sat at the other side of the narrow bed. "All of you. So many truths."

"Kil." Sehina's voice was hoarse with tears, but firm. As strong as she had always been, her friendship old and essential in his life, her statement carried quiet weight. "We've never needed to know more than you've shared. We don't need it now, unless telling us would ease something in you."

He closed his eyes, and the tears slid harder down his face. How had he been so lucky in his life as to have such friends? The truth of Sehina's words was one he had long known. Even Cleod had never asked, never needed to know. But the thought of being able to at last share all of who he was with those he loved...a new ache swelled his chest, a blend of relief and grief like none he had ever known. To no longer have to lie...and to have the price of that freedom be the loss of so many he loved... The suffering of his racked body was nothing in light of that horrible truth.

"I have so much to tell you," he said.

"All right, Kil." Retta leaned forward and brushed his hair from his forehead "But it doesn't have to be now."

"It does." Cleod was gone, along with any chance to speak the truth, to share as friends were meant to share. That loss was lesson enough about the fragilities of time and mortality. Kilras forced energy into his voice. "Help me sit up."

Amhise shook her head firmly. "No. If you insist on speaking, you'll do it from where you are."

He shifted his attention to Sehina, seeking support, but she shook her head. Taking quiet measure of his body, he sighed. They were right. He closed his eyes again, and settled into old pain and new.

Perhaps, somewhere along the chain of light, Cleod would also hear the story.

"My name is Kilras Hantyn," he began quietly, and let the history he had long held secret slip forth along with fresh tears.

Whatever came now, however his friends responded, a new road lay open before him, and for once he would tread it as all that he was.

63

Leiel

ON SHE FOUGHT, AND ON, ATTUNED ONLY TO WHAT WAS BEFORE HER—
the sweep and pound of battle, the heat of flames and rage
and sorrow flashing through the city and through her heart. She
allowed in no thought beyond the idea that now they *must* win.
If the thousand reasons that had been true before had always
been enough, now the need for victory was tied to her soul and,
perhaps, her very sanity.

Distant yet powerful, the other Draigon crowded the edges of her mind, until she knew their anger, and exhaustion,
their fear and their determination, as if all of it belonged to her,
moved through her. Every decision they made, every action,
every blow struck or received, flowed with each of hers, until
Kinra's gleaming awareness centered her own. In a silvered instant, understanding blossomed, and she bent the lesson of her
connection with Cleod and Kilras into the present, flooded the
other Draigon with the power of it, the nuanced intensity and
possibility. A shudder crashed through her, through them all, as
they accepted her insight.

Leiel let go, and *Kinra's* experience filled her, guided her,
until the battle around her, the battle *everywhere* came clear. As
Leiel passed Cleod's knowledge of the Farlan plans through the
revelatory connection, layers of strategy and response revealed
themselves by the instant, wherever she looked. She took it in,
felt the others do the same...and turned anguish into the unrelenting need to *triumph*. And if she remembered little of the

night or the dawn or night as it fell again, she knew she fought. That they all fought, to make the price of rising loss, among the people they fought with, among themselves, worth every drop of blood and suffering that suffused them all.

On the morning of the second day, Kinra's unflagging awareness whispered that their battles were ended, at least in the moment, and Leiel came completely back to herself to find that she stood, bloodied and bruised, great wings spread wide, on the plains east of Adfen. Before her, the tattered remains of an army fled down the ancient stone road, broken bodies littering the space around her. When she had flown from the tower and how she had rendered such destruction—of those things she had no memory. Behind and beside her knots of cheering people raised spears and axes and farm tools in victorious celebration. How...? She let the thought drift away, as grief crashed in upon her, she swayed, and the small crowd around her backed away, shouting.

Steadying herself, she raised her long neck and turned her gaze back toward Adfen. Draigon vision picked out a strange gathering before the Old City's gates—Gydron and Kinra and the king named Rawden. Negotiation? Victory? At what cost? What cost beyond that which already overwhelmed her?

Whatever passed between the group standing in the shadow of Desga Hiage's greatest work, the fate of the city, of all Arnan, now seemed to lie in words as much as actions, in promises and papers across which they would be recorded.

Have we won? She sent the vital question across distance, across the thoughts of all with whom she had shared the last days in action and mind. The overwhelming response echoed both bottomless fatigue and astonished hope. From Gydron came a vision of a framework of new stories to be written across the land, laws and conditions and change to reorder lives. Possibility loomed—of peace, of quality lives, and of freedom for those to whom it had been so long denied—the very things Leiel had spent her life working toward. The dream she had spun as a girl and envisioned in the warp and weft of her prismatic vision hung on the horizon like the brightest star.

Intellectual recognition of the wonder of those things, of all they could mean for the future, shone in the back of her mind. But the unfolding storm of shock and grief that slowed her heart in her chest and wrung her tears dry, smothered the light, drowned her in a raging sea.

Because Cleod was gone. And though Gweld had allowed her to follow his journey along the chain of light until the moment he passed beyond what a mortal, world-bound mind could comprehend—the knowledge that beyond that blazing place lay the promise of peace eased nothing within her. Nothing at all.

With a roar that scattered the human fighters, she took wing, launched herself into the sky and made for the Spur with desperate speed. Up and up, until the scene on the great granite peak came clear in all its horror and all its wonder.

The broken, bloated corpse of Trayor Draighil lay among shattered boulders, his pale hair streaked with debris and frozen blood. The burdening relief that should have filled her at the sight, did not come, because the shining, amber body of a strange, new Draigon seeped crystalline blood over the stony summit. A Great Shape that had once been her old friend. Cleod Woodcutter. Cleod Draighil. Cleod Ruhelrn. Cleod *Draigon*.

She plummeted to earth beside the stunning form, took in both the horror and the wonder of its existence. And grief spiraled through Gweld in darkening rainbows, bleeding into deepening shades of grey that blended night and the tempest within her as she shrieked her pain and fury into the sky.

More than her own breath she wanted her born form, wanted Cleod in his. Neither could claim the moment, any more than the Great Shape could offer tears. But her heart wept in the shelter of her chest—for the loss of all that could never have been, and of all that could never be.

Without his friendship and the hope it knitted between them, the dark whirlpool of her childhood would have dragged her under, drowned a thousand times over, like cup after cup of water drunk too quickly, burning as it choked. How many pointless, unrequited dreams of *them* had sustained her through her lowest days? How much, long before Gahree had entered her life, had Leiel's love for Cleod's laughter, and his wit, and his caring hugs, given her reason to believe in something besides the bitter moment before her?

Could anything measure the ache of loss that swallowed all dreams of the future, broke all promises made within a daring heart? Loss hung in the air, bitter and acrid as death itself—copper and iron and the otherworldly scent of Draigon blood shimmering the burned earth.

She stamped a mighty, clawed foot into the crystalline pool of crimson and it shattered into the wind, shattered like the deepest part of her that had always reserved itself for a desperate, senseless wish, a care-filled fantasy. One replete with long, comfortable silences, and easy laughter at silly things, with meals shared and stories told, and beauty created on the wind of imagination and the freedom of passionate dreams. Gone now without ever truly being tasted, red dust in a dying storm.

Through brutal conversation and tears both shed and denied, they agreed, she and the others who loved Cleod—the traditional burial services of Arnan could not unfold atop the Spur, not for this great form. That left only fire able to claim their friend, to return his body to the land.

And it fell to Leiel to set the blaze.

She stood, wings folded tight against her back and sides, beside the unfamiliar form, searching the strange and mighty shape sprawled before her for anything familiar, anything that spoke of the born-form she had known so well, yet in so many ways, known not at all. But the lifeless being was both more and less than Cleod had been. More in scale and power and eternal physical capacity—just as *she* was in this moment—but did that measure the true depth of what he had been—of his will and his joy and his focus? No. All that had passed beyond her reach. Beyond all of their caring ability to touch and love and soothe.

From Adfen, she took in the full impact of Kilras's regret, and the rolling ache of Sehina's grief, that melded with her own.

And from across the land, distant and astonishing, reached the deep connection to all the other Draigon. The weight of their awe burned through her, at the truth unveiled this day. At the cost of it. At the potential it unleashed across Arnan.

She raised bronze wings above her glowing body, closed her heart to piercing anguish, and blazed focused heat over the lifeless body. Focused and relentless, the inferno washed over Cleod Draigon, set him to smolder, ignited, and engulfed. And with the blaze unquenchably aflame, she shrieked agony that echoed and rebounded into her bones as the air filled with ash blowing wild upon the wind.

64

Leiel

A WOOL CLOAK DYED THE DEEPEST GREEN OF FIR TREES, STIRRED TO beauty in Delhar's vats. Books, only favorites, the ones that came with her from Adfen so long ago—she held, for a long moment, the book Cleod had stolen for her so long ago. Socks, warm and soft, knitted by Gemda's hands. A tiny, knotted bag full of seeds plucked from Gahree's greenhouse. A bundle of maps. A battered tin cup. A wooden bowl and matching spoon. A broken, twisted ring. Each, she tucked carefully into place in the pack, among shirts and pants and a knife Wynt had made for Kinra, now gifted into Leiel's care, to honor memory and the long fight—both behind, and ahead.

At last, Leiel checked the straps on the pack, straightened, and gazed slowly around the little cabin. Since the day Shaa—Gahree—carried Leiel north on that first magnificent flight and delivered her into the embrace of Cyunant, this cabin had been home. As much as her mother's arms, and Gahree's stories, and the mountain itself, this small house had eased her heart. Here, she always belonged. One wish among a thousand, thousand others, to be able to show this place to Cleod.

Could it really be that a whole month had washed by since he and so many others had passed along the chain of light? Seven Draigon lost to the war—Shore and Resor and Dahlie among them. Others, like Kinra and Gydron, forever scarred in body. All of them scarred to the depths of their souls. And how many hundreds of ordinary people? Thousands. And every Enclave member who refused to surrender or to unlearn.

An ache crowded her chest, and she closed her eyes and breathed deep. Neither regret, nor exactly resignation, was the feeling that wrapped her heart and her thoughts in weight and contemplation. Breath flowed into breath, until at last, she opened her eyes and continued what must be done. Not because the pain had eased, but because the thought of it hampering the future was intolerable. That for so many she loved, the cost of the potent alteration of the world had been written in blood and suffering, in loss so profound that its hurt cut beyond healing, rang anguish through her bones. Too much had been lost. Too much sacrificed. But she could not surrender to it because, as well, too much remained to be done. And the future that could rise from all the loss was good, and powerful.

If the King had negotiated in good faith, a chance existed that peace might hold. If not...hopefully the work they were about to begin would ease any need for another war.

She would find the Enclave documents, no matter how long it took. But the level of attention and caution needed to seek those secrets must wait a little. Opportunity, almost insurmountable in its depth and breadth, spread over Arnan in the rolling wake of change. Honoring what brought that into being meant all her focus must, for now, be on the good they could build, the freedom and joy of creating it. She owed all of herself to remaking Arnan in the light of hope bought by staggering sacrifice.

She needed a final look at Cyunant. She smiled the faintest bit. Perhaps not *final*, but the last for a long, long time. She draped the pack over her shoulder, crossed the small space, and stepped out into the shining morning.

Pulling the cabin door closed behind her, she set her feet on the path. Where her little track met the main trail, she paused. Down-slope, to the right, the others gathered at the main Cabin: Ilora worn from days of assisting Teska in healing myriad wounds, Gemda her hands calloused from the work of digging graves, Kinra's face scarred anew by the marks of all they had lost and won. All readied to make the journey out into Arnan, to reclaim the Draigon's place in the land.

Leiel turned left. Time soon to say farewells, but she was not ready for them yet. Instead, she climbed toward the ravine. At the bottom of the great sweeping bowl, she gazed up the scree field, toward the waterfall, toward the arched top of the mountain. So many hours spent exploring this land, learning how to be...everything she had dreamed to be. All possible because she chose this place. Chose. One choice among so many leading to this very moment, when leaving was as healing as arriving had once been. She climbed higher, moved right at the next fork and followed the trail until the wide entrance of the cave that sheltered the library came into sight.

At the top of the steps leading to the cave, two figures stood against the shadowed opening. Gydron raised a hand, and Leiel returned the gesture. Greeting and goodbye. A moment of silence held, then Gydron turned to descend into the library. Teska waited a moment more, then nodded, and followed Gydron.

Tears welled, and Leiel blinked them back. Teska—so powerful, and with so much still to learn before she claimed her Great Shape. The healing the other woman had already rendered, echoed day by day. How much more lay ahead? The potential prosperity that might unfold in the path of Teska's fully unleashed gifts—that held worth beyond measure, and lay ahead to be benefit to all Arnan. Healing and hope.

Moving on. Leiel resumed climbing, set one foot after the other in steady rhythm up the steep slope, until the trail vanished in a tumble of boulders that must be scrambled over, the way marked only by small cairns. The hard way. The long way. To the summit of the great peak, she ascended with steady determination, traveling upward with the skillful assurance of long practice. How strange to think that once such climbing had seemed difficult.

The wind picked up as she climbed, and the sun beat brighter, clearer in the thinner air. Granite and fir and chill patches of last season's snow filled her nose with scents distinctly *mountain*. Around her, trees turned to scrub, then faded behind her. At last, she crested the top and the world opened around and beneath her, an unending horizon that freed her, bounded her, and made her small, all at once. Other peaks rolled away toward the edges of the sky, gulfs and valleys fell and sprawled. Green bled into grey and brown and blue, spring spreading upward from the lowlands, from the south into the north, fragile bloom by fragile shoot by fragile bud.

She gazed south, as though she could see Adfen, the Tower, the farm, the pond. The places where so many things had begun and ended. The places where *she* had begun, and where she would continue. Adfen—where so many things that mattered through history found root and grew and spread. Desga Hiage. The library. Gydron and Ilora and Gahree. The Enclaves. Cleod.

She and Cleod. The long roads of their lives, their choices, their changes. Tangled and brutal. Loving and hopeful. What friendship could become, when tested and tried beyond all reason. What love could mean, even in the face of pain. So much to carry—for herself, for Kilras, for all who had cared for Cleod. So much to miss. So much to, in the end, be grateful for. And too much possibility filled the days, the years, ahead, for grief to overwhelm her completely.

Leiel closed her eyes. Nothing died. Not really. That which could not be mended, remained, in heart and in memory, an unrelenting ache. But it neither passed beyond caring, nor lost meaning, nor vanished from the future. She folded her arms across her waist, opened her eyes, and took in the view of Arnan, of a new world where the impossible would soon be born for all to see.

Hope.

Dreams.

Promises.

A story for the vast land to share with all its children—the legacy of true sacrifice and the bittersweet splendor of its rebirth. A tale that broke as it mended, cut deep and healed with scars like risen mountains, places of awe and mystery that demanded exploration and understanding. Precious history re-written in the blood of the benevolent and the brave.

It was up to those who remained to make sure what they forged would be worthy of what had been given to create it. Such change could weight, could unnerve, but instead filled her chest with spreading warmth. What better purpose to guide her, to guide them all?

Leiel smiled just a little through the tears spilling down her face, and put her feet on the path that led back down the mountain, toward family and freedom, and the wild, unfolding future.

GLOSSARY

Term	Definition
Adfen (AD-fen)	The major city of the Spur region. Originally settled and built by Desga Hiage and her followers in the time before the Farlan came to Arnan.
Afonaedor	Land of the snaking river.
Annaluft Rayyat (anya-LOOFT Ray-YAT)	The Great Desert in southwest Arnan. Desert bordering the trade roads and down the southwest coast toward Bajor.
Ardrows Dur	Western Ocean, also called Across Water.
Bajor (BAY-jor)	The major trading port on the west coast of Arnan. Western end of the trade roads. Largest city in Ceardedur.
Blayth Hound	Wild dogs not native to Spur region, trained for guard dogs/attack dogs.
Brekko	Face cover made by the desert traders designed to keep out dust and debris in desert wind.
Brenenti	Central region of Arnan, where the capitol city, Sibora, is located.
Bynkrol (BIN-krol)	Draighil Enclave located near Bajor. One of two remaining, fully active, Draighil training sites.
Ceardedur	Western region north of Annaluft Rayyat and south of Gwinlad. Know among traders as "The long walk to water."
Cefreid (KEH-freed)	Farlan term for someone not of Farlan descent.
Clumnis	Small island near shore of southwest coast.
Clyfsirth	Coastal town at the western end of the southern trade road.

Crosswell	Town on far southern trade road, located at river crossing.
Crubanis	Island east of Hernis, known as Turtle Island.
Cruwigros	Land of low, wet walking. Marshland region in northeast Arnan.
Cuila (CUE-la)	Vision Mint, used to poison awareness to change brain chemistry for permanent changes allowing Gweld state to be maintained. Used early in Draighil training.
Dehir Dur	South ocean, also called Long South Water.
Dinist	Draighil Enclave located between Inris and Giddor, destroyed, and no longer active.
Diflan	Draighil Enclave north of Oryok, abandoned, and no longer active.
Dolencul Dur	Southern strait known for dangerous tides and currents.
Dorn	The trail lead of a merchant caravan.
Draigfen	Draigon Woman - Draigon Touched Woman. A woman who has been influenced by a Draigon.
Draighil	Draigon slayer trained by the Enclaves.
Draigon	1) Gigantic flying creature to which the Farlan sacrifice women to counteract Dragon Weather; 2) Teacher women who take Draigon-like form as needed.
Draigon Weather	Extreme drought conditions caused by the presence of Draigon.
Draigre (DRAIG-ray)	Candidate for the position of Draighil.

Draigdyn (DRAIG-den)	Draigon Man – Draigon Touched Man
Drearloc	Carnivorous insects that travel in large groups underground, and emerge to devours any animals above ground. Travel in large groups.
Ehlewer (EH-lewer)	Located in The Spur - One of the Enclaves in charge of training Draighil
Enclave	Farlan organizations in charge of training Draighil.
Eroganke (ER-oh-GANK-ay)	One of the two gods worshiped by the Sanctuary priests—"The God of Belief."
Ercew (ER-kew)	Strong alcoholic beverage that is highly addictive.
Farlan (FAR-lann)	Descendant of the Far Landers.
Fen	Fennar word for woman.
Fennar	The language of the old people of Arnan and of the Draigon - Woman's Words
Gernis	Island east of Giddor, very near the coast.
Giddor (GIHH-door)	Port city on the South-Southeast Coast, major city of Plynduirn region.
Glasvetal	Central grasslands.
Gweld	Trance state allowing expansion of senses, and hyper-natural physical and mental response. Also, allows limited connection of multiple consciousnesses and projection of illusions.
Gwindor	The major city of the Gwinlad region. Accessed mostly by water.
Gwinlad	Wine region.

Hantyn (HAN-ten)	Someone of mixed heritage.
Hernis	Long island south of Giddor and Gernis.
Hlewlion	Mountain cat, cunning and very dangerous.
Ilris (ILL-ris)	Southern Central city, south of Melbis. North of the Trade Roads where Spur country fades into the plains.
Kee's Ferry	Ferry crossing and riverport.
Kittown	Town located in Ceardedur, two days ride east of Bajor on the edge of the Anyaluft Rayyat. Known for its glass artisans
Lesuthcwithnis	Large island off southwest coast of Arnan. Sometimes called Left Boot Isle.
Longshore	Fishing village on the south shore of Hernis.
Nearshore	Fishing village on north shore if Gernis.
Northship	Small shipping port and fishing town north of Bajor. Established by the Farlan.
Nys	Draighil Enclave located on Tahnis. Abandoned due to volcanic activity, no longer active.
Orlis	Large town in far northeastern Arnan, the Cruwigros region.
Oryok (Or-yok)	A major east coast trade city and port, located in Afonaedor. Eastern end of the trade roads.
Overlash	The physical and psychological backlash that comes as the aftermath of using the Gweld state.
Plynduirn	Eastern plains region.
Poit	Steam-based bathing chamber similar to a wood-fired, dry sauna.

Ruhelrn (RU-hellern)	The Lead Sword of a Caravan.
Seebo Ferry	Ferry crossing of the Seebo River, located on the trade road west of Melbis.
Sibora (She-BORRA)	Capital of the Land of Arnan in the Brenenti region. Location of the Palace of the King. Central City known for arts and wine and fine food and drink. The largest city in Arnan. Known also for fine Inns, spas, and Memorial Garden.
Sowd	Fishing village on the east shore of Lesuth-cwithnis.
Tahnis	Island of southwest coast. Known as the Fire Isle for its active volcano. No longer inhabited.
Trachwant (TRAYK-want)	One of the two gods worshiped by the Sanctuary priests—"The God of Desires."
Waymete	Crossroads town on the far southern trade road.
Wedill	Draighil Enclave located in the mountains near Orlis. Only a few Draighil trainers remain. Mostly used as an archive site.
Wyntoc Dur	Eastern ocean, known for strong, gusting winds near shore.

Raised in Maine, **Paige L. Christie** became obsessed with books after falling in love with the movie, *The Black Stallion*. When her mother presented her with a copy of the book the movie was based on, worlds opened up. It had never occurred to Paige that there was more to a story than what a movie showed. Imagine her joy at learning that novels had more to say than movies.

What followed was a revelation that stories could not only be read, but *written*. This led to decades filling notebooks with stories.

Two random Degrees later (in English and in Web Technology), the gentle prodding of a friend urged Paige into an experiment that broke loose Paige's writing in completed-novel-form for the first time. (No she was not bitten by a radioactive anything.)

Along the road to authorship, Paige had adventures in everything from weatherstick making to cross-country ski racing, white water raft guiding, wedding photography, website design, and the dreaded 'retail'. (Lots and lots and lots of retail.)

Her current obsessions include the study of Middle Eastern and North African folk dances, costume design, and dreaming up new ways to torture... err...*explore* her characters.

Paige resides in the mountains of North Carolina where she runs a small art gallery and wine shop. She spends her evenings writing speculative fiction, walking her dog, and being ignored by her herd of 3-legged cats.

A believer in the power of words, Paige tries to tell stories that are both entertaining and thoughtful. She enjoys stories with intense impact, and strives in her writing to evoke an emotional response in her readers. Especially of interest are tales that speak to women, and open a space where adventure and fantasy are not all about romance and happy endings.

CPSIA information can be obtained
at www.ICGtesting.com
Printed in the USA
BVHW091551061022
648776BV00004B/10